PUREBRED
DEAD

Previously published Worldwide Mystery titles by
KATHLEEN DELANEY

DYING FOR A CHANGE
GIVE FIRST PLACE TO MURDER

PUREBRED DEAD

KATHLEEN DELANEY

W⦿RLDWIDE.

TORONTO • NEW YORK • LONDON
AMSTERDAM • PARIS • SYDNEY • HAMBURG
STOCKHOLM • ATHENS • TOKYO • MILAN
MADRID • WARSAW • BUDAPEST • AUCKLAND

Recycling programs
for this product may
not exist in your area.

Purebred Dead

A Worldwide Mystery/July 2017

First published by Severn House

ISBN-13: 978-0-373-28414-6

Printed in U.S.A.

PUREBRED
DEAD

ONE

MARY MCGILL STOOD on top of the library steps, trying to hear the person shouting at the other end of her
cell phone. She could only make out every other word.
It sounded as if they said the cow had run away. She
should have learned to text.

'Where did the cow go?' She listened for a minute as the growing crowd made their way through the
park toward the Victorian Christmas Extravaganza on
Maple Street, one block over, wondering, not for the
first time, why she'd agreed to once more chair the organizing committee for this event. 'Why we ever let
the Maids a-Milking bring a real cow, I'll never know.
Can you catch it? It what? Oh, oh. Keep me posted.'

She hung up, hoping Bobby Connors was right and
he could keep the cow out of Mrs Wittiker's mums.
She was pretty proud of those mums. Oh, well. It was
a bit late for them anyway.

It was getting dark fast. Clouds were coming in.
The forecast was for rain, but not until later tonight.
Mary sent up a silent prayer it would hold off until at
least midnight. It would take that long to get everyone
out of their costumes, make sure all the animals were
accounted for and back in their barnyards or kennels
and any stray children found and returned to their parents. No matter how hard you tried, children strayed.

Her cell phone rang again. 'Mary here. Everything's

fine. No, no sign of the cow. You tell Bobby to get on
it. We can't have a cow running—Oh. Good. Where's
the *posada*? The donkey did what? Is Luanne all right?
Take care of her. She's about as far along as Mary was
when they got to Bethlehem and I have no intention
of closing this event tonight birthing a real baby.' She
listened a moment. 'All right. I should hear the singing any time now.'

The library Mary stood outside of was in the middle of Santa Louisa's town park, almost directly across
from St Theresa of the Little Flower Church, where the
posada was supposed to end. Mary and Joseph would
finally be welcomed someplace after all the inns set
up along the procession route had rejected them. Mary
would lay baby Jesus in the manger, the children's choir
would sing a hymn, the people who had followed the
procession would join in and a party would immediately commence. Libations were supposed to consist
of lemonade and hot chocolate. Mary fervently hoped
that was all that was served.

Many California towns had recently included *posa-
das* in their Christmas celebrations, but this was Santa
Louisa's first attempt. St Theresa's had decided to hold
the *posada* as their contribution to the annual Victorian Christmas Extravaganza and the plan, or at least
the hope, was that after the singing and the breaking
of the *piñata*, all the pilgrims would leave Main Street
and move over to Maple Street and enjoy the extravaganza. Every house on Maple Street was lit to the hilt
with Christmas lights, and almost every house offered
some kind of tableau. This year it had almost gotten
out of hand. The Maids a-Milking were really going
to try to milk that cow while the lords were leaping

all around them. How they could do that every fifteen minutes while people walked up and down the street, gaping at the exhibits, she didn't know, and was afraid they didn't either.

They weren't the only ones taking the 'extravaganza' seriously. Mimes, Morris dancers, a barbershop quartet, a storyteller, a group wearing Dickens-era costumes while singing Christmas carols, even Ebenezer Scrooge, were all making an appearance. Evan Wilson played Scrooge every year. He came out on his balcony, dressed in a bathrobe and stocking cap, shaking his fist at the children, telling them to 'get off my property.' Then he'd throw down gold-wrapped chocolates. The children loved it. Mary didn't know how he did it. Evan was usually such a mild-mannered man.

The *posada* would come down Maple Street, turn the corner on 11th, a block before the extravaganza started, continue up Main Street and stop on the church lawn, where the manger scene was set up, just to the right of the church steps. Joseph, portrayed by Stan Moss, led the procession, walking alongside Luanne Mendosa who portrayed Mary. She was perched worryingly on the Bates' donkey, an animal that wasn't mild in the least. Shepherds walked behind, followed by the Three Kings, who had thankfully not been able to come up with any camels. They were mounted instead on Irma Long's three most elderly and unflappable mares. The townspeople came next, singing traditional Mexican songs, and in this case, traditional English Christmas hymns as well, pausing only to howl in disappointment each time they were refused entry by one of the inns along the route. They should make it to St Theresa's manger scene in—Mary checked her watch—about fifteen minutes. The crowd was already moving her way.

So many people. She thought back to the first extravaganza, over twenty years ago. She'd managed that one, too, but the crowd had been considerably smaller. Only a few houses were lit that year, the entertainment limited to a living manger scene, a barbershop quartet on the Martins' lawn and the high-school choir. Where they had set up she couldn't remember. What she did remember was her middle-school home economics class making Christmas cookies. How Samuel had laughed when he'd seen the few she'd brought home. Their nieces and nephews hadn't minded how uneven they were or how sloppy the frosting. They'd gleefully added them to the Christmas breakfast Mary and Sam hosted every year. Sam had been gone some seven years now, but she still missed him dreadfully. Her days teaching home economics were also gone but not missed nearly as much. However, she still presided over the extravaganza, which now attracted visitors from all over the state. She sighed and shifted her weight. Why she'd allowed herself to be talked into coordinating this mob scene 'just one more year,' she had no idea. Yes, she did. It was either that or prance around in a reindeer costume. The choice had been clear. She surveyed the crowd and checked her cell phone again. All quiet.

'Mrs McGill?'

Mary looked down at Dalia Mendosa. The child had climbed the steps without her noticing.

'Dalia. What are you doing here? Aren't you supposed to be over at the church waiting for the *posada* to arrive?'

Dalia nodded. 'I was. We have the doll and everything, but he won't get up and I don't know what to do. Ronaldo's there. He's holding the doll.'

Mary surveyed the ten-year-old and shook her head slightly. 'What are you talking about?'

'It's Doctor Mathews. He's lying in the manger, asleep, I think. He won't get up.'

The child's eyes were large and a little frightened. 'Old Doctor Mathews? The vet? Are you sure?'

Dalia nodded, her large green eyes wide with apprehension. 'We called his name, but he won't get up.'

Oh, Lord. Cliff Mathews. He'd been so good too. Why did he have to pick this night, of all nights, to fall off the wagon? Why did he have to pass out in the manger? She clicked on her cell phone. 'Tony? I think we have a problem. Can you meet me at the manger? No. St Theresa's. Now. Cliff's been drinking again and it looks like he's passed out in it. The *posada* will be here in just a few minutes. I can't get him out of there by myself.' She listened for a moment. 'Thanks.' She hung up and took Dalia's hand. 'Let's go.'

They crossed the street with some difficulty. People were everywhere. Strollers decorated with battery pack Christmas lights were pushed by parents who weren't looking where they were going; dogs on leashes, even though outlawed, wound themselves between people's legs, doing their best to trip someone. The traffic lights were off tonight and the sea of people that flowed in all directions, laughing, talking, kept Mary and Dalia from making much progress. Finally, they stood in front of the church. The lawn was clear of spectators. There was, so far, nothing to see, but as soon as the *posada* got closer... Was that singing coming their way?

'Where is he?'

Dalia pointed to a rough-built lean-to, open to the street. Inside, where the manger was set up and the animals were housed, was in shadow. Spotlights were ready, sitting at both the inside and outside corners, for the arrival of Mary. The place would radiate light, the North Star would shine from the oak tree and angels would appear. But for now, everything was in shadow. Mary could just make out the outline of what looked like a goat. It bleated as she came up. A couple of other animals hung their heads over small pens, staring at the figure overflowing from the manger in the middle of the display, waiting for Mary and Joseph to appear.

'Cliff Mathews, you promised.' Mary let go of Dalia's hand and marched up to the manger. 'Get up right this minute. How you could—'

She stopped abruptly. Cliff wasn't going to get up, now or ever again. He lay in the middle of the manger, eyes staring up at nothing, the shadows failing to hide the front of his gray hoodie, stained bright red.

TWO

'So, THERE YOU ARE.'

The voice made Mary jump. She wheeled around. Father D'Angelo bore down on them.

'I told you two to stay where I could see you. I was scared to death. Why did you—Oh. Hello, Mrs Mc-Gill.'

'Good evening, Father.' Mary glanced down at Dalia. Why had she been out here, with the animals, unsupervised? It didn't matter. There were other things more pressing, like a whole procession of people following Mary and Joseph on their quest to find a place for Mary to have her baby. It couldn't be here. There was no longer any room in this inn, either. 'We have a problem. Can you call St Mark's right now and tell them we are rerouting the *posada* over to their crèche? They're right around the corner. Theirs is a big one, so please, do it now.'

The priest looked for a second as if he didn't understand, then, as her words sunk in, he began to shake his head. 'No.' He shook it emphatically as he thought about it. 'Why? We've planned this for months. It's our first. Why would we...'

Dalia moved closer to Mary and reached for her hand as she watched Father D'Angelo. It gave him his first view of the manger. His head stopped shaking and he drew in his breath with a hiss. 'What's that? There's someone in the manger.' He took a step closer. 'He has to get out. We can't—'

Mary's hand closed on Dalia's. She pulled her close and stepped in front of Father D'Angelo, blocking his assault on poor, dead Cliff. She thrust Dalia at him, making sure the child had her back to the gruesome scene. 'Please, Father. Take the children inside and make that call. Tony's on his way, and I'm going to call Dan right now. Or Hazel.' She looked around. Where was Ronaldo? He needed to go... There. Standing beside the sheep pen. One sheep had her head over the railing, watching them with what seemed to be great anxiety.

'Dan? Dan Dunham? Hazel? She's the dispatcher for nine-one-one. What are you saying?' Father D'Angelo quit trying to move around Dalia and stared at Mary.

She gestured toward the children and once more gently pushed Dalia toward the priest. The children needed to get out of there before the police arrived; before they realized what they'd found wasn't a living, breathing drunk but a very dead man. 'Ronaldo's got the baby Jesus doll. They can put it in St Mark's manger.'

The eight-year-old boy watched them with the same anxious expression as the sheep. Eyes wide, seemingly trying to decide if he should be scared, he clutched something tightly to his chest; something smaller than the doll, something that squirmed. Mary squinted to see better, but the lighting was dim. What... No time. She'd find out later. She turned back toward the priest. 'Maybe you, or one of the ladies, can take them over to St Mark's. Only, as soon as their mother gets off that retched donkey we're going to need you back here.'

Father D'Angelo took another look at the body in the manger, crossed himself, walked the few steps over to Ronaldo and reached for his hand. The boy backed up a step and clutched his bundle tighter.

'It's all right. You can take the doll with you. We're just going to St Mark's. We'll meet your mother there.'

Ronaldo stared at the priest but he didn't move and didn't speak.

Father D'Angelo glanced over at Mary, a helpless look in his eyes. He'd always seemed so calm, so collected when they'd worked together on events like the Cancer Run or the Special Olympics, but he wasn't collected now. However, Mary suspected he'd never found a dead body before.

She sighed. It was equally obvious he'd never taught school. 'Ronaldo, please go with Father right now. Dalia's going also. The *posada*'s not coming here, and you have to hurry to catch them.'

She was interrupted by a whimpering noise. The bundle Ronaldo held so tightly squirmed harder.

'What's that?' Father D'Angelo bent down.

Ronaldo backed up farther, pushing against the sheep pen.

'That's not the doll.' Mary also took a step closer to the cowering child.

'It's a puppy.' Dalia sounded torn between pride and fright. 'We saved it.'

Mary and Father D'Angelo turned toward her as one. 'You what?'

'Saved it. We came out to make sure the doll was here, ready for when Mom rode up on the donkey, and heard the puppy crying. That's when we saw Doctor Mathews. I called to him, but he wouldn't get up.

Ronaldo picked up the puppy and I went to get Mrs McGill.' She paused, as if she hadn't yet told the most important part.

Mary held her breath. Surely they hadn't seen…

'It's black and white.' Dalia looked at her brother, as if for corroboration.

Mary let her breath out in a sigh of relief.

Ronaldo nodded and shifted the wiggling puppy.

'We can't…' the priest stammered.

'You have to.' Mary put as much determination in her voice as she'd ever used in her seventh-grade home economics classes. 'Take the children and the puppy. We'll sort it all out later.' She reached into her pocket and pulled out her cell phone. 'I'm going to call Hazel now. We'll get the procession rerouted, but the people at St Mark's need to know they're about to get several hundred people they hadn't counted on.'

Father D'Angelo took another quick look at the body in the manger, took each child by a shoulder and herded them back toward the vestibule of the church. 'I'll go right now,' he tossed over his shoulder.

Mary sighed and turned back toward the body as she clicked open her cell phone. Cliff. Poor old Cliff. What could possibly have happened?

'Hey.'

She almost dropped her cell. 'Tony! You scared me half to death.'

The tall, dark-haired man grinned. 'Sorry about that. Where's Cliff ?'

Mary took a deep breath and let it out slowly as she'd learned in her Silver Sneakers exercise class, hoping it would keep her hand from shaking. 'In the manger.'

'In the—He would pick tonight.' Tony turned

slightly to stare at the crumpled body. 'He's really out cold. Do we need an ambulance?'

'We need the coroner. He'd dead.'

She ignored the shocked look on Tony's face and spoke into her cell phone. 'Hazel? Mary. We have a problem. I'm at St Theresa's and Cliff Mathews is dead. In the manger. Send Dan and the troops and can you call Sister Margaret Anne? She's walking with the *posada*, but she's got her cell. Her number should be on your sheet. Good. They have to go to St Mark's. Don't let them come here. Father D'Angelo is going over there right now.' She paused. 'No. I don't know what happened, but the last thing we need is a few hundred people milling around while Dan and his people try to find out. Thanks, Hazel.'

Tony hadn't taken his eyes off the body. 'Where are my kids? They were supposed to wait in the church, with the choir, until the procession arrived. Are they still here? Inside?'

'They're with Father D'Angelo.' Mary paused.

Tony continued to stare down at the body as if transfixed. He'd made no move to touch anything but seemed to be taking in all of the details.

Mary had seen all the details she wanted or needed. 'I asked Father to take them with him to St Mark's and stay there until Luanne gets off the donkey.'

Tony managed to tear his eyes away from the awful tableau. 'She's the most stubborn woman—she's due any minute. Why she insisted on riding a donkey half a mile up the street is beyond me.' He looked back at the body. 'Did you find him?'

Mary hesitated. Tony wasn't going to like this. 'No. Actually'—she took a deep breath again—'Dalia came and got me. She and Ronaldo found him. They thought he was asleep.'

Tony's face got red and he seemed to sputter. 'My kids saw that? That old man lying there—blood all over his... Why weren't they in the church, with the choir kids?'

'I don't know. I don't know anything right now. The children are all right. I don't think they realize what happened, and Father got them out of here so quickly they can't have seen much. Right now let's concentrate on keeping anyone else from seeing this.'

It took a minute but Tony finally nodded. 'Can you wait here? I'll head down the street and make sure the procession goes the other way. Dan should be here any minute.'

'Please go. I'll be fine here.'

'My kids—you're sure they're—'

'Father had them in tow. They should all be at St Mark's by now.'

Tony took another look at the manger and shook his head wonderingly. 'Why would anyone want to hurt poor old Cliff?' He turned and almost ran out of the lean-to.

Mary kept her back to the contents of the manger. She felt a little shaky and another look at Cliff's dead body wasn't going to help her feel better. Why would anyone hurt Cliff, indeed? He was a wonderful vet in his day; everyone in town said so. Everyone loved him. At least they had before he'd started drinking and had all that trouble. She sighed heavily. But he'd never been a mean drunk. Just a sad one.

A tear started to form. She blinked rapidly. She couldn't cry now, no matter how much she felt like it. They had a lot of the evening left and at least a thousand people wandering around the six blocks of lighted houses, most with tableaus on their front lawns, through the downtown displays and in and out of the restaurants. Crime scenes weren't in keeping with Christmas pageants. There was no way to keep this one a secret but maybe she could... She dialed again. 'Wilma. Have you got the choir in there? I need them. Now. Can you get them out here? They need to march down the street, singing, and meet the *posada*. Then they can lead it back to St Mark's.' She moved the cell phone a little away from her ear. 'You heard right. The *posada*'s going to St Mark's, and I need a distraction to keep people away from here. Those kids can be my Pied Piper.' She listened. 'We've had an emergency, that's why. I'll tell you about it later. Right now, I need those kids out on the street. Get their candles lit and get them out here. Hurry.'

Almost immediately, the church doors opened and children, dressed in long red robes topped with white Buster Brown collars, gilded halos bobbing precariously above their heads, spilled out onto the church steps, laughing and talking. As one, they looked at the manger scene, chattering. Wilma Goodman, her graying bun starting to unravel a little, clapped for attention.

'We'll start our first song, children, and walk down the steps while you sing. Turn on your flashlight candles now and hold them just the way I showed you. Then I want you to follow me down the street, four by four. Just as we practiced. Now. On my count of three.'

The children formed themselves into rows of four,

most quit their giggling and, on Wilma's count, started to sing.

A shiver ran through Mary as she recognized the hymn. 'Away in a Manger.'

How appropriate.

THREE

'TONY, I'M GOING to have to talk to them.' Dan Dunham, Santa Louisa's chief of police and Mary's nephew by marriage, faced Tony Mendosa and sighed.

Tony was out of breath from his sprint to St Mark's and back, but he had enough left to flatly refuse to allow Dan to talk to Dalia and Ronaldo. 'They're little. They don't know anything and all you'll do is scare them to death.'

'Tony.' Mary didn't think she'd ever heard Dan's voice more patient. 'We have to know why the kids left the choir room and what time they came out to the manger scene. Was anyone there… Was Cliff already… Did they touch him? We have to know what they saw. You and Luanne can be there the whole time.' He turned to Mary. 'Will you come? The kids love you.'

Mary didn't know what to say. The Mendosa family lived only two houses down from her, and the Mendosa children visited her kitchen often. They seemed to have a sixth sense when it came to cookie baking day, but she was still needed out on the street. The *posada* hadn't turned the corner yet. Many of the other displays were just getting started and she still didn't know where that blasted cow had gone.

'I can't. You can't have the kids yet, either.' She looked around. A crowd had started to gather to watch the *posada* appear, only now they stared at the police

stringing yellow crime-scene tape that cordoned off
the church lawn around the manger and started mur-
muring among themselves. The word would go out
any minute that something not scripted was happening
at St Theresa's, and Maple Street would be deserted.
Every person able to squeeze anywhere close would
be over here, wanting to know what happened. Not a
good idea. 'We need to finish the *posada* and all the
other events, find that damn cow and get this crowd out
of here without completely overwhelming your crime
scene. The kids are waiting for Luanne. Tony needs
to go back there. I need to be back on the library steps
and try to make sure nothing else goes wrong. The
way things have gone so far, that doesn't seem likely.
When this is over, Luanne, Tony and the kids can all
come to my house. We'll wait for you. Bring Ellen.
I'll make coffee.'

'You better have more than coffee.' Dan's face was
grim but he nodded. The kids could wait. 'Tony, don't
let them out of your sight. I have no idea what they
saw, but if they caught even a glimpse of whoever did
this… Don't leave them alone for a moment.'

Tony visibly paled.

Mary's heart pounded. If those children saw the
killer… No. They couldn't have. They saw Cliff in the
manger, though, and they saw the puppy. Where had
it come from, anyway? Thoughts of the puppy van-
ished as a new noise intruded. What was that? Mary
listened. The *posada*? The singing was close, too close.
This wasn't the *posada*; it was another noise—laughter. A lot of laughter.

Mary glanced at Dan. It seemed he'd also heard it.
They walked toward the front of the lean-to. A Jersey

cow leisurely trotted down the street, swinging her head, making the broken lead rope hanging from her halter sway. She looked with seeming curiosity at the crowd gathered around the yellow police tape, loudly wondering what had happened in the manger scene. Almost as one, they turned their attention to the cow.

'You'd think they've never seen a cow before.'

'Some of them probably haven't, and I'll bet no one has seen one leading a *posada*.' For that was exactly what was happening. The cow ambled down the center of the street, turning right on cue toward St Mark's. Rounding the corner, right behind her, came the St Theresa's Children's Choir, halos swaying, flashlights making their faces glow like angels in an antique Bible, belting out 'We Three Kings' with gusto. Mary, perched precariously on her donkey, Joseph right beside her, came next, followed by four shepherds trying to keep a band of six sheep together with the help of Ben McCullough's black-and-white Border collie. The Three Wise Men, mounted on Irma's Arabian mares, were close behind, followed by a crowd of what Mary supposed were pilgrims, most of them in medieval costumes, singing 'O Little Town of Bethlehem' at the top of their lungs. They paused as they got to St Theresa's, puzzled when the cow, Joseph, Mary, the donkey and the angels headed toward St Mark's. Most looked over toward Mary, who waved them on. It wasn't until Sister Margaret Anne appeared, arm raised in a forward motion, that they obediently fell back into rows and, with only furtive glances at the police occupying the lean-to, disappeared around the corner.

FOUR

MARY SAT IN her overstuffed reading chair, shoes off, slippers on, surveying the people in her living room. She'd begun to think she'd never get away. Did the straw go on the fire truck, which was in charge of tearing down the inns along the *posada* route, could the maids leave the cow overnight in the Blake's garage…that one was easy. No. But finally all the questions stopped, the streets were empty and she was home. Luanne sat on her sofa, a child on each side, the puppy on what was left of her lap. It was asleep. The children weren't, but their yawns and half-closed eyes gave signs sleep wasn't far away. Her niece, Ellen McKenzie Dunham, was in the kitchen getting coffee, hot cocoa and the chocolate-mint cookies Mary had made that morning. Ellen. Her only blood relative left in this small town. There had been only one streetlight when Mary was growing up, and only one grade school. Today there were three grade schools, a much expanded middle school and more street lights than she thought necessary. The growth was largely due to the vineyard and wineries that had sprung up all over the county. They brought in large groups of tourists but the town remained small enough so she still knew almost everyone who lived here. Growth had been good for Ellen, a talented and hardworking real estate agent. It hadn't been as kind to Dan. A growth in population usually meant an increase in crime, and the gray that sprinkled Dan's light brown hair and mustache testified to the truth of that. He should be here any time now. He'd better hurry up if he wanted to talk to the children.

Tony paced.

'Tony, for heaven's sake, sit down. Or, better yet, go help Ellen with the drinks. Dan will be here soon. The kids can tell him what little they know and then you can all go home.'

Luanne moved one of Mary's pillows into the small of her back and leaned against it. The children moved closer to her. The puppy slept on.

'He'd better hurry. The kids aren't going to last much longer.'

Both children looked at him with half-closed eyes, as if determined to prove him right. Ronaldo's head slumped against his mother's arm.

The front door opened and Dan entered. He looked as tired as the children. The sight of Ellen coming out of the kitchen, carrying a tray filled with white porcelain mugs and the cookie plate, visibly brightened him. She smiled at him, walked across the room and set the tray down on the coffee table in front of the children. 'I put marshmallows in your cups. Is that OK?'

The two children sat up straight, their now wide-awake eyes darting from their mother to the cups and cookies. Ellen picked up a mug and walked over to Dan. 'Here. You look like you need coffee. Let the kids get a sip or two of their cocoa down before you start grilling them.'

'I don't grill children.'

'Oh, yeah?'

'Yeah.' Dan smiled, gave her a quick kiss on the cheek and took his mug.

Mary watched with satisfaction. It was a good marriage. They'd both had problems with their first marriages, but this one was working well. She glanced at Tony, who scowled at Luanne. Worry about her and the child she carried showed on his face. He adored the other two and was the only father they remembered, and they seemed to love him back. However, he had a hot temper and a tendency to think his way was the only way. She hoped this marriage worked out as well as Ellen and Dan's, but she sometimes had her doubts.

Dan set his mug on the tray and squatted down in front of the coffee table. 'Nice puppy. Where'd you find him?'

The children looked at each other then up at their mother.

'Tell him.' She squeezed Dalia a little closer and dropped a kiss on the top of Ronaldo's head.

'By the sheep.' Dalia squirmed until she sat up straighter, while holding her mug tight against her front.

Mary held her breath, but the child didn't spill a drop.

'He was crying.'

Dan shifted his weight slightly. 'Is that why you left the choir room? Did you hear him?'

Ronaldo shook his head. 'No. You couldn't hear him until you got out there, where the manger was.'

'Then why did you go?'

Mary watched Dan carefully. She'd never seen him work with children before and was surprised at how neutral he kept his voice and how quiet he kept his body. Nothing there to frighten two small people who'd already been frightened enough. Dalia, in particular, seemed to be coming around.

'We wanted to make sure the doll would fit in the manger. Ronaldo couldn't remember if anyone had tried it.' She paused and glanced over at her brother. 'I couldn't either.'

Dan nodded. He reached for a cookie, picked up three of them and held out two. 'You guys get a cookie yet?'

Dalia hesitated but Ronaldo reached out. He took one before he looked up at his mother. She sighed and nodded. Dalia transferred her now almost-empty mug to the coffee table and took the other one.

'So, what happened when you got out by the manger?'

'We saw someone in it.' Dalia talked around a mouthful of cookie, swallowed quickly, picked her mug back up and washed the crumbs down with the last of the cocoa. She gave no sign of wanting to say more.

Dan's jaw tightened. 'What did you do then?' He turned to Ronaldo who, up to now, had said nothing. It didn't look as if he was going to begin now, either. Dan turned back to Dalia. 'Did you walk over to the manger?'

She shook her head. 'At first, we stood there. We didn't know what to do. He wasn't supposed to sleep there.'

'Could you see who it was?'

Dalia shook her head again. 'Not right then. That part came after we heard the puppy and the other man ran out.'

Mary forgot to breathe. They'd seen the murderer.

Tony stopped pacing and stared down at the children. Luanne gathered both of them tighter. She bit her lip, hard, and stared at Dan. He rocked back on his heels a little and waved his hand toward Tony, who looked as if he was about to speak.

'OK. You watched a man leave, is that right?'

The children nodded in unison.

'Then you went over to the manger?'

They shook their heads together. 'We heard the puppy.'

'He was crying real loud.' Ronaldo seemed to come alive in his concern for the dog. He turned toward his mother and laid a hand on the puppy's head. It looked up, as if to see who was there, seemed reassured and dropped his head back on Luanne's lap and closed his eyes once more. 'We started looking all around. We found him, too. He was in with the sheep.'

'Did you climb over that fence into the pen?' There was not only disapproval in Luanne's voice, but a tinge of horror.

'Didn't have to.' Ronaldo looked at his mother with wide-open eyes. 'He was right by the gate. We just opened it a little, grabbed him and backed out.' He paused and gave them all a proud smile. 'I put him under my sweatshirt and he liked it. I know, because he got real quiet.'

So did everyone.

Finally, Mary spoke. 'Then what happened?'

'We went over to the manger.' Dalia leaned over and started to rub the puppy's ears. There was a tremor in her voice, and Mary was certain tears pooled in her eyes. The child had seen more than she thought. Should they be putting her through this?

Mary could see just the side of Dan's face, but it was enough. He looked as agonized as she felt. So did Luanne. Tony looked as if he was going to stop this. But they couldn't stop. Not now. The children had seen something—a man, quite possibly the murderer. The next question had to be asked.

'Dalia, honey, I know this is hard, but I'm counting on you. You walked over to the manger and then what?'

'We saw Doctor Mathews lying there, all crumpled up. He had blood on his sweatshirt.'

Mary's stomach lurched. Luanne's hand shook as she put her coffee mug back on the tray. A strangulated sound came from behind her. Tony. He'd walked around behind her sofa and stretched out his arms along the top, as if trying to envelop all three of them.

'Can you go on?' Dan no longer looked neutral. The lines around his mouth had tightened and his eyes had narrowed. He looked like a man fighting profound anger and losing.

'We didn't know what to do. That's when I told Ronaldo to hide back by the sheep and I'd go find you.' She lifted her head and looked into Mary's eyes. 'I knew you'd know what to do.'

Dan glanced at her and the lines around his mouth briefly softened into a sliver of a smile before he turned back to the children. 'Why didn't you go into the church and find Father D'Angelo?'

'We were scared.' Ronaldo looked as if he still was.

'With good reason.' Dan nodded. 'But the church was closer than Mrs McGill and the library. Why didn't you go in there?'

The children looked at each other. Ronaldo closed his mouth with an expression that clearly said he wasn't saying another word. Dalia's voice wasn't much louder than a whisper. 'Because we were scared to. The man who ran out?'

Dan nodded, encouraging her to go on. 'Did you recognize him?'

Dalia nodded then stopped.

'For heaven's sake, Dal, tell us.' Tony apparently couldn't hold it in any longer, but it didn't help.

The frightened look in Dalia's eyes intensified.

Luanne sent Tony a warning look and crunched Dalia closer to her side. 'It's OK, baby. We know how hard this is, but we have to know. Who did you think the man was?'

Dalia took a deep breath and, as she let it out, the name came with it. 'We think it was Father D'Angelo.'

FIVE

MARY'S LIVING ROOM had never felt so still. It was as
if time somehow stopped, leaving them all frozen in
place.

It was Dan who finally broke the spell, only his
voice didn't sound quite right. Cracked, somehow.
'Why did you think it was Father D'Angelo? Did you
get a good look at him?'

Dalia and Ronaldo glanced at each other across their
mother, who had them each squashed tightly into her
sides.

'He had on a hood.' Dalia made the simple statement
with confidence and Ronaldo nodded his agreement.

Dan waited a moment and took in a long breath
and let it out before speaking again. 'A hood. Is that
the only reason you thought it was Father D'Angelo?'

Dalia nodded. 'He doesn't usually wear it up 'cause
it makes him look like something out of a scary movie.
That's what he says.'

Father D'Angelo was a Franciscan priest. He wore
the centuries-old long brown robe tied at the waist
with a heavy rope and sandals. Mary couldn't remember ever seeing his hood—they called it a cowl, didn't
they?—up either. She didn't attend St Theresa's so only
knew Father D'Angelo from the events she helped put
on for the church. He'd always seemed like such a nice
man, never angry, so good with the children. A bit fraz-

zled from time to time, especially when they were setting up for the church bazaar, but that certainly wasn't abnormal. Or frightening. He couldn't have…could he?

'Father D'Angelo never murdered anyone.' Tony's faced was flushed with anger, his hands rolled up into fists. 'He wouldn't harm a fly. You kids don't know what you're talking about.'

Luanne pulled the children tighter, if that were possible. Dalia gasped; Ronaldo gave a little groan; even the puppy yelped.

'For heaven's sake, Tony. They only said what they saw. There's no need to yell at them.'

'I wasn't yelling.' Tony glared at them then walked away from behind the sofa to stand behind Dan. 'Only, they're wrong. I don't know who they saw, but it wasn't the good Father.'

Dan sat back a little on his heels before pushing himself to his feet. He never took his eyes off the children, who had theirs firmly fixed on Tony. They both looked scared.

Dan sighed. 'Tony, let the kids tell us what they think they saw. Scaring them to death won't get us anywhere.'

Tony stiffened; the veins in his neck stood out.

He's going to explode.

But he didn't. His hands unclenched, he filled his lungs with air and let it out slowly, his shoulders dropped and he nodded. 'Sorry. It's just that—Go on. Tell Dan what you saw. I'm not going to say another thing.'

Luanne smiled at him and relaxed as well. The kids didn't, much.

Dan studied them a moment then smiled. He got no

smiles back. 'OK. Tell me again about the puppy. Do you know why it was there? Was'—he glanced up at Tony—'the person you saw looking for it?'

The children looked at each other. Dalia shrugged. Ronaldo stayed mute. Dan sighed.

'All right. I think that's all for tonight. Luanne, could you bring the kids—'

'Not the police station.' Ellen hadn't said anything until now, but there was no maneuvering room in her voice. 'Aunt Mary won't mind if Luanne brings them back here, or you could go to their house.'

'Why don't you do that?' Luanne looked at Tony, silently asking if he agreed, or perhaps telling him that was what was going to happen.

Mary wasn't sure.

'They're exhausted, and they'll feel more comfortable at home. Right after lunch tomorrow?'

Dan nodded and picked up his coffee cup. 'I'll be there. Right now, I've got to get back.' He drained his cup and handed it to Ellen, along with a quick kiss on the cheek. 'Don't wait up.' He turned back toward Luanne but made sure he included Tony. 'Please don't question the kids. Don't talk about it with them at all, unless they get upset and need to talk. The more you question them, the more they'll forget what they really saw.' He turned back toward the children, as if reluctant to leave them, but Ronaldo's head had dropped to his chest and his eyes closed, the cocoa mug dangling from one hand. Dan shook his head and turned to go.

He got to the door just as it opened.

'Hi. We thought we'd find you here. What happened out there tonight?'

Karl and Pat Bennington walked into the room,

shedding coats as they came. Pat enveloped Mary in a huge hug, wiggled her fingers at Ellen and zeroed in on Dan. 'You're not leaving, are you? We want to know what happened to Cliff. Is it true he was murdered?'

Dan looked at Pat, then at Ellen. The Benningtons were their best friends, and Pat, as well as Ellen, didn't believe for one moment the police had any reason to keep anything from them. The press, of course, and other townspeople, maybe, but they were family, or as good as, so, of course, he should confide in them. 'Oh, a puppy.' Pat walked over to the sofa and bent down to touch the puppy on its head. 'Isn't he—she?—cute. Where did you get him?' She touched Ronaldo on the top of his head as well, but he didn't look up. Dalia looked at her through half-closed eyes but said nothing. Pat grinned at Luanne. 'So you're going to have two little things to housebreak.'

Luanne laughed, but it didn't last long. 'We're not keeping it.'

That woke the children.

'We saved her. We can't let her go now.' Dalia's eyes started to pool and she reached out for the puppy.

'I got him out of the sheep pen. He would have gotten trampled if I hadn't. He needs me.' Ronaldo's eyes had snapped open. He glared at his mother, his face set in stone. He also tried to grab the puppy.

It yelped.

Karl had followed Pat to the sofa. He reached out for the puppy and, without a word, the children let him have it. He spoke softly, stroked its long, black, curly ears while he held it in his other hand then turned it over. 'Sorry, Dalia, she is a he. Where did you say you got him?'

'The girls will tell you all about it. I've got to get back.' Dan looked at his phone, texted something, struggled into his jacket and reached once again for the door. He paused, his hand on the knob. 'I can understand you not wanting to keep the puppy, Luanne, but someone needs to. I want it close, at least for the time being. I suppose it's possible it strayed into the manger scene by itself, but I think it's a whole lot more likely it was brought there. I'd sort of like to know by who, and why.' He looked at the kids for a minute then smiled. 'So, keep him safe at least for tonight. OK? I'll see you guys tomorrow.' The door closed with a firm click behind him.

The children looked at their mother with hope written clearly on their faces. She shifted the pillow behind her back and sighed. 'He's too young to be housebroken. I really can't...'

'Your mom's not doing anything else today, or tomorrow, either. She's done way too much. That damn donkey jolting her all over—we're not keeping the dog.'

Both faces started to crumble.

'Why don't I take him home tonight and then tomorrow, we'll see,' Karl said.

All eyes turned toward Karl, even Pat's.

'You'd do that?' Tony looked torn between relief and skepticism.

'I'm a vet, remember? I have a clinic and am well equipped to house a puppy. We'll give him a nice, comfortable bed and lots of dinner. He'll be fine. Then, tomorrow, after you talk to Dan, we'll see.' He looked at the puppy, turned him over again, pushed his ears back and ran a soft finger over his nose and down the back of his head. He picked up each front paw and examined it before letting the puppy withdraw it. 'I'll need to look him over, anyway, to make sure he's healthy—all that.'

He'd already done a pretty good job of looking him over. Why? Professional compulsion? Or something else? Karl had a strange look in his eye.

'Luanne, I think you need to take these children straight home to bed.' Mary looked at her a little more closely than at Tony. 'You all look as if you could use a little time in bed. Go on, scoot. All of you. We'll see you tomorrow.'

The yawn Luanne gave was testimony Mary was right. She smiled, reached out for Tony's hand and got to her feet. 'Come on, kids. Let's go home. We'll visit the puppy tomorrow.'

'Promise?' Ronaldo scrambled to his feet as well and grabbed his mother's other hand.

She nodded.

Dalia sat for a moment, evidently thinking it over. Finally, she pushed herself up but bypassed her mother and walked over to Karl. She placed her hand on the puppy's little head then bent down and gave him a kiss. His tongue went out in search of her and landed on her nose. She laughed. Tony didn't.

'His name is Sampson,' she told Karl.

'How do you know?' Ronaldo let go of his mother to stand beside Dalia. He gave the puppy one last pet as well.

'Because I just named him.'

Mary almost laughed at the finality of that statement. However, now wasn't the time for a discussion on the merits of a name for a puppy they probably weren't going to keep, and Ronaldo's mouth was open with what Mary was sure was a protest.

'Where are your coats?' That ought to serve to get them moving.

'Mary, can you come over tomorrow when Dan comes? Before would be even better. I have some questions…' Luanne gave a quick glance at the children.

Mary nodded. 'We do have a few things to talk about. I'll see you all then. Tony?'

'Probably not. We're starting to prune the vineyards, and I have to be there to supervise the crew. I'll try to make it home for lunch, but I don't know yet.'

Mary nodded and held the door as they all walked out into a night that had started to spit rain.

'Hurry, it's starting.' Tony, clutching Luanne by one arm, shooed the kids ahead of them. He glanced back, gave a small wave and resumed guiding Luanne down the sidewalk.

Mary watched until they turned onto their front walk before she closed the door and turned to face the room.

Ellen made the rounds with the coffeepot. She poured the last drop into Karl's cup. 'I'm going to make another pot. I'm pretty sure we're going to need it. Don't say one word, any of you, until I get back.'

Mary walked across the room, sank into her chair and picked up the oversized NPR cup she always used.

'What on earth happened tonight?' Pat leaned forward slightly from the seat she'd taken on the sofa. 'I've never heard so many rumors in my life. Is Cliff really dead? Murdered?'

'How did that cow get into the act?' Leave it to Karl to zero in on an animal.

Mary almost laughed, but it wasn't really very funny. 'The Maids a-Milking brought the cow. They were going to try to milk it during their performance. Evidently, the cow took one look at all the people acting out the song and decided she wanted no part of it. How she came to lead the *posada*, I have no idea. Did anyone ever catch her?'

'Bobby Connors did. Tell us about Cliff.'

Ellen walked back into the room, crossed it and settled herself in the rocking chair beside the TV. She picked up the full mug of coffee she'd put down beside it. 'Coffee's perking. Yes. Tell us about Cliff. Was he really murdered? Did the Mendosa kids really see the murderer?'

A shudder ran through Mary. They'd seen something—or someone—and whatever, or whoever it was, it wasn't good.

'Yes. Cliff was murdered. I don't know how, but there was blood all over the front of his sweatshirt. The coppery smell filled the air.' She stopped, reliving the horrible scene. She fervently hoped the children hadn't seen as much as she had.

'Blood on the front of his sweatshirt?'

Mary nodded. 'A lot of it.'

Karl absently stroked the puppy as he watched her. 'That means he probably wasn't shot. If he was, he'd have fallen backward into the manger and all of the blood would have been around the exit wound. Maybe someone stabbed him with something and pulled it back out.'

The rest of them just looked at him.

'That was more information than we needed,' said Pat, finally.

'Why would anyone kill poor old Cliff? He wouldn't harm a fly, and now that he'd quit drinking…' Ellen paused to wipe the corner of her eye. 'I remember when I was a kid and my cat got hit by a car. Cliff was wonderful, let me hold Fluffy's paw while he set her back leg, kept talking to me the whole time, telling me she'd be fine. She was, too.'

'Fluffy?' Pat's eyebrow rose.

'Fluffy. I was about Dalia's age.'

'She came up with Sampson.'

'Yes. I wonder where she got that.'

'Bible story.' Mary's tone left no doubt that was as far as they were going with that conversation. 'What I want to know is what Cliff was doing in the empty manger scene. He didn't go to St Theresa's, so he wasn't there to help.'

'Cliff didn't go to any church in town, at least, not on a regular basis.' Karl set the puppy down but immediately picked it back up. 'Mary, do you have any newspaper? I think we're going to need some, and soon.'

Papers were found and the puppy obliged, but the conversation didn't resume.

Ellen looked at her watch and said she'd better go. Unless she would rather have someone with her tonight?

Whatever for? Mary hadn't seen Cliff killed, or the murderer. It was the children she worried about.

Ellen smiled at her aunt as if that was the answer she expected, and pushed herself to her feet, empty mug in hand. So did the Benningtons.

'It's after eleven,' Pat said. 'We need to drop the puppy off at the clinic—unless we're taking him home?'

Karl smiled.

Pat sighed. She hugged Ellen and kissed Mary on

the cheek. 'You did your usual wonderful job. Don't know how you do it, but nothing in this town would ever go right without your help. Ellen, you'd better call me.'

Ellen nodded and reached for their mugs. 'I'll just drop these off in the kitchen.'

'You'll do no such thing. I'll take care of them. You get yourselves home. You must be done in, all of you.'

'You're not?' Ellen looked at her aunt with a small smile. 'It won't kill me to stick these in the dishwasher.'

'It won't kill me, either. Get.'

Ellen obediently set the mugs down on the coffee table.

'Don't forget to lock this,' was Ellen's last remark as they went out the front door, running toward cars as they tried to avoid the rapidly increasing rain.

Mary closed the door, locked it, slipped the chain into its holder and leaned her back against it. The stillness suddenly seemed ominous. Why, she couldn't imagine. Unless, of course, the horror of the last several hours was just setting in. Poor Cliff. Why now? He'd been so good for…how long? At least two years. He had to be in his late sixties, early seventies. Certainly not a threat to anyone. Any fallout from the mistakes he'd made when he was practicing were long… well, maybe not forgotten but certainly tempered by time. Who could possibly have wanted to kill him, and in that bizarre way? Who'd brought the puppy into the manger? Mary agreed with Dan. The puppy hadn't wandered in. It had been brought. By who? Why? She sighed and pushed away from the door. Answers to those questions weren't going to come tonight. She picked up the coffee mugs and headed for the kitchen.

SIX

THE PHONE RANG. Again. Mary paused in the act of slipping another tray of pumpkin/cranberry muffins in the oven and glared at it. Who was it this time? She'd already answered it six times and it was only nine in the morning. Why did all these people think she knew what had happened to poor old Cliff? She shut the oven door and looked at caller ID. Bonnie Blankenship. She needed to talk to her.

'Hello?'

'Mary, it's Bonnie.'

'Bonnie, yes. You're on my list to call. Did you manage to get the dog food?'

'Six cases.' She sounded pleased with herself. 'And, Mary, I talked to Evan at Furry Friends pet shop into donating some dog collars and leashes. He's going to throw in some food dishes too.'

'Great. There are so many families out there that have pets they can't really afford to feed. Adding pet food and supplies to our Christmas Can Tree Food Drive was brilliant. When can you deliver what you collected?'

'That's one of the reasons I'm calling. I can't. Todd took our truck to the hardware store this morning, my van won't start and all I have is the MG. Can you possibly come out and get this stuff? I think we can get it all in your trunk.'

Mary blanched. She had to get these muffins over to the Holiday Bake Sale at the St Stephen's Lutheran Church, be back in time to meet Dan at the Mendosas and be at city hall to open the Christmas Can Tree Food Drive by two. They were going to lay the first layer for the Christmas Can Tree. All the local press would be there. As chairperson, she was going to put down the first can. She also needed to make sure the city crew cleaned up Maple Street as promised. The extravaganza was fun; the mess it left the next morning wasn't. The homeowners cleaned up their yards. The city did the street, but not without some persuasion. She didn't really have time but they needed that pet food. She'd promised the Humane Society that this year pets would be included in the yearly food drive, and she'd been the one who'd pressured Bonnie, as president of the Santa Louisa Pure Breed Dog Club, to help out. If she didn't have that pet food today, their contribution wouldn't be in the paper or on the local TV nightly news, which was part of the deal she'd cut. If she hurried, she'd have just enough time for a shower before these muffins had to come out of the oven. She set the timer, told Bonnie she'd be there in an hour and sighed. She was getting too old for all this.

There were three new messages on the machine when she got out of the shower. She didn't bother to listen to them until she had the muffins cooling on the rack. Her box was already almost full; these could go in just before she left. The Lutherans were raising money for the Shelter for Abused Women and their children so they'd have something special for Christmas, a cause close to Mary's heart. The thought of what those women went through—but then, most of the causes she helped raise money for were close to her heart. She'd felt guilty when she had to turn down the chairmanship for their fundraiser, but between the Victorian Christmas Extravaganza and the Christmas Can Tree, she couldn't do it. But she could still help by donating some baked goods, and pumpkin muffins always sold well. Hoping three dozen would be enough, she turned her attention to those messages. One was from the Santa Louisa *Post*, wanting an update on how she thought the Victorian Christmas Extravaganza went. Another was from the city maintenance department. They were on the job, but Dan's people wouldn't let them near St Theresa's, and it wasn't their fault if that part of the street didn't get cleaned. The third was from Evan. Could she stop by and pick up the leashes and things he was going to donate? He couldn't leave the store. No one asked what she knew about Cliff, thank God. Not that he'd been out of her thoughts. She couldn't seem to shake the picture of him, lying there, the blood... Why? That was the question that kept going round and round in her head.

If this had been a few years ago, she would have wondered if it had been someone who suffered from one of his 'mistakes.' Was it three years since he'd lost his license? No, closer to five. That was a long time to hold a grudge over what happened to your cat or dog, no matter how beloved they were. Although spaying Alma Maxwell's Champion cocker spaniel bitch, who was in the vet's for a pregnancy exam, was pretty close to unforgivable. Cliff had got her mixed up with another cocker spaniel because he'd been drinking. There had been several others, she couldn't remember them all, but that had been the mistake that had cost him his license. Father D'Angelo had also testified against Cliff at the veterinary board hearing. What was it Cliff had done? Whatever it was, Father D'Angelo's cat had died, and he'd been distraught. How distraught? Father D'Angelo was hardly the murdering type, even though the children had thought the man in the manger scene was him. He'd really liked that cat; he'd told her once it was his best friend. Mary shook her head as if to clear all those memories. That was five years ago. Cliff no longer practiced as a vet; he'd paid for his sins and stayed sober for, well, at least two years now.

If any of those people wanted to kill him, and she wouldn't have been surprised if, at the moment it happened, the thought had crossed more than one mind, they would have done it then. No one would carry a grudge that long, surely? So, what had he done to get himself killed now? She sighed. Dan was going to have his hands full with this one. She put the last few muffins in the box, closed the lid, reached for her car keys and purse and headed out the back door.

SEVEN

MARY SLOWED THE CAR, conscious of those behind her, impatiently wanting to pick up speed on Hwy 46, that were forced to slow. Her directions said turn left at the Golden Hills Winery. There it was, and there was a left-hand turn lane. She thankfully took it. The winery was large and impressive, and she slowed to admire it, but not for long. She'd been meaning to come out here for some time. Naomi Bliss and her husband, Bill, owned it. She and Naomi were on a committee together at St Mark's, but somehow she'd never made the time to take the tour. It wasn't going to happen today, either. She was already behind schedule.

The women at the Lutheran church fundraiser wanted information along with their muffins. Most of them knew—had known—Cliff and were visibly upset. How could anyone… Was he really… Was Mary sure he hadn't had a heart attack? He hadn't been well for some time—surely he hadn't… Did Mary think… Was she really the one who found the body? Only one person mentioned the children. She glossed over the question about them quickly. The rest of the questions she tried to answer as best she could, but she didn't have any real answers. She'd broken away as soon as possible. She wanted to get the pet food Bonnie collected so she could sit in on the interview—she refused to think of it as questioning—Dan was going to conduct with the children. Dan would never bully them, but he needed to find out what they saw. Sometimes the police—well, zeal could take over good sense. She wasn't at all sure those kids knew what they'd seen, and too much questioning was only going to muddy the waters. They were sure about one thing: the puppy. Where he came from, she had no idea, but somehow he was important. So was finding the right street. This area was new, built up over the last year, and she had no idea where she was. She didn't know anyone who lived out here. It was a new experience for her and one she found unsettling.

'Blast.' Mary glanced at her watch. She was running late. She hated being late. Her mother always said— There it was. Mary Beth Lane. Bonnie had said her place was a yellow Spanish-style stucco house set close to the street at the end of the cul-de-sac. A dry fountain and a flower bed that needed weeding sat between the street and the circular drive. A high board fence defined the boundaries of Bonnie's pie-shaped lot, broken only by a wide gate along one side. It opened to reveal Bonnie, waving at Mary.

'What? I can't hear you.' Mary rolled down her window and leaned out a little.

'I said, come in here. It'll be easier to load up the dog food.'

Mary eased the car through the gate. Bonnie trotted ahead, gesturing for her to stop in front of a long, shed-type building. High-pitched barks serenaded Mary as she climbed out of the car.

'These are my kennels.' Bonnie gestured at the long, one-story red board building. There was a white door in the middle, with several windows on each side, trimmed in white boards. The barks came from wire-fenced runs barely visible along the back.

'The food's in here.' Bonnie opened the white door and entered. Mary assumed she was to follow but paused to look around. Bonnie's property backed up to a vineyard, the vines just visible as they rose up the hill. Golden Hills? Probably. There was an old two-story barn inside Bonnie's back fence line. The long metal pole once used to hoist hay bales into the loft was still there. So was an old rooster weather vane perched on top of the barn roof. The dirt driveway she'd entered on ran down the side of the property, past the kennel building, turned in front of the barn and continued down the far side of the property, toward the street, and ended in a parking area of some sort right behind the house. The driveway in front of the kennels was evidently a small spur. Did Bonnie keep dogs in that old barn as well? It would be a good choice. She doubted grapevines cared if dogs barked.

She entered the doorway and was in the middle of a wide aisle that ran the length of the building, chain-link fencing on the side facing her, closed doors into rooms that faced the drive on the other. The fencing on the kennels side was interspersed with gates leading into individual pens separated by smooth board fencing that ended a little more than halfway to the ceiling. Sliding doors open along the back revealed the long-fenced runs visible when she parked. What appeared to be a large exercise yard in the middle separating the runs contained a low automatic water bowl, an assortment of well-chewed toys and four puppies running circles, yelping as they ran. There were two black-and-white ones, one black and one a soft golden brown. The golden-brown pup was delicate looking, with an exaggerated indentation between the nose and forehead and large liquid-brown eyes. It looked at Mary, walked over to the fence, sat and cocked its head to one side. Her heart lurched. *Quit it. The last thing I need is a puppy.*

A single black dog stood by the kennels next to the exercise yard. He stared at Mary without moving, his ears long and silky, feathers on his legs and sides without a tangle.

'Oh. He's beautiful.' Mary didn't know much about dogs, but there was no mistaking this one was special, and knew it.

'That's Champion Seaside Manor Over the Moon. Better known as Bart.' The dog's stub of a tail wagged slightly and his head came up. 'He's used to being admired.' Bonnie's tone changed as she smiled at the dog. 'Aren't you, big boy?' The stub wagged harder. Bonnie's smile faded. 'He's bored. He likes to show. He also likes to breed. He's not scheduled to do either, which is a shame. A couple of bookings or a little prize money would help right now.' She ran an arm over her brow, leaving a faint streak, then looked down at herself. 'I've been cleaning pens.'

That explained it. Bonnie wore jeans that needed a trip to the washer, a sweatshirt that had been there many times and running shoes. Her usually immaculate red hair didn't look as if it had been combed yet this morning. It was the first time Mary had seen Bonnie without a full face of makeup. She had to be somewhere in her fifties, and today it showed.

Bonnie flushed a little under Mary's scrutiny and opened a door across the aisle from the majestic black cocker. 'The food's in here. If you'll go pop your trunk,

I'll carry it out. I'm sure there will be someone at the can tree who'll unload them for you.'

Mary glanced into the room, which seemed to be a feed and grooming room. There was a bathtub at one end and a table in the middle with a clipper that looked large enough to shear a sheep hanging from a hook above it. The side of the room closest to the door held brown sacks clearly marked 'Stillman's Special Mix Dog Food.' The shelves above them were stacked with clean metal bowls along with pails and measuring scoops. Six cases of canned dog food were piled up close to the door.

'Are you giving us all your dog food?' Surely Bonnie wouldn't do that, but she didn't see any more around.

'I don't feed canned. The dry food in those sacks is specially formulated. We start the puppies out with the little pieces, then they graduate to the adult food, and that's what they get the rest of their lives. Most people buy the kind you get in the grocery store, and that's fine, but these are show dogs.'

That seemed to say it all. Mary nodded, walked out to her car and popped the trunk. Bonnie staggered out of the kennel building with two of the cartons in her arms. She grunted as she thrust them in the trunk and let them drop with a clunk. Mary winced but decided the floor of her trunk was designed to bear heavier burdens than a few cartons of dog food. Bonnie was back almost immediately with two more. This time she seemed a little out of breath.

'Let me get one,' Mary said.

Bonnie barely glanced at Mary. 'I'm fine. I'm used to this.' She disappeared and returned with the last two. This time she leaned against the car, pulled a handkerchief out of her jeans pocket and wiped her hands meticulously.

What should she say? 'You have a wonderful place here.' That seemed safe.

Bonnie smiled for the first time since Mary arrived. 'Thanks. We've only been here a little over a year, but it's working out great.'

'Do you have dogs in the barn as well?'

Bonnie shook her head. 'Too far away from the house. Todd uses it to store inventory for the hardware store.'

'Oh.' Mary couldn't think what else to say. She needed to go, but Bonnie still leaned against her car. Mary tried not to fidget. Finally, Bonnie stood upright. Mary tried not to show her relief as she held out her hand, ready to thank her once more.

However, Bonnie wasn't ready to let her go. 'I'd like to ask you—'

Mary knew what was coming; the only surprise was she hadn't asked before.

'I've heard that Cliff—that you found him… Mary, was he really murdered?'

Mary studied Bonnie's face. The red-rimmed eyes. The tired lines around her mouth. Grief ? Cliff was Bonnie's vet when she first started to breed cocker spaniels. She was now one of the most successful breeders in Central California and showed her dogs all over the country. She'd even taken one to Westminster. She was a local judge and evidently in much demand. Losing Cliff, whom she'd known much better than Mary, must have been a terrible shock.

Mary hesitated. What should she say? She didn't know much, and what she did know was bound to be on tonight's news and was probably already in the local paper. 'There was blood all over his front, and I don't think it came from natural causes.'

'Who would want to kill poor old Cliff? He suffered enough from all the…mistakes he made. I know he was trying to make up for some of it. How, I don't know, but he was always there for me, even after he lost his license. He came out when one of my bitches whelped to make sure she was all right and check out the puppies, even though he knew I'd take them all in to Karl. He loved purebred dogs in particular and felt awful about the…what he did.' She looked past Mary as if her eyes registered a scene only she could see. Then her eyes shifted back and she was her usual brisk self. 'Was there really a puppy in the manger scene? Do you know how it got there?'

Startled, Mary didn't answer for a moment.

Bonnie's eyebrows narrowed.

'Yes.' This came out slowly. How did news of the puppy get out so fast? As far as she knew, only Dan and the group at her house last night knew about it. No. That wasn't right. Father D'Angelo knew. Ronaldo had the dog with him when the *posada* stopped for the last time. Someone else must have seen it. She sighed. Probably lots of someones. 'There was a puppy. Where it came from, I don't know.' That was absolutely true. What she suspected was another matter.

'What kind of puppy?'

'Kind? A black-and-white one. Cute.'

'No.' Impatience showed on Bonnie's face. 'What breed? Or was it just a puppy?'

'Oh.' Evidently 'cute puppy' wasn't enough of a description for someone who knew about dogs. 'Karl says it's a cocker spaniel.'

Bonnie had let her hand rest on the side of Mary's car. She now jerked it away as if it was burnt. 'A cocker! No. That can't be right.' Her horrified expression softened a little, replaced with puzzlement. 'Karl thinks it's a cocker puppy? Did Cliff bring it?' That last statement was almost an accusation.

'I have no idea. I don't think anyone does.'

'Is Karl sure it's a cocker?'

Mary fished her car keys out of her purse and edged past Bonnie toward the driver's door. 'Bonnie, it's a puppy and it was in the sheep pen. How it got there and what kind of dog it is, I really don't know.' She managed to get the door opened and started to slide in.

'Where's the puppy now?'

Leave it to a dog lover to put the puppy before everything else. 'Karl and Pat took it. I guess they'll keep it until its owner shows up.'

Bonnie didn't say anything. Finally, she nodded. 'I'd better hit the shower if I'm going to make the can tree thing. Don't worry about the gate. I'll close it.' She turned and walked away.

Mary shook her head as she started the car. Bonnie was often abrupt, usually because she was absorbed in what she was doing. She was president of the Santa Louisa Pure Breed Dog Club, head of the committee responsible for the all-breed dog show they put on every year, wrote a column for the paper about dog care and breeding, did volunteer work with the Humane Society and was largely responsible for the no-kill shelter the town recently instituted, as well as taking care of her own breeding business. Her husband, Todd, ran the only independent hardware store left in town and put in long hours. Bonnie was left pretty much on her own. Her almost rudeness just now was probably due to overwork, grief and concern about Cliff. This wasn't going to be easy on anyone in town.

Mary pulled out onto the street, heading for town and the Mendosas' house. Her hands tightened on the steering wheel. There was something about that meeting with Bonnie that was very uncomfortable. The interview with the children wasn't going to be easy, either. This was turning out to be a very difficult morning, indeed.

EIGHT

DAN LOOKED UP as Mary came in the door with obvious relief. His smile seemed strained. The children sat at the kitchen table, the remains of their breakfast in front of them. Luanne sat on a straight chair squeezed between them.

'I thought you'd got lost.' Dan faced them, an untouched cup of coffee cooling at his elbow.

She shook her head. 'I was out at Bonnie Blankenship's collecting dog food for the Christmas Can Tree Food Drive. Before that, I baked some muffins for the Lutheran Christmas craft show today, their fundraiser for the women's shelter. Want to try one?' She put the small box of muffins she'd kept back on the table and opened it.

The tantalizing aroma of pumpkin escaped, surrounding the table. The children smiled.

'Oh, can we?' Dalia crooned.

'May we,' corrected their mother. 'Yes. But only one each.'

Small hands reached out and worried faces dissolved into smiles.

'You make the best muffins.' How Ronaldo made that understandable with a mouth full of muffin, Mary had no idea.

She handed him a napkin. 'How are you two this morning?'

Ronaldo was busy picking cranberries out of his muffin and didn't answer.

'We're fine. Chief Dunham said we didn't have to go to school this morning and Mom let us call Doctor Bennington. He says Sampson is fine too. We can come and visit him, if we want.' The bite Dalia took of her muffin was small. She put it down and stared at her mother expectantly. 'We can, can't we, Mom?'

'We'll see. Coffee, Mary?'

'You sit where you are. I'll get it.' She set her handbag down, slipped out of her jacket and headed for the cupboard where the mugs were kept. The first time she'd been in this kitchen was when Luanne's mother died of breast cancer. Even though Luanne went to St Theresa's, it was Mary who'd made sure everyone was fed, that family coming in from out of town was met at the airport and a list was kept of those who sent flowers or condolences. She'd been here, helping, when Luanne brought Dalia home from the hospital and when Ronaldo was born. She'd also been here when Cruz, the children's father, died in that terrible accident on Hwy 46. She'd organized food donations to take Luanne and her family through that terrible time and had made sure, along with some of her other friends, that errands were run, floors washed and laundry done until Luanne was able to function again. This kitchen held no mysteries for Mary.

She brought the coffeepot back to the table and waved it over Dan's still-full mug. He shook his head. Luanne did as well. *Watching her caffeine intake, probably.* Mary wasn't.

She poured her mug full and returned the pot to the machine. 'Are you two helping Dan?'

Ronaldo smiled. 'Yep. We told him everything.'

Dan looked at him with an impassive face. 'They're both trying really hard.'

Mary wanted more than that. What had they said? More importantly, what had they seen? Had a good night's sleep, which she fervently hoped they'd had but somehow doubted, helped their memory, or had facts slipped in that were somehow tinged with fiction? 'Can you tell me too? Remember, I came over late.'

Dan glanced over at her. Was that relief in his eyes? 'Now, that's a good idea. Why don't you tell Mrs McGill what happened?'

Ronaldo looked dubious, but Dalia seemed more than willing.

She put down her muffin and turned toward Mary. 'Like we told you last night. Ronaldo was worried the doll would be too big to fit in the manger. It is kinda a big doll. Besides, we both wanted to see Mom ride in on the donkey. I've never been on a donkey.' She looked thoughtful, glanced at her mother and tore off a bite of muffin, which she put in her mouth. She swallowed. 'Ronaldo picked up the doll and we went outside to the manger. It was pretty dark in there.'

'It was scary.' Ronaldo looked up quickly and just as quickly dropped his eyes.

Dalia nodded. 'You could hardly see the animals. At first, I thought the man was a cow. He stood right beside the cow. She was in a pen by the sheep.' Dalia paused.

Mary nodded.

'Then we walked over toward the manger and I saw something was in it.'

'What did you do?' Mary held her breath, waiting for the answer.

'Nothing. We just sort of stood there. Then the man moved toward us and I saw he wasn't a cow.'

The corners of Dan's mouth twitched.

Not Mary's. There was nothing amusing in this story. 'Did the man say anything?'

Ronaldo shook his head.

'Yes, he did,' Dalia corrected her brother.

'Did not.'

'Did so.'

'What did he say?' Mary inserted that forcefully. She hadn't taught middle school all those years for nothing.

Dalia's face got red. 'I can't tell you.'

'Why?' Dan's face showed confusion for the first time.

Dalia looked at her mother and bit her lip. ''Cause it's a word I'm not allowed to say.'

Luanne glanced over at Dan then at Mary. She reached over and patted Dalia on the arm. 'You can say it just this once. Chief Dunham needs to know, but this is the only time. What did he say?'

The word came out in a whisper. 'Shit.'

'Shit?'

Dalia looked at Dan disapprovingly but nodded.

'Then what happened?'

'He brushed past us and ran out. That's when we heard the puppy and started to look for it.'

Brushed past them. He was that close. A shudder ran through Mary. 'Did you see his face?'

Dalia shook her head.

Ronaldo looked up from his pile of cranberries. 'His hood was pulled way down.'

'I felt his skirt. It was sort of swirling around his legs, he was going so fast.'

'His skirt?' Luanne's expression changed from confusion to awareness to something like despair. 'The man had on a skirt?'

Dalia nodded. 'A robe. Like a bathrobe with a hood. Or like that robe Father D'Angelo wears. He ran out so fast he didn't even know his stick hit me on the leg.'

'Stick?' Luanne tensed. This was the first anything had been said about a stick.

'What kind of a stick?' It came out before Mary knew she'd spoken. She tried to signal her apology to Dan, but he was too absorbed in the little bombshell the children dropped to notice. 'How long was it? Did you get a good look at it?'

The children looked at each other across their mother. Dalia shrugged.

Ronaldo shook his head. 'It was pretty dark in there.'

Dan sighed but looked thoughtful. 'I think we just expanded the range of our crime scene.' His fingers started across the keyboard of his phone so fast Mary thought flames would surely fly up any minute.

'Is that when you, ah, saw who was in the manger?' Mary was thinking as fast as Dan typed, trying to picture what happened.

'No. We heard the puppy and started to look for it.'

'*I* heard the puppy. You said I was hearing things. I found it too.' There was no room for argument in Ronaldo's tone. He didn't exactly glare at his sister, but the stare he gave her was just one notch short of one.

'I opened the gate so you could get him.' Sweetness

dripped from Dalia's voice. She might not have actually saved the puppy, but her contribution was not to be overlooked. She smiled at Ronaldo, who sat back in his chair and sighed.

Luanne looked at both of them and also sighed.

Dan looked confused.

Mary almost laughed. 'Then what happened?'

This time Dalia got in first. 'I let Ronaldo hold Sampson and went over to the manger to see what was in it.' She paused. Her face grew white. So did her knuckles as she squashed the remains of her muffin. She didn't seem to notice. Her voice was soft and there was a little tremor in it as she went on. 'That's when I saw it was old Doctor Mathews. There was blood on him.' Her eyes locked onto Mary's and the fright in them was heart-wrenching. 'I called to him, but he didn't move. I thought maybe I should shake him, but I didn't want to. I told Ronaldo I thought Doctor Mathews was sick or hurt and asked what we should do.'

'I said we needed to get help.'

Mary thought he probably had said it in that same matter-of-fact tone. 'You didn't go back into the church, though.'

Ronaldo looked wary, as if somehow that decision got them in trouble.

Dalia shook her head. She didn't look any happier, but she seemed ready to defend their decision. 'We aren't really in the choir and we don't know the lady leading it. And—' She looked over at her brother. There seemed to be some silent communication between them before she went on: 'The man who ran out—he didn't go back to the church that we could see, but you can get into it from the side door. If it was Father D'Angelo…

We talked about it and Ronaldo said he'd hide by the sheep and I should go get Mrs McGill. We knew she was on the library steps, ordering everybody around.'

Mary gave a little gasp at that one but swallowed it quickly to glare at Dan. His smile was just a bit too broad.

'You did the right thing. Tell us more about the man. He had on a robe like the Father wears and he carried a stick. Was there anything else that made you think he was Father D'Angelo?'

Together, the children shook their heads.

'Just the long robe with a hood,' Dalia stated.

'Excellent point.' Dan reached for his coffee and took a huge swallow. He held onto it, looking down into the mug as if the coffee were tea leaves that would tell him what to do next. The thought that Father D'Angelo might be a murderer clearly didn't make him happy.

'A good point for any day of the year but yesterday.'

Dan looked up from his coffee to stare at Mary. 'What do you mean?'

'Half the town was dressed in robes. The shepherds in the *posada*, also the Three Kings. A bunch of the *posada* followers got into the mood and dressed in medieval robes. The adult choir from St Mark's United Methodist was dressed in robes. There were three other living crib scenes along Maple Ave. They all had people who were shepherds, kings and heaven only knows what else. There was some kind of display or pageant on the lawn of most of the houses on our six-block tour. Even Evan had on a hooded bathrobe while he played Scrooge. Anybody in town could have been dressed like that and no one would have paid them any attention.'

Luanne, with no little difficulty, pushed back her chair and struggled to her feet. She swept up the pile of cranberries and crumbs in front of Ronaldo, handed Dalia a napkin and headed for the kitchen sink. 'Mary's right. It could have been anyone. People came and went during the procession. People watching us wore costumes, and everyone milled around so much... The only person it couldn't have been is Santa Claus. Dan, if you're finished, I have a doctor's appointment and need to get going. I don't think they have anything more to tell you.'

Dan pushed his chair back. 'We're done. Kids, you did a good job. Thank you.' He picked his coffee mug up. Luanne reached to take it from him, but he set it down and grabbed her hand instead. 'I'm going to tell your mom something and I want you to listen. For the next couple of days, you're to stay with a grownup. No park, no playground. Mom will drive you to school and pick you up. You need to play here, in your yard. In your backyard. Do you hear me?'

Two faces stared at him, their mouths slightly open, but no sound came out.

Finally, Dalia nodded. 'Because of that man? Because he's bad? Do you think he might try to hurt us?'

Luanne gasped.

Mary didn't. She expected something like this. They'd seen him. Whoever he was, he couldn't be sure the children hadn't recognized him, or had seen something that could lead police to him. Whether he'd hurt them or not, she had no idea, but Dan was going to make sure they were protected. However, he could have gone about it a little more tactfully.

Mary looked Ronaldo and Dalia in the eyes, one at

a time. 'No one's going to hurt you, or even try. Chief Dunham wants you to be careful for a couple of days until we know what really happened.'

The worry seemed to fade from Ronaldo's eyes. But not from Dalia's.

'Old Doctor Mathews. He was dead, wasn't he? He had blood on his front. That man we saw who ran away, he killed him, didn't he? Is he going to kill us too?' Dalia's voice rose and gradually faded.

Ronaldo's eyes got round. He looked at his sister first, then at Dan, then his mother. All it was going to take was one more scary statement and he'd burst into tears.

Luanne, blinking back tears, walked over and put her arms around him then reached out and gathered up Dalia. 'No one's going to hurt either of you. They'd have to get through me first, and that wouldn't be easy.' She looked at Dan. 'They'll have to stay in the waiting room when I go to the doctor. They can't come in with me. Is that all right?'

It might have been all right with Dan, but it wasn't with the children.

Ronaldo's eyes clouded over. Tears threatened but the set to his mouth was stubborn. 'No. I'm going in with you.'

Dalia didn't say anything, but she started to bite her lip. Tears appeared at the corners of her eyes. One more minute and the whole room would be awash.

'There's no need for them to go with you. Why, they'd be bored to death. I'm going to the Christmas Can Tree Food Drive opening ceremony and they can come with me. After that, I want to go see Karl. I need a donation from him. You kids can play with the puppy while I talk Karl into giving it to me.'

Fear evaporated. Smiles appeared. 'Can we, Mom?' Ronaldo looked at his mother, pleadingly.

Dalia was more practical. 'What's a can tree?'

'We're collecting canned food for the food bank. That's where poor people—homeless people—go to get something to eat. So, people who want to donate bring their cans to city hall and we're going to build a big tree out of them then give all the food away before Christmas.'

The children looked dubious but willing. It obviously beat waiting in the doctor's office and there was the puppy to visit.

'Good idea.' Dan smiled at Mary with visible relief. 'Can't think of a better place for them to be, or a better person for them to be with. That all right with you, Luanne?'

Luanne didn't look as if it was, but she'd been outmaneuvered and she appeared to know it. The kids would be happy and safe. 'Are you sure?'

'Positive. All right, we have to leave in'—Mary looked at her watch—'five minutes. Go get washed up and comb your hair. Both of you. You aren't going anywhere looking like ragamuffins. Put on sweaters. It's getting cold outside. Scat.'

They did, their mother right behind them, issuing instructions.

Dan grinned at Mary but immediately turned serious. 'Don't let those kids out of your sight. Not for one minute. Someone drove something sharp and nasty into Cliff's chest. We haven't found it, so we don't know what it was, but it was long and pointed. It went in...'

He shook his head. 'I think whoever it was hadn't left because he was looking for the puppy. Dalia said he was over by the sheep pen. He wasn't expecting those kids to show up. They must have startled him big time because he left fast after that. If he thinks they recognized him, well, I don't want to scare them, but I don't mind scaring you. Don't let go of them for a second.' He paused. 'You're going to see Karl?'

Mary nodded. She wasn't capable of speech right then. The picture Dan had painted of Cliff was more graphic than she'd needed to hear. She swallowed, hard.

'Ask him about the puppy.'

'Ask him what about the puppy?'

'I don't know. Only, I think it was brought there, and I'll bet Cliff brought it. Why, I have no idea. Why was he there? I've got a lot of questions and not even one answer. Just…ask Karl.'

He gave her hand a quick squeeze and left. Mary was out of breath and strangely weak in the knees. This wasn't good. Not good at all, and somehow she was certain it was going to get a lot worse before it got better. She turned, gathered up the remaining dishes on the table and headed for the sink.

NINE

MARY SLIPPED INTO a parking space in front of Furry Friends pet shop right behind a van that pulled out loaded with kids. What a stroke of luck. She had fifteen minutes to get in there, get the donations Evan agreed to make and get to the opening of the Christmas Can Tree Food Drive. There were so many people in town she was afraid she wouldn't be able to find another spot. She glanced in the backseat. Could she chance leaving...of course she couldn't. Anyway, the decision had already been made. Seat belts were off and the rear door opened.

'We don't have time to look at the pets.' She used her sternest middle-schoolteacher voice. 'I have to be at the Christmas Can Tree Food Drive in ten minutes.'

Dalia stood on the sidewalk and looked across the street. 'It's right there, in front of city hall. Why don't we just walk across the park?'

Why, indeed? 'We have to unload all that dog food, which means finding another place to park and someone to help, so don't get involved.'

Ronaldo opened the shop door and waited as she and Dalia walked through. *Unusual for an eight-year-old.* Someone had taught that boy well. That kind of politeness usually came later, when they, and the girls they were interested in, were more grown-up. She smiled and thanked him.

'Look!'

There was a low pen just inside the front door filled with newspapers and puppies. Black and white curly haired puppies. The children couldn't have been drawn more effectively with magnets.

'This one looks just like Sampson.' Dalia leaned a hand over the low side of the pen. A puppy immediately came over to investigate and started licking her fingers. She giggled.

'Mary McGill. I'll bet you're here for the donations, aren't you?'

Mary swung around.

Evan grinned.

She smiled back and nodded, thinking how unlike Scrooge he looked this morning. No nightcap covered his thinning blond hair, no bulky bathrobe gave substance to his skinny frame, and Scrooge wouldn't have been caught dead in the long-sleeved mauve polo shirt Evan wore, or the sandals he'd buckled over white socks.

'We're in a hurry, Evan. Sorry, but today's been a blur. I'll make sure the paper knows these are from your shop, though.'

'Not a problem. I've got everything right here.' He picked up a large shopping bag with rope handles and handed it to her. Mary almost dropped it. 'My goodness, you've given us a lot.'

Evan's face reddened. 'Had some food dishes that didn't sell very well. Thought some of those kids would get a kick out of having a special dish for their pet. They need collars and stuff too. You know, I've seen dogs running around with kids, no collar, no leash.

That's no way to keep them out of the street. Maybe this stuff will help.'

'Is that why you've put in squeaky toys and a couple of balls?' Mary had the top of the bag open and pulled out a green elf. It squeaked as she squeezed. Evan reddened more. 'Well…' His voice got more muffled as his face got redder.

'Thanks, Evan. All this will be greatly appreciated, I know.' She patted him on the arm as she turned to go. 'Come on, kids. We have to go.'

'Come look. This puppy is just like Sampson.' Dalia held the puppy high for Mary to see.

'Who's Sampson?' Evan walked over by Dalia, gently took the puppy out of her hands and put it back in the pen.

'Ah…' Dalia backed up a little; a worried look took the place of the smile. 'Just a puppy.'

'We found it,' Ronaldo said.

Mary cringed. This was exactly what Dan didn't want to happen. She took Ronaldo by the hand, motioned to Dalia with the shopping bag dangling from her wrist and headed for the door. 'Will we see you at the can tree opening ceremony?'

Evan was right behind them. 'No. I can't leave the store. Where'd you find a puppy?'

Dalia looked at Mary, fright in her eyes. Mary shook her head just a little and kept on toward the door.

'Aren't these the Mendosa kids? I see them playing outside sometimes. They're just down the block from me. Someone said they found poor old Cliff. Is that right?'

'They live right down the block from me also, Evan. They're staying with me this afternoon. Their mother is

at the doctor. I've got to get over there and find a place
to park. My trunk is full of dog food. Thanks again.'
She pushed the door open and the children scampered
out. She followed them, letting the door swing shut.

'Wait.' It was Evan, half in and half out of the doorway. 'Wait a minute. How many cartons do you have?'

'What?' Mary turned back.

Evan held the door open, gesturing at her. 'Dog
food. How many cartons? I can get eight on my hand
truck. I'll take them over for you. I can lock the store
for a few minutes and that way you won't have to move
the car.'

Mary looked across the park to the library. The can
tree was to be built in the area between the library
building and the city offices. TV trucks were already
there. People carrying cartons of cans poured through
the glass double doors. All the real estate offices in
town had challenged each other to see who could contribute the most cans and, of course, get their names
in the paper or on the local news. Banks, doctors' office employees, the Chamber of Commerce and the
local markets were all turning out for this event. There
wasn't a parking spot in sight. She sighed.

'Thanks, Evan. I'll take you up on that. Kids, let's
go. I'm supposed to lay the first can and, at this rate,
I'll be the last one there.'

After Evan had loaded his hand truck, Mary hustled
them all across the park toward the library/city hall
building, her purse and the shopping bag with the dog
dishes in it slapping her leg the entire way. She was
puffing when they got to the steps. So was Evan, but
the cartons were all still on the hand truck.

'What do you want me to do with them?'

Mary looked at the steps then down at the heavily laden hand truck. 'Take them up the handicap ramp and into the building. We're going to build the tree right in the middle, between the library and the city offices. I've got to get up there and see what damage all those people are doing to my plan. Kids, stay with me.'

Telling each child not to dare leave her side, she forged up the stairs and through the doors.

'Here she is now!' A TV camera appeared in front of her. 'Mrs McGill, can you tell us how many cans you expect to get this year?'

Another voice and another microphone came at her from the left. 'Mrs McGill, are you only collecting cans? What about fresh fruit and vegetables? Turkeys?'

Someone out of sight commented, 'They can't collect fresh stuff now and keep it in the lobby for two weeks.'

Mary stretched her neck to try and see who it was making the first sensible comment she'd heard. 'All fresh food donations go directly to the food bank, as do all donations of money. We're here to collect canned goods or boxes of things like cereal or rice.'

'We were told you're collecting dog and cat food this year too. Is that right?' It was the roving reporter for Channel Two, the one who always looked like she disapproved. True to form, she looked like she disapproved right now. Maybe she didn't like dogs and cats. Or children. Or poor people.

'That's right. Pets are important for children. All the experts say so.' There. Let her disapprove of that. 'So, with the help of the Pure Breed Dog Club of Santa Louisa, we're collecting pet food so families who can't otherwise afford to have a pet, or have one and can't

afford to keep it will get some help. Furry Friends pet
shop has kindly donated some pet food bowls, leashes
and collars, as well as some other things. There's Evan
Wilson, the owner, bringing in the food.'

The TV cameras and the reporters turned as one
to focus on Evan, who struggled to get his hand truck
through the glass doors. He turned beet red as they
gathered around him, peppering him with questions,
flashbulbs going off in his face. He didn't object, however, when the questions centered on his store. Mary
sighed in relief, checked to make sure she had each
child safely secured and headed for the middle of the
vestibule.

'Are we all set?'

'Hey. I thought you'd gotten lost. We're ready to go
when you are.' A young man with long blond hair swept
back in a ponytail knelt on the floor doing something
with chalk. 'I've got our circle drawn out so all your
people have to do is fill it in.' He stood up, stretched
and looked at Dalia and Ronaldo. They looked back
at him, mouths slightly open, as they stared at the diamond he wore in one ear. He grinned at them. 'Who
are you guys?'

'I'm Dalia. This is Ronaldo. He's my brother.'

The young man nodded. 'I'm Luke, from the library.
Nice to meet you. Why does Mrs McGill have you so
tight by the hands? She afraid you'll get away?'

Ronaldo laughed but Dalia answered in her most
serious tone. 'No. There are lots of people here. She
doesn't want us to get lost.'

'In that case, you'd better help her lay the first
can. As chairperson, she's going to do the honors.'

He looked at Mary, smiled and nodded. 'You look really nice.'

Heat climbed up Mary's cheeks. She'd taken extra pains because she knew the newspaper and TV people would be here. She tucked her cranberry blouse a little tighter into the waistband of her best black pants. She'd hesitated before she'd bought it. It was only two dollars at the last St Mark's rummage sale, but it fit and didn't look used. She smiled her thanks at Luke, who grinned back and picked up a microphone that lay on an amplifier box with speakers next to a large pile of food cartons. 'Let's do this thing.'

Mary put up a hand to stop him. She suddenly doubted she wanted the children out in the open where everyone could see them, or that she wanted their pictures spread all over the local news, but she was too late.

'Ladies and gentlemen, we want to thank you for coming this morning and for all of the wonderful contributions you've made.' Luke was the master of ceremonies. The microphone squeaked but immediately settled down, throwing his voice all around the vestibule. People stopped talking and started toward the large chalk circle. 'This year we especially need to make our can tree the biggest and best it's ever been. The food bank is almost empty, and we have more families that need help than we've had in years. Your generosity is going to make a huge difference. The first layer of our Christmas Can Tree will be laid by the people in this community who have been instrumental in getting our food drive organized, along with our beloved city officials. So, gather round while I introduce them. Our mayor, ladies and gentlemen, Harlan Campbell.'

There was the appropriate applause, accompanied by laughter when the mayor started pulling cartons of Campbell's soup into the center. He waved at the TV cameras and the newspaper flashbulbs.

'That your company, Harlan?' quipped one of the reporters.

'Closest thing my side of the clan ever got to this soup was eating it.' The mayor beamed a practiced smile while he unloaded the first carton.

The rest of the city council was introduced, then the head of the food bank and the president of the Chamber of Commerce. The children were starting to fidget when it was finally Mary's turn.

'And now, ladies and gentlemen, I'd like to introduce the person who made all this happen. The person who organized it all, who personally coordinated all of the committees, and without whom this Christmas Can Tree Food Drive would never have happened; the person who will chair our next Friends of the Library fundraiser, the person who is always there when help is needed, let's have a cheer for Mrs Mary McGill, ladies and gentlemen, and her two elves.'

Mary stepped into the circle, holding tight to Dalia and Ronaldo's hands.

'Where are the elves?' Ronaldo looked around the edges of the crowd, flashbulbs going off in his face.

'He means us, silly,' Dalia whispered loudly. She didn't ignore the cameras or the flashbulbs. Her smile was bright and broad as she faced them.

'Now, ladies and gentlemen, our dignitaries, led by Mrs McGill, will lay the bottom layer of cans for our tree, and we hope it grows as high as the ceiling. Drop by every day with your contributions and watch it grow.' He motioned for the children to come to him. Mary let go of their hands and they both sprinted toward Luke. He handed them each a couple of cans. 'Set them upright along the chalk line and come back for more.'

It didn't take long for the children to get the hang of it and they were soon lying cans around the edge— Ronaldo going one way, Dalia the other.

When the entire perimeter of the large chalk circle was covered with cans, the mayor took over. 'We'll get ourselves locked in the middle if we do it this way. Let's fill in as we go and work ourselves through the middle toward the doors.' He pointed toward the large glass doors that led to the steps. Everybody grabbed cans and started laying them out, Dalia and Ronaldo in the thick of things. Mary pushed herself up off her knees, a hand on the small of her back. Kneeling on the hard floor was not as easy as it had once been. She backed up toward the edge of the circle and stepped over the outer layer to join the crowd of watchers. She wouldn't be missed. There were too many hands in there anyway, and she could still keep an eye on the children. She stood beside Alma Maxwell.

'Mary, I see you've done your usual wonderful job.'

'My goodness, Alma. I haven't seen you in ages. How are you?'

Alma gave a small, sad smile. 'Feeling my age. As a matter of fact, Mary, I've decided to move down south with my sister. Your niece, Ellen, is coming over next week to talk about listing my house. I'm putting it on the market right after Christmas.'

Mary was rarely stunned, but she was this time. Alma moving away from Santa Louisa? Why, she'd always lived here. They'd gone to high school together. They'd married within a year of each other and lost their husbands within two. They'd never been close friends, but they'd known each other. Always. Why would Alma leave? 'Why?'

Alma sighed. 'You know my sister, Eva, moved to Atlanta.'

Mary nodded. Eva moved thirty years ago.

'Her husband died recently, she has a big house and she's invited me to come live with her. I don't have any family here, what with both my girls married and moved away, so I thought, well, this seems best.'

'What are you going to do with your dogs?'

Alma had raised cocker spaniels for as long as Mary could remember. She was a junior handler when they were growing up, had dogs during her marriage and delivered puppies right along with her two girls. Mary couldn't envision her without her dogs. Alma's dogs weren't as 'good' as Bonnie's, which she thought meant they hadn't won as many ribbons, but then, she didn't think Alma took them to as many shows either. There was that one dog, however. The one Cliff…

Alma sighed, a deep, heavy sigh. 'I sold the ones I had left to Bonnie.' Her eyes got misty and her hand shook ever so slightly. 'I'm taking Belle. She can't be bred and she's way too old to be shown. Besides, I love her and my sister likes dogs. The others… You know, Mary, after what Cliff did to Belle, I sort of lost heart. I've been thinking about this for a while and decided now is the time. Bonnie will be good to them, and she has that wonderful male. His bloodlines should blend nicely with my last two bitches.' Her chin had a determined, almost defiant set to it, but there was sadness in her eyes. 'Bonnie will be good to them.' She made a little choking sound before she went on: 'I'm going down to Atlanta to spend Christmas with Eva. Sort of a trial run. We'll work out the details then.'

Mary nodded slowly then reached over and gave Alma a hug. 'We'll miss you.' There wasn't much else to say. She understood how Alma felt. All of her hopes had been tied up in Belle, the best dog she'd ever had, and certainly the best one she'd ever bred. She'd paid a lot to breed her to some special black cocker and eagerly awaited the puppies. Only, instead of doing a pregnancy test, Cliff had got her mixed up with another cocker and spayed her, aborting the puppies and leaving her unable to have another litter. Alma had almost had a breakdown when she found out. She'd never totally recovered, and her interest in her dogs gradually diminished. She must also be feeling her seventy-some years, a feeling Mary understood, and no longer wanted to work so hard or go through the stress breeding and showing dogs put on you. Mary could only wish her friend well.

'Is it true Cliff was murdered?' Alma lowered her voice as she pulled Mary back through the small crowd so they could talk more privately. 'I heard you found him. How awful. Do you have any idea what happened?'

Mary shook her head. 'I'm having a hard time making myself believe it's true, even though I saw him there. It was awful. Poor old Cliff. I can't imagine anyone doing such an awful thing.'

Alma didn't say anything. Instead, she looked at

Mary, her usually soft gray eyes hardening to the color of steel. The lines around her mouth tightened and the words she spoke were equally as hard. 'I can.'

TEN

KARL BENNINGTON'S Five Oaks Small Animal Veterinary Hospital was in the north end of town, tucked away behind the Almond Tree Motel and Café. Mary had made the drive many times and drove it now on autopilot. Her conversation with Alma had shaken her more than she liked to admit.

The children sat in the backseats, faces still encased in smiles. They had had a wonderful time, placed cans with unbridled enthusiasm and took over from adults who no longer wanted to bend down. Now they sipped chocolate milk and argued over who laid out the most cans and who was going to pick the game they were going to play with Sampson. Mary ignored them. Her thoughts were consumed with Alma and the grudge she'd carried against Cliff all these years. She'd blamed him not only for the monetary loss she suffered when he spayed her prize bitch, but for the mental anguish she'd suffered and the loss of interest she'd had in rebuilding her kennels. Alma had let her hurt fester until it was like a boil under her skin. If she was younger, stronger, and a man, Mary would have considered her a suspect, but it made her realize how deep a hurt like that could go and how long it sometimes took to heal. Who else was out there, holding onto a grudge against poor old Cliff? He'd made some pretty awful 'mistakes' during those years when he'd systematically drowned his career in alcohol. In the process, he'd inflicted pain on a lot more people than himself. She hoped Dan found out who murdered him quickly. This was reopening old wounds she had hoped were closed for good. Alma's weren't. She wondered who else had an open wound.

She swung into Karl's parking lot. There was only one car other than Karl's SUV with the dog crate in the back. The office closed at noon and reopened at two, so their timing should be great.

'Don't you dare open the car doors until I'm parked and say you can.' She didn't care how empty the parking lot was, she didn't want the kids running across it. True to her expectations, the office door opened and a woman Mary didn't know walked out with a cat carrier. She barely glanced at Mary, who had pulled in beside her, but took a good look at the kids before she opened the back door and set the carrier on the seat. The cat yowled.

The woman walked around and got in the driver's seat. When she was clear of the parking lot, Mary spoke. 'Now you can…' That was as far as she got. Both children shed their seat belts, had doors opened and were at the front door before Mary had the keys out of the ignition. They didn't have to open the door. Karl did that for them.

'Perfect timing. Sampson's in the puppy pen, waiting for you.'

Karl's bald head shone pink in the sunlight, the little freckles on it almost glowing through the few thin strands of hair. He smiled as he pushed the door open wider. 'Pat's inside. She's got sandwiches made and some apple slices. You two hungry?'

Mary started to follow the children into the building but Karl stopped her. 'Wait. I need to talk to you.'

She turned to face him, surprised the smile was gone. The look on his face was serious. No. Worried. Karl never looked like that unless he was worried about one of the animals. Mostly, he looked mildly pleased with life, which, Mary was sure, was how he felt. But he didn't look pleased right now.

'What's the matter?'

'Do you know where Dan is? I have…something happened… I think he needs to know.'

'I have no idea where he is. What is it you think he needs to know?'

Karl looked at her for what Mary felt was a long time. 'I don't know if this is important or not, but…' He stopped, evidently mulling something over in his mind, trying to decide. His expression changed. 'Come into the office. I want to show you something.'

It was with more curiosity than dread that Mary followed him. The office smelled faintly of dog. That wasn't surprising. There were two dog beds in one corner, both currently empty. Bookshelves were crammed with veterinary books. Framed diplomas filled the space between two of them, along with pictures of dogs, cats and one horse. Mary looked twice at that one. Karl made no secret of the fact that he only took small animals as patients. A large glass tank held— No, she wasn't going to look. She didn't like reptiles and was sure they didn't like her. Instead, she took the only chair in front of Karl's freestanding-and-totally-loaded-with-papers desk.

'Well?'

Karl pulled out his desk chair and sank into it. He

looked as if he was having a hard time finding a place to begin. 'A few weeks ago, Cliff came by to see me.'

That surprised Mary. Karl and Cliff had never been friends. Karl had been openly critical of Cliff's actions in the years before he lost his license. Cliff knew it and resented it. They'd never argued that Mary knew about, and she was sure she would have known if they had, but there was a coolness—no, more like a winter frost between them. 'What did he want?'

'He wanted a favor.'

'Really.' Now, that was a surprise. 'What kind?'

'He wanted me to send a DNA sample to the American Kennel Club to verify parenthood.'

'To do what? Parenthood? For a dog?'

Karl smiled his mildly amused smile, but there was worry underneath it. 'Most purebred dogs that are registered sires have their DNA on file with the AKC. It's required for most breeds, especially if the dog sires more than a couple of litters a year. Keeps things honest. If someone buys a purebred puppy and suspects the sire on the papers isn't the real one, they can request the puppy's DNA be checked. There are other reasons—verifying the identity of a dog when it's sold, things like that. Anyway, Cliff asked me if I'd send in his sample.'

'Why didn't he do it?' Mary tried to absorb all of this. She'd never heard of DNA testing for dogs, or for any animal, but then she knew next to nothing about dog breeding or showing. Why would Cliff want a dog's DNA tested? He no longer had anything to do with dogs of any kind, or did he? He'd been, when he was a young and eager vet, the doctor of choice for all the purebred breeders in this part of California; at least that was what she was told. No longer. So, what would he want with this test? Why didn't he send it in himself? The last two questions she asked aloud.

'He said,' Karl's words came out slowly, 'that he didn't think the AKC would let him send in a request because he lost his license and wasn't practicing anymore.'

'Is that true?'

'I think he just didn't want anyone to know what he was doing.'

'Why? Do you think it could have something to do with why he was killed?'

'Mary, I have no idea. I don't know what Cliff was after, who the dog was, anything. He didn't tell me and, honestly, I didn't ask. Just told him sure, I'd do it. A few days later he brought the sample, had all the paperwork filled out, gave me a check made out to me and asked me to send mine in with the package and to please call him when the results came back. They came back yesterday.'

Of all the odd things. 'Did you call him?'

Karl shook his head. 'Didn't have a chance. It was a busy day and we wanted to end early so we could see the *posada*. Besides, I was the vet on call for the extravaganza.'

Mary nodded. She knew that. She'd arranged it. 'You never talked to him?'

'No.'

'Have you looked at the results?'

'I didn't yesterday. It was Cliff's test and his business. I had no intention of opening it. However—'

'You opened it today?'

Karl nodded.

'For heaven's sake, Karl, do you know the dog? Or the owners? Don't sit there, looking mysterious. Tell me what's bothering you about this.'

Karl took a deep breath and let it out slowly. 'Do you remember last year when the Blisses' poodle got stolen?'

'The little black dog Naomi took everywhere? Yes, I do. They looked all over and finally concluded someone who visited the winery took him. Why?'

'That dog was a finished champion and was much in demand as a sire for poodles that size.'

'What does that have to do with—No. It isn't.'

'It is. Only, there's been no trace of that dog for almost a year. He can't be shown, and if whoever took him tried to stand him at stud...' Karl smiled at the puzzled look on Mary's face and explained, 'Used him to breed to other dogs, especially poodles... He's hidden someplace around here. He must be and somehow Cliff found him. I think he wanted the DNA test to make sure he was right.'

Mary sat stunned. Had Cliff stumbled onto something that got him killed? But, what? The puppy. Could he somehow... 'Sampson. The puppy. Is he a poodle?'

There was no longer even a trace of a smile on Karl's face. 'I think Sampson may be a very cute cockapoo.'

'A what?' Mary sat up straight and stared at Karl. Maybe she hadn't heard him right.

Karl smiled faintly. 'I can see you don't keep up with the latest "designer" dogs. A cockapoo has one parent who's a poodle and the other a cocker spaniel. They're becoming pretty popular. At least with everybody but those who don't believe in mixing purebred bloodlines.'

Mary tried to make sense of that but couldn't. However, it wasn't what she wanted to know. 'You think Sampson is a cockapoo? Is that what you said?'

'It's hard to tell with a puppy Sampson's age, but he sure looks like one to me.'

A picture swam into Mary's mind. Black puppies, black and white puppies. 'Evan has puppies in his shop. Black and white furry puppies. Is it possible Sampson is one of those?'

'The world is full of black and white furry puppies. If you're asking me if Sampson could be related to Evan's puppies, I couldn't begin to tell you. I don't know where Evan gets his puppies and have no idea where Sampson came from. All I can tell you is he's cute and appears healthy. However, I've started him on his shots. Just in case.'

Mary tried to hide her smile. Just like Karl, always thinking about the animals first. 'What are you going to do with him?'

Karl sighed. 'Hold onto him for a while, I guess. At least until Dan's satisfied he's not evidence of something. Then I suppose we'll try to find him a home.'

'Karl, do you think either of those dogs, the Blisses' poodle or Sampson, have something to do with Cliff's murder?'

Karl leaned forward on his desk. Mary had never seen him look so troubled.

'I have no idea. It seems too much of a coincidence for there not to be a connection, but I can't think what. I'll tell Dan about this test as soon as I find him and then bow out.' He looked directly at her. 'I think we need to keep this to ourselves. That sample is from Naomi's dog, but it doesn't tell us where the dog is or who has him, and it certainly doesn't tell us why

Cliff was killed or by whom. Let Dan sort this out. All right?'

Mary nodded but slowly, and without conviction.

He got up and headed toward the door. 'I need to get back to work. It's after two and I have patients in the waiting room.'

Mary nodded again and followed him out the door. She needed to pry the kids away from Sampson, and she wanted another look at the puppy. Why, she had no idea. He could be part Beagle for all she knew, but she'd promised Dan she'd find out what she could. She wasn't going to do that by looking at him, though. There had to be another way.

ELEVEN

THE PHONE RANG as Mary pushed open her back door, her arms full of groceries. She set her full cloth bags on the floor and stared at the phone. She didn't want to talk to anyone. She was tired. It was after three and she'd been talking to people all day. The children were safely deposited with their mother and right now all she wanted was a cup of tea.

The phone kept ringing. She must have forgotten to set the answering machine again. With a snort of disgust, she picked it up.

'Mary, thank goodness. I've been trying to get you for hours.'

'Isabel. What's wrong?'

She sounded rattled. Pastor's wives weren't supposed to sound rattled. They had to deal with everything from committee women with their noses out of joint to distraught parents of a sick or dying child. Isabel usually handled her role with calm dignity that Mary found admirable. There was nothing calm about her now. 'Cliff and what we're supposed to do about him, that's what's wrong.'

Mary felt herself stiffen. Do? About Cliff ? What was Isabel talking about? She set her handbag on the kitchen table and walked over to the stove. She checked the teakettle. It was full. She turned the fire under it full on blast and headed for the cupboard for a mug. 'What are you talking about?'

'I'm talking about Cliff Mathews. Everybody's asking me about the funeral. I called Dan's people and they said as soon as the autopsy was finished, so were they. Someone has to claim the body and arrange for burial. They won't. What are we going to do?'

Cliff's funeral. It'd never occurred to her. Her hand didn't get any farther than the cupboard door. It seemed frozen on the knob, incapable of pulling it open. Surely his family—only, she couldn't think of any family. His wife was dead, had been for over ten years. They had one daughter, but Mary didn't think she'd seen her since her mother's funeral. She'd had some kind of falling out with her father and Cliff hadn't mentioned her since. She'd almost forgotten about her, couldn't even remember her name. Where was she now? Mary had no idea. Had Cliff any siblings? She couldn't remember him mentioning any. Cliff wasn't a native of Santa Louisa but had bought his practice after he'd graduated from vet school. He'd moved here from… Where? They'd have to find out and find his next of kin as well. Everybody had someone. Surely it was just a matter of locating them. 'What about his family?'

'Don't know. Les is working on it. There's a daughter, but where she is… Anyway, the autopsy is scheduled for Monday and it won't be long after that before the body's released. We have to do something.'

'What do you mean by "we"? Cliff wasn't a member of St Mark's, and if you mean you and me, I'm sure he had closer friends.'

'Cliff didn't officially belong to St Mark's, but Les said he'd do the service. Eloise, his wife, was a member for years and Les officiated at her funeral. If memory serves, you and your committee did the food for the reception after her burial.'

Isabel was right. Mary remembered that day. Cliff had looked like a lost child, dazed, uncomprehending. A vague picture of the daughter came up. A thin woman, boney actually. Her hair was pulled back in a severe ponytail, her black dress a little too large through the hips, as if she'd lost weight and hadn't bothered to replace the dress, or even take it in. Only, she couldn't remember anything else. Nothing she said, no one she talked to, not even her father. Her memory put the woman at the grave site. She couldn't remember if she'd even been at the reception. So sad.

'They bought two plots and Les says we're going to bury Cliff beside her. Unless, of course, someone comes along and says different.'

If Mary's memory of the daughter was correct, she thought that highly unlikely. That Reverend Lestor McIntyre was going to give Cliff a proper send-off wasn't. It solved one problem, one she hadn't thought about. There were plenty of others. 'What does Les want us to do? Provide food for the gathering afterward? Flowers?'

'Well, a little more, I'm afraid. He wants you to contact the funeral home and make the arrangements. Dan wants you to meet him at Cliff's. He needs to look through the house. While he's there he thought you could collect the, you know, clothes and things like that, for the burial.'

The teakettle started to scream. Mary removed it, took a mug from the cupboard and a tea bag from the canister, plopped the bag into the mug and filled it with hot water. It started to turn a rich brown almost immediately. This was going to take a few minutes, though. She pulled out one of the chairs by the old white table that sat under her kitchen window, sank down onto it and tried to push the shoe on her left foot off with her right one. She almost groaned with relief when it slipped to the floor. Now for the other one. 'Why me? I knew Cliff, of course, but not that well. It was Eloise I knew. After she died I didn't see Cliff all that often.'

'You're the chairperson for St Mark's Hospitality Committee.'

'Arranging other people's funerals doesn't come under the heading of Hospitality.'

'Visiting people in the hospital. Sending people cards and flowers. Making sure people have food after a funeral—that kind of thing does. It's the closest committee we could think of to do this. You will, won't you, Mary?'

Oh, for heaven's sake. Mary took a deep breath, willing herself not to be huffy. She'd had a long, exhausting day and she wanted to sit here, sipping her tea, alone, letting the day just slip away... There wasn't one thing about any of this she liked or wanted any part of.

'First, I'm the co-chairman of that committee. Naomi Bliss is the other one and all she does are the cards and flowers. I do the food and all the organizing. Neither of us signed on to arrange funerals.'

'Well, if you don't want to do it, tell Les and Dan. Not me. But, Mary, I'm a little surprised. You're always the one we can count on when we need help.' Isabel sounded surprised and more than a little hurt.

Mary sighed and got up to get her tea. It looked black and strong. She fished the teabag out and put it in the sink before gingerly taking a sip. Too hot. It would be another couple of minutes. Drat. She needed that tea. 'I'm sorry, Isabel. I guess I'm a little tired. The extravaganza and the can tree thing have worn me out. Then all this with Cliff. I suppose Les wants to use O'Dell's Mortuary.'

'Who else?'

Who else, indeed. The O'Dells had been members of St Mark's for three generations and took care of all the funerals for the congregation. They'd also volunteered their services in cases like this before. Not in murder cases—at least, Mary couldn't think of one, but in cases when someone died without the necessary funds or if there was no family. They'd waived their fee when the Ryans' little boy died. Pat Ryan had been out of work for almost a year and the child's hospital bills had gotten out of hand. The Ryans were in danger of losing their home as well as their child. Mary sighed. If the O'Dells were willing to help, she guessed she was too. That didn't make her feel any better, though. There was something creepy about arranging a funeral for someone who wasn't a relative, someone who you knew only casually, whose wishes you could only guess at. Was she supposed to pick out the casket as well as Cliff's last outfit?

She shuddered and tried a sip of tea. 'All right. I don't like this one bit, but I'll do it. When am I supposed to meet Dan?'

'He said he's at Cliff's right now and could you come there. I have the address. It seems there's a problem with the landlady and Cliff's things need to be taken care of by tonight.'

'Tonight!'

'That's what he said. He's called Ellen as well.'

'Oh, all right. I'll see what I can do. But, I'm finishing my tea before I do another thing.'

Isabel laughed and hung up.

Mary looked at the clock and at the groceries she hadn't unpacked and groaned. The last thing she wanted was to go out again. Her back hurt, so did her feet, and she wanted to put on her slippers, sip her tea and watch the local news. Well, maybe she still could. It wasn't quite four. If she left now she could run by and see what it was that Dan needed. Maybe most of it could be done tomorrow. With a deep sigh, she opened the cupboard that held vitamins and other everyday medications, shook two Tylenol out and popped them into her mouth, picked up her mug, drained it and put it in the sink. She pulled the orange juice, butter and fish out of the sack and put them in the refrigerator. She'd do the rest later. She had to make a phone call before she left. No, two. O'Dells needed to be put on alert. And Naomi. She wasn't doing this one alone.

TWELVE

MARY PULLED UP to the curb and stared at the row of townhouses. She looked down at the address written on the back of her grocery list then again at the tired-looking building. So this was where poor old Cliff lived after he lost his wife, his house and his practice. She sighed, unsnapped her seat belt and climbed out of the car.

'There you are. Dan's inside.'

Naomi came down the stairs of the middle town-house, the one with the dead bush in the pot on the front porch. Mary shook her head in wonder. Naomi was the only woman she knew that still wore high heels. High, high heels. She wasn't much taller than Mary, at least Mary didn't think so. It was hard to tell because she wore those torture chamber shoes all the time. How she stayed on her feet all day in those things, Mary couldn't begin to fathom. But then, she was younger than Mary and didn't have her soft curves. In fact, she had no curves at all. Naomi was practically straight up and down. Mary sighed. *She* wasn't. She ran her hand down the side of her sweatpants, the ones that fit snugly over her hips. Why was Naomi the only person she knew who made her feel self-conscious? She'd put on her new—to her—Santa Claus sweat-shirt before she left, thinking it was nice and warm and would wash easily. Perfect for packing up someone's belongings. Naomi wore knit pants that wouldn't dare bag at the knee, a silk shirt Mary was sure wouldn't wrinkle, and her makeup wasn't mussed. Mary wore no makeup. Was the fifty cents she paid for her sweatshirt at St Mark's rummage sale such a good deal after all? Deciding this wasn't the moment to worry about her wardrobe, she climbed the stairs.

'Have you already been in there?'

Naomi nodded. 'Did you call O'Dells?'

'Yes. They're going to take care of everything but the casket. We have to pay for that, so we'll have to go over tomorrow after we find out how much we have to work with and pick one out. I have a budget from the church charity fund but it's not much. I hope Cliff left something.'

'I don't imagine he did.' Naomi sighed deeply, turned on her spiked heel and headed for the front door. 'I still can't believe…' The rest of her sentence was lost in the squeak it made as she wrenched open the door.

Mary followed her inside with reluctance. She couldn't shake the feeling she was intruding, walking into someplace she had no business being. However, there didn't seem to be an alternative, so she continued on into the middle of the room, stopped and looked around. There was only one way to describe it. Depressing. A sofa, whose flowered pattern had long since faded into nothingness, sat against a long wall. A square end table of no particular design sat beside it and a matching coffee table in front of it. The end table held a wooden lamp that looked like a Walmart special and a collection of magazines. Dog faces looked up from the front covers. The coffee table was equally sparse. Aside from dust, it held nothing but a TV remote and a plate with what were probably the remains of Cliff's last meal. No pictures graced the wall behind the sofa, no pillows softened it. A recliner, its vinyl worn through on the arms, sat at an angle facing the small TV. It was a flat screen, the only new thing in the room, and easily fit on the small table that separated the two bookcases on the wall opposite the sofa. A small dining set that also looked suspiciously like Walmart almost filled the tiny dining area. A lovely old mahogany buffet was wedged along the back wall. There was nothing about it that suggested Walmart. It was the only piece, and the only wall, that held anything personal or decorative. The top was covered with pictures. So was the wall above it. The only other available space in the room held a battered rolltop desk and an elderly swivel chair. In the chair sat Dan.

'You finally got here. Good.' Dan turned from the scarred old desk he'd evidently been searching through and smiled at her. 'Did you talk to O'Dell's?'

Mary nodded. 'All I have to do is find a casket that fits the church budget. I don't suppose Cliff left any money we can use?' She looked at the piles of bank statements, bills and letters and blanched. 'Dan, should we really do this? Go through all of Cliff's things?'

His voice was grim. 'I got a warrant. The courts might frown on us if we didn't follow all the legal steps.'

'Oh.' Mary wasn't sure being legal made her feel any less like a snoop, but there didn't seem to be anyone else to do this. Besides, there might be a clue as to who killed him and the other question that plagued her: why? 'Do you think there's enough to bury him?'

'Doesn't look like it.' Dan put a checkbook down

on top of a pile of bank statements. 'Cliff's landlady paid me another visit before you got here. Seems he was about three months behind on his rent and she had served him eviction papers.' He picked up an official-looking sheet of paper with a heading in red screaming 'Notice to Pay or Quit.' 'She wants his stuff out and wants it out now. I think she feels bad, but she says these apartments are her only income and she needs to get this one rented. I talked her into giving us until sometime tomorrow. Les says we can store all his things in the storage room at St Mark's until we can find his daughter. We're going to have to pack up all of Cliff's belongings and get them over there by to-morrow afternoon or she'll put them out on the curb.'

Mary looked around the apartment once more. It shouldn't take long. But the storage room? She knew it well. She used it for many of the events that went on and had planned to use it again to store the donations they would soon be collecting for the annual rummage sale. She groaned inwardly, wondering how they were going to manage. That they would, somehow, she had no doubt, but hoped Dan found the daughter soon. 'Did he leave a will?'

'Not that I've found.' He frowned and waved a hand at the piles of paper stacked on the desk.

'I haven't found an address book either, and no one I've talked to can remember the daughter's married name or even what state she lives in.'

He was stopped by a sharp intake of breath. They both turned. Naomi held a picture in her hands, star-ing at it.

'Did you find something?' Dan pushed his chair back and started toward her.

She didn't answer, just kept staring at the picture.

Mary followed Dan. She caught only a glimpse of a small poodle before Naomi clutched the picture to her breast. That it was of a dog wasn't a surprise. Naomi's reaction was. She looked over at the buffet. The top was covered with pictures of dogs. Mary didn't recognize any of the animals, but she knew a lot of the people.

'Why, that's Ray Blackburn. I'd forgotten he had a police dog.' A beautiful German shepherd sat beside a slender young man with bushy black hair, almost dwarfed by his police equipment. He grinned from ear to ear. His dog looked equally happy. 'That was taken the day Ray and Spike graduated from the canine academy. I've never seen Ray so happy. Before or since.' Dan paused to stare at the picture. 'Where did… Ray must have given it to him. Cliff took care of Spike.'

Mary nodded, but her attention had been caught by another picture, obviously taken in a show ring. 'Isn't that Luke? Luke from the library? My goodness, he looks so young.'

Naomi, her picture still clutched tightly to her breast, glanced up. 'Why—yes. That's Luke when he was a junior handler. That was years ago. Why would Cliff… He was the one who ruined Luke's chances for a scholarship. Neither Luke nor his parents ever forgave him. What's he doing with that picture?'

Luke must have been in middle school when it was taken. There was no mistaking that slightly awkward look so many of them, especially the boys, had at that age. Luke looked more put together than most. He also looked happy. Happy and about to burst with pride. He held a huge blue ribbon in one hand, a dog lead attached to a large and elaborately groomed poodle in the other. A scholarship? At that age? What was Naomi talking about? She didn't get a chance to ask.

'What's that picture you're holding, Naomi? You'll have to put it back. We'll have to do an inventory of all this stuff and...'

Naomi turned the picture over and held it out for them to see. A small black poodle stood proudly in front of an elaborate sign bearing the words, 'Best in Show.' A woman in a black and silver pantsuit knelt beside him, holding his lead. A distinguished white-haired man holding a large silver cup stood next to them. 'It's Merlot,' Naomi whispered. 'This was him winning the West Coast Specialty last year. It was the last show he went to before he was stolen.' Her eyes clouded over with tears, her words almost buried in the sobs she tried to suppress. 'I had it at the winery, up on the wall in the tasting room. One day, a couple of weeks ago, it was gone. We looked everywhere but couldn't find it. Cliff must have taken it. Only, why? Why?' Her voice became stronger. Her eyes no longer threatened tears. Instead, they radiated anger. 'Bill was sure I'd lost it. He was sure I lost Merlot too. As if I could. He kept asking why would anyone take his picture, or him, for that matter? The dog was famous. No one would dare. But someone did. Todd Blankenship saw him in the backseat of a car. He said he didn't realize what dog it was until later. Cliff didn't steal the dog. So why did he take the picture?'

Mary looked from Naomi's angry eyes to the picture of the lovely little dog to Dan.

He didn't look any happier than Naomi, but his voice was soft. 'I have no idea, Naomi, but I'd like to find out.'

THIRTEEN

'ELLEN, I CAN'T thank you enough for doing this. I simply couldn't face it last night. I know it's early, but Dan's arranged for Ricker to bring his truck by at two, and I would never have finished by myself.'

Mary turned from the pile of clothes she had spread over the bed, sorting them into two piles. She and her niece had easily chosen the clothes Cliff would be buried in. There was only one dress shirt that had all of its buttons and one pair of pants that didn't have stains of some sort. It seemed a shame to bury the only halfway nice things Cliff had left, but then he deserved to be dressed this one last time in something decent. Mary packed them carefully in an old suitcase she'd found and started sorting the remaining clothes into a pile to throw away and another that could potentially go to St Mark's next rummage sale. The throw away pile was growing faster than the one for St Mark's.

'I know this isn't much fun, going through a murdered man's clothes and things, but there doesn't seem to be much choice. After Naomi found that picture, she announced she was going home and couldn't come back this morning. Dan sent Agnes over to help but...'

Her niece interrupted. 'Will you look at this?'

'What?' Mary dropped the shirt she'd folded into the carton box packed with the clothes going to St Mark's.

She ran her hands down the sides of her pant legs and walked over to see what her niece had found.

'It's a diary.' Ellen thumbed through the well-worn brown leather-bound book. 'It dates back'—she flipped back to the front page—'about five years ago.' She handed it to Mary. 'Go to the end.'

Mary took the book but made no move to open it. She didn't want to know Cliff's thoughts, what made him happy or, more likely, what saddened him. She felt she had intruded enough cleaning out his closet and packing up his meager kitchen supplies. Something as private as a diary… 'Can't we give this to Dan?'

Ellen picked up a pile of sheets, towels and pillow-cases off the end of the bed and put them into a carton box. 'Just a sec.' She wrote what she had packed on the inventory sheet they would attach to the box when it was full. 'Yes, but you need to read the last few pages.' She left her box, walked over and gave Mary a squeeze. 'I know. It feels creepy. Like we're spying on him, or something. But I think you need to read some of that. I want to know what you think.'

Mary looked at Ellen, who nodded, then down at the book. Its soft cover appeared like it had been held, opened and read a lot. She sighed. There was a purple ribbon attached to mark the owner's place. She let the book fall open to where the ribbon separated the pages. The date was 27 November this year, the weekend after Thanksgiving. The day Cliff's landlady had handed him his eviction notice? Mary counted quickly. Yes, the number of days allowed on the notice had passed. Cliff had to be out. Mary's hand shook as she read the entry.

Just got an early Christmas present. Only, if I don't come up with some money, I won't be here for Christ-

mas. Where I'll go, I have no idea. Don't know how I'm going to get money, either. Or, do I? I've been wondering about this for some time. If I'm right... I know I'm right. Now, if I can prove it, Christmas might turn out merry after all.'

Mary almost dropped the book. She looked at Ellen then flipped the page and read the next entry. And the next. 'What's he talking about?'

'I have no idea. That's why I wanted you to read it.' Ellen held out her hand.

Mary put the book in it.

'He didn't post every day and most of them are just short sentences. They don't make much sense. Look. *"Father D'Angelo's got a new cat."* Why should Cliff care? And here. *"Alma's bitch had a litter. Does she know?"* Who's Alma, and if it's her dog, how could she not know?'

'I think I can answer that one. Alma Maxwell. She bred cocker spaniels for years, probably before Bonnie Blankenship started, but Cliff...'

'Oh, no. She isn't the one who had the dog Cliff spayed, is she?'

Mary nodded. 'She held on for a long time but told me yesterday she sold all the dogs she had left, except for that one, and is moving to Atlanta to live with her sister. She might not know one had puppies, but Cliff makes it sound like it's a big deal. I'm not sure why it should be.'

Ellen frowned. 'I know about her move. I'm going over this afternoon to talk about listing it. I didn't know about the dogs, though.' She looked at the book and flipped to another page. 'Listen to this. *"Should I do something about Luke?"* What does that mean? Then he has one about Evan. He owns Furry Friends, doesn't he? He wonders if Evan knows. Knows what? They're all like that. There's even one about those people who own the winery. Bliss—Bill and Naomi, right? He's got this one liner about them. *"Don't think Naomi is in this, but Bill? I don't know."* In what?'

'The Blisses are the ones who lost the little poodle. He was a champion and, I guess, very valuable. Naomi was devastated.' Mary thought of Naomi holding the picture of the little dog to her breast, her eyes filled with tears.

'I heard'—Ellen held up her hand to stop Mary's protest—'I know, no gossip, but this might be important.' Ellen looked from Mary to the book and then waited.

After a second, Mary nodded.

'I heard Bill Bliss wasn't nearly as devastated as Naomi and the dog was insured to the hilt. I don't know what "this" is or what Cliff's talking about, but he seems to think Bill could be implicated.'

Mary felt a little lightheaded and the notion to sit down was suddenly strong. The edge of Cliff's bed was all that was available and she took it. 'Implicated in whatever it was that got Cliff killed. That's what you mean, isn't it?'

Ellen nodded. 'Cliff's got a lot of comments in here that could mean nothing, just him rambling, or that he found out something. Something someone didn't want known. He mentioned money.' Ellen paused and took a deep breath. The look on her face plainly told Mary she didn't like what she was about to say. 'Do you suppose Cliff tried to blackmail one of these people and it backfired?'

'What?' Mary thought of all the people mentioned in Cliff's diary. She knew them all, had known them for years. 'What could any of those people possibly have done that would result in blackmail?' She paused and shook her head emphatically. 'Or murder?'

'I have no idea. Cliff must have been pretty desperate to have tried blackmail.'

'Who's blackmailing who?' A large carton box appeared in the bedroom door. It almost totally obscured the person who carried it. 'I've got everything packed, sealed and inventoried in the living room and had a box left over.' The box fell to the floor, revealing a short, rather round gray-haired woman tightly encased in dark blue police pants, a wide black belt and a light blue long-sleeved shirt tightly buttoned around a dark blue tie. 'Now, what's all this about blackmail?'

'We found Cliff's diary. It sounds—odd.'

'Like he was blackmailing someone?' Agnes stopped in the middle of the room, spread her feet apart slightly, hooked her thumbs in her belt and stared at Mary.

Mary inwardly sighed. Agnes had recently been hired by the police department to do office work. She answered the phones, had learned how to contact the few squad cars Santa Louisa owned, took messages, handed out forms and did everything that wasn't an emergency or had to do with actual crime. Today she was here helping Mary and Ellen at Dan's request, but she'd somehow turned it into official police business. She checked everything Mary and Ellen packed as if she thought they might run off with something, a thought that made Mary shiver. She'd insisted they put the contents of each box down on an inventory list and sign each one before it was pasted on top. The inventory would come in handy when they needed to make a final disposal of Cliff's things, but Agnes' attitude was beginning to wear thin. She was not now, and never would be, law enforcement, a fact that seemed lost on her. More and more, Agnes reminded Mary of Barney Fife from *The Andy Griffith Show*.

'Who was he blackmailing?'

'We don't know that's what he did.' Mary looked at the book Ellen still held and shuddered. 'How much more did you read?'

'Not much. I didn't want to go any farther.' Ellen put the book down on Cliff's dresser and stepped back from it.

Agnes walked over and picked it up. 'Where does it say he was blackmailing someone?'

Mary's fists clenched. 'It doesn't. He says, toward the end, that he needs money and maybe knows how to get some.'

Agnes blinked. She stared at Mary, then down at the book. 'How?'

Ellen snorted with what Mary thought was an interrupted laugh. 'How was he going to get money? He doesn't say. Agnes, it's all innuendos. We don't have any idea what Cliff meant. Except, he seems to be sorry for all the things he did while he was drinking. Talks about how he wants to make up for what he did.'

It was Agnes' turn to snort. 'That's hard to believe. I've known Cliff Mathews ever since he set foot in this town, and I'm here to tell you, he was a much nicer man drunk than he ever was sober, and that's a fact.'

Mary glanced over at Ellen, who reached out and

took the book back. She looked confused, exactly how Mary felt.

'Agnes, what are you talking about? Everything we read in that book says Cliff regretted all those things he did when he was drinking. Why, he even talks about Luke and how he should do something. He got Father D'Angelo a new cat. I don't know what he did to the old one, but he seemed to feel responsible.'

Agnes laughed. A loud and not very mirth-filled laugh. 'He got him a cat all right. The meanest, most cantankerous cat I've ever seen. I think Cliff did it on purpose. Blasted thing attacks Father every time he comes in the room. The cat's taken over Father's favorite reading chair, and the good man lets him. He—the cat—rules the house.' She paused for breath.

Mary and Ellen stared at her then at each other.

'Why does Father let him?' Ellen asked.

Agnes shrugged.

Mary's question was more direct. 'Did Cliff know what the cat was like?'

'He must have.'

This was not the Cliff Bonnie talked about. But Cliff had taken Naomi's picture of her poodle. Why? He'd brought Karl a DNA sample of that same dog to identify. What was that all about? Had he hidden the dog? No. He couldn't. Only... 'You make him sound mean.'

Agnes reached out and touched the diary, then withdrew her hand and let it drop to her side. 'Cliff was a nice man when he came here. He was nice when he started drinking. Even when all those things happened, all those "mistakes," he seemed sorry. He seemed kind. Then his wife died, his daughter left, he lost his practice and he got sober. I don't think he liked being sober.

He got morose. He blamed everyone but himself for all the bad things that happened, and every year he got angrier. What're you going to do with that book? It should go in with the other books.' She reached out her hand.

Mary withdrew hers. 'No. I don't think so.' She looked over at Ellen, who nodded.

'What are you going to do?'

'There's only one thing to do.'

As one, Mary and Ellen said, 'Give it to Dan.'

FOURTEEN

MARY SAT IN a straight-backed chair opposite Dan's desk, trying not to fidget. Ellen wasn't doing as well. She shifted her weight in her chair beside Mary, picked up her Styrofoam coffee cup, put it back on the corner of Dan's desk and sighed heavily.

'All that isn't going to help me read faster.' Dan didn't take his eyes off the page he was reading.

'First-graders read faster than you.' Ellen squirmed again.

Dan closed the diary and surveyed them both before reaching for his coffee.

'Well?' Mary leaned forward, almost not noticing the toll the chair's hard surface had taken on her behind.

'What do you think?' Ellen leaned her elbows on the edge of Dan's desk and stared at him intently.

'What do you want me to say?' He took a sip of the coffee, made a face and put it back on his desk. 'That after reading a month's worth of Cliff's ramblings I now know who murdered him and why?'

'Yes.'

Dan smiled at his wife. 'I appreciate your faith in me, but it doesn't usually work that way. Wish it did.'

'Dan, you must have some idea what Cliff was thinking. We only read a few pages. They weren't very clear, but it sounded...'

'As if Cliff was contemplating blackmail?' He picked the book back up and held it as if he could squeeze more information out of it. 'He may have. However, he never comes right out and says so. He rambles. Talks about how sorry he is for some of the things he did, how Alma Maxwell still, after all these years, won't speak to him. He says he can't blame her, only he doesn't know how to fix it for her. He talks about how he knows Father D'Angelo felt terrible about losing his cat and he guesses he's responsible. So he found him another one.'

'He found him another one, all right.' Mary paused, coffee cup halfway to her mouth. 'According to Agnes, he got Father D'Angelo another cat without even talking to him.'

'That seems a little high-handed, but at least it was well meant.'

'Not the way Agnes tells it.' Ellen stretched out her legs and sat back. 'She says it's meaner than a bobcat. Says he gave Father D'Angelo the cat on purpose. I guess Father doesn't know what to do with it, but it's terrorizing him and Mrs Farrell.'

'Who's Mrs Farrell?'

'His housekeeper.'

'Oh.' Dan shook his head a little. 'Most of what's in here are lamentations on the hurt he caused people and what he can do to make it up for them. Doesn't sound as if there was much.'

Ellen and Mary looked at each other. 'Who else?'

'Who else what?'

'You know very well what I'm talking about.' Mary used her best middle-schoolteacher voice.

Dan grinned. 'Who else did he think he'd hurt and what did he plan to do about it?'

'Luke, for one.'

'Luke who?' Ellen looked mystified. 'Do we know a Luke?'

'Luke from the library.' Mary turned toward her. 'You remember him. Young, ponytail, diamond earring.'

'Oh. That Luke. What did Cliff do to him?'

'I'll read it to you. It's one of the most poignant.' Dan opened the diary and flipped through pages, pausing at a couple before stopping. 'This is it.' He glanced up at the two of them, both waiting, sighed a little and started.

'"*Every time I think of young Luke, I want to cry. It's hard to realize what I'd do for a drink back then. I don't think Liam MacDougle really asked me to rig that junior handler class. I remember him telling me he'd spot me a bottle if I helped his kid, Ronnie. He meant coach him. I used to be a good coach. There was just about nothing I couldn't get a dog to do and I could teach the kids how to handle the dog too. The kids I coached won a lot. Liam is an honorable man. That day—it's still foggy. Why I thought... Then, after it was all over and Luke got thrown out for trying to show a drugged dog, the look Liam gave me, I'll never forget that. Ever. I don't remember if his kid won or not. I sure remember Luke not winning. Why, oh why, did I do those things?*"'

Mary sucked in her breath, hard. It made her stomach hurt. So that was what happened. 'I wonder if Luke knows how Cliff felt.'

'Not if Cliff hadn't approached him yet.' The look

on Dan's face was speculative, as if he, too, was mulling a possibility over in his mind.

'Cliff seems to have tried to make amends to everyone else he could think of.'

'Or at least have thought about it. His writing about it in his diary doesn't necessarily translate into action.'

Mary nodded. Ellen was right. There was nowhere in the part of the diary she read that mentioned any overtures Cliff had made to anyone. 'That's true. He talks about making amends but doesn't say how. Except for Father D'Angelo's cat.'

'That doesn't sound much like making amends.' Ellen bent down to pick up her purse, took out her cell phone and checked the time.

'You know, the more I think about it, the more his comments sound speculative.' Mary spoke slowly, as she tried to remember how Cliff phrased his cryptic sentences.

'As if he was assessing his chances for blackmail?' Ellen looked over at Dan, who shrugged. 'All those people he mentions, they were all victims, them and their animals. He may have been sorry, but he doesn't say he did anything to ask for their forgiveness. People like Alma, like Father D'Angelo, don't seem like potential blackmail victims. To the best of my knowledge, they're both squeaky clean and neither of them has any money. He could hardly blackmail Luke. He mentions the Blankenships but they were good friends and no comment he makes refutes that. He talks about the Blisses being involved in something, but he doesn't say what and it doesn't sound ominous. So, who was he thinking about?'

'I have no idea. If he had decided to try to blackmail

someone, I can't see who from his diary.' Dan shut the little book and laid it on his deck. 'Where did you find it? Sergeant Ricker and I searched that place pretty thoroughly yesterday afternoon. I got all his papers and personal things from his desk and brought them back here. We went through everything, I thought.'

'It was in his pillowcase.'

Dan stared at his wife then burst out laughing. 'His pillowcase?'

Ellen nodded. 'I was stripping the bed, packing up all the linens and it fell out. I picked it up to see what it was and it fell open. I read some and then called to Aunt Mary. It sure sounded as if he planned to blackmail someone.'

Dan nodded. 'It does. Only, who?'

Mary shrugged. 'That's why we brought it over. We thought you needed to see it right away.'

Dan leaned forward, resting his chin on his hands. Mary and Ellen waited.

Finally, he sat up straight. 'Have you finished packing up all his stuff ?'

Mary shook her head. 'Almost. We've finished the kitchen, and Agnes did the living room. We were working on his bedroom when we found the book.'

'OK. Are you going back? Cliff's landlady wants everything out this afternoon, and Ricker will be there…' he glanced at the digital clock on his desk…'in a little more than an hour. Is Agnes still there?'

'I can't go back. I have an appointment to list Alma's house and I need to go home and change.' Ellen pulled out her cell phone and glanced at the time. 'I really need to get going.'

'I can for a little while, but I promised Luanne I'd

pick up the children after school. She does the book-keeping out at Golden Hills winery. It's Friday and she has to close out the books and can't get away until about five. I want to be there when they come out of their classes.' She paused and took a deep breath. 'Dan, do you really think the children are in danger? Luanne is worried sick. So is Tony, and they're trying so hard not to let the children feel it. Today is Renaldo's soc-cer practice and he pitched a fit when they told him he couldn't go. I said I'd take him, but they both felt that—well, the field is big and the kids are all over the place. Hard to keep them in sight, so they decided he needed to skip it. I have errands to run, and they can tag along until I can deliver them to Luanne at the winery.'

It was as if a cloud settled on Dan's face. 'I don't know much of anything yet, and I don't want to take a chance they've spooked this guy. We know the kids saw him. He's got to be wondering if they can iden-tify him. I'd rather have Ronaldo mad at all of us for making him miss soccer practice than see him hurt, or worse.'

A shiver ran through Mary, from her head to her toes. The very thought of anything happening to those children…'Ronaldo will have to deal with it. How long do you think we're going to have to keep this up?' She ran her calendar through her head, wondering how much Luanne would need her and which com-mittee meetings wouldn't bore them to tears. All of them would.

'Dan,' Ellen was on her feet, her tote bag slung over her shoulder, 'have they done the autopsy yet?'

'As we speak.' He paused, as if trying to decide what to say next. 'Doc did tell me one thing.'

Ellen stood still; so did Mary.

Dan smiled. 'You two watch too many crime shows. He says he was stabbed with something long, thin and pointed. It went in through the rib cage and he's pretty sure right into his heart. He'll know more when he gets in there.' He leaned over his desk, pushed some buttons on his desk phone and picked up the receiver. 'How long will it take to finish boxing up all his things? I have to get them out of there and over to St Mark's this afternoon. It was nice of Les to say he'd store them. When we locate the daughter, we'll know what to do with them. I wouldn't be surprised if most of his things end up in your next rummage sale, Mary.'

Mary had a little trouble making the shift from long, sharp murder weapons and possible harm to the children back to Cliff's old dishtowels. 'Oh. An hour or so. Agnes may be finished by now.' She thought about the lovely old buffet and hoped Dan found the daughter soon. She got to her feet and steadied herself. 'You'd better get this solved, and fast. We're not going to be able to keep those kids under wraps forever.'

FIFTEEN

MARY PARKED THE car as close to the school as she could. Cars were parked two deep in front of it. She had no idea that many parents picked up their children. Then again, this was St Theresa's, a Catholic school. No school buses. She wondered what the mothers did who worked. She didn't think St Theresa's had an after-school program. She shook her head as she made her way through the parked cars and the chattering mothers. They must have quite a car pool system worked out. She pushed the front glass doors open and headed for the office. She hoped Luanne hadn't forgotten to send a note to the secretary authorizing her to sign out the children. The school would never hand them over to anyone who didn't have written permission from the parent, no matter how well they knew them.

The school secretary was on the phone. She wiggled her fingers at Mary while she agreed with whatever the caller had said. Mary found a chair, sank into it gratefully and waited.

She didn't wait long.

'Mary.' Sister Margaret Anne poked her head out of her office and waved at Mary. 'Can you come in for a moment?'

Mary nodded. She'd expected this. 'Good afternoon, Sister. It's been a while. Wasn't it the fundraiser for the new children's wing at the hospital we helped organize?'

Sister Margaret Anne nodded absently, obviously not interested in what happened since she'd seen Mary last. Her only interest was in what happened today. 'What's going on with the Mendosa children?'

She closed the door, walked behind her desk and sat, motioning for Mary to do the same. 'Luanne called here, her voice practically shaking, saying you'd pick them up and no one, emphasizing no one but you, Mr Mendosa or her was to come near them. Oh. Dan Dunham could. Mary, he's the chief of police!'

Mary tried to swallow her sigh. She didn't blame Luanne one bit for being upset, but falling apart wasn't going to help. However, Sister Margaret Anne needed to know what happened. They needed her to help keep the children safe.

'It's about Cliff Mathews. I'm sure you've heard.'

Sister Margaret Anne nodded, but she didn't smile. 'He was murdered. In the manger scene on St Theresa's lawn, of all places. What a wicked thing to do.'

She sounded more outraged than scared. That might change, soon.

'The Mendosa children saw the person who did it.'

Sister Margaret Anne didn't say a word. She stared at Mary, her mouth slightly open, her eyes wide. Finally, she blinked. 'Good Lord.'

Mary nodded. 'No one knows this, except whoever killed Cliff. It has to stay that way.' Mary relayed the events of Wednesday night.

Sister Margaret Anne sat rigid, her clasped hands increasingly tightening. 'You really think the children might be in danger from this man?'

'We have no idea. We don't know who he is. If he thinks they recognized him, well, I can't say what he might do. We just don't know.'

Sister Margaret Anne nodded but her hands didn't relax. 'You can't rule out the possibility he might do something here, on the school grounds. Shoot them, perhaps.'

'Oh, I don't think so.' Mary shook her head vigorously. 'I really don't think so.' But she did think he might do *something*. Wasn't that why she was here? 'It's more likely he'd try to take them—grab them. Or something.' Her voice got weaker as she wound down.

'You have no idea what might happen.' Sorrow and fear were in Sister Margaret Anne's voice and in her eyes. 'I'm responsible for all these children. If there is even a remote possibility of danger… I'd better call Chief Dunham.'

Mary wished she'd never opened her mouth, but she'd had to, just as Sister Margaret Anne had to call Dan. That was one phone call he wasn't going to enjoy.

The bell rang, announcing the end of the school day with enough noise to send shock waves through Mary. Sister Margaret Anne almost seemed not to have heard it. But she had. She got to her feet. 'I need to help make sure the kids get in the right cars. It's hard to keep track, and sometimes the older ones don't tell us when plans change. Come on. I'll help you find the Mendosa children.' She paused as they got to the door. 'Tell Luanne I'll talk to her this evening.' She took a step but turned once more, this time with anger in her eyes. 'This is outrageous. Those innocent children and poor old Cliff.' She paused and her voice softened. 'We had a dog at the convent once, a wonderful little dog we found one morning on the front porch. Cliff took care of that dog for years and did it with kindness and patience. Well, until those last few years. He didn't deserve this, though. And the children! They must be terrified. The police had better catch that man, and fast. This is just too much.' She wheeled around, her skirt and short veil flying, and left the room.

Mary followed. It didn't sound like Sister Margaret Anne had any recent memories. If she had, would she be as sympathetic? Probably. She was a kind woman. One thing they could agree on, the police had better catch whoever killed Cliff, and fast. As for the children being terrified, she wasn't so sure. They'd been pretty scared at first, but now she thought they were beginning to enjoy all the excitement. Which was not a good thing, not a good thing at all.

SIXTEEN

'WHY ARE WE going here?' Dalia sounded confused and not too pleased.

Ronaldo already had his seat belt off and his door half open.

'You said we were going to the pet shop.'

'We are.' Mary glanced in her rearview mirror. 'Ronaldo, don't you put one foot in the street until I tell you.'

The boy stopped, his foot half in and half out of the car. He looked like a runner ready to take off as soon as the gun fired.

Mary sighed, released her seat belt, reached over to the passenger seat and picked up a folder. She found the paper she wanted, extracted it and opened her door. 'Stay with me, both of you.'

Ronaldo pushed open the door to the Village Hardware store and the three of them entered. The store appeared to be empty.

'Mary McGill. I haven't seen you in here in ages.' The man seemed to appear out of nowhere, grinning from ear to ear. He looked like a lumberjack in his blue jeans, lace-up tan boots and plaid flannel shirt, sleeves rolled up to the elbows. His head was covered with thick black curls and his deeply muscled forearms with black hair that extended down to the knuckles of his stubby fingers. 'Hope that sink isn't blocked again.'

'No, Todd. The sink is working fine. I hoped you could take this home to Bonnie. It's a receipt for the donation the Pure Breed Dog Club made to the Christmas Can Tree. They'll need it for their taxes.'

Todd Blankenship glanced at it but made no move to take it. 'I don't suppose you'd consider driving this out to Bonnie.' He looked at Mary forlornly. 'Bonnie needs some company right about now, some cheering up. She's taking Cliff's death pretty hard.'

'Oh.' She didn't know what to say. Stopping at Bonnie's wasn't on her schedule, but she'd wondered if she was all right. Cliff had been Bonnie's vet and friend for many years. 'I have to go to Evan's then drop the children off at the winery—I can stop by your place on the way back.' She glanced at her watch and tried not to let Todd see her reluctance. She'd planned on going home early, taking off her shoes and doing nothing harder for dinner than heating up the chicken and rice soup she took out of the freezer this morning. But if she could help Bonnie… 'She's taking it hard?'

'Very hard.' Todd didn't look too happy. He shook his head in bewilderment. 'How could anyone do such a thing?'

'I don't know.' Mary tucked the paper back in her carryall and looked around for the children. They were by a large bin filled with sale items and were intently examining something that looked like barbeque tools. 'What are you two doing?'

'Looking for a Christmas present for Tony. We want to get him something with our own money. Mom too.' Ronaldo returned his attention to the bin.

'Do you think Tony would like this? He loves doing barbeques.' Dalia held up a barbeque apron embossed with a chef's hat, a whiskey bottle and a saying Mary didn't think appropriate for a gift given by two small children.

'It has a broken apron string.' She removed the apron from Dalia's hand.

'It's only two dollars.'

'It's still overpriced.'

Ronaldo dug a long-handled spatula out of the jumble of things in the bin. 'I'll bet he'd like this. Where's the fork thing?'

Todd removed the spatula from Ronaldo's hand. 'It's gone. I've priced these things so low because parts are missing or the packages are torn, or something. I'm not sure this is where you want to shop for a Christmas present.'

Dalia looked at him then down at his boots. A slight frown passed over her face. 'We only have five dollars and we don't want to get any money from Mom if we can help it.' She turned back to the bin, moved stuff around and came up with a package of barbeque skewers, long, thin ones with heavy wooden handles. 'Look! These are nicer than the ones Mom and Tony have and they're only three dollars.' She held the package aloft, grinning.

'Oh. That package is torn and one's missing.' Todd reached for it but Dalia clutched it to her chest.

'Mom can find a box.'

'Aunt Mary will find one.' There was no doubt in Ronaldo's voice. 'We'll give it to both of them.'

'Would you?' Dalia's expression was hopeful as she looked at Mary. 'They're only three dollars. We can get something for the baby with what's left.'

'Of course I will.' Mary's thoughts whirled. How

was she going to wrap those wicked-looking things? The ends were sharp. They'd go through any wrapping paper... The long, awkward box under her bed. She'd been certain it would come in handy someday. She examined the skewers. Five of them. Should be six but Tony and Luanne wouldn't mind. That was more than enough for their family and the baby wouldn't be eating barbeque food for some time. 'Ring them up, Todd.'

Todd looked at Mary then down at the children, reluctance evident in his furrowed brow and his tight shoulders. 'That's mighty thoughtful of you kids, but are you sure? Someone destroyed the package and there are only five skewers.' His voice trailed away as the children said nothing but showed no signs of replacing their prize in the sale bin.

Mary glanced at her watch. 'They'll do fine. Ring them up, Todd. Dalia, where's your money?'

Distress passed over the little girl's face. 'My wallet's in my backpack in the car.'

'I'll go.' Ronaldo beamed at Mary. 'The car's right outside. Can I?'

Mary's car was parked outside the store window in plain sight. Nothing could possibly happen to the boy with her eye firmly glued on him. Had she locked it? No. She never did, not in this town. She nodded and he was off.

'We're going to the pet shop next. They have the cutest puppies.'

Ronaldo was half in and half out of the car and Mary gave Dalia's statement only half her attention.

'You like puppies?'

Mary turned quickly away from the window.

Dalia nodded. 'We found one, Ronaldo and me. We're trying to get Mom and Tony to let us keep him.'

Todd's next question was sharp with surprise. 'Where?'

Mary quickly intervened. 'Over by the church. They found it over by St Theresa's. A stray, I guess.'

'Where is it now? Is it OK?'

Another dog person. Mary wondered if he'd act this concerned if the kids had found a newborn baby. That wasn't fair. There were more stray dogs than lost babies, and it was a good thing people cared about them. 'It's at the Benningtons' clinic.'

That wasn't enough for Dalia. 'Doctor Bennington's going to keep him until he's bigger and learns to—you know—go to the bathroom outside. He's real cute. He's got one white foot and white down his front and all his toenails are white and his ears are curly. He looks like the puppies over at the pet shop. You can go look at them, if you want, and you'll know just what Sampson looks like.'

Todd might be a dog person, but he didn't seem to have any interest in Evan's puppies. He opened his mouth ready to ask another question, but Ronaldo burst in the door, panting slightly but proudly waving Dalia's wallet over his head. 'Got it.'

Dalia handed Todd a five-dollar bill. He rang up the sale, gave Ronaldo the package and Dalia the change. She gravely counted it and put it in her wallet.

Mary hid her smile. 'We've got to get going if we're going to meet your mom at the winery.'

The children beamed as they carried their treasure out to the car. Mary put the skewers in the trunk and took both their hands, and they walked across the street to Furry Friends pet shop. She glanced back. Todd Blankenship watched them from the door of his shop. Mary waved. He waved back, turned and walked back into the store.

to Party Friends, yet alone. She glanced back. Paula Foundation was worried, looking from the parking lot. Mary turned. Hopwood Track turned, and walked back into the store.

SEVENTEEN

THE CHILDREN SKIPPED as they crossed the street, at least Dalia did. Mary could hardly keep up with them. She didn't drop their hands, however, until they were inside. They immediately headed for the puppy pen.

'Where's the one who looks like Sampson?' Dalia turned toward Evan, who approached at almost a trot, followed by two men who couldn't have looked more unalike. 'Is he all right?'

'That puppy sold. He's going to be a little girl's Christmas present from her grandma.'

He smiled at her. So did the two men who stood behind him. Mary watched relief flood Dalia's face. Ronaldo knelt beside the pen and put his hand over the top, ready to scratch the ears of any puppy who came close. They all did.

Mary finally looked closer at the two men. 'Why, Glen Manning. John Lavorino. I haven't seen you two in ages. Where have you been and what are you doing here?'

John, short and swarthy, with what Mary thought an unfortunately large nose, looked across at Glen. John fiddled with the gold chain that hung around his neck, clearly seen through his unbuttoned lavender Henley. Today his jeans were black and very tight. John's jeans were always tight. He glanced back at Mary, then at Evan and back at Glen, but he didn't say anything. Instead, he knelt down beside Ronaldo, reached into the puppy pen, picked one up and handed it to him. The puppy immediately started to lick Ronaldo's nose. The boy giggled and sat on the floor, Indian style, the puppy wiggling in his lap.

John looked over at Dalia. 'You're the Mendosa children, aren't you?'

Dalia nodded, her eyes glued on the remaining puppies.

'You want to hold one too?'

She nodded again, a smile playing around the corners of her mouth.

'Sit down.' John reached into the pen and pulled out the smallest puppy, almost equally black and white, with a pink nose. She had white feet and shiny clear toenails.

'She looks like she had her nails done.' Dalia laughed and held the puppy close to her face, where she also got a kiss on the nose. She laughed again, lowered the puppy into her arms and started to rock it back and forth, humming under her breath.

'Starts early, doesn't it?' Glen was tall, thin and dressed in well-pressed chinos and a blue button-down collar shirt, cuffs turned back once over the sleeves of his navy blue pullover. Brown leather sandals over white socks completed the picture. Mary blinked at the sight of him. She'd never seen Glen in anything but the carefully tailored suits he wore at the bank. Shouldn't he be at the bank? Evidently he was starting his weekend early.

He smiled at the picture the girl and dog made. Mary didn't. It was appealing, but she couldn't help think the child was growing up too fast and fear for her made her throat close. The fear wasn't for her growing up but that something might happen so she didn't. Whoever killed Cliff would have to get by Mary first before he harmed one hair on the head of either of these children. She shifted slightly and saw Evan out of the corner of her eye. He wasn't smiling. Glen saw him as well.

'Lighten up, Evan. It's good for the puppies to be held and good for the kids to hold them. They're not going to hurt them.'

Evan almost wrung his hands and his face was contorted with anguish. Little beads of sweat appeared on the edges of what hair was left on his scalp. He kept glancing at the door as if he expected someone to burst in any minute. What was the matter with him? Almost as if he'd read her mind, he said, 'Those aren't my puppies. They're here for sale. I'm responsible for them. The'—he paused, as if he'd caught himself just in time—'owners might not like them being held.'

Ronaldo looked up, alarm in his eyes. 'Do we have to put them back?'

'No.' John was emphatic. 'Evan gets nervous. You can hold them for another couple of minutes.' He looked at the crestfallen faces and knelt down once more between the children. 'Tell you what. When Glen's and my next litter of cockapoos are ready for Evan to sell, we'll let you know and you can come hold them as much as you want.'

Ronaldo grinned but Dalia held her puppy up and examined it closely. 'Is that what these puppies are? Cockapoos? What does that mean?'

'It means they have a cocker spaniel for one parent and a poodle for the other. Cockapoos.' Glen bent down and took the puppy out of her hands. 'Evan is right. It's time to put them back.'

The children groaned but handed over the puppies. Evan leaned against the counter and ran a hand over his damp scalp.

Mary looked at her watch. 'It's after four. I told your mother I'd have you out at the winery before five. We'd better get going.' She looked at them. 'If she sees you looking like that she'll never trust me with you again. You need to wash, and Dalia, you have to comb your hair. Do you have one?'

Dalia cheerfully shook her head.

'You're in luck. I do. Evan, do you have a bathroom where the children can wash up?'

Evan pointed toward the back of the store. Mary handed Dalia the small brush she always carried and the two dejectedly walked in the direction of the bathroom.

'Don't dawdle, either. We have to get going.'

She dived into her carryall and pulled out the receipt for the donations Evan had made and handed it to him. 'This is why I came in. You'll need this for your taxes, and I want you to know the entire can tree committee thanks you.'

Evan smiled a weak smile and took the paper. Mary didn't smile back. Two questions had occurred to her and she wanted answers before the children came back.

'Evan, where do you get the puppies you sell?'

'What do you mean?' Evan's eyes shifted and he ducked his head. She'd seen that look on every seventh-grader she'd ever taught when they were trying to avoid answering a question.

'Where do the puppies come from? Who owns them? What do you know about them?'

'Why?' The reptile tank suddenly seemed of supreme importance. Evan walked over, put his hand in and moved a fake green tree a little to the left, much to the annoyance of the lizard asleep under it.

'She wants to know if you buy puppies from a puppy mill.' John propped himself up by leaning on the counter next to Evan. He lounged back against the counter, letting his elbows hold him, and looked at Evan over the top of his sunglasses, which he let fall from the top of his head where he'd pushed them.

'Straighten up, John.' It sounded like something Glen said often.

John grinned but straightened up. When he looked at Mary, all trace of a smile was gone. 'He doesn't, you know. He knows every breeder who brings dogs, cats or anything else in here to sell. He makes sure every animal has its shots, or whatever they need, and demands a vet certificate to prove it. I think he'd shoot anyone who tried to bring an endangered animal in the door. Our Evan is a good man. We wouldn't bring our puppies to him if he wasn't. We wouldn't keep bugging him to sell us part ownership in the shop, either.' He looked over at Glen, who stood, not moving, smiling or talking, next to a tank that held small turtles. 'Would we?'

Glen shook his head. 'No, we wouldn't.'

Mary glanced toward the bathroom, but there was no sign of the children. No screams came from that direction, either, so she decided it was safe to ask her next question.

'I haven't seen any of you in church for, oh, several

weeks. I heard—I haven't talked to Reverend McIntyre but… I hope I'm wrong.'

Glen, John and Evan exchanged glances. Evan left the lizard alone and turned back toward the puppies. Tension was evident in his back muscles, even through his blue long-sleeved polo. John's face seemed to turn black. His eyes snapped and his nostrils flared. He appeared about to say something when Glen laid a hand on his arm. 'You're not wrong. There was a little… unpleasantness. We didn't want it to get out of hand and didn't want the congregation to start choosing up sides, so we thought—we decided—to start attending services at a church in San Luis Obispo. We're going down there tonight. They're having a potluck, with music and dancing after.' He paused and glanced at the other two men before going on. 'Attending the dances at St Mark's is a little awkward.'

Mary couldn't remember when she'd felt as sick, as humiliated for her friends. Where had Les—Reverend McIntyre—been in all this? How much did he know? Should she do something? Say something? She should, and would. 'I can't tell you how sorry I am and how appalled. What can I do to help?'

'Nothing, Mary.' Evan tried to smile but it didn't work very well. 'Some things are just the way they are.'

'Surely we can do something. Who is it that's acting this way? I'll talk to them; I'll get Les, Reverend McIntyre, to talk to them also. You must know that most of us don't… What is it?'

The three of them looked at her with almost identical expressions of wry amusement, sorrow and fury.

Finally, it was Glen who spoke. 'You want to know who stirred up some of the congregation against us.'

Mary nodded, a feeling of dread creeping up her throat.

'Cliff.'

EIGHTEEN

MARY DROVE ALMOST on autopilot. The children sat in the back, discussing the merits of the puppies they'd held, the other critters offered in Evan's pet shop and what they could get for the baby for two dollars. Mary barely heard them. Her thoughts were on Cliff. What had he done, and why? John and Glen had been members of St Mark's for years. Everyone knew them, knew they were a couple. No one cared. At least, Mary didn't think anyone cared. Evidently, she was wrong. But what could Cliff have done to make them change churches? He wasn't even a member. Well, not an active member. It must have been something pretty uncomfortable. What that was, Mary silently vowed to find out.

The light changed, she made her left-hand turn and entered the winery parking lot. It was after four, but the lot was still half full. Mary stepped out of the car and waited for the children, who joined her almost immediately. She took each by the hand but didn't move. Instead, she looked around. She'd heard the winery was impressive but still wasn't quite prepared for what lay before her. The building sprawled out on top of a knoll, covering most of it. The stucco was painted a pale creamy yellow, the shutters on the long windows were a bright blue and the door leading into the building from the cobblestone courtyard was massive oak,

its handles hammered wrought iron. A tiled terrace was
to the right of the building, iron tables and chairs scattered over it. The umbrellas were tied down, the tables
empty. Why, wasn't hard to guess. The early winter
breeze made sitting outside uncomfortable. Mary let
go of the children and pulled her jacket tighter around
her, took each child's hand again and started toward
the doors.

Dalia pulled away and stared at the vineyard that
trailed down the hill toward the highway. Houses could
just be glimpsed between the highway and where the
vines ended. 'Look. There's Tony's truck.' She pointed
toward a dirt road that ran between the vines. A group
of men piled into the back of a dirty brown pickup.
Another group stacked branches at the end of a row of
vines. 'They must be done pruning for the day.'

They watched for a moment as the truck slowly
made its way up the hill. It turned off, headed for what
looked like an equipment barn about halfway up the
slope. It disappeared through blue double doors.

'Come on.' Mary tugged at the children. 'Tony will
be up here soon enough. Let's go find your mother.'

Mary had been in half the wineries in Santa Louisa but she'd never seen one like this. The room they
entered was huge and filled with light. The wall that
overlooked the terrace held a series of French doors,
showcasing the panoramic views of Santa Louisa and
the hills beyond. There were brightly striped canvas
roll-up canopies on the outside to protect the room, and
those who sat on the patio, from the hot summer sun.
This afternoon they were pulled up to show the beginnings of what promised to be a beautiful winter sunset.

A large round display table stood just inside the

windows, piled with majolica pottery and pewter platters, all in some sort of grape pattern. Books were featured on another, and there was one full of crystal wineglasses. The one closest to the door where Mary stood offered cookbooks. Main courses made with wine, pasta dishes from Tuscany, artisan bread recipes, straight from the grill delights. There was a book for every taste. There was also a goodly display of barbeque tools, baking dishes, kitchen implements and cork pullers. Mary looked at the barbeque skewers and wondered if she should try to talk the children into another choice. She strained to read the price tag and gave a gasp. What they had already purchased would do just fine. She turned as the children tugged her toward a hallway that opened up on the far side of the long and very crowded tasting room bar. People stood against it, resting their feet on the brass rail, making notes in small booklets with stubby pencils as they sipped tiny amounts of wine from long-stemmed glasses. For many folks it would not be a dry Christmas.

'Mom's down this way.'

She was being tugged down the hallway toward what looked like offices. She'd seen people tasting wine before. That wasn't what held her attention, or caused her to drag her feet. It was the cookbooks. She wanted to look at them. Maybe later.

'Mary.'

Naomi stood in an open doorway of a spacious room that held two large desks, back to back, in the middle. Bookshelves lined the far wall, loaded with bottles of wine, pictures, plaques and long-stemmed glasses. There were a couple of upholstered tub chairs, a cre-

denza and a load of electronic equipment. The Blisses'
office.

'What are you doing here?' She looked down the
hall past Mary to where cries of 'Mom' and soft laughter sounded. 'Oh. You had the Mendosa children.'

Mary nodded. 'Glad you're here. It'll save me a trip.'

'A trip?' Naomi looked blank.

'Yes. Cliff's memorial. We talked about it yesterday.' Mary was beginning to feel tired and faintly irritated. 'We've finished packing all of his things and
some of the church people are picking them up to take
to St Mark's. Les has agreed to store them temporar-
ily. Now, we need to decide what we're going to do
about the service.'

'Nothing.'

'What?' Mary wasn't sure she'd heard right. Nothing? 'What are you talking about? Les, Reverend Mc-
Intyre, asked us to—well, Isabel asked us.'

'I talked to Bill about this. He thinks, and he's
right—Mary, I can't do it.'

The words weren't making any sense. 'I don't understand.'

'Come in the office.' Naomi turned her back on
Mary and walked into the room.

Mary glanced down the hall, nervous she hadn't
personally delivered the children to their mother, but
another burst of laughter reassured her. They were with
Luanne. Mary followed Naomi and sat herself in one
of the chairs. 'Now. What's all this about?'

Naomi sat behind her desk, a gold pen in her hand.
She didn't look at Mary but stared at a yellow legal
pad set squarely in the middle of her desk. 'I can't
do it. Memorials mean saying nice things about the

dead person. Friends gather, console the family and each other and remember things they'd done together, good things.' She made some marks on the legal pad, drew a figure of what Mary thought might be a dog, then a bottle, then a stick man. Finally she let the pen go slack in her hand and looked up. 'There aren't any good memories.'

Mary had no idea what to say. She didn't need to. Now the difficult words were out, Naomi seemed eager to explain.

'We've only been here about four years. We never saw the Cliff so many of you remember. The kind one, the one who was a good vet. The sober one.' She picked the pen back up and started rolling it around in her fingers, keeping her eyes resolutely fixed on it. 'The first time we met Cliff he showed up here, drunk. It was our grand opening. Bill was all for throwing him out, but the mayor was here and a couple of other people who knew him. They got him out before he caused a disturbance. He kept coming back. Sometimes he was sober, sometimes not, but always he came because he wanted to see Merlot, the little poodle who...disappeared. It got to the point where I'd lock the dog in my office when I saw him coming.' She laid the pen on the paper and looked straight at Mary for the first time. 'It wasn't any better after he got sober. He didn't come as much, but when he did he hung around, not saying anything, just picking up bottles, putting them down, looking for the dog. Mary, he was weird. He wasn't very good for business, either.' This last she said with a rueful little laugh well mixed with bitterness. 'I got to the point where I almost hated him. I hated seeing that old car of his drive into the parking lot.' She paused again and this time sighed deeply. 'Bill thought I was overreacting. Maybe I was, but I'll tell you something…' She paused again, as if choosing her words carefully. 'I've wondered if Cliff had something to do with Merlot's disappearance.'

Mary sucked in her breath quickly. 'Oh. Oh, no. Why would he?'

Naomi shook her head. 'I don't know, but he was here that day.' Her eyes filled with tears. She pulled her desk drawer open, pulled a couple of tissues out of a box Mary couldn't see and slammed it shut. 'He was so damn weird about the dog, always telling Bill we should breed him, even. I've always wondered, and when I saw that picture yesterday, it all came back. Mary, there is no way I can help put on a memorial for that man. I don't have even one good memory to share.' She dabbed both eyes, blinked away any remaining tears, straightened herself and laid her folded hands on the desk. 'I'm sorry.'

The person Naomi described wasn't the one Mary knew. Or thought she knew. Why would Cliff act like that? But then, why would he complain to Reverend McIntyre about John and Glen? Why would he give a half-wild cat to Father D'Angelo? The cryptic sentences in his diary—what did they mean? A throbbing started in her temples. 'I'm sorry, also. Of course you don't have to do anything. I had no idea—I'll talk to Les.' She had a lot to talk about with Les.

'Oh. I didn't realize you had someone—hello, Mrs McGill.'

Mary twisted in her chair at the sound of the man's voice. The sun was almost finished for the day and a shadow obscured the doorway. At first, she didn't recognize the man who stood there. He walked into the room and she knew him immediately. Bill Bliss. Naomi's husband. He wasn't a man you easily forgot. Tall, solidly built, he wore his gray wool slacks, open-necked blue dress shirt and soft navy jacket with an easy confidence. Mary was surprised he remembered her. They had been introduced once at church and had nodded at each other a few times, but she'd always felt it was cursory. Maybe she'd been wrong.

She smiled and nodded. 'Nice to see you, Bill.' She would have sworn he blinked at the 'Bill' but covered it quickly. Her smile widened.

'We're leaving now.' Dalia skipped into the room and skidded to a stop when she saw Bill Bliss. 'Oh.'

He turned to look at the child, a frown narrowing his eyebrows. They looked like brown and gray caterpillars.

Dalia looked back, her mouth still forming a small 'Oh.'

Ronaldo almost ran into her as he entered. 'Why are you standing—Oh.' He, too, stared at Bill before he glanced at his sister.

Their eyes met, then they looked at Mary, soundless. Soundless, for them, was not a normal occurrence. The moment didn't last.

Luanne walked into the room, carrying a briefcase. 'I'm going now. Oh, Bill. I didn't know you were back.' She nodded, but it was Naomi she addressed. She looked tired and didn't seem to notice as the children backed up to stand close, one on each side of her.

Ronaldo reached for the briefcase. 'I'll carry that for you, Mom.'

She squeezed him with her free arm. 'That's all

right, sweetie. That's my laptop. I think I'd better hold it, but I forgot my tote bag in my office. Can you carry that?'

Ronaldo beamed and headed out the door. Dalia gave Bill Bliss one more look, ducked out from under her mother's arm and followed. Mary watched them go. So did Bill.

'Brenda's closing out tonight. I'll make the bank deposit Monday. The payroll's ready, all except the hourly people, and the inventory is up to date. I'll go over that with Brenda on Monday. She's going to be fine.'

Naomi nodded. Bill frowned. Mary heaved a silent sigh of relief. She hadn't known if Luanne and Tony worked weekends or not. The first committee meeting for St Mark's spring rummage sale was tomorrow. She wouldn't mind missing it. She'd attended more than her share. However, try as hard as she might, she'd once again been elected chairman. She needed to show up. 'What about Monday? Do you want me to pick up the children?'

Luanne glanced at Bill then over at Naomi. 'Let's see what happens. Can you drop by the house after church on Sunday? Tony should know his schedule by then. And Mary, thank you.'

Mary smiled and nodded. She was happy she could help but secretly relieved she wouldn't be needed until Monday. There were things she had to do besides the committee meeting. At some point in the next couple of days she wanted to talk with Les. She wanted to know what to do about Cliff's memorial. If a lot of others felt the same way Naomi did John and Glen wouldn't be coming, and she didn't think Evan would either. What had happened with them? What had Cliff done? Yes, she had to talk to Les. Right now, however, she had to go see Bonnie, and then she was going home. Did she have a bottle of wine in the refrigerator? She couldn't remember. Well, she was in a winery.

'I need to go as well. However, I hear your Chardonnay is exceptional. May I buy a bottle?'

Bill Bliss smiled for the first time since he'd come in. 'You may indeed. Let me get one for you.' He took her by the arm and they headed toward the tasting room. Mary looked back. Luanne was right behind them, but she turned the other way down the hall.

'Mary, thank you again. We'll see you Sunday.'

NINETEEN

THE DRIVE TO Bonnie's was too short for Mary to sort out all of her thoughts. Why had the Mendosa children fallen quiet when they saw Bill Bliss? The children were many things, bright and fun, but never quiet. Had they recognized him? Or thought they did? No, not possible. They hadn't looked scared. Wary perhaps, but not scared. Well, he was their mother's boss, and their stepfather's as well. Could that account for it? Someone had said something, though. What was it? Something…insurance. That was it. Ellen said the little poodle the Blisses had was insured to the hilt. Could Bill really have done something to the dog, made it disappear somehow, and collected the insurance? Could Cliff have found out and decided to blackmail him? She shook her head. This was beginning to sound like a made-for-TV movie.

She turned into Bonnie's driveway and paused. The big gate was open. She drove through.

No one seemed to be around. Bonnie's car was parked by the kennel building. Her van wasn't, but that didn't mean anything. Some people actually kept cars in their garage. She got out, stretched and let the car door slam. Immediately dogs barked. Yelped. Demanded to know who was on their property. If Bonnie was here, she knew that Mary, or someone, was also.

She'd heard. She appeared in the doorway of the

kennel bulding, peering into the dim light of the yard. 'Mary! I didn't know you were coming.'

'I was at the winery and thought I'd stop off and give you the receipt for the donations. I didn't know if you were a nonprofit or not but thought you should have it. The Christmas Can Tree Drive is very grateful for your help.'

'Nonprofit?' Bonnie looked a little surprised then laughed and nodded. 'There are times.'

Mary held out the paper she'd carried out of the car with her, but Bonnie shook her head again. 'Can you put it on my desk inside? My hands—I've got gloves on.'

For the first time, Mary noticed the thin gloves Bonnie had on. They were the same kind the nurse and doctor wore when she went in for a check-up. The ones the dentist and his assistant wore—even the people at the bakery wore them when they filled your order. What was Bonnie doing with them? Mary looked closer. The knees of her jeans were damp, as if she'd been kneeling in something wet, her T-shirt was stained and there were streaks of dirt on her face. What was she doing?

'Whelping.' Bonnie smiled as if Mary had spoken out loud. 'Mindy is having her babies. You're just in time to see. Come on in.'

She headed back through the kennels' doorway, Mary close behind. She'd only seen puppies born one other time, years ago when one of her sister's dogs had produced a litter. She had obligingly let the entire neighborhood watch. It had been fascinating; she remembered that but not much else. She hurried a little faster.

'Put that down on my desk then come in the last

kennel. Try to be quiet. She's a first timer and is doing well, but she's a little nervous.'

Tiredness forgotten, Mary placed the tax statement on Bonnie's cluttered desk, hesitated as she wondered how to keep it from getting lost in the pile of papers already there, placed a clear glass paperweight with a cocker spaniel etched on one corner of it and tiptoed down the aisle to the open kennel. Bonnie knelt in the dirt beside a large slat-sided box filled with shredded newspaper.

'Is she all right?'

'She's fine. So are the pups. Come look. She's got three already. She's taking a little rest before she does it again.'

Bonnie sat back on her heels. Mary looked at her, sighed, then lowered herself down on one knee, placed a hand on the ground and got down on both of them. This was only going to last a short time. She hoped she'd be able to get back up.

However, while she was here, there were three puppies laying, wiggling by their mother. One was already sniffing the air, pulling itself around while making soft mewing sounds. 'Where is he going?'

'He's trying to find his mother's nipple. He can't see yet, that will take a while, and can't really get up on his feet, but he can smell and he knows he's hungry.'

They watched the pup in silence while it tried to find its first meal.

Finally, Mary asked, 'How many more will she have?'

'One. At least, if that ultrasound we took is right. Probably is. Cliff said she had four and I've never known him to be wrong. She'll lick these guys a little more, let them try to find a nipple then go back into labor. She'll kind of shake off anyone who's figured out how to latch on, break the sack on the new one, break the cord and lick the pup until it's breathing on its own and starts to wiggle around. I never tire of watching this. It's like a miracle, each time.'

Mary had no trouble agreeing with that. So tiny, so perfect, and both mother and babies seemed to know just what to do. 'Who's the father?'

'The dog you saw the other day. This is his first litter, for me, that is, and I already have all of them sold.' There was great satisfaction in Bonnie's voice and obvious pride.

Mary thought back to the puppies she had seen at Evan's pet shop earlier that day. Those puppies looked a little like these and the older pups she'd seen here when she'd collected the dog food for the Christmas Can Tree. That honey-colored one still stuck in her mind. So sweet, such long, silky ears, so... 'Are these purebred cocker spaniels?'

From the expression on Bonnie's face, Mary thought she'd just said something blasphemous. 'Of course. That's what we do. Breed cockers. I'm known for my cockers. Why would you think they would be something else?'

Mary was taken aback by how upset Bonnie seemed to be. 'I didn't mean—only I don't know much about dogs and the puppies we saw at Evan's shop look a little like these and they were only part cocker. So, I wondered if you ever did that.'

'No.'

Mary had never heard a more emphatic one.

'The dogs you saw at Evan's are cockapoos. Part

poodle, part cocker. People pay huge amounts for them but I wouldn't consider breeding them. When people buy my dogs, they know they're getting the best pure cocker spaniel bloodlines they can find anywhere.'

That seemed to be the end of that subject, and it was just as well. Mary could feel her knees protesting. The dirt was hard, her knees were used to a soft garden kneeler when she worked in the yard, and they were not happy. Neither was her back. It was time to go. She put her hand on the ground and started to position one leg under her, hoping she could get up in one movement, when Bonnie grabbed her arm. 'Look. She's getting ready.'

The little dog contracted. She lay on one side and pushed. A small, greenish sack appeared from under her tail. The dog paused, panted a couple of times, looked back at the sack, laid her head back down on the newspaper and pushed again. The sack slid out a little farther, enough so Mary could see a nose. A little black nose. With a groan, the dog pushed one more time and the sack was almost out. The puppy it contained didn't move. Neither did the mother. Mary forgot her knees, her back and how to breathe. Were they dead? The beautiful mother, her head limp on the damp newspaper, and the puppy entrapped in the thick membrane sack would surely die as well. They had to do something. Why was Bonnie not...

She was. 'Tired, aren't you.' She reached under the dog's stub of a tail, gently pulled the sack all the way out and broke it open. Liquid poured out along with a puppy. A black puppy with white feet, with white across its shoulders, its flanks and a white diamond mark on its chest. 'Will you look at that. A parti-color. I wasn't expecting that.'

The puppy started to shudder. At least, that's what it looked like to Mary. The mother picked up her head, looked back at her baby, turned so she could reach it and started to lick. The sack was off completely, the cord disappeared and the puppy started to wiggle.

Mary breathed again. 'How many times a year do you do this?'

Bonnie laughed. 'I have three bitches and I only breed them once a year. She's got four beauties. Time to leave her alone. Come on, I'll help you up.' She stood, reached out to Mary and helped her to her feet. They stood for a moment, looking at the mother dog as she let the first puppy nurse while she licked the newest one. The other two sniffed the air and headed for their first supper.

'Even three times would be a little too much drama for me. I'm wrung out.' Mary stretched and flexed her knees. They were fine. 'Does that include the dogs you bought from Alma?'

It was almost as if Bonnie hadn't heard her. 'Cliff used to be with me when I had a litter born. The first time I thought I was going to pass out, but he walked me through the whole thing. The dog was fine. I almost didn't make it. He taught me so much, not just about whelping but about breeding, about caring. He knew what to look for in a dog. He was the one who taught me how to judge. He went to dog shows with me. Even after... He would have been here with me today. It's hard to believe he's gone.'

Bonnie wiped her eyes with the back of her hands, seemed to realize she had on gloves, stripped them off, threw them in a close-by trash can and headed out the kennel building's doors into the now-dark yard.

Mary followed. 'Alma's dogs. You have three including hers?'

Bonnie stopped and looked around. 'Oh. Alma's dogs. No. I haven't bred them yet. I'm not sure what I'll do. They're nice but not quite…' She seemed a little lost once more. Grief. Grief and strain.

Only, from what she had read in Cliff's diary… She must have misunderstood. Or Bonnie had. Anyway, it wasn't important. What was important was that she went home and took off her shoes.

'Is there anything I can do for you?' She fervently hoped not and immediately felt guilty. Bonnie was grieving. If she needed help, Mary would give it, but she really wanted to go home.

Bonnie shook her head. 'No. Thank you for asking, and thanks for coming by. Actually, it helped just having someone else here. Todd will be home soon, and even though he doesn't know it yet, he's taking me out to dinner.' She pushed back a strand of hair and left a grayish streak on her cheek.

Mary got in her car and rolled the window down. Bonnie rested her elbows on the door and leaned on them. 'You're close to the Mendosa family, aren't you?'

Mary nodded. What had brought that on?

'I heard the Mendosa children were in the manger when Cliff…' She shuddered. 'I heard they saw the man who killed him and that's where they found the puppy. Is that true?'

Mary felt as if she'd been hit in the chest with a meat mallet. 'Who told you that?' She could barely get the words out.

'It's all over town. Do they know who the man was?'

Mary wasn't sure what to say. All over town? No. It couldn't be. If the murderer heard that, if he thought those children really knew who he was... She had to stop this rumor, right now. Starting with Bonnie. 'They don't know anything. They did go out to the manger. They wanted to see their mother ride in on the donkey, and that's when they found Cliff's body. They have no idea—they saw a shadow. It might not even have been a man. Dalia thought it was a cow.' She tried to laugh a little. It came out as a giggle. 'The only ones who might know anything are the police, and so far they haven't said much. As for the puppy, no one seems to know where it came from. I don't see how it can be connected.' Mary was babbling. She didn't approve of lying and wasn't very good at it. 'You tell whoever's spreading this they're wrong. Dead wrong.' Oh, that wasn't good. Never mind. Was she convincing? She hoped so. She needed Bonnie to spread the word that the children knew nothing. If whoever did that to Cliff thought they could identify him... Goose bumps broke out on her arms. It was a long shot, but the best she could do right now. She smiled. 'You're sure there's nothing I can do for you?'

Bonnie stepped away from the window and shook her head. 'No. Thanks, Mary. I'm fine. I'll go feed the dogs and wait for Todd.'

Mary nodded. She tried to read the expression on Bonnie's face but couldn't. Did she believe her? Would she tell whoever was spreading the rumor they were wrong? Would she even talk to that person? Mary ground her teeth, slipped the car into gear and drove out through the gate opening.

She turned into the street with one hand and fished in her tote bag for her cell phone with the other. She knew she shouldn't drive and talk, but this was important. There was one person who needed to know about this rumor going around and needed to know right now. She dialed the police station.

'Hello, Agnes? Did they get the apartment cleaned out? Good. Agnes, I need to talk to Dan. Now.'

TWENTY

'TELL ME THAT AGAIN. Bonnie says it's all over town the kids saw a man in the manger? That they know who he is?'

Mary picked up her water glass, looked at it and held it in front of her. 'That they saw someone, yes. That they know who it is I'm not sure. However, the way rumors work, by tomorrow the story will be they not only knew him but shook his hand on his way out.' She put it down and picked up her wineglass. 'What are we going to do?'

Mary sat at Ellen and Dan's dinner table, along with Pat and Karl Bennington. She had no more than walked in her door when the phone rang. It was Ellen. Dan was home, had gotten her message and wanted to talk to her. Since she was coming over, she might as well stay and have dinner with them.

Mary thought about her feet for a moment, but she wanted to talk to Dan as well. She accepted and offered to contribute the bottle of wine she'd just purchased. So, here she was, sipping wine and waiting for someone else to bring in dinner. Somehow, that didn't feel right. However, she was tired. Ellen was a good cook. She'd taught her, and it would be fun to see what she produced. But she felt uneasy. She should be standing over the stove, supervising, stirring, mashing, not just sitting here doing nothing. *Get over it.* She'd try. She took a small sip of the wine.

'I guess it was inevitable.' Dan sipped his wine absently. He looked directly at Mary but she didn't think he really saw her. He was probably going over the night of Cliff's death, wondering if there was anything they could have done better to protect the children. What it could have been, she didn't know. Father D'Angelo had taken them directly to St Mark's, where they waited in front of the manger for their mother to arrive. It had taken the crowd a little while to realize the *posada* was going to St Mark's, that something unexpected had happened at St Theresa's. She'd spent some time pointing toward the corner and making shooing motions, but finally the crowd had mostly turned the corner. It had evidently taken no time at all for them to see Ronaldo held a puppy. Coos and goos had apparently come from all sides, accompanied by 'Where did you get him?' She'd been told the children only said they found him, but somehow where they found him had quickly become public knowledge. So did the fact all those police cars and all that yellow tape was because Cliff Mathews was dead and the children had found him as well. Murdered. Mary fervently hoped none of them knew they'd not only found the body but had actually seen the murderer. It seemed she'd hoped in vain.

'How did that piece of information seep out?' Evidently Dan was struggling with the same puzzle.

She shook her head.

The swinging kitchen door opened and Ellen and Pat appeared, bearing plates. Ellen put one in front of Mary. Pat sat one in front of Dan and another in front of Karl.

'What is this?' Mary looked at her plate. It held a small piece of chicken breast topped with prosciutto and covered with a sauce that gave off a slight tangy fragrance. Mary had never seen chicken done that way and it smelled delicious. Whipped sweet potatoes and fresh green beans completed the picture. A basket of crunchy French rolls appeared along with a bowl of spinach salad. She'd come to talk to Dan. This was an unexpected bonus.

'It's Balsamic chicken.' Ellen stood back a little and surveyed the plates with satisfaction. 'It's a new recipe I got off Williams-Sonoma's website. It sounded wonderful and it was easy. So, you're my guinea pigs. Tell me what you think.'

The rapidly emptied plates spoke louder than any words. Mary pushed back her chair and started to clear the table, but Pat took the plates out of her hands before she could make for the kitchen. 'You're off duty. I think both Dan and Karl want to talk to you. I only hope the conversation doesn't spoil your appetite for dessert. I brought over brownie pudding.'

'Oh, goodness. I haven't had that in ages. It's a perfect winter's night dessert. Can I make the coffee?'

'You can sit right there and help these two try to figure out what's going on.'

Ellen and Pat disappeared through the swinging doors. Dan poured Mary a little more wine and offered the bottle to Karl, who nodded. Dan topped off his glass then poured the last few drops into his own.

'There was no useful forensic evidence in that whole damn manger scene. Lots of people had been in and out, but we did find one whole footprint.'

'Whose?'

Dan didn't answer Mary right away. He seemed to weigh how he wanted to answer. 'It was a sandal. A man's sandal.'

'Where was it?'

Dan actually smiled. 'In a cow pat.'

'In a…oh.'

'Father D'Angelo?' There was no smile on Karl's face. 'No one else wears sandals this time of year. That can't mean much. He's been in and out of the manger for days.'

Dan nodded. 'It doesn't implicate him, but it doesn't eliminate him, either.' He held up a hand before Mary could say anything. 'Whoever stabbed poor old Cliff didn't leave right away, which might. Father was pretty much in evidence all evening. Our murderer was by the animals, the darkest part of the manger scene, when the kids saw him. Well away from the manger and the body. Logic would say he would have left immediately. Why did he stay? There's only one answer.'

'And that is?' Karl looked as if he knew the answer.

Mary thought she did also.

'He wanted the puppy. The kids interrupted him, probably startled him pretty bad. We're just lucky he didn't do anything when he saw them.'

Mary looked into her wineglass, shuddered and picked it up. Her hand started to shake at the thought of what might have happened and she set it back down. She ran her fingers up and down the stem instead. 'There's one other person I know who wears sandals.'

Both men turned to stare at her.

'Who?' Dan said.

'Evan Wilson.' She thought back. Wasn't there someone else? Was it Glen? She wasn't sure. 'He helped me take the dog food to the library the day we started the food drive. He wore sandals and white socks. Only, why would he kill Cliff and what would he want with the puppy?'

'I have an idea about that.'

Dan and Mary turned their attention to Karl. He had been quiet through most of dinner, through all the conversation, contributing almost nothing. Now he pushed his glass aside, clasped his hands on the table and leaned forward.

'Mary knows this but I haven't been able to catch you. Remember that little poodle stolen from Golden Hills winery last summer? Belonged to Naomi and Bill Bliss?'

Dan nodded. 'Cliff had a picture of it. Naomi had broken down when she saw it, claimed he took it from the winery. Why is another mystery. I'm afraid that dog is long gone.'

'No. He's not.' Karl raised his head and looked directly at Dan. 'He's very much alive and I think someone close is using him for breeding. That puppy the kids found? I think that poodle is its father.'

The room was so quiet the faint clink of dishes in the kitchen could be heard. A laugh from Pat broke the stillness, but Dan didn't say anything. He simply stared at Karl. A loud meow from Jake, Ellen's yellow Tom, announcing his presence as he passed through the dining room on his way to the living-room bookshelves finally seemed to restore Dan's speech.

'How do you know that?'

'Two things. Cliff brought me a saliva sample from a dog he wanted the AKC to test for DNA. He asked me to send it in. I did. The results came back the day he died, so he never saw them. The dog was the Blisses' poodle, so he's alive. At least, he was when Cliff took the sample. Alive and close.'

'What's the second?'

Mary didn't think she'd ever seen Dan look so intent.

'I got to looking at Sampson a little more closely. I'm sure he's a cockapoo. And his toenails aren't right.'

'His what?' Mary wasn't sure she'd heard right. 'His toenails?'

Karl nodded. 'Dogs have either clear or black nails. A black dog will have black nails. A black dog who has a white paw will have clear nails on his white paw, black ones on his black paws. If the paw is only partly white, the nails will probably be mixed as well. There are a few poodles who have a recessive gene for clear nails. Merlot, the Blisses' poodle, has that gene. He's passed it on to several of his pups. He's the only dog I know, personally, who does. Sampson has clear nails on all four paws even though two of his paws are black.'

Dan didn't say anything. Mary found she couldn't.

Dan found his voice first. 'You think Cliff found the poodle and took a puppy from whoever has him to do…what?'

'Blackmail somebody.'

Mary almost dumped what was left of her wine on the tablecloth. She hadn't heard Ellen and Pat come back into the dining room, but they must have been there a few minutes, long enough to hear what Karl had said. 'Oh, you startled me.'

Ellen grinned, pulled out her chair and sat. 'I could tell. You jumped a mile. Coffee's brewing.' She turned toward Karl. 'You think Cliff found the Blisses' poodle?'

'No doubt about that.' Karl gave one decisive nod. 'The question is, where?'

'I hope not in a puppy mill.' Dread filled Pat's voice.

'We've had no reports of one for some time.' Dan looked over at Karl as if for corroboration. 'That dog has been missing for over six months. Usually we hear when the first pups show up.' He paused, as if thinking it through. 'What's the gestation period for a dog?'

'About twelve weeks. Add six weeks for the pups to be weaned and Sampson could be Merlot's.'

'I'll put out feelers.'

'What's a puppy mill?' Visions of a stream, water wheel and sacks of grain filled Mary's head. She didn't think that's what they were talking about.

Karl voice was heavy with disgust. 'It's a place that turns out puppies like a factory. They vary in awfulness. Some buy second-rate pure breeds, but some don't care how they get their breeding dogs. They're interested in one thing only: puppies. Little things like health, clean conditions and the quality of the dog don't matter. If it can pass for a purebred, they can sell it for one. Papers aren't included, but lots of folks don't care.' He paused, looked over at Dan and shook his head slightly. 'But I think it's more likely he's local, servicing some backyard breeder's dogs and possibly producing cockapoos.'

Dan nodded. 'It makes sense. Keep Merlot under wraps, bring just one or two bitches to him and sell the puppies out of the area.'

'Sampson wasn't out of the area.' Ellen pushed back

her chair and headed for the kitchen. 'I'll bring in the coffee. Don't solve this thing until I get back.'

'She's got nothing to worry about.' Dan sounded glum. He picked up his teaspoon and started to tap it on the table.

Mary reached over and took it away. 'We're on edge enough.'

He smiled and let her. 'The rest of Sampson's litter could be in Southern California, for all we know. Maybe they kept him back for some reason.'

'Or the rest of them could be right here.' Mary became lightheaded. Sampson and the puppies in Evan's shop were about the same size, and they looked alike. Could Cliff have stolen him to blackmail…who? Evan hadn't said who the puppies belonged to, but he knew. He had to. He'd looked nervous when the children were handling them. Why? If Merlot was the father, then the mother had to be a cocker. Did Evan have a cocker? Mary had no idea. He lived just about a block from her, but she'd never been to his house. Evan, mild-mannered Evan, who ran an immaculate and seemingly honest store, a man who wouldn't steal a dog or condone anyone else's doing it. A man who enjoyed playing Scrooge at the Christmas extravaganza during which he wore a long bathrobe, tied at the waist, a bathrobe that had a hood, and sandals. No. It couldn't be. Who else had cockers? Half the people in Santa Louisa. Maybe not half, but they were a popular breed. Glen Manning and John Lavorino. They had at least one female cocker. Maybe Cliff making trouble for them at St Mark's had nothing to do with lifestyle. Maybe it was about dogs. Could that be? Should she say something?

'What do you mean, they might be here?' Dan set down his spoon and looked at her suspiciously.

'I mean—well...'

'She means Evan has puppies for sale that look like Sampson,' Pat answered for her. 'I saw them when I was in there a few days ago.'

'He does, does he?' Unfortunately, Dan looked interested.

Mary nodded.

'Are they cockapoos?'

'Evan says so.'

'Who owns them?' Ellen seemed as interested as her husband.

Mary shrugged. 'Evan didn't say.' She didn't add Evan seemed determined not to say.

'Odd.' Karl pushed his dish away. 'Evan usually gets me to check out any of the animals he sells. He doesn't care about papers and breeds, and if the dogs don't have papers, he'll say so. However, he's careful about shots and health. He doesn't want anyone to buy an animal from him that's going to go home and die.'

'How about goldfish? Susannah won some at the fair a couple of summers ago. They only lived a day.'

'Fish are tricky, especially fair fish. Still, Evan wants everything alive and healthy when they leave him. I wonder why he didn't call me.'

'Hmm.' Dan attacked his pudding with gusto. 'Maybe I'll drop in on Evan tomorrow. Take a look at those puppies.'

Should she say something about John and Glen? No. Those two had been through enough. She'd corner Evan tomorrow, right after her committee meeting, and make him tell her who owns the puppies. If he wouldn't tell her, she'd have to investigate further. If it turned out they belonged to John and Glen, she'd... she'd decide what to do then. Right now, saying anything would be the same as idle gossip. She looked at the brownie pudding Pat put before her and her stomach lurched. She reached for her coffee instead.

TWENTY-ONE

It HAD NOT been a good night. She had fallen into bed almost as soon as she closed the door. She hadn't paused to admire anyone's Christmas decorations as she drove home, hadn't even bothered to put her car in the garage. She'd staggered into the kitchen, thrown her coat over a chair, her purse on the table and gone to bed. But not to sleep. Every time she started to doze off, a dog barked. All night. As the night wore on, the dog became more frantic. She'd gotten up a couple of times, worried it might be in trouble, but she had no idea where it was. Down the block somewhere, probably. She wasn't the only one who couldn't sleep. Lights went on and off in several houses. On toward morning, it stopped. Either its owner had come back or it was exhausted. She hoped the owners had gotten it. She'd never heard it before and fervently hoped she wouldn't again.

Mary watched the coffeepot drip out enough for one cup. Thanking Ellen, who had given her this pause and pour coffeemaker, she poured. The coffeemaker paused. She reached for the Tylenol and washed down two of them with a small mouthful of way-too-hot coffee.

As she sipped, she reviewed the schedule she'd mapped out during those wide-awake hours. The first meeting for the annual St Mark's Spring Rummage sale was at nine. Evan's shop wouldn't be open yet. What time had he gotten home last night and had the blasted dog kept him up? She hadn't been by the can tree in at least two days. Her committee was great, but she needed to check in. The volunteers with pickup trucks would arrive midweek, dismantle the tree and take all the food to the food bank. In the meantime, she needed to make sure the stacking volunteers arrived daily, making the tree grow. The press would return right before they started tearing it down and hopefully those people who hadn't donated or had somehow not been aware of the food drive would come through. Then she would visit Evan. First, a little breakfast and a shower. Where had she put those folders? On the kitchen table. One folder for each committee with a to-do list and a timeline for completion. Each sub-committee head would get one. She'd keep the master list. Things should go smoothly. She drained the last of the coffee and headed for her shower.

The morning was chilly, the meeting informal. Gray sweatpants and the green sweater with Mrs Claus appliquéd on the front would do fine. The sweater had been a gift. Why, she wasn't sure, but it seemed appropriate for today and was soft and warm.

She slowed as she passed Evan's house. No car in the driveway. Had he already left for the shop? Probably. There were a lot of animals and she supposed cleaning before the shop opened was the best time. She noted, with satisfaction, the street in front of St Mark's contained nothing. No trash, no animal droppings, nothing to show that hundreds of people had been tromping through the streets and on the lawn only a few days ago. She must remember to drop the city maintenance people a thank-you note.

The meeting was in the small room off the main hall called, appropriately enough, the all-purpose room. It was used for Bible study, Sunday school, the breakfast prayer group and a meeting place for a variety of committees and clubs. Today a round table took up the center, with folding chairs around it. A large coffeemaker gave off gurgling noises, along with an inviting smell; thick white mugs were stacked beside it. Mary laid her folders on the table and headed its way.

'Guess we're a little early.'

Mary nodded and filled her cup. 'Good morning, Joy. Glad to see you. Which committee do you want?'

'Same as always. I'll take charge of the pricin', sortin' and settin' out.'

Mary nodded once more. Joy had been doing that for years. She knew how much to charge for just about anything. Antique brooches, slightly used high chairs, an out-of-date suit donated by a still-grieving widow who claimed it had 'plenty of good wear in it,' baby clothes stained with God alone knew what, really nice lamps and not-so-nice end tables, even wedding and prom dresses. Joy put a price on them that would see them out the door and still make their cash box rattle pleasantly at the end of the day. She smiled at her over the top of her coffee mug. She didn't get one back, but then, she hadn't expected one. Joy didn't live up to her name. She looked to be about Mary's age, early seventies. That she was only fifty-seven, Mary knew for a fact. Joy seemed to take a perverse satisfaction in presenting herself as a neat, clean, plain no-nonsense homebody. Her haircut certainly looked home done, her nails were chewed off, not cut, and her hands were always a little red and chapped. Today she had on a shapeless plaid dress covered with a sweater that had been washed so many times Mary couldn't guess its original color. Her stockings were thick, and so were her lace-up brown oxfords. She could, however, make an angel food cake from scratch that was so light it almost floated away. Her buttermilk fried chicken was second only to Mary's and her biscuits were incredible. How such good food came out of a home so dour, made by a person who seemed to find no pleasure in its creation, Mary wasn't sure. However, Joy was a person you could count on, and Mary did. Often.

'Heard you were there when they found Cliff Mathews.' Joy pushed her plastic glasses back on her nose and blew into her coffee mug. The steam immediately fogged her glasses. She set the mug down on the table and cleaned them with a paper napkin. 'I was no fan of his, but he didn't deserve to die that way.'

Mary felt a little start of surprise. Somehow, she hadn't associated Joy with a pet. 'You knew Cliff ?'

Joy's expression didn't change. She took a sip of her coffee, set it back down and put her glasses back on. 'You could say that. Not well, but I knew him. I got a little black cocker from Bonnie. She said she wasn't show quality and if I wanted her for my granddaughter, who was sick a lot back then, I could but I'd have to pay to have her spayed. I agreed and took her to Cliff.'

A jolt made Mary's hand shake. She knew about Alma's bitch, but she hadn't given any thought to who owned the other dog. 'It was your dog Cliff was supposed to spay? But he did Alma's?'

Joy's face looked even more disapproving, if that

was possible. 'After that I took the dog to Karl Bennington. You know Karl, don't you?'

Mary nodded.

'Good man, Karl. He's taken real good care of that little dog. I don't hold with dogs in the house but have to admit, it sure helped my granddaughter. Perked her right up. Never saw much of Cliff after that, but I heard plenty.'

'Are you talking about Cliff ? That was the most horrible thing. The manger! How could anybody do such a thing? Hello, Mary, Joy.'

Annie Wilkes shed her coat and dropped it on a chair and reached out for a mug. 'It's getting chilly out there. Amelia couldn't come. She's got a cold. I'll take her folder to her.'

It didn't matter. Amelia had headed up the donations committee, along with Annie, for the last five years. Mary knew there'd be no lack of items donated to sell. 'Tell her I hope she feels better. This is no time to get sick.'

'I know. I'm so far behind. We haven't even put up the tree yet. It's sitting in the backyard in a tub of water. I don't want to do it unless we can all be there, but the kids are going in different directions and we can't seem to all get together. This teenage stuff is for the birds.' Annie filled her mug, added a generous amount of sugar and looked around for a spoon. 'Don't we have any—Thanks.'

Joy produced a white plastic one and silently handed it over.

Mary watched the small interplay. She'd known both these women for years. Neither had changed much. Joy had always been dourly competent, her household run with the rigidity of Mussolini's train schedule. Annie's house was filled with kids, dogs, activity and laughter, but she always got the job done. People were, indeed, interesting. 'Before I forget, we have all of Cliff's stuff for the sale. Well, all his furniture and some of his kitchen stuff.'

Annie lowered her mug and stared. 'How'd we get that?'

Joy said nothing but her frown deepened.

'He was being evicted. His landlady had filed the papers and it was past time for him to be out. She was going to put all his stuff out on the street but said if we wanted it for the sale we had to come get it. Agnes, from Dan's office, helped, so did Ellen, and we got it all packed. It's all here, somewhere.' Mary looked around but no boxes, TVs, toasters or really bad pictures were in evidence. 'Maybe they're in the storage room. It's a start.'

'I thought he had a daughter. Wouldn't she want some of it?' Disapproval deepened the wrinkles across Joy's forehead.

'No one knows where she is. Dan's trying to locate her.'

'She lives in Charlotte, NC.'

Annie and Mary stared at Joy.

'She does?'

'How do you know?'

'She and my daughter were friends. They still keep in touch.'

'Does she know about her father?'

'Don't know. I don't pry into other folks' business.'

Mary tried to bury her sigh. No, Joy wouldn't pry,

but this hardly qualified. 'Do you know her married name or how we can contact her?'

'No.' That came out of pursed lips which relaxed just enough for the next sentence to arrive. 'I guess I could ask Charity, though.'

'Better yet, ask Charity to contact Dan.' Mary barely remembered Joy's daughter, although she usually remembered the children in her middle-school classes. However, if she grew up anything like her mother, Dan was better equipped to get the information than Mary was. She wondered if this let her off the hook for organizing Cliff's memorial. She fervently hoped so. Packing up his meager possessions had been bad enough. 'I'll tell Les to hang on to his things. If she wants to donate any of them, fine. I'll feel a lot better taking them from her instead of Cliff's landlady.'

Annie glanced at her cell phone. 'Mary, it's almost nine thirty. Can we get started? I have to pick up my kids from band practice in an hour and I need to go to the grocery store first.'

'Where's Leigh Cameron? She said she'd…'

The door flew open and a rather shapeless woman with a nervous expression rushed in. Her hair was the color of goldenrod and was almost as stiff. It fell, without moving, just above her shoulders. Her pink and mauve track suit didn't appear to have ever been near a track, or a gym. Neither did her running shoes. However, her panting sounded as if she'd just come in from a brisk run. Mary knew it was nervous energy, not exercise that caused the stitch in her side she now dramatically covered with her hand.

'I'm sorry I'm late. I had to pack Dave's lunch—he's going on some kind of hike with the boy scouts and

Emily has dance class this morning, so I was rushed and then the dog threw up. The kids wouldn't clean it up so I stopped by Evan's Furry Friends, but it's closed. He has that special food—I was going to get some last night but that stuck-up Bill Bliss went in the store and I didn't want to talk to him so I bought food at the grocery store. Do you think that's why she threw up? Maybe I should take her to Karl. Are you all done already?'

Leigh had been the head of the advertisement committee last year and had done a terrible job. Press releases had never made the paper, flyers hadn't been distributed and promised radio spots hadn't gotten their copy; Mary had ended up doing it all. She vowed then that if Leigh volunteered again, things would be different.

'Actually, we were just getting started. The folders are over on the table. Leigh, I have a special favor to ask. I don't have anyone to organize the volunteers the day of the sale. Could you do that? I'll give you a list of them, with all of their assignments. You'll just need to make sure they know where to go.' All of the volunteers already knew their jobs and they all knew Leigh.

'As well as the publicity?' Worry creased the pancake makeup on Leigh's face.

Mary was briefly distracted. *Where does she get that? I didn't think anyone made that thick stuff anymore.*

'Oh, no. Kay Epstein, over at the newspaper, offered to do the publicity. She deals with it all the time.' *And gets the job done on time, and well.* 'You'll be so much more valuable handling the volunteers.' Mary held her breath. She didn't want to insult Leigh, but she couldn't go through another year like the last one.

Different expressions crossed Leigh's face until finally she smiled. 'That's a great idea. I have so many other committees that this will fit in easily.'

Relieved, Mary headed for the table and the folders. 'OK, let's see where we are so we can all get out of here.'

She spread out her lists. What was Bill Bliss doing in a pet store? Naomi hadn't said anything about another dog. She forgot about him in a blur of who was going to be in charge of what, and when.

TWENTY-TWO

MARY STOOD IN the doorway of the atrium between the library and the civic offices and gasped. The can tree had grown to at least twice the height it had been the last time she saw it but it wasn't going any higher. It ended at the ceiling with one large can of beans topped with a red velvet bow. There were paper streamers, obviously made by small hands, draped over the tiers of cans, interspersed with lopsided green and red, as well as blue and white, bows. The local grade school children had been busy. Boxes of cans were placed around the perimeter of the tree that could hold nothing more. Mary's smile beamed satisfaction as she looked at the food they'd collected. It would make the difference between a full belly on Christmas Day and beyond for many families who would otherwise go hungry. Hungry! In this country! In her own county, town! The thought filled her with rage, but the sight of the tree made her smile grow broader. They'd done good work, but it wasn't finished. The press was scheduled to take pictures of the tree and do a follow-up article on Tuesday, after which it would be dismantled and everything moved to the food bank. Maybe the cases and sacks of cans piled around the tree could be moved now. She needed someone with a pickup. Todd Blankenship had one. Would he help? He never had before. Who else? Bob MacIntosh ran the food bank. He had a van. Maybe he could take some of it, and he must know someone with a truck. The town was full of trucks.

The door to the library opened and Luke walked out. 'Mrs McGill. I was going to call you. What do you think?'

'I'm overwhelmed. I hope Toys for Tots is having as much luck. It's going to be a Merry Christmas for a lot of families.'

Luke grinned, a wide, expansive grin. 'I know. Half the real estate offices in town have been here, piling up cans. A lot of them got on the phone and called their clients. They collected money too. There'll be turkeys and a lot of fresh produce this Christmas. Some of the money is going to the Meals on Wheels people to pay the hospital for some special meals for those old folks who can't get out.'

Mary stood in front of the tree, examining it and the boxes of food in front of it. Luke stood beside her.

'Are all those cartons all right with you? I don't want anyone tripping, trying to get into the library.' There were cartons stacked behind the tree, more behind the library doors and some over by the elevator.

'Should we get someone to take these over to the food bank right away? It doesn't look safe.'

'I thought so too. You want me to ask Bob? He's been over here almost every day, watching this thing grow. You can almost hear him purring, he's that pleased. He'll figure out how to get them over there. I'll get some pictures before he removes the extras.'

Mary nodded. 'That would be great. The newspaper will be out Tuesday to take pictures. Then we can start tearing it down. I'll try to get some of the children who made the decorations in the picture. Let's see. Harry Waters is head of the committee to get the cans moved. I'd better call him...'

She stopped as Luke's smile grew. 'Harry and a bunch of other Realtors have already been here, planning the dismantling. I'll take pictures of it coming down as well, and we'll post them in the library later.'

She laughed. 'This committee is the best I've ever worked with. I'm going to quit worrying about all of you.' She stopped, not sure how she should phrase what she wanted to say next. 'I—well, I wasn't over here yesterday because I helped pack up Cliff's things. He had a picture of you at a dog show, holding onto a poodle and a blue ribbon. I thought you might like to know where it is and how to get it back. If you want it back.'

Luke didn't say anything for so long Mary thought maybe he hadn't heard her. Or understood.

'It's in a box with a lot of other things at St Mark's. I can ask...'

'I heard. And thanks. It's just that... I gave Cliff that picture. It was my last showmanship win before the show where everything fell apart. The Pure Breed Dog Club of Santa Louisa gives a thousand-dollar scholarship every year to the junior handler who wins the most points in showmanship at California dog shows. Cliff was my coach. I needed just a few more points to win. I'd already planned what I'd do with it. I was going to be a vet, just like Cliff, and that money would have helped me pay for it. The poodle, Jester we called him, was a great dog, but a clown. He loved to show, but he sometimes got distracted and blew it for me. We practiced and practiced. If I won that show, the scholarship was mine. Then Cliff gave the dog tranquilizers. I guess he thought he was helping me, but I got blamed and kicked out of the club. Cliff never admitted he'd done it. I haven't been in a dog show ring since and, as you can see, I didn't go to vet school. I think I'll pass on that picture, Mrs McGill. The memories it brings back aren't exactly pleasant.'

There was no trace of a smile on Luke's usually cheerful face and the bitterness in his voice was deep and old. Another unsettled score Cliff had left behind.

After all these years, had Luke's bitterness erupted? Only, in Cliff's diary, he'd said…she couldn't remember exactly what he'd said. However, it seemed unlikely it was Luke Cliff had tried to blackmail, and that seemed the most logical motive for his murder. She shifted her purse to her other shoulder and surveyed the tree once more.

'Let me know if you can get the children over here for photos. What time is the press coming?'

'Don't know. I'll find out. I'll call you Monday.'

'Will you call Bob?'

He nodded.

Mary smiled at him. 'Thank you, Luke. You've been invaluable. I'd better run. I need to stop at Evan's for a minute.'

She could actually feel Luke wondering why she was stopping at Evan's. She didn't have a dog or a cat or even a bird, but all he said was, 'Tell him I'll be in later for some of the special dog food he carries. He knows what kind. Same as he feeds his little dog.'

Mary came to an abrupt halt, turned and faced Luke once more. 'Evan has a dog?'

He nodded and a trace of his smile was back. 'A cocker. Pretty little thing. Not show quality, but a sweet dog. He got her from Alma.'

'Alma? I thought she sold all of her dogs to Bonnie Blankenship.' Mary became a little lightheaded. Not only did everyone in this town seem to have a dog, they all seemed to be related.

'She sold the last two bitches, her best two, to Bonnie. Earlier, she sold one to Evan and the other two bitches to John and Glen.'

John and Glen again. They had two female cockers and they bred cockapoos. The same kind of dogs Evan had for sale. Sampson, whose sire was—might be—the missing winery dog, was also a cockapoo. 'Do you have one of Alma's dogs also?'

Luke shook his head. 'I'm still a poodle man. Actually, I have one of the Blisses' dogs. He was in the first litter Merlot sired. It was a real tragedy when that dog disappeared.'

Mary didn't say a word. She stared at Luke for a moment, turned on her heel and headed out the door. She was still shaking her head as she walked down the stairs and started across the park toward Furry Friends. It was time to have a long conversation with Evan.

TWENTY-THREE

THE SHOP WAS CLOSED. It said so on the sign that hung in the glass door and in the lowered blinds that covered the windows on each side of it. Inside, soft barks, a rustling noise, other stirrings, but no voices, sounded. Where was Evan?

She stood for a moment, trying to decide what to do. Evan's car hadn't been in his driveway when she passed. Of course, he could have put it in the garage. Just because hers was full of rummage sale boxes, her washing machine and other assorted things didn't mean others filled theirs the same way. Only, why wasn't he here? She checked her watch and double-checked that against her cell phone. Ten thirty. Past time for him to open. She rattled the door. The barking intensified, but no one came. Could he be sick? He could be hung over. She had no idea what the three of them did last night.

She briefly wondered if John and Glen were home. The bank was closed on Saturday, so she couldn't run over there to check with Glen, the branch manager. They must have come home last night, though. John was a surgical nurse at the hospital and was probably… no. He took a leave of absence. She knew where they lived. Should she stop by? Better to go back to Evan's house and see if he was there. See if his car was in the garage. Then, well, then she'd decide. This was bound to be something simple. Something easily explained and Evan wouldn't thank her if she went off half-cocked.

She walked back across the park, avoiding the vendors set up for the Saturday Farmers' Market, but turned to look back before she entered the parking lot beside the library. The closed sign still hung on the door and the blinds still covered the windows. It was with a growing sense of urgency that Mary climbed into her car and headed for Evan's.

The driveway was still empty. She pulled her car in far enough to clear the sidewalk, stopped, got out and stood by it, staring at the house. Now what should she do? Go up and bang on the door? Tell Evan to get up, he was late? Ask if he was all right? That she was worried because the shop was closed? That would go over big. She wasn't his mother and, even if she was, he was beyond needing one to monitor his movements. It wasn't like him to be late, though.

Reluctantly, she walked up on his front porch and rang the bell. Noise exploded from the backyard, the same noise she'd listened to all night. Mary hurried down the steps, around the house and into the backyard. There, in a large chain-link dog run, was a small black cocker spaniel, running back and forth like an insane thing, barking the whole time. The dog stopped and stared at Mary. Mary stared back. She walked closer. So did the dog. There was a small doghouse in the run and also a stainless-steel, empty dog dish. Another one, upside down, lay close to the gate. The dog pawed at it and looked back at Mary. This must be the bitch Evan had bought from Alma. It was also the dog that had barked all night. Why was she out here, with no food or water, coat tangled, toys torn to shreds?

The dog came toward the gate and jumped up on it, her paws pushing the wire, and whined. That she wanted Mary to do something was obvious, but what? Fill her water dish? Feed her? Let her out? Find Evan. That's what she needed to do, and right now. She started to back up. The dog whined more.

'Oh, don't.' Mary didn't know when she'd felt so helpless. She walked back and stuck her fingers through the wire. The dog put her nose against them and gave a gentle lick.

'You poor thing. Are you thirsty? Is that it? I can't believe Evan would—well, I'm sure he won't mind if I give you water. Only, I'm not sure…' The dog cocked her head as if listening to Mary then jumped on the gate again. The snap wiggled but held. Should she open the gate? What if the dog ran out? She couldn't catch it. Damn Evan anyway. She turned to look at the house once more. No sign of movement. Surely, if he was here he would have heard the dog barking, the doorbell ringing. Where was he? She had no idea. She turned back toward the dog and spotted a hose. That solved one problem. She stuck the end of it through the wire fence. It just reached one empty bowl. Mary filled it with water. The dog drank greedily, her long ears dipping into the bowl along with her tongue. She came up for air and shook her head. Water drops sprayed everywhere. Mary laughed. The dog looked at her and seemed to smile. Mary stopped laughing. The dog sat down and stared at her again.

Now what? She'd check the garage for his car. The door was down and there was no handle. That meant an automatic opener. A window. There, on the side. Only, the window was higher than Mary, and she wasn't at all sure she could see over the sill. There must be something she could stand on. There was. A gardening kneeler, the kind you turned over and it became a seat. She dragged it under the garage window, turned it to the highest position and wiggled it. Unfortunately, one end wanted to sink into the slightly damp soil, but all she needed was one peek. She put one foot on the kneeler then looked over her shoulder. The dog sat in the corner of the run, watching her with what seemed to be great interest. Mary sighed, grabbed the windowsill, put her other foot on the kneeler and pulled herself up. The garage was empty. Gingerly, she let herself down and abandoned the kneeler. Evan truly wasn't here. Where was he?

She walked back to the dog run, where the dog waited for her. She once more jumped on the gate, making it clear she wanted out.

'I can't do that,' Mary told her.

The dog rattled the gate once more.

'Look, I'm going now. Maybe Evan's at the shop. Maybe he stayed down in San Luis Obispo for some reason and he's back at the shop right now, opening it up. I'll find him, I promise, and then we'll get you out of there.'

The dog whined. Mary sighed. She turned toward her car. The dog started to bark, loud, insistent barks, letting her know she didn't appreciate being abandoned.

'I'll be back,' Mary shouted, then started her car and backed out of the driveway. Evan had better be at the shop. If not, she was going to go to John and Glen's and bang on their door until they answered and helped her figure out what was going on.

TWENTY-FOUR

THE SHOP WAS still closed. Mary found a parking spot in front of it, a rare occasion on a busy Saturday, but she didn't get out. Nothing had changed. Now what? She pulled back out and her spot was immediately taken by a large SUV filled with laughing children and a flustered-looking woman. Mary turned the corner. She'd go down the alley. Furry Friends backed onto it. A car was parked out the back of Evan's shop. What type of car did Evan drive? Was that it? There was an open spot next to it. Mary pulled in and got out. She walked over to the car and looked at it as if it could tell her something. The car remained silent. She peered in the driver's window. Nothing. Not even a candy wrapper. She walked around the car, trying to look in the rear windows. This was an SUV of some type so there would be a storage area in the back. The windows were darkened but she could make out a shape—a dog crate. This had to be Evan's car. How long had it been here? What was it they did in mystery novels? Tested to see if the hood was warm. If it was, the car had recently arrived. She laid her hand on it. It was cold. She looked around, but there was nothing to see. The dumpster looked like a dumpster. Boxes stuck out of the top, sacks of something were barely visible, smells, definitely, but nothing you wouldn't expect of a dumpster.

The back door of Evan's shop looked undisturbed.

Mary walked closer. She wasn't sure what she was looking for. There wasn't anything to see but a closed door with no window. There was, however, a window next to it. Bars. Probably practical on a shop, but not very helpful to her. Could she see into the back of the shop through the window? There probably wouldn't be anything to see, but that uneasy feeling had turned into out and out worry. Something was wrong. Very wrong. What, she didn't know, but she was certain she needed to find out.

This window wasn't any lower than the one in Evan's garage, and there was no garden kneeler in sight. However, there was a slatted box. It appeared to have contained lettuce or maybe flowers, but if she stood it on one end it might be tall enough. Not too sturdy, but then, she wasn't planning on standing on it very long. Besides, she could hold onto the bars to steady herself. All she needed was to make sure… Make sure what? She didn't know, only that she had to look.

The sense of urgency kept getting stronger. So was the urge to call Dan, but right now she had nothing to tell him. She dragged the box under the window and put one foot on the solid wood end. The side slats groaned but held. She grabbed the bars and slowly pulled herself up, put her other foot on the box and leaned forward, closer to the window. The back room was dim. She could make out a few shapes but not much more. Cartons of what were probably unpacked merchandise sat in one corner, an empty fish tank and a couple of chairs in the other. A half-open door must be the bathroom. Something lay on the floor in front of it. A bundle of rags? Dog blankets? No. That pile of cloth had a person inside it. It couldn't be. Surely it wasn't.

She shifted her weight and leaned into the bars for a better look. It *was* a person. Wasn't it? Evan? Could it be? She didn't know, but she now had something to tell Dan. She needed to call him right now. Did she have her cell phone? She let go of the bars and slid her hand down into her jacket pocket. Yes. There it was. She'd better get down off this box before she tried to punch any buttons. She lifted one foot, letting it drift in midair as she shifted her weight. The slats in the box groaned alarmingly, followed with a resounding crack, and the box collapsed. It was the last thing Mary heard as she crashed to the ground, the box in splinters around her.

TWENTY-FIVE

'DON'T MOVE.'

The voice sounded familiar, but she couldn't place it. What did he mean, don't move? She needed to find Dan. She started to roll over but immediately stopped. A pain shot down her leg like a thunderbolt and another one tried to drill a hole in her head. Maybe she wouldn't move after all.

Mary opened her eyes, which for some reason were closed, and looked into the smiling face of a young man she remembered quite well. He was doing something to her leg, something that seemed to involve cutting her sweatpants and blood. She tried to repress the shudder that ran through her, but it wasn't a success.

'Almost done. Remember me?'

'Of course. Only, last I heard, you moved down south.'

'We did. My folks, I mean. I went to college in LA, got married and decided this was a better place to live. I took your advice, you see. Actually, your order, and got my act together. Stay still. I'm almost done.'

'Thank you, Randy, for helping me. My leg feels…'

'It's your head I'm more worried about, and as for helping you… I owe you. You spent plenty of time helping me.'

'What about her head?'

That voice she knew. Dan.

'I was going to call you. Something's wrong and I can't find Evan. No, that's not right. I think I saw him, only I can't remember. Where am I?'

'In the alley behind Furry Friends. Remind me to ask you later what you are doing back here. In the meantime, you've earned yourself a trip to the emergency room in an ambulance. If you're lucky, they may run the siren.'

'What?' Mary tried to sit up but was immediately pushed down.

'Don't move. You've got a nasty bump on your head as well as this cut on your leg. The nail that got your leg was huge and nicely rusted. Now, we're going to put you on this stretcher and lift you up into the ambulance. We can sound the siren if you want, but you don't really need it.'

'Randy Johnson, you'll do no such thing. I'm not going to any hospital, and furthermore...'

That was as far as Mary got. Pain from her leg shot through her, accompanied by a throbbing in her head and neck. Instead of finishing her protest, she groaned. Damn! 'Was it Evan?'

'Yes.' There was more than a trace of bitterness in Dan's tone.

'Why? Why would someone hurt Evan?' She tried to lift her head to see Dan, but pain and the collar Randy was fastening around her neck made that impossible.

Dan's face, however, appeared above her, looking down as Randy tucked a blanket around her and fastened thick yellow straps to hold her in place. She wanted to protest but somehow couldn't.

'Just a minute, guys. Mary, how did this happen? Did someone attack you?'

Mary gasped. That thought hadn't occurred to her. Worry and anger showed in Dan's face.

She almost preferred his version to the truth, which, as she thought about it, was embarrassing. However… 'No. I was looking for Evan. I was worried, especially after I found his dog. So, as the shop wasn't open, I stood on the box to look in the window and, well, it sort of collapsed.'

Dan didn't say anything for a moment.

Randy, who stood beside him, blinked. 'Huh?'

'It all makes perfect sense,' Dan said finally. 'Take her away, guys. I'll meet you at the hospital as soon as I can get there.'

'On my count of three.' Randy and another man bumped the stretcher against the back of the ambulance, the legs collapsed and Mary rolled in.

Before the doors closed all the way, she managed to call out, 'Dan. Send someone over to Evan's place to get that little dog.' The doors shut firmly behind her.

TWENTY-SIX

MARY LIMPED INTO her house by the back door, ignored the kitchen, for perhaps the first time in her life, and headed for the sofa in the living room. She sank down on it, raised her legs as she had been told in the hospital, and propped her head up on one of the sofa pillows. What an ordeal! They'd stitched her leg, given her shots, put IVs into her hand, pushed her through some kind of tunnel machine to take pictures of her head and finally told her she was fine and could go home. She knew she was fine. A couple of butterfly bandages would have taken care of the leg and two super strength Tylenols would take care of her head. That and an ice pack. Ellen brought the ice pack.

'Tea?'

Mary started to nod but thought better of it. 'Please.'

Ellen paused long enough to put another pillow under Mary's head and an afghan over her knees before returning to the kitchen. Mary lay still and fumed. If that stupid box had held together one more minute, none of this would have happened. She closed her eyes and let her drifting thoughts take over. Evan. Killed. Lying all night, dead, in his shop. She hoped he'd been dead. The thought of him lying there, no one to help him, perhaps in pain, was too much. The only possible good thing she could think of was it meant Evan hadn't killed Cliff. Didn't it? It must, but somehow that was no consolation.

She let her thoughts move on to what was now the most important question. Why? It had to have some connection to Cliff's death, didn't it? Something to do with the dogs, with the missing poodle. Only, what? Evan didn't have anything to do with the poodle. He sold cockapoos in his shop, though. He sold them for John and Glen. He sold his own puppies. Were they cockapoos? What a silly name for a dog. Why would anyone…? The puppies were so cute. She thought about Sampson. Where had he come from? Was he part of the litter Evan had in his store? How did you go about finding out? Who owned those puppies, anyway? Poor Evan. What a terrible thing. This had to stop before anyone else—oh my God. The children. Mary sat up abruptly, holding the ice pack to her head. If the same person killed both Cliff and Evan, were the children next?

'What are you doing? You're supposed to be lying down.' Ellen set two mugs of tea on a magazine on the coffee table and walked over to her aunt. 'I'll help you.'

'I don't need any help, and I can't drink tea while I'm lying down. Quit fussing.' She took a deep breath and let it out slowly. 'Ellen, do you think the same person killed both Evan and Cliff?'

Ellen didn't say anything for a moment. She picked up both mugs of tea, handed one to Mary and sat down in the rocker. 'Ouch. This is hot.' She passed her mug back and forth between her hands. 'It seems likely. But why? Evan didn't have anything to do with Cliff. At least, I don't think so.'

'I don't know of any connection between them, either. Do you think whoever it is will try to harm the children?'

Ellen almost dropped her tea. 'Oh, my…twice. This person, whoever he is, has murdered twice. At least, we think so. But children?'

'They saw him.'

'They didn't recognize him, though.'

'The murderer doesn't know that.' Mary blew into her tea. She thought about the children and their reactions through all this. How much danger, if any, might they be in? They had to find the murderer, and fast, before something else terrible happened. The children's reactions. The Blisses' winery. 'Bill Bliss.'

'What?' Ellen looked at her aunt as if the bump might have done something more than cause a headache. 'What about him?'

'Reactions. I was thinking about Dalia and Ronaldo's reactions. When we were in the Bliss winery, they stopped short when they saw him. Just skidded to a halt and stared at him. I've been thinking about it. Maybe it was because of his size.'

The expression on Ellen's face clearly said that bump had done some damage. 'His size? Bill Bliss isn't fat.'

'No. But he's tall. They described the murderer as tall. Father D'Angelo is tall. So was Evan.'

'We can eliminate Evan as a murderer.' She seemed doubtful but willing to try to follow Mary's train of thought. She took a sip of her tea as she thought about what Mary said. 'That's not much to go on. There are a lot of tall men around. Dan, for one.'

Mary put down her ice pack and reached for her

mug. 'I think we can eliminate him also. I know it's not much, but it's the only place I can think to start.'

'So, you think Bill Bliss could be the murderer? Why?'

'Insurance money. Maybe he didn't want to kill the dog so he handed it off to someone, claimed it was stolen and collected the insurance. Cliff found out, so he killed him. We know the dog is still alive somewhere.'

'OK. But how do you explain Evan?'

Mary couldn't. 'Bill Bliss went into Evan's shop right about closing yesterday. Why he might want to kill Evan, I don't know, but he had the opportunity.'

'He was probably going in to buy dog food. That's where I buy Jake's cat food.'

'They no longer have a dog. Naomi said so.'

Ellen started to shake her head but stopped when her tea sloshed. 'It seems so improbable. The Blisses have plenty of money. Why would he do such a thing?'

'I don't know. I wouldn't have even considered him if the children hadn't had such a strange reaction when they saw him.'

'The children. We have to talk to Luanne and Tony. It's obvious they can't be left alone, even for a moment. I have a hard time believing they could be in danger, but I wouldn't have believed Evan could be either.'

She didn't say it, but Mary knew what Ellen was thinking. She had the same thought. Evan was dead. It didn't matter what they believed, or had a hard time believing. What mattered was what they did, at least until they knew beyond any doubt the children were safe, and that wouldn't be until they knew who murdered both Cliff and Evan.

The front door opened and Pat appeared. 'Ellen, could you help me, please?'

'Sure. Help you do what?' Ellen set her mug down and walked toward the door. 'What's all this?'

Ellen backed up, her arms now full of a dog bed, a sack of dog food, a bowl and a leash draped over one of her arms. A large dog carrier followed her into the room, pushed by Pat Bennington.

'This thing is heavy.'

A whine emanated from the carrier in response.

What do you have? Mary was on her feet, staring at the dog crate. It couldn't be, could it?

Pat answered as if Mary had asked her question aloud. 'We'd better get this little girl out of there and in the backyard before we do another thing.'

A loud bark emanated from the crate, a bark Mary was sure she recognized.

'Is that...'

'Evan's dog? Yes.'

'Why did you bring her here?'

'Dan called. He told us what happened to Evan.' Pat stopped pushing the crate and ran the back of her hand over her eyes. It looked suspiciously as if she wiped away tears. Her voice broke. 'He said she was all alone and you were worried about her.'

'Well, yes, but I didn't think you'd bring her here.'

'It'll just be for a day or so. We're full up at the clinic, and I didn't know where else to take her.' Pat opened the door of the crate and waited.

The dog poked her head out and looked around. Evidently she didn't think any of them looked dangerous because she took a step into the room.

Pat immediately removed the leash from Ellen's arm

and snapped it onto her collar. 'Come on, baby. There's a whole lot of nice grass out there, just waiting for you.' She started for the kitchen, the little dog trotting at her heels, when she stopped and looked back at Mary. 'You don't mind, do you? Dan said you got hurt, but not badly, so I thought it would be all right.' She looked more closely at Mary. 'I don't know. That's a pretty good-sized lump on your head. Can you handle this?'

Mary bristled. If she could handle just about every difficult woman in town, she could certainly handle one small dog. 'Of course I can. It's just that, well, I've never had a dog.'

'I'll teach you.' Pat smiled and walked on toward the back door.

Mary followed. If Pat was going to teach her, she'd better start to learn.

There wasn't much to it. Pat let the little dog loose and watched her wander around the yard, dragging her leash. The dog squatted, Pat picked up the leash and they both headed back toward the house. Mary stood aside as they came in then closed the door. She followed them into the living room and went back to her sofa and mug of tea. If that was all there was to dog ownership, why had she put it off so long?

Pat accepted the mug of tea Ellen handed her. The dog, no longer dragging the leash, curled up on the living-room rug and went to sleep. They all looked at her for a minute.

Pat looked at Mary. 'OK. What happened?'

'I don't know.'

'You must know something. You were in the alley getting yourself a cut leg and a goose egg on your head and poor Evan is dead. Something happened.'

Mary sighed. 'Something did. I just don't know exactly what.' She drained the last of her tea and sat back, resting her head on a pillow and stared at the dog, who snored. 'She barked all night.'

'Who did?' Ellen looked down at the dog.

So did Pat.

'That dog?'

Mary nodded. The dog slept on. 'I didn't know it was her. I had no idea where the dog was, but it was the first time I'd ever heard it. Anyway, in the morning I went to my rummage sale meeting then over to see how the Christmas Can Tree was coming along.' She paused and smiled. 'You wouldn't believe how much food we've collected.'

'Never mind that. What did you do then?' Ellen's tone left no doubt the Christmas Can Tree had lost all interest for her.

'Well, after I talked to Luke, I went over to Evan's shop. I wanted to know who owned the puppies he had for sale. Only, the shop was closed and it was after ten.'

'And?' Pat's tone said let's get to the point.

'I was worried, so I went to Evan's house. He and Glen Manning and John Lavorino were supposed to have gone to San Luis Obispo to some church function last night. I thought maybe something had happened.' She felt herself get a little shaky as she relived those anxious moments. She had been so certain something had happened and had been so right. 'His car wasn't there but the dog'—she nodded toward the still sleeping dog on her living-room rug—'was. She had no food or water. That really got me worried. It wasn't like Evan to neglect an animal. I went back to his shop and found his car parked out the back.'

'That's when you got attacked?' Pat leaned forward in her chair, her hands clasped, her eyes anxious.

'I didn't get attacked.' Mary stopped. Her cheeks heated. It really was silly of her to climb on that box. She should have found something stronger. 'I found a packing crate and stood on it to look in the window. Poor Evan was lying on the floor right by the bathroom and then, well, the box collapsed. That's all I remember until I woke up and Randy was trying to put me on a stretcher to take me to the hospital. Totally unnecessary.'

Pat and Ellen looked at each other and grinned. The grins turned into giggles, which dissolved into gales of laughter.

'I fail to see anything funny in this.' Mary bristled.

Ellen grabbed a napkin and wiped her eyes. 'Debbie from the flower shop next door said she heard a loud crack. She thought it was a gunshot. She peeked out her back door and saw you lying in the alley, bleeding. She was sure you'd been shot so she called nine-one-one. Poor Hazel, our unflappable dispatcher, almost had a heart attack. She darn near gave Dan one too. By the time I heard about it, they knew you weren't dead.'

'Oh.' Mary couldn't think of anything else to say. She had no idea she'd caused so much fuss. Why on earth hadn't the silly girl come over and looked? She would have seen she was very much alive. Shot, indeed.

The dog lifted her head and stared at the front door. So did Mary. It opened and Dan appeared. He looked tired and profoundly irritated. He stopped when he saw the dog, glanced over at Pat, stepped over the dog and squatted down beside the sofa. 'How are you?'

Mary lowered her ice pack and smiled. 'I'm not shot.'

He smiled back. 'Glad to hear it. So far, neither is anyone else.' He patted her hand, nodded with what seemed to be approval and stood. 'I don't suppose there's any coffee?'

'We're having tea, but it won't take a minute.' Ellen headed for the kitchen. 'We've got about a thousand questions, so don't start until I get back.'

'Why am I not surprised.' Dan stood over the dog, looking down. The dog sat up and returned his stare. 'I see you got it.'

Pat nodded. 'She was glad to see me.'

'What are you going to do with her now?'

'Mary's going to keep her until we can find other accommodation.'

Dan turned toward Mary with a quizzical look. 'Are you sure you can handle that?'

Mary's hackles rose. If one more person asked her if she could handle something… 'It's a little dog. I think I can manage.'

A smile played around the corners of Dan's mouth. 'I imagine you can.'

'OK. Now, tell us what happened.' Ellen walked back into the living room, wiping her hands on a dishtowel. 'Coffee will be right up, but in the meantime, who killed Evan and why?'

Dan gave a little start then started to laugh. 'Nice to know you have that much faith in me, but I don't know yet. We know how he was killed, like Cliff. Stabbed with something long and sharp. I have no idea who did it. Well, I have some ideas but no proof.'

The three women all looked at him, puzzled. The

dog just looked. 'That requires an explanation. Sit down and tell us.'

A lifetime of obeying Mary was not to be denied. Dan sat, seemingly gratefully. 'This is what we know so far.'

'Wait.' Ellen held up her hand. 'I don't want to miss a word of this. That coffee should be ready. If it's not…'

Dan settled himself in her large reading chair. Ellen would be back immediately. The pause and pour coffee machine was coming in handy. She was right. Ellen appeared with a mug filled with freshly brewed coffee which she handed to her husband. Mary sniffed. It smelled good. Maybe her next mug full would be coffee as well. In the meantime…

'Talk,' was all Ellen said.

'We think he was killed after he closed the shop.'

'What makes you think that?' Mary thought so as well, but she wanted to know why Dan did.

'We have reports of people seen leaving the shop after the closed sign was up and the blinds pulled down.'

'Oh.' Ellen and Pat looked at each other than at Mary.

We're all thinking the same thing. 'Who?'

Dan's frown was deep and unhappy. 'Father D'Angelo for one.'

Ellen groaned.

'John Lavorino and Glen Manning came out carrying something, and John looked furious. Luke, from the library, was there as well.'

'How do you know all this?'

'Our little friend at the flower shop. She evidently wasn't very busy Friday afternoon.'

'Sounds like he was having open house.' Pat sounded as distraught as Ellen.

'Bill Bliss was there around closing time. Did anyone see him leave?'

'No. No one mentioned him. How do you know that?'

Mary thought Dan looked unusually interested in that piece of information. 'I heard it at the rummage sale committee meeting. Leigh Cameron told me. She needed dog food, but when she saw Bill Bliss, she went to the market instead. She doesn't like him—thinks he's stuck up.'

'Mmm.' Pat didn't offer a comment but from the muffled sound she made, Mary thought she agreed.

'Anyone else?' Ellen's remark sounded a little sarcastic.

Pat wasn't far off the mark when she said it seemed like open house. It sounded as if half the town had been in and out of Evan's store yesterday afternoon.

'Todd Blankenship, but he didn't get in. The door was locked by the time he went over,' Dan answered.

'Who saw all this?' Ellen made it sound as though someone had had the place staked out, watching all the comings and goings.

'I had someone asking questions in all the stores. Todd claimed he needed to buy dog food but the door was locked by the time he got there. He knocked but there was no answer. He assumed Evan had left, so he did also. Mary's savior, Debbie from the flower shop, saw Father D'Angelo go in but didn't see him come out. That was probably after John and Glen left. Luke says he went over right after he closed up the library, at five. He walked over so he'd get there before Evan closed. He says John and Glen were still there, talking to Evan rather heatedly. He didn't see Father D'Angelo so doesn't know if he came after him or before.'

'What were Evan and John and Glen talking about?'

'He doesn't know. We'd ask them, but we can't find them.'

Dan's tone when he said that was mild but the statement sent shockwaves through Mary.

They weren't home? Where were they? Surely not still in San Luis Obispo? They also had dogs to take care of.

'What is it?' Dan looked directly at Mary and his voice was a lot sharper. 'What do you know?'

'Nothing really.'

'Uhuh. Suppose you tell me about nothing.'

Mary sighed. It really was nothing. 'John and Glen were in Evan's shop on Friday. They said they were going to San Luis Obispo to a church function, Evan too. Did they stop by the shop to pick Evan up? Only, he didn't go. Where are they now?'

'Good questions.' Dan looked increasingly thoughtful.

'Wouldn't they have picked him up at home? He'd want to shower and change, wouldn't he?' Ellen walked around, picking up empty mugs and headed for the kitchen. 'I'm surprised they're not home now.'

'They may have gone somewhere else today and haven't heard the news yet.' Pat followed Ellen toward the kitchen. 'Mary, more tea? Coffee, Dan?'

They both shook their heads.

'If they haven't heard yet, they soon will. At least, they will if they're close to a radio. The local news will be all over this.'

Mary nodded but her thoughts weren't on John and Glen. At least, they weren't right that minute. 'Dan, why would anyone want to kill either Cliff or Evan? Well, I guess Cliff gave people reasons to hate him, but Evan…the most disagreeable I've ever seen him was when he played Scrooge in the Victorian Christmas Extravaganza and he wasn't too mean then. Why would anyone do such a thing?'

Dan sat very still then shook his head. 'I don't know. Yet. But I'd guess Evan knew something. Maybe something about why Cliff was killed.'

'Dogs. It's got to have something to do with dogs.'

'Maybe. Maybe not. But one thing is clear: whoever's doing this isn't shy. Cliff was killed in a place about to be invaded by literally hundreds of people. Evan was killed in his own shop, a busy shop. My team is going over the shop right now, hoping to find something, but it's not going to be easy.' He pushed himself to his feet. 'I came by to make sure you were all right, but also, Mary, I'm worried about the Mendosa children. I'm going to talk to Tony and Luanne, but until I know who's doing this, I want those kids with someone. Day and night. If you don't feel up to it, then I'll help the Mendosas cover them. Maybe Agnes can stand in when Luanne is at work or at the doctor. Sister Margaret Anne called and after she gave me an earful, we worked out something for the school. But—' He never got to finish.

'I'm just fine. When did a little scratch on the leg stop me? I will, of course, help with the children. Tell Tony to stop by here and we'll make a plan. Now, go back to finding out who's behind all this. I'll tell Ellen…'

'You'll tell Ellen what?'

'That I probably won't be home for dinner.' He put his arm around his wife and kissed her on the nose.

She smiled at him. 'I hadn't planned on you being. I figured you'd be a little busy. Just be careful, OK?'

'I think I can manage that.' He gave her one more squeeze, turned, gave Mary a very careful kiss on the cheek and headed for the door. 'I'll call the Mendosas when I get back.'

'Dan, wait.' Pat stood in the doorway to the kitchen, looking worried.

Dan stopped, looked at her and waited.

'The animals in the shop. The puppies, and I think there are still a couple of kittens. There are turtles, lizards and snakes. Who's taking care of them?'

'I called Karl. He sent someone over. Cute girl. Doesn't seem to be afraid of any of them, even that ugly lizard who hisses.'

'Pam. Thank goodness. She's a vet student. Works for Karl sometimes. That's perfect.'

'She also follows directions, which is helpful. My guys are trying to take fingerprints and look for anything that might give us a clue, and she keeps out of their way. Pretty hopeless job considering the number of people in and out of that store, but you never know.' He turned and was out the door.

The three of them watched him go. Even the dog raised her head, stood, stretched and looked around expectantly.

'Does she have to go out?' Mary suddenly found she was nervous watching her. She had no idea what the dog had in mind. She could tell by the way a child sat in class whether they were paying attention or planning mischief. She could tell by the gleam in an eleven-year-old boy's eyes if he was thinking about tripping his arch enemy as he walked down the aisle, or if a twelve-year-old girl hadn't heard a word Mary said but had gotten every nuance directed her way by the boy two seats in front of her. Suddenly, she was afraid she was out of her element with a dog. 'Should I take her outside?'

'Feed her.' Pat grinned and started for the kitchen. 'Come on. I brought the food I found on Evan's back porch. I brought her dinner dish and water bowl as well. We'll set her up on your back porch. She'll feel right at home.'

Mary followed Pat into the kitchen. The stainless-steel bowls she'd seen earlier that morning were now on her counter beside a huge bag of dog food. Pat filled one bowl with water and carried it onto the back porch. The dog followed and started to lap. Mary watched her for a moment then picked up the other bowl.

'How much of that stuff does she get?'

'I don't know what Evan fed her, but for a dog this size one scoop should do it.' She produced a red plastic scoop out of the bag and handed it to Mary. 'Scoop away.'

Mary had to stand on tiptoe to get the scoop into the bag. 'We'll have to put that sack somewhere lower. Is this enough?' She poured the food into the other dish. There didn't seem to be very much. Mary was used to feeding people and did it with a generous hand. This didn't look very generous. It didn't look very appetizing, either.

'It's plenty. Just set it down beside the water.'

They spent the next few minutes getting both Mary

and the dog settled in. The dog ate, went outside, came back in and looked around.

'What's she looking for?'

'Her bed if she's got any sense. She's likely tired after the night she put in.' Ellen pushed herself away from the doorjamb she'd been leaning against while she watched the dog-settling program. 'Where is she going to sleep?'

That caught Mary by surprise. She hadn't given it a thought. Where did dogs sleep? Some of her friends let their dogs sleep on their beds. She wasn't quite up to that.

'I brought her basket. It's on the front porch. Tell me where you want it. Wherever you start her off, that's where she'll stay, so decide.'

'Unless she changes her mind.'

'There's always that.' Pat headed for the front porch and almost immediately was back. 'Where do you want her to sleep?'

Mary felt a bit helpless, an unfamiliar feeling and one that was not welcome. 'I don't know. Where do dogs usually sleep?'

'Depends. You can put her bed beside yours or you can put it in the living room, or you can put her on the back porch and close the door. You can even put her bed out on the back steps.'

Horrified, Mary stared at her. 'On the back steps? She'd be lonely. Scared. Do you think she'd like her bed in the living room?'

'She'd like it better if you put her bed beside yours. She'd be less lonely that way.'

It took Mary a minute. 'You're setting me up. That damn dog doesn't care if she's next to me or the TV.'

'I don't think that's true, I really don't, but I think you'll feel better if she's right beside you. Try it tonight and see how it goes.'

Unconvinced, but also not sure what else to do, Mary agreed. It took no time at all until Pat had the dog's basket, with the dog bed in it, set up beside hers. The dog sniffed it, decided it was indeed hers, got in, curled up and promptly fell asleep.

Mary stood for some time after Ellen and Pat left, staring down at the sleeping dog, wondering how she'd gotten herself into this, wondering what 'this' was. Cliff dead, Evan dead, the children in danger, well, perhaps in danger. What was going on? She wasn't going to figure it out tonight. She was exhausted and she hurt. She also needed to eat, but the bowl of soup she ate while watching a rerun of *Antiques Roadshow* didn't help much. Tylenol was needed. She walked back to the kitchen, conscious she was moving slowly. She rinsed her bowl and put it in the dishwasher, poured a glass of water and swallowed two pain pills. She slipped off her, by now, very dirty sweater, examined it closely, decided it would recover from a good washing and laid it over a chair. She'd wash it in the morning. The same could not be said of her blood-stained and torn sweatpants. They went into the trash. Clad only in a bra and panties, she headed for the shower. That pleasure was denied her, at least for tonight. Don't get either bandage wet, she'd been warned. The hot washcloth she applied liberally to her body was a poor substitute for a hot shower, but it was better than nothing, and it got off a little of the hospital smell. Her nightgown warmed and soothed as it settled over her and, slowly and carefully, she crawled into bed. Her head still hurt, and so did her leg, but her brain refused to succumb to pain and exhaustion. What had happened to Evan? Where were John and Glen? Why wasn't Evan with them last night? Did they know he was dead? What was Bill Bliss doing at Evan's shop? What was Father D'Angelo doing there? Buying cat food? Maybe. Bill Bliss wasn't. And Luke. He'd said he needed dog food. What else did he need? Her thoughts went round and round until finally the painkillers worked and sleep wiped away all of her worrying thoughts. The last thing she remembered was her hand creeping over the side of the bed, reaching out, finding and stroking the silky black fur of her very new friend.

TWENTY-SEVEN

HER HAND WAS WET. Something was licking her. Mary bolted upright and looked at her hand. Wet. What... The dog sat on the floor, looking up at her. She made a soft whine, stood up and headed for the bedroom door. She couldn't have made it plainer. Mary slid out of bed, thrust her feet into fur-lined moccasins, grabbed her robe off the end of the bed and followed. The kitchen clock said eight thirty, late for her. She yawned and opened the back door. The dog bolted out. Mary returned to the kitchen, looked at the coffeepot. Should she push the button or go back to bed? She pushed the button.

The dog returned to the kitchen, sat down and looked at Mary.

'It's too early for breakfast. I haven't had my coffee yet.'

The dog walked over to her empty bowl, looked inside and made a whining sound.

'Oh, all right.'

She bent over to pick up the bowl and immediately the room started to spin. 'Oh, that isn't good.' She dropped the bowl on the countertop and leaned against it until her head cleared. 'Why did that happen? I don't have a concussion.'

'Probably because you banged it hard on asphalt and have six stitches in your leg. Go back to bed.'

Mary's hold on the counter slipped as she swung around to face the owner of the voice. 'How did you get in here?'

'You didn't close the door after you let the dog in. Go sit down. I'll get your coffee and feed the dog.'

Ellen crossed the kitchen and put an arm under her aunt's and led her to the kitchen table. 'Sit.'

Mary did. Much to her annoyance, her leg was on fire and her head hurt. The dizziness was gone, but the side of her head, where the goose egg hadn't retreated, ached. 'Damn.'

'You can't expect to fall through boxes onto asphalt and come out unscathed.' Ellen put a full mug of coffee in front of her aunt, turned and set a bowl of food in front of the dog. The dog started to eat and Mary immediately picked up her mug. She put it down almost as fast as she picked it up. 'Hot.' She tried to smile but suddenly even that seemed too much of an effort. She needed pain pills. Two white pills and a glass of water appeared in front of her.

'What's this?'

'You look like you need them. Did you sleep?' Ellen set her mug on the table, pulled out a chair opposite Mary and settled into it.

'Better than the dog did. I heard her prowling around a couple of times. I had to get up to use the bathroom and offered her a chance, but she ignored it. She just prowled around.'

Ellen sighed. 'Looking for Evan. Poor little thing. Are you going to keep her?'

'I don't know.'

Mary had never had a dog. She'd never felt the need, even after Samuel died. Lots of her friends took comfort in their pets, treating them almost as they would, or had, their children. Mary had had all the children she needed while she taught middle school and, after she retired, her volunteer work and her closeness to her niece and her family and her many friends fulfilled her. She didn't need the added work of a dog. But this one… The dog left her now-empty bowl, pushed close to Mary's leg and sighed.

'Maybe.' Mary reached down and rubbed the dog's ears, soft and silky under her fingers. 'We'll see.' She glanced up just in time to see a smile hastily wiped off Ellen's face. 'What are you doing here at this time of morning, anyway? Church doesn't start for another hour.'

'I came to see how you are and to bring you a message from Les. He says he doesn't want to see you in church this morning and if you show up he will personally escort you back out the door and bring you home, even in the middle of a sermon. I'm to make sure you don't try.'

'You're all making a terrible fuss over a little accident. I'm fine.' She took another sip of coffee and hoped burying her face in her mug would hide her relief. As much as she wanted to talk to Les, she really didn't feel like getting dressed and going downtown.

'The hole in your leg isn't small but the knot on your head's bigger. What made you climb on that crate, anyway?'

Mary absently scratched the dog's ears. Why had she? 'I was worried about Evan. When I saw his car in the parking lot and realized the engine was cold…'

'You felt the engine?'

Mary nodded. 'I wanted to know how long the car had been there.'

Ellen shook her head. 'Dan's right. We've got to stop watching *CSI*. OK. The engine was cold. Then what did you do?'

'Tried to look in the back window of the shop but it was too high. I was beginning to get nervous, so when I saw the crate, I used it. It wasn't very sturdy.'

'No.' Ellen shook her head again. 'Why didn't you call one of us?'

'I didn't have anything to say. Just an uneasy feeling that something was wrong. This dog was barking all night. When I found her and realized Evan wasn't home, I was sure something was wrong. He's not— wasn't—the kind of person who'd neglect his dog. Do you think she misses him?'

'What? Who? Oh.' Ellen looked at the dog, who stared back. 'I don't know much about dogs, but she must be pretty confused. So am I. Why would anyone want to kill Evan? He wasn't victim material.'

Mary squelched the laugh that threatened to erupt. It was guaranteed to make her head hurt. She had to agree with Ellen, however. Evan was the last person she thought would be a murder victim. This was no random mugging, no bullet going astray and killing an innocent bystander. This was a deliberate act intended for Evan and him alone. Why? What could gentle, slightly nervous but always kind Evan have done that made someone angry enough to kill him? 'What does Dan say?'

'A lot, but none of it very useful.' Ellen grinned. 'He's furious. First poor old Cliff, now Evan, and he doesn't have a clue for either who or why. When he thought you were shot, that really sent him over the edge. I wouldn't want to be in the murderer's shoes when he catches him, and he will catch him.'

'I'm sure you're right.' Mary sighed deeply. She looked at the dog who hadn't moved from her side. 'This all seems so senseless. Unless...'

'Unless, what?' All traces of a smile were gone from Ellen's face. 'What are you thinking?'

'About dogs.' The vague thought forming disappeared under the insistent ringing of her front doorbell.

'Good grief. Who is that at this hour? Are they trying to push the bell through the wall? Ellen, will you go?'

Ellen was already halfway across the kitchen. 'Whoever it is, they better have a good reason for trying to push that bell through the wall.' The ringing turned into knocking. 'I'm coming. I'm coming.' Her step quickened with extreme irritation. If whoever that was didn't have a good reason for making all that noise Ellen was likely to make a little of her own.

'Where is she?' Mary was sure that breathless shout belonged to Glen Manning.

Ellen's exasperated 'what on earth' was loud enough to reach Mary in the kitchen. She was prepared when Glen appeared at her side. He was dressed in the same chinos he'd had on when she saw him late Friday afternoon, only now the sharp crease down the pant leg had disappeared. But the sandals he'd worn hadn't.

'Are you all right? Oh, your poor head.' He squatted down beside her and reached out his hand, but stopped before it made contact with the bump pushing up through the shaved part of Mary's scalp.

'Don't touch it.' John was right behind Glen, his voice sharp, almost as sharp as the welcoming barks the little dog gave as she circled the two men, her stub of a tail wagging her rear end. John knelt down and was immediately plied with wet kisses. 'Oh, Millie, oh, poor Millie. Are you all right? Have you been nice to Miss Mary? She got hurt too.' He gathered the little dog in his arms and looked at Mary. 'We came as soon as we heard.'

'Heard what?' Ellen leaned against the doorjamb leading from the dining room into the kitchen, her face devoid of expression.

'Why, about Evan's death, of course, and about poor Mary getting attacked by the murderer.' John, still on the floor, held the dog a little tighter as he looked from Mary to Ellen and back.

The dog yelped.

'We spent the night in San Luis Obispo. We'd been trying to reach Evan—he always feeds our dogs when we're gone—but he didn't respond to any of our messages, so we got an early start back. We walked in the door and our answering machine was blinking like crazy. We still can't believe it. Are you all right, Mary?' Glen once more leaned in toward Mary, this time touching her on the shoulder. 'Do you know who attacked you?'

Ellen smiled and pushed herself away from the door. 'She was attacked by a wooden box. Would you two like coffee?'

'What?' Glen stood and stared at Ellen.

'A box?' John let go of the dog and also got to his feet.

The dog went back to Mary, put her front legs in her lap and let her head drop down into it. Mary trailed her hand through the soft curls on one ear. 'I was worried about Evan. I thought he'd gone to San Luis with you two, but his dog barked all night. I didn't think he'd leave her out like that, without food or water, but I couldn't find him. It was after ten and he hadn't opened his shop, even though his car was there, so I tried to look through the window. I stood on the box and it collapsed.' Her face heated. 'It was a very flimsy box.'

'You two spent most of the weekend down there?' Ellen poured coffee into two mugs, her back to all of them. Her stance looked rigid and her voice unnaturally careful. Ellen liked John and Glen and thought John was funny in spite of his not-funny job as a surgery nurse. She banked at the local bank which Glen managed and had nothing but good things to say about how he ran it, so why, now, was she being so cautious? Or was it something else?

Ellen turned and handed Glen one of Mary's blue and white mugs. She walked across the room, avoided stepping on the dog still glued to Mary's side and handed John the other one. Then she picked up her cup and resumed her seat across from Mary.

John and Glen looked at each other over the tops of their mugs. John took a tentative sip.

Glen looked into his. 'Yes. We'd planned to come home Friday night, after the dance, but one thing led to another and, well, driving home wouldn't have been a good idea. A friend offered us a bed and we took it. We left Evan a voice message, asking him to take care of the girls.'

'That was Friday night, wasn't it?' Mary's tone left no doubt that she wanted to know where they were last night as well.

John shrugged. 'A bunch of our friends decided to

go to the beach. It's nice over there this time of year. We called Evan, but no one answered. We thought he was still pouting but knew he'd take care of the girls, so we went along and ended up spending the night.'

'Pouting?' Ellen walked over to the sink and ran water in her coffee mug. 'What was he pouting about?'

'Evan was supposed to come with us but begged off at the last minute.' Glen didn't look at either Mary or Ellen but studied his mug intently. 'I think he had an attack of shyness. He didn't know any of the people we were going to be with. We put a little pressure on him—he'd never get to know them if he didn't try, but that sort of backfired. We stopped by one last time to persuade him to come, but he wouldn't, so we went without him. When he didn't answer, we thought he was…' There was a catch in his voice. He cleared his throat. 'I—we—couldn't believe it when we got home this morning and heard the messages on the machine.'

Neither Mary nor Ellen said anything while Glen cleared his throat again.

'I still can't. Why would anyone want to hurt Evan?'

John set his mug on the table, walked over and took Glen's hand. He squeezed it before he looked at them. 'Evan was our best friend.' A simple statement, but the emotion in it was raw. He blinked several times, dropped Glen's hand and walked over toward Mary and peered at her head. 'Did they put stitches in your scalp?'

Mary had to think about that. 'I think so, but not many. They shaved off my hair and put me in that awful machine to see if I had brain damage. I could have told them I didn't.'

'You did. Several times.' Ellen walked back over to

the coffeemaker and turned her attention to the two men. 'So, you didn't know about Evan until you got home this morning?'

'Not exactly.' Glen joined Ellen at the sink. He took the empty pot out of her hands, rinsed it, filled it with water and handed it back to her. 'We went out for an early breakfast. There was a TV turned on to the local news. We couldn't believe it.'

'We left right away and came home. Our answering machine was full. Someone said you had Millie.' He paused and scratched his head as if thinking. 'Can't remember who. But they also said you were hurt. Or was that someone else?'

Glen interrupted. 'Anyway, we're here and so glad you weren't attacked. What happened was bad enough. Did you, ah, see anything before the box collapsed?'

'Evan's body on the floor right in front of the bathroom.'

John gave a visual shudder.

Glen's face paled. 'Do you know what happened?'

'Someone stabbed him, just like someone stabbed Cliff.' Ellen's tone wasn't quite as frosty but it wasn't especially friendly. Why?

Glen's face hadn't regained any color and he clutched his coffee mug closely to his chest, but his voice was steady. 'Any idea when?'

'The coroner thinks sometime between six and eight on Friday evening.'

Mary turned a little too quickly to look at Ellen. 'When did you learn that?'

'Dan talked to him this morning.'

'That means he was killed shortly after we left.' Glen's tone was soft and thoughtful.

John's wasn't. 'That's awful. I can't believe we no more than got out the door than someone stabbed poor Evan. Who would do such a thing?'

The dog looked up at the half-hysterical tone of John's voice then curled up as close to a ball as she could, one paw on Mary's foot.

'Who was in the shop when you left?' Mary looked at the dog. She, at least, looked peaceful. The rest of them didn't.

'Father D'Angelo came just as we left. Luke Bradshaw was there too, buying dog food.' Glen paused and finished off the coffee in his mug. He looked over at the coffeemaker, but it hadn't finished dripping coffee into the carafe.

'Evan and Luke were arguing.' John dropped that into the conversation as if it were a juicy bit of gossip he'd saved just for this moment.

'Arguing? What about?' Mary glanced at Ellen, who almost imperceptively nodded. Evidently Ellen was going to keep out of this conversation.

'About purebred dogs, as usual. Evan wanted Luke to let us breed one of our cockers to his poodle. Luke wasn't having any of that. He thinks cockapoo is a four-letter word.'

'I beg your pardon?' Mary felt this conversation was getting away from her. What was wrong with cockapoos? They were adorable. They reminded her of those cute stuffed animals all the teenage girls loved. What could be better than having a live one?

The look Glen shot John was razor sharp. 'Most breeders of purebred dogs don't like hybrids. They're interested in trying to improve the breed they've chosen and don't want to muddy up their precious bloodlines. Horse people aren't too much different. People who breed cockapoos are trying to get them recognized as a breed by the ACK, but so far that hasn't happened. So people like Naomi Bliss and Bonnie Blankenship never let their dogs cross bloodlines. Luke bred his dog to a cocker once. Evan thought he might again. He's not going to show the dog or stand him at stud, even though he's an especially nice one.'

Ellen held her coffee mug in both hands as if it might escape if she let it go. Her face had lost its stony look. Instead, it had the intense look of a bloodhound who had picked up the scent.

'Why did Evan think Luke might be willing to have his dog father puppies for you two?'

Glen and John exchanged looks again.

'Because he let Evan breed Millie to him.' Glen sounded as if each word was pulled out of his mouth against his will.

Mary's foot was going to sleep under the weight of the dog's head and she moved it a little. The dog looked at her, moved a little closer and let her head drop back down on the foot again.

Mary wiggled her toes. 'If Luke let his dog father one litter of cockapoos, why did he balk at doing it again?'

Both men shrugged.

'I always thought it had something to do with Cliff. He was so adamant about never crossing breeds. Some of that rubbed off on Luke when he was young.'

'Then how did Evan get Luke to let his dog father Millie's pups?' Mary looked at the still sleeping dog, trying to picture her as a mother. She was sure the puppies had been adorable.

'We never could get Evan to say,' John said, 'and Lord knows, we tried.'

'We have to go. Mary, we're so glad you aren't hurt any worse. This is all so terrible. I'm still in shock. It doesn't seem real, but it is.' Glen set the cup on the drain board, paused, his back to them, his shoulders rounded, his head slightly bowed before he turned. 'We have to meet with Les after this morning's services and plan Evan's funeral. Is it all right if we leave Millie here for a little longer? We'll be back to get her as soon as we can.'

Mary felt a jolt go through her. They were going to take the dog? 'Why?'

'Why, what?' John paused on his way to deposit his mug in the sink.

'Why take her? I like her and think I'd like to keep her.' Mary looked at the black head, still firmly planted on her foot. She trembled a little when she realized what she'd just said. A dog was a commitment. Taking responsibility for any pet was one she'd never been willing to make before. So, why now? What was there about this dog…she didn't know. But she wanted her. 'I'll take good care of her.'

'I don't know…' John began slowly.

'Is it up to you to say?' Ellen sounded a little short, as if she thought John had overstepped his bounds.

'Actually, yes.' There was something in Glen's tone…asperity? Impatience? Certainly a little sharpness. 'We are Evan's executors.'

Why Mary felt stunned, she didn't know, but somehow that wasn't expected. 'Executors? What about his family?'

'Evan was an only child,' Glen said. 'His father is

dead and his mother has dementia and is in Shady Acres. She has no legal capacity over her affairs. Evan was worried about what might happen if he had an accident or something. We worked this out last year.'

'I'm taking over the shop.' John seemed, for the first time, serious. No gushing over the dog, no almost hysterics, no waving about of arms, just a short, simple statement. He and Glen again exchanged glances. Glen nodded slightly.

'I've wanted Evan to sell part ownership to me for ages. I was totally burnt out at the hospital and wanted something else to do. He wouldn't make up his mind, but he did make us the trustees of his estate. The shop will be open for business again very soon. We'll let you know about the dog.' He walked over to Mary and gave her a light pat on the shoulder, repeated the pat on Millie's head and nodded at Ellen.

Glen dropped a feathery kiss on Mary's cheek, patted Millie, smiled at Ellen and they were gone.

'Interesting.' Ellen stared at the empty kitchen doorway.

'I don't think they want me to keep the dog. Why?'

'I have no idea. I didn't know they were that close to Evan, either.'

'Neither did I.' Mary let her hand drift down the dog's ear, who had lifted her head as the men left. 'I'd heard John left the hospital but had no idea he wanted to run a pet shop.' She paused. 'I wonder how badly he wanted to.'

Ellen shrugged, picked up Mary's now-empty cup and headed for the sink. She stopped midway; turned to face Mary again. 'Wasn't John a surgical nurse?'

Mary nodded. 'Yes. Why?'

'Just thinking. He'd certainly know where to insert something long and sharp that would penetrate the heart, now, wouldn't he?' The look on Ellen's face was more troubled than Mary thought she had ever seen. 'They were at Evan's around five thirty or so. Right?'

Mary thought about it and nodded.

'Most dances for adults start sometime between seven and eight. San Luis Obispo is just a little over thirty minutes away. I'd like to know why they left so early and what they did for that couple of hours.' Ellen dropped a kiss on her aunt's forehead and turned toward the kitchen door. 'Dan and I'll be back later this afternoon to check on you. For heaven's sake, try to rest.'

Mary could think of nothing to say as the door closed firmly behind Ellen.

TWENTY-EIGHT

MARY SAT FOR quite a long time after Ellen left, thinking. A long, thin, sharp instrument slid into someone's chest between their ribs and into their heart. She didn't think she could do that and doubted many people could. What kind of skill would someone need? Ellen was right. John would have it, but why would he want to kill Cliff? And Evan? He and Glen had been close friends of Evan's, if not of Cliff's, so, why? Could it have something to do with the pet shop? She shook her head but immediately stopped. It felt better but still wasn't up to shaking. She needed food. The dog had eaten, but she hadn't. Two cups of coffee were having an effect on her empty stomach. The thought of an egg, or anything else she had to cook, overtook her hunger pangs. With a sigh, she pushed herself to her feet and headed to the refrigerator. The dog raised her head from her position beside Mary's chair and looked hopeful.

'You already ate.' Mary opened the refrigerator door and looked in. 'Besides, mocha yogurt isn't on your dietary program.' She took out the yogurt and looked at it. She'd bought it last week at Trader Joe's but hadn't yet tried it. Was she up for a new adventure this morning? Even one as mundane as yogurt? She peered again at the contents of the refrigerator. There was nothing else that she didn't have to fix. Even toast seemed like too much effort. There was one rather tired-looking orange in the hydrator. She sighed, closed the door and took the yogurt back to the table.

The dog hadn't taken its eyes off her.

'Not a chance.' She took a small mouthful. 'I wish you could talk. I'd love to know what happened between your other owner and John and Glen.'

Other owner? She had to smile. 'I guess you're going to stay. At least, I hope so. I sort of like having someone to talk to.'

The dog cocked her head.

'Did Evan really leave everything to John and Glen?'

The dog said nothing but saliva built up at the corners of her mouth.

'How about the house? Do they get that too? Or are they just the executors?'

The dog whined softly, her eyes watching every spoonful Mary put in her mouth.

'Did you go to the shop much? Did Bill Bliss come in often? I can't think why he was there. They don't have a dog. I'm pretty sure they don't.' She thought about that.

Millie seemed to be thinking as well, but not about Bill Bliss. Tiny drops of saliva hit the floor as she stared at Mary's yogurt carton.

'Maybe they have a cat. That would be a sensible animal for a winery.'

The dog whined softly.

'Luke was there last evening. I don't understand all this about using his poodle. Why wouldn't he let John and Glen use his poodle? People generally pay to do that, don't they?' She took another spoonful. How much could one charge for such a service? 'As for Cliff influencing Luke, I doubt if he's been able to do that in years.' She took another spoonful and looked into the carton. It was empty. 'You didn't mind having pups with a poodle, did you? Cocker spaniels and poodles, they're both darling dogs.'

Millie looked crestfallen as Mary put the empty carton on the table. She stood, staring at the yogurt cup, as if daring it to move her way, and gave one sharp bark.

'You want the empty yogurt cup? I'm pretty sure I heard dogs aren't supposed to have chocolate. Besides…'

The dog barked once more and scratched at Mary's knee.

'Oh, well. There's not enough left in there to hurt you.' Mary put the cup on the floor. The dog picked it up and headed for Mary's bedroom. Mary hoped she planned to take it to her basket in her bedroom and not her living-room sofa. She pushed herself up to follow and the doorbell rang. And rang again. And again.

'What is there about this morning that makes everyone so insistent?' She hobbled toward the front door. No sign of the dog on the sofa. She pulled the door open.

Dalia and Ronaldo stood there, their faces beaming. Tony and Luanne stood right behind them, holding a large donut box.

'We came to bring you a donut so you'd feel better.' Ronaldo's grin seemed to go from ear to ear.

Dalia's face was more serious. 'Are you all right? Mrs Dunham said you had a knot on your head and stitches in your leg but were OK. Are you?'

'I'm fine. What are you doing standing on the porch? Come in. Come in. Coffee's hot and I'll bet I can find some hot chocolate. It's a cold morning. Something hot will go good with donuts, won't it?'

A black bomb exploded out of the bedroom, barking and wagging at the same time. She skidded to a stop behind Mary, making a huge fuss as the children drew back. Then she stopped, looked up at Mary as if for approval, and sat down.

'This is Millie.' Mary wasn't sure if she should laugh or be alarmed. She'd never seen the dog act like that. Should she put her outside? Would she bite the children?

'Millie.' Dalia was already cooing at the dog, calling her name softly, squatting down and holding out her hand.

The dog stood and inched toward her, sniffing at the open hand, wagging her stump of a tail harder as Dalia rubbed her ears.

'I want to pet her too.' Ronaldo knelt down beside his sister and reached out for the dog.

Mary held her breath. Luanne grabbed Ronaldo by the arm.

Tony smiled. 'She's fine. That's Evan's dog, isn't it? She makes a lot of noise but she's never bitten anyone I've heard of.'

As if to prove his point, the dog planted a wet kiss on Ronaldo's face. He laughed. Dalia scowled.

The children played with the dog for a moment before Mary looked at Tony and Luanne. They also watched the children but with no joy on either face. Stress lines framed both of their eyes.

'Why don't you kids take Millie outside to play? Just in the backyard. I don't know how well she does on a leash yet. Ronaldo, I think there's an old tennis ball on the shelf above the washing machine. Why don't you see if she likes to play fetch?'

Both children were on their feet, calling Millie and heading for the back door.

Dalia paused to look at her mother. 'Can we?'

Luanne nodded.

No hesitation there. She'd been right. Luanne and Tony wanted to talk and she didn't think it was about her failed encounter with the slated box.

TWENTY-NINE

It took a few minutes. Ronaldo couldn't reach the ball and implored Tony to help him. Dalia pronounced the grass too wet for her shoes then assured them all that the dog didn't want to play ball. It took the promise of hot chocolate and another donut to finally get all three of them into the backyard. They promptly started a loud game of fetch in which Millie gleefully participated.

The three adults watched for a few minutes.

Finally Tony turned to Mary. 'We've got to talk.'

Mary nodded and gestured toward the kitchen table. 'Let's sit in here so we can see the yard.'

Tony pulled out a chair for Luanne, who lowered herself slowly onto it.

Mary headed for the coffeepot, rinsed out the remaining few drops and filled it with water. 'Luanne, can you drink regular?'

'It's the only caffeine I allow myself. I had half a cup with breakfast so I'm ready for more.'

She looked as if she needed it. There were black circles under her eyes and her mouth was pinched and worried. Mary glanced over at Tony. He didn't look much better. His usually immaculately groomed black hair stuck up in the back and a five o'clock shadow had advanced to ten o'clock stubble.

Mary poured the last tablespoon of coffee into the

filter, flipped the switch and turned back to face them. 'OK, what's happened?'

Tony managed a small smile as he tore his eyes away from Luanne to look back at Mary. 'How did you know?'

'All I had to do was look at you. Besides, you didn't come bearing donuts so you could examine my stitches. What's wrong?'

Tony sighed. Luanne swallowed a sob.

'I'm not sure,' Tony finally said, 'but we think someone tried to break in last night.'

Mary almost dropped the mug she'd reached for. Clutching it tightly, she whirled around to face him. 'Someone tried to do what?'

'Tony found footprints under Ronaldo's window.' Luanne looked as if she was going to break down or have hysterics, or both, and soon.

'Footprints? Under his window? How did you…?' Mary took a deep breath to quell the panic that was beginning to rise, took down another mug, filled them both and set one in front of each of them before refilling her own. 'Tell me what happened.'

Tony put his hand around the mug but made no attempt to pick it up. He glanced over at Luanne, who held hers halfway to her mouth, staring at the steam that rose lazily toward her pale cheeks.

'I'm not sleeping too well. It's hard to get comfortable.'

Mary nodded. She certainly didn't look too comfortable.

'It must have been around midnight. I'd gotten up to use the bathroom and was having trouble getting back to sleep when I heard a noise.'

'What kind of noise?' Mary envisioned scratching at the window, glass breaking, something dramatic.

'A sort of rustling noise. Like someone or something was in the bushes by the side of the house.'

'Most likely a cat.' Mary heaved a silent sigh of relief. Their nerves were all on edge. This was sure to have been a false alarm. But hadn't Tony mentioned a footprint?

'That's what I thought. I was sure I heard it meow. Only, cats don't whisper or break branches off bushes.'

Mary made a soft 'oh' with her mouth. 'You heard someone whispering?'

The sound Luanne made was somewhere between a sigh and a sob. 'It sounded like a whisper. It sounded like someone said "damn it." Then a branch broke. That's when I woke up Tony.'

He nodded. 'It's funny how fast you can wake up. One minute I was sound asleep, the next wide awake. I heard the rustling too. I told Luanne to go into Ronaldo's room but not to turn on the light and I'd see what was happening.'

'Why Ronaldo's room?'

'The sound seemed to be coming from outside his room. I started for the back door, but it was dark and I bumped into a chair in the kitchen—one the kids hadn't put back where it belonged, and knocked it over. By the time I got the door open and turned on the light, no one was in sight. I looked around but couldn't see anything. I decided it was a cat, that we were all getting paranoid and went back to bed. But I didn't sleep very well. This morning I went out to look. I found the broken bush and a footprint.'

'How could someone leave a footprint? The rain the other night was barely enough to dampen the sidewalk.'

'I'd just mulched the beds.' Tony smiled. 'Loose compost takes a good footprint.'

Mary's scalp tingled. Another footprint. She had to ask. She didn't want to. She didn't want him to have anything to do with this, but she had no choice. 'Could you tell anything from it?'

'It was a sandal.' Tony seemed to stumble over the words. 'What was he doing in our bushes in the middle of the night? Priests don't prowl around in bushes. They don't—I can't believe—but I don't know anyone else who wears sandals in the middle of winter.'

'Luke does.'

Almost as one, the adults wheeled around to stare at Dalia, who stood in the doorway, watching them, her brow furrowed, her eyes wide with anxiety.

'Who's Luke?' Tony sounded a little taken back but also a little hopeful.

'Luke from the library. He had them on the day we built the can tree. Only he wasn't barefoot, like Father D'Angelo. He had on white socks. Ask Ronaldo. He saw them too.'

They didn't have to ask him. He stood behind his sister, Millie at his heels, and nodded. 'Dalia's right. Luke wears sandals. I'd like to wear my sandals like that. With socks.'

Tony looked over at Mary. 'Is that right? This Luke, does he wear sandals?'

Mary shook her head. 'I don't know. I've never looked at his feet. Why would Luke be rummaging through your bushes?'

Tony's face was grim, his eyes large and angry.

'Why would anyone? There's only one answer I can think of.'

The stillness in the room was oppressive, as if Tony's remark had somehow sucked all of the air out of it. Then, suddenly, they all started to talk at once.

'Why are you talking about sandals?' Dalia's voice held deep uncertainty, her eyes more than a little frightened.

'No reason. We were just talking.' Luanne made what Mary thought a valiant attempt to be casual. But it didn't appear to fool Dalia.

'Actually, we were talking about Mrs McGill's accident. Good thing she had on running shoes. If she'd had on sandals…' Tony smiled at Dalia.

She just stared. She appeared to be buying none of it.

'Millie's real good at catching a ball.' Ronaldo's interest in sandals ended when the conversation didn't include him. 'Aunt Mary, are you picking us up from school tomorrow?'

'She can't.' Luanne made that statement emphatic. Did Mary hear a little wistfulness in there?

'Of course I can. You don't think I'd let a little cut on my leg stop me from collecting you two, do you? We'll go see how the can tree looks before it gets torn down. I want a picture of you both in front of it. After all, you helped build it.'

The children looked at each other and giggled. 'Can we get Sampson and have him in the picture?'

That, of course, came from Dalia.

'No.' Tony and Luanne gave one horrified gasp together.

Mary didn't say a word but thought that wasn't a

bad idea. Someone might see it and identify him. She'd suggest it to Dan. In the meantime…

'How long before Christmas break?'

'Next week.' Luanne sighed. 'Christmas is coming fast and I'm not ready. So much has happened…' She looked at the children, then at Tony.

'My mom is coming out next week. She's going to stay until after the baby is born.' He looked at the children with an uncertainty Mary hadn't seen before. 'It'll give the kids a chance to get to know her. However, if you can help out until she gets here…'

A surge of different emotions ran through Mary. She, too, was worried about the children and if she could help keep them safe, she would. However, she wasn't ready for Christmas either. She hadn't even dragged out her decorations. Maybe she could get the kids to help. That would keep them busy and under her watchful eyes. As for this latest development, she wasn't sure what to think. Had someone really been under Ronaldo's window with the idea of breaking in? Tony seemed to think so, but Mary thought it seemed a foolhardy thing to do. Whoever killed Cliff and Evan could hardly think he could sneak into their house and…do what? Kidnap the children? That wouldn't have been successful. Harm them? That was a thought too awful to be considered. Besides, he couldn't realistically have expected to get away with it. However, the other two murders had been pretty brazen. A shudder ran through her. She needed to talk to Dan. Tony had called him, hadn't he?

'You did call Dan?'

Tony nodded his head slightly.

Luanne looked stricken. She turned toward the children, who were listening intently to every word. 'What are you two doing back in here? I thought you were out playing with the dog.'

'We were, but we thought we'd better tell you.'

Dalia's tone was matter-of-fact but there was a spark of something in her eyes that Mary couldn't quite identify. Fear? Certainly uneasiness. 'Tell us what?'

Dalia took a deep breath and turned her gaze on Ronaldo as she slowly let it out. 'There's a man in our bushes. I think he's looking for something.'

Luanne put her hand on her stomach. 'What makes you think that?'

'He's behind the bush outside my window, and he's bending down doing something. I don't like having someone outside my window.' Ronaldo looked as if he was torn between anger and fright. Anger was winning. 'Who is he?' The look he gave Tony was almost a glare.

Tony didn't answer. 'We have to go if we're going to make ten o'clock Mass.'

Luanne pushed herself forward in her chair in preparation to pushing herself to her feet. Tony was there ahead of her, holding out a hand, pulling her up. The smile he gave her and the hand carefully holding onto her elbow as she steadied herself were tender, caring. No trace of the impatience and the sometimes quick anger he was capable of.

He motioned to the children. 'Let's go. We'll walk, so if you have to go to the bathroom, do it now.'

'Good heavens, look at you.' Luanne held Ronaldo at arm's length, examining the dirt on the child's cheeks and the hair that had escaped whatever she'd combed it with earlier. 'How do you do it? You were clean when we came over here.' She turned to Mary, who had no trouble anticipating Luanne's request.

'Of course you can use the bathroom. Dalia, go with your mother. You don't look much better.'

She and Tony watched Luanne herd the children down the hall.

When the door closed, Mary turned toward him. 'OK. What's that man doing in your bushes?'

'Taking a cast of the footprint, I suppose.'

Mary nodded. Forensics. That made sense. 'Does Dan really believe someone tried to get in last night?'

Tony ran a hand through his hair. 'I don't know. He didn't say much when I told him. Just that he'd investigate.' He paused, shook his head and seemed to stare through Mary. 'Someone was there. Who it was and what he wanted, I don't know. The thought he may have tried to get in, to do...' He broke off, looking a little sick. 'This whole thing is unreal. Luanne is trying hard not to show it, but she's worried sick. That's not good for her or the baby. I'm not much better.'

He was probably worse.

'I can't concentrate on anything. I keep thinking about Cliff and wondering why...and Evan. Why would anyone... Do you think someone would really try to hurt my kids?'

His kids. Mary was sure Tony thought of them that way. He wanted this baby, badly, but he'd been a close friend of Cruz, the children's father, and had known both since they were born. He was the only father they could remember. Mary was positive he loved them deeply.

'I don't know, but with you, Luanne, Dan and me

on the job, he's going to have a hard time getting near them.'

'We can't even begin to thank you enough for what you've done, but I—we—feel so guilty. Are you sure you're up to picking up the kids tomorrow?'

Mary thought if one more person asked her if she was up for something she'd scream. Or attack someone with a rolling pin. She was fine. Almost fine. She hurt, but then, when you got to be her age, hurting was nothing new.

'Of course I am. I'm certainly not going to let a couple of stitches hold me down. Now, about tomorrow. I'll pick them up from school. Then what? Do you want me to bring them to the winery or do you want me to bring them here?'

Tony looked blank. 'We'll have to ask Luanne. I'm not sure what her schedule is. It's probably better if you drop them off at the winery, even though I'm sure they'd love to help you, take the dog for a walk and feed it, that kind of thing.'

Feed it. Something stirred in Mary's head. Someone had said something—Bill Bliss. He'd gone into the pet store. At least he had if Leigh was right. 'When did the Blisses get another dog?'

Tony looked blank then totally confused. 'A dog? What gave you the idea they have another dog?'

'A cat then?'

Tony shook his head emphatically. 'Not even a hamster. Why?'

'No reason. Someone said… I must have heard them wrong.'

Tony's eyebrows narrowed as he looked at Mary. 'I hope they never get another dog. At least, not a little one like Merlot. I'm surprised he lasted as long as he did.'

'What are you talking about?'

'Naomi let him run loose. That wasn't so bad when he stayed up by the winery, but he'd taken to roaming the vineyard. We have machinery in the vineyard. Tractors, cultivators, sprayers, all kinds of things. That dog was little. No way could someone on a tractor see him. Or stop the sprayer from spewing insecticide on him. I told them both, he had to stay out of the vineyard, but neither Bill nor Naomi listened. She thought it was cute that he roamed all over. Bill just couldn't be bothered. When he went missing, I was sure we'd somehow killed him and we'd find his body down by that damn fence he patrolled. Instead, he was stolen. I feel sorry for the dog, but I'm glad my crew had nothing to do with it.'

Before Mary could make a comment, Luanne appeared, towing the children behind her. They looked much better. Sticky donut sugar mixed with backyard dirt was gone from both faces and hands and both heads were damp from the water Luanne had liberally used on the comb.

'We're ready whenever you are.'

Tony smiled at her and at the children. 'You look a lot better.'

From the scowl on both faces, Mary doubted they thought so.

'Let's go.' Tony headed for the door, the reluctant children slowly following.

Luanne paused to give Mary a kiss on the cheek. 'If you don't feel up to dealing with them tomorrow, give me a call. I might be able to tuck them away in my office for a couple of hours. You've done so much, and been through so much, I'd certainly understand. I'm sure Naomi wouldn't mind.'

Mary doubted that. Naomi might not have minded if her little dog wandered all over the winery and vineyard, but Mary was pretty sure that indulgence didn't extend to children. 'I'll be fine. I'm going in right now to shower and get dressed. And I'm going to try to get into the beauty shop in the morning. I'd feel a lot better if I can get some of this sticky blood out of my hair.'

Luanne was on her way to the open front door but stopped and turned back to face Mary. 'I thought you couldn't get stitches wet for a few days.'

'Irene can at least see where they are and wash around them.'

Luanne looked doubtful. 'Just be careful, won't you?' She sighed. 'You won't, though. You're going to do whatever you want. OK. Call if you need anything. Otherwise, I'll see you at the winery tomorrow afternoon.' She blew Mary another kiss and was out the door.

'"Need anything."' Mary addressed Millie, who looked at her as if to say, *What?*

'Exactly what I was thinking. What could I possibly want her to do? I'm fine. Just fine.'

Only she didn't feel too fine. In spite of the Tylenol, her leg hurt—burned would be a better way to describe it—and her head still throbbed. She wished she could stand under the shower and see if it could wash away any remaining blood from her hair. But, since she couldn't, she was going to find out more about that footprint. Maybe Dan was still there, looking for more. If she hurried, she could catch him.

'Stay here,' she instructed Millie. Limping only slightly, she walked out her front door and headed for the Mendosa house.

THIRTY

'Mrs McGill! What are you doing here?'

Mary had known Gary Roberts all his life, had applauded his choice when he joined the Santa Louisa police department, had seen him in action during several police investigations but had never seen him look so stricken.

'Why? Is there something I shouldn't be seeing?'

'No. Not at all. It's just that… You shouldn't be out of bed. Should you?'

Mary stopped herself from saying something she'd regret. She didn't want to snap Gary's head off. She wanted information and he wouldn't give it to her if she got his back up. She took another look at his closed face and sighed. He probably wasn't going to give her any no matter what she said. Or didn't say.

Luckily, Dan appeared. 'What are you doing here?'

'He already asked me that. I want to know about that footprint.'

'So badly you couldn't wait to get dressed?'

Mary looked down. Her pajama bottoms peeked out from underneath the bottom of her heavy bathrobe, the one with the reindeer romping around on it. She'd gotten it at St Mark's semi-annual rummage sale for less than a dollar several years ago and had been wearing it ever since. She'd actually forgotten she had it on, so many things had happened.

She shrugged.

Dan smiled. 'Come on. I'll walk you home.

'I don't want to go home. I want to know—'

'About the footprint. I'll tell you what we know while we walk.' He took her by the arm and gently but firmly turned her around. 'This wasn't exactly the way I wanted to spend my Sunday, tromping through bushes looking at footprints.'

'Did you find one?'

'We did. Also some freshly broken branches. Someone was there, in front of Ronaldo's bedroom.'

Mary's breath caught in her throat. Tony was right. 'Was it a sandal?'

Dan nodded. 'A big one. Belonged to a tall man.'

'Oh, no.' She stopped and clutched Dan's arm. 'Do you know whose it was?'

'If you mean, have we matched it with Father D'Angelo's, no, not yet.' He gently removed her arm from his sleeve and propelled her up her front walk.

'Whyever not?' Mary didn't want Father D'Angelo implicated, but the thought that someone had been outside the children's windows, trying to get in, made her sick to her stomach. She couldn't believe Dan wasn't going to do something to find out who had been prowling around.

'We're taking a cast of the footprint and pictures, besides examining the branches broken off the bush. We'll compare the footprint with the one we took in the manger. If they match, we'll have a little talk with Father D'Angelo. Until then…'

They were on the porch.

Dan opened the door. A small, yelping whirlwind

immediately descended on them, barking, whining and welcoming them home.

Dan caught Millie just as she tried to jump into Mary's arms. 'Here, stop that. You're going to knock her down.' He held onto the wiggling dog while closing the front door with his foot. 'For Pete's sake, go sit down so I can let go of this thing. You'd think you'd been gone a month.'

Mary sank down on the sofa with more than a little gratitude. She hurt more than she'd thought.

Dan let go of the dog, who immediately jumped up on the sofa, buried her head in Mary's lap and sighed.

'She gets upset. I think she misses Evan.' Mary stroked the silky ears and gave a small sigh of her own. 'All right. What happens if the footprints don't match? Even if they do, how do you know the sandal is Father's? How do you know it's a sandal?'

Dan looked around, grabbed the back of the rocking chair, pulled it closer to the coffee table and sat down. He leaned forward but didn't let it rock. 'We know it's a sandal because of the tread and shape of the sole. We also know whoever was outside didn't try to get into the house. Never touched the window.'

Mary stopped stroking the dog's ears and stared at him. 'How do you know that?'

'We dusted both Ronaldo's and Dalia's windowsills for prints. Nada. Nothing.'

'None at all?'

'Remnants of old ones, half washed away. We had rain the night of the Victorian Christmas Extravaganza. Not much, but enough to leave nice fresh dirt on the windowsill but no fresh prints.'

'Then why...?'

'Don't know. Someone was there, behind the bushes all right, but whatever he was doing it wasn't trying to break into the house.'

The dog nudged Mary's hand with her nose. Absently, Mary resumed stroking. 'Luanne said she thought she heard a cat. Could it have been...?'

Dan shook his head. 'It was a man out there. A fairly big man. He wears about the same size shoe I do. I don't know any man who would wander around in the bushes looking for a cat. Most would figure the cat could get along fine without them. I doubt I'd go out looking for Jake, and I'm pretty fond of him.'

Mary buried her smile by looking at Millie. If Jake was outside when Ellen didn't want him outside, Dan would go looking. Of that, she was certain. However...

'If whoever it was wasn't trying to break in or look for his cat, what was he doing? Wandering around in someone's bushes in the middle of the night isn't a normal pastime.'

All traces of amusement left Dan's face. 'You're right. We don't know what he wanted.'

'Do you think it was the murderer?' Mary could hardly get the words out around the tightness in her throat. 'Did Tony scare him off before he could do anything?'

Dan shook his head. 'Don't know. That's certainly a possibility but since nothing happened...'

'You have the footprint.'

'We do, but we can hardly go house-to-house asking every man over six foot tall if he has a sandal and can we see if it matches our casting. This isn't Cinderella. Even if we found the right person, which is more than doubtful, what do we do then?'

'Ask him what he thought he was doing prowling around under the windows of small children.' Mary sat up as straight as the soft sofa cushions would allow. Worry and indignation made her forget the pain in her leg.

'I don't think we'd get an answer. Right now we'll just keep as close an eye on them as we can and keep working on finding whoever killed Cliff and Evan.'

'Are you making any progress?' Suddenly, tiredness overtook Mary. The sight of the bundle of blood-soaked rags that had been Cliff swam into her memory, followed closely by the crumpled body of poor Evan laying half in and half out of the tiny shop bathroom. A shudder ran through her, one strong enough to make her head ache.

The look on Dan's face didn't help any. 'Not much. Half the people in town were in and out of Evan's shop. Trying to sort out all those prints is impossible.'

'How about the people who were there yesterday?'

'Yesterday was Saturday. Evan was killed Friday late afternoon or early evening.'

Mary nodded. Dan was right. Yesterday was Saturday. She'd found Evan mid-morning and had fallen off the crate around then as well. It hadn't been her best day.

Dan grinned. 'Town was full of people. We're interested in the ones who were there in Evan's shop last, but that's proving a little confusing as well.'

Mary let her hand drop off the dog's ears as she concentrated on what Dan said. 'What do you mean?'

Dan shrugged. 'We've talked to most of the shop owners and, of course, to Luke. The flower shop girl—what's her name—Debbie? Anyway, business was slow and she evidently spent part of her time looking out the front door. She remembers seeing Luke go in, also John and Glen, but not exactly what time and can't remember who came out first. She didn't see Father D'Angelo coming out but remembers him going in.'

'How about Bill Bliss? We know he went in, but I can't for the life of me figure out why. They don't have a dog. They don't even have a cat.'

Dan looked at her curiously. 'You mentioned him before. How do you know they don't?'

'I asked Tony. He said he was glad they didn't. The little dog that disappeared, Merlot, was always running through the vineyard and he was scared he'd get hurt, or killed, because they couldn't see him. He said he didn't want to go through that again.'

Dan sat back and ran his fingers through his hair as he stared at Mary. 'Sometimes I wonder why I have detectives on staff. What about Luke? From the library Luke. What do you know about him?'

'Other than what we found out the other day? He has a poodle but doesn't show him. However, he does breed him. Or did once. He let Evan use the dog on his cocker to have puppies…' Mary looked at the little dog then back at Dan. 'It was Millie who had the puppies.' She ran her hand through the curly hair on the back of Millie's neck. 'Wasn't it?'

The dog didn't answer.

'I know it was her. Luke said it was, and she is the only dog Evan had.' Mary felt stricken for no good reason she could understand. Dogs had puppies all the time. Millie looked perfectly healthy and she certainly looked happy. At least, she did right now.

'What's the matter?'

Mary could feel Dan's eyes on her, curious about her sudden change of mood. 'I don't know exactly.' Her words came out slowly as she tried to sort out her thoughts. No. More like emotions. 'It's just that, well, John and Glen were here earlier. I guess they're Evan's heirs, if that's the word, and they intimated they wanted to take Millie. They said they thought she might be too much for me.' Mary snorted.

Dan laughed.

Mary shot him a look. 'They breed little dogs called cockapoos.'

Dan looked blank. 'Why does that matter?'

'I don't know that it does. Only, Millie—' Mary let her hand once more caress the dog's ears, who sighed with pleasure and wiggled deeper into Mary's lap. 'Millie had puppies and Luke's poodle was the father. John and Glen wanted to use him on their dog but he refused. Evidently Cliff had something to do with that, but I'm not sure what.'

'And your point?' Dan watched her, his head slightly cocked to one side, his expression dubious.

'I'm not sure, but everything about Cliff and Evan seems to revolve around dogs in some way. I can't help but feel…'

'I can't say we're coming up with anything any better, but somehow dogs don't seem a very good reason for murder.' The expression on his face changed as he, too, seemed to follow a thought. 'However, financial gain might. From what Les says, John and Glen are the heirs to whatever Evan had, and that was more than appeared on the surface. The house is free and clear. He also owned the building where his shop is. The only stipulation is that they keep his mother in Shady Acres.'

'How do you know that?' John and Glen had told Mary they would take over the shop, but they hadn't mentioned any of the financial arrangements. Not that they should have. It was none of her business. But now she wondered. Was she wrong about the dogs? No. She didn't think so, and she refused to believe that either John or Glen would murder someone. They might have a motive, of sorts, but what about Cliff ? Surely the same person was responsible for both murders. However... 'Oh.' She gasped.

'What?' Now Dan leaned forward, his hands resting on the arms of the chair, ready to push himself up. 'What have you remembered?'

'John and Glen. They were here this morning.'

'So you said. What about it?'

'Glen. He had on...he's usually so carefully dressed.'

'Mary, get to the point.'

She could hardly get the words out, but she had no choice. 'Dan, Glen had on a sweatshirt over some kind of workout pants.'

'I don't think workout pants made you go white. What else did he have on?'

'White socks.'

Dan raised one eyebrow. 'And?'

'Sandals.'

THIRTY-ONE

MARY SAT FOR a long time after Dan left, running dozens of thoughts through her mind. It seemed as if there were a whole lot of different threads running through this story and she couldn't untangle them. She was convinced the same person had murdered both Evan and Cliff. There were several people who might have wished one of them dead, but she couldn't think of anyone who might want both of them out of the way. There had to be something that connected them, but what! She needed more information. She also needed a shower. She still smelled like a hospital, despite using the washcloth.

'Down you go.' She tried to pick up Millie, but she was heavy. However, the dog took the hint, jumped down and headed into the kitchen where she stood beside her dish and looked hopeful.

Mary followed. 'It's only three thirty. Are you sure you eat this early?'

The dog wagged her stub of a tail.

Still dubious, Mary picked up the dish, pulled out the dog food sack from the broom closet where Ellen had stashed it and scooped some into the dish. The dog drooled on the floor.

'Shades of Pavlov.' Mary set the dish in front of Millie, who evidently didn't care about Russian scientists. She buried her head in it and proceeded to devour the food. Mary watched her for a moment, returned to the closet and stuffed the sack back in. She rummaged through the boxes on the floor and brought out a large black trash sack. 'Just the thing to put over the bandage on my leg, don't you think?' She got no answer, but then, she hadn't really expected one. She started to close the door but stopped. Dog food. What kind was it? She pulled the sack back out. It didn't seem to be one of the commercial dog foods they sold in the grocery. This food was in a large, tough brown paper sack stamped the same way as the bags in Bonnie's feed room. She wasn't sure but thought the name of the company was also the same of a company in Los Angeles.

'Bonnie has these kinds of sacks in her feed room.'

The dog paid no attention. She put one foot in the empty bowl and started licking the edges.

'Do you suppose she bought all that special food she talked about from Evan?'

The dog gave up licking the immaculate bowl, sat down and yawned.

Mary continued to stare at the dog food sack. 'Half the dog owners in town seem to have bought their food from Evan. Is it really so much better?'

The dog got up and walked to the back door. She looked back at Mary and gave a sharp bark. Mary hurried to open it. The dog walked through it and down the stairs without a look back.

'You've adjusted well.'

She sniffed around the grass, evidently looking for a perfect spot, but Mary's mind wasn't really on the dog. At least, not Millie. It was occupied trying to figure out what Cliff and Evan had in common that could have gotten them killed. She wasn't coming up with anything. Except dogs. Cliff was a vet. He cured sick dogs. Evan ran a pet store. He sold dogs and the things people needed to take care of them. There had to be more to it than that. In a way, Evan also took care of dogs. Bonnie had been adamant about what she fed her dogs, a food Evan evidently supplied. Luke, from the library, fed his dog the same food. So did John and Glen and Leigh, spacy as she was. A lot of people did. However, Evan could hardly have been killed over dog food. She sighed, watched Millie come in, closed the door and headed back into the kitchen to tie the trash bag over the bandage on her leg. Sponge baths were well and good but she didn't feel clean. She wouldn't until her hair was washed, but she'd leave that to Irene.

'I'm taking a shower, but I need to make a phone call first.'

Millie looked at her and stared with apparent interest at the sack but made no comment.

THIRTY-TWO

'YOU HEARD ME. Dog food. What's the difference between what Evan sells…sold…in his shop and the kind you buy in the market?'

Mary held the phone gingerly against her right ear. The wound on her scalp was a little more sensitive than she'd thought. Maybe she shouldn't have dabbed at it with that washcloth, but the dried blood around the bandage was sticking to her hair and driving her crazy.

The question seemed to have left Karl speechless for a moment and his reply wasn't helpful. 'Why?'

Mary carried the phone into the living room and sat down in her oversized reading chair. She felt the need to get off her feet, but she wanted an answer. Not for the first time, she was grateful for the cordless phone. The dog jumped up and sat beside her. 'I'm trying to find some connection between Cliff and Evan, something that might have resulted in their murders.'

'I doubt you'll find it in dog food.'

'Maybe not, but lots of people around here bought their dog food from Evan. Is it so much better than the commercial ones?'

Karl's voice had lost its faintly amused sound. 'Depends.'

'That helps.'

'There are some excellent foods out and there are some full of fillers.'

'Fillers?'

'Yes. Stuff that takes up volume but is hard for dogs to digest. There are some that sneak by the government inspectors and are made from ground-up dead animals. That kind of thing.'

'Yuck. Really?'

'Most kinds you buy at the store are just fine, but Evan was a fanatic about food. There's a company in Los Angeles that makes several special mixes. Evan carried four kinds: one for puppies, another for pregnant and lactating dogs, one for most dogs and the last for seniors. He praised the nutritional value in those mixtures to the hilt and sold a lot of people on their benefits. It's probably the only food Millie has ever had.'

'So I should continue to feed it to her?'

'You could switch her over to something else, but slowly. However, if John and Glen continue to stock it, yes, stick with it. She looks great.'

Mary switched the phone to her other ear and scratched behind Millie's ear. The dog sighed and laid her head on Mary's lap. 'You said Evan was a fanatic about feeding. John and Glen said he was very selective about the animals he took into his shop. Made sure they had their shots and whatever else they needed to be healthy. He must have really cared about them.'

'He did. Evan was a kind man. He even took good care of that blasted lizard, who'd just as soon bite your finger off as look at you.'

'What lizard?' Mary couldn't remember any lizard large enough to put a finger at risk. Only the one who'd been napping under the plastic tree and it didn't look dangerous to anything larger than a fly.

'He had him in a glass cage in the back of the store. Evan was afraid a child would get hurt if he put it out front. Nasty creature. Should be in a zoo somewhere, but Evan took good care of it. All God's Creatures, Great and Small, that was his motto. It wasn't Cliff's.'

'What do you mean?' Mary's hand slipped off the dog's ear as she sat up straighter. The dog raised her head and looked at Mary with reproachful eyes. Her hand dropped once more onto the dog's head. 'I thought Cliff loved animals, especially dogs. Bonnie had nothing but praise for how he helped her. Even Luke said how good he was at coaching...' Somehow those incidents didn't really translate into universal love of animals.

'Cliff loved to win. He helped Bonnie because she had good dogs who won. Luke was a talented kid with an excellent poodle who also won. Cliff believed in purebred dogs and the people who bred or owned them. He was nice to his patients and their owners, but he only really cared about the prestigious ones. I don't approve of his attitude but I have to give him credit. He knew his dogs. Naomi should have listened to him.'

'What?' Surprise almost brought Mary to her feet. The dog raised her head and waited for Mary to settle back down. 'What are you talking about? Listened to Cliff about what?'

'He wanted her to stand her little dog, Merlot, at stud. He was a finished champion and, according to Cliff, an especially fine dog. He told Naomi she could make a lot of money standing him and if she didn't want all of the hassle, boarding the bitches, paperwork, all that kind of thing, he'd manage it all.' Karl paused. 'I think Bill was for it, but not Naomi.'

Mary thought back to Naomi's description of Cliff, his old car, his showing up half drunk, his many 'mistakes' as a vet and didn't blame Naomi one bit. Cliff had proved over and over again he wasn't capable of accepting responsibility for getting his own dinner. He certainly wasn't capable of running a dog-breeding business. At least, Mary didn't think so and, evidently, neither did Naomi. Only, why hadn't she said that was why Cliff kept coming around? Karl's next sentence brought her back to their conversation.

'Both Cliff and Evan were involved with dogs but from an entirely different direction. I don't see any common motive for murder.' Karl sighed deeply. 'I don't see any motive at all. Cliff—maybe. He made some horrific mistakes and upset some people pretty badly. But Evan, I can't imagine who'd want to kill him. He was a truly kind person.' There was a pause. Mary thought she could hear a catch in Karl's voice before he went on. 'We'll miss him a lot.'

'Yes.' She looked at Millie, who had gone to sleep on her lap, and vowed to give her the best life possible. Another thought struck her. 'Karl, is Millie spayed?'

'No.' Another pause. 'I talked to Evan after her puppies were born and asked if he wanted to, but he said no. I think he was going to breed her again.'

'To who?'

'I don't know.'

'Luke's poodle again?'

'Evan never said. Only that he was thinking about breeding her.'

'I wonder if Luke would have agreed.'

'He did once and I heard he made out pretty well on that deal. Why wouldn't he do it again?'

'I heard…someone said…Cliff gave him grief because of it.'

Karl heaved a heavy sigh. 'I doubt if Luke paid any attention to anything Cliff said.' There was a pause and Mary heard a voice in the background. 'Mary, I've got to go but Pat wants to talk to you. Hold on.'

She moved the dog's head off her leg, which had gone to sleep. Millie opened her eyes and gave her another reproachful look. She wiggled closer and put her head back where she evidently thought it belonged. Mary gave up and moved the phone to her other hand.

'Are you there?' Pat spoke into the phone.

'Yes. I was trying to move the dog's head off my leg. She seems to think that if I sit down she gets to sit on me.'

Pat laughed. 'You can make her get down.'

'I suppose so, but I keep thinking if it gives her comfort…she must be so confused, wondering where Evan is, when he's coming back, when she's going home. It just breaks my heart.'

'It doesn't sound as if she's falling apart too badly. How are you? I'm sorry I didn't get over there this morning, but I went to church and got sidetracked.'

'I'm fine. A little headache but other than that…did you by any chance talk to Les?'

'That's why I wanted to talk to you. They found Cliff's daughter.'

Mary heaved a sigh of relief. 'And?'

'Oh, Mary, it's so sad. She's not coming. She has children, says she can't afford the airfare, every excuse she could think of. She said a graveside service would be fine. No one will come to a funeral. All he left behind was bad memories and, by all means, put his stuff in the rummage sale. Except the buffet. She has enough money to ship that to North Carolina.'

There was no lack of bitterness in Pat's voice as she relayed the sad tale. Poor Cliff. He hadn't left much of a legacy.

'Did Les mention Evan? I guess John and Glen are in charge of those arrangements, but I'll bet we get called in to do the food.'

'Count on it. Evan will fill the church. He was as popular in this town as Cliff was not.'

'John and Glen stopped by. They were in San Luis Obispo. Returned this morning when they heard the news about Evan. Glen says they're going to run the pet shop. I guess Evan left them everything.'

'Including his mother.'

'What do you mean by that?'

'Evan was an only child. His mother was over forty when he was born. Sometimes older mothers dote on their child to the point of ruining them. Not her. Anyway, she's in Shady Acres Alzheimer unit. From what I hear, they get the shop, the house and whatever money there is but have to take care of her until she dies. They'll earn every bit of it. She's not an easy woman. Wasn't when she was younger and now she's a real terror. Didn't recognize Evan the last few months when he came to visit. Doesn't know much of anything anymore except how to make life miserable for everybody around her.'

'How do you know all that?' This time Mary pushed the dog off her lap and onto the floor and stood. Her leg felt like it was being stuck with pins. She stomped on it.

'What's that noise?' Pat sounded alarmed.

'Me trying to wake up my foot.' She stomped on it again.

'The hurt one?'

'No, the other one. How do you know all that about Evan?'

'Irene—you know Irene. At the Beauty Spot?'

'Of course. She cuts my hair.'

'She cuts mine also. And, she cuts both John's and Glen's. I doubt she gets much information out of Glen, but John has loose lips and Irene loves to gossip.'

Mary didn't. She knew almost everyone in town and knew quite a lot about most of them. After all, it was a small town. She didn't, however, deal in speculation about them or spread rumors. Mary approved of facts. And facts were what she wanted right now.

'I assume that includes Millie?' For some reason the words were hard to get out. Why, for heaven's sake? She'd only had the dog one day and dogs were a lot of work. Hair everywhere, yards to clean up, all kinds of things. She wouldn't miss the little thing one bit. But, looking into the soft brown eyes, a pang of loss she hadn't experienced in a long time went through her.

'Millie? I guess. I don't know why they'd want her, especially. They have two of Alma's other dogs and one they bought from Bonnie a couple of years ago. Millie's sweet but not near the quality of the other dogs. Her cockapoo pups were cute, but I can't imagine anyone feeling bereft because she wasn't in their cocker breeding program.'

'Is that what John and Glen do with all their dogs? Breed them?'

There was a pause so long Mary thought Pat hadn't heard. She continued, 'I mean...'

'I know what you mean and I don't really know. They only breed one dog each time so they have two litters a year. I know they love them and certainly don't keep them in kennels all the time—are they pets the same way you'd make Millie one? I'm not sure. However, if they keep Millie and breed her, it will have to be for cockapoo pups, and that's how they got into disfavor with so many purebred dog people in the first place.'

Mary blinked. 'What are you talking about?'

'The fuss the purebred dog people made when they bred one of Alma's bitches to a poodle. Some of them, led by Cliff, think if you breed a purebred dog to one of another breed, you are bastardizing the pups. Not only do they not have AKC papers, the offspring can't be bred back into either the cocker or poodle registries. There are no AKC specialty shows for them, so what do you do with them?'

'Love them.'

Pat laughed. 'That's what most of us do with our dogs.' Her voice got serious. 'That's not what I wanted to talk to you about. Do you have your tree yet?'

It took Mary a minute. 'What tree?'

'Your Christmas tree, of course. The Humane Society people decided to sell them this year as a fundraiser. So far they haven't raised many funds. In fact, they're in danger of going in the red, so, of course, Karl bought what looks like half a truckload.'

'What are you going to do with all those trees?' Mary's voice sounded a little faint even to her. Did Pat want her to help sell them? It was a good cause, but…

'We're giving them away. We took some down to the food bank, we're giving some to the various homeless shelters, one to the hospital and another to Shady

Acres, but we're giving most of them to clients and friends. Can we bring one over to you this afternoon? I'm making chili and I'll bring you some of that as well. That way you won't have to cook.'

'Why, that would be wonderful.' Mary was a little out of breath. She usually had her tree up by now, but this year, for some reason, or maybe for several reasons, time had gotten away from her. A tree would be most welcome. 'Do you think Karl would mind putting it up? Not the lights or anything, just in the stand?' That was the part that always flummoxed her. The blasted thing never stood up straight when she did it.

'He's counting on it. About four?'

'That would be fine.'

'See you then.' The line went dead.

A smile spread. Her Christmas tree was coming. She hadn't planned to do much decorating. There wouldn't be nearly as many people around as there had been last year when Ellen and Dan were married, but she had wanted a tree. It was a long-standing tradition that everyone came to her place for Christmas breakfast, and it wouldn't feel right without one. She needed to get out her decorations. She'd bought a set of beautiful cardinal ornaments when she was in Colonial Williamsburg last spring. They were too big to go on a tree, so she'd planned to put them on the mantel after she draped it in fresh branches. She'd put them away...where? The cranberry wreath she purchased years ago would go on her front door. She put her hand up to touch the bloody bandage on her head. It would have to wait until morning. However, she could get in a shower. She'd better hurry, though, if she didn't want to get caught in her nightgown. Maybe Karl would pull all those cartons of Christmas decorations out of the spare room closet. The tree lights were in the garage. So was the tree stand. She patted Millie on the head. Where was that trash sack she planned to use to keep her leg dry? In the kitchen. She headed that way, but the dog stayed where she was, watching her.

THIRTY-THREE

MARY PUT HER hands on her hips and turned slowly in a circle, surveying her living room. One of the prettiest trees she'd ever had, blazing with light and covered with ornaments, sat in her living-room window, also outlined with lights. The cardinals sat on the mantel, their little feet buried in fresh pine branches interspersed with tall white candles in small crystal candleholders. Her crèche, the one Samuel bought for her the year they married, sat on her round table by the front door; her cranberry wreath, complete with a fresh bow, adorned the outside of it. All of the other decorations she'd collected over the years were scattered around the room in the spots they occupied every Christmas, put there by people who had been in her house every Christmas for most, if not all, of their lives. She looked around at them and smiled. It had been a hard week, but this afternoon had turned out special.

Ellen walked over and slipped her arm around her waist. 'It looks pretty good, don't you think?'

'It's beautiful. The whole room is just beautiful.'

Pat walked in carrying three wineglasses and an open bottle. 'I love this room. It looks just the same— well, almost the same—as it did when I was a little girl. The only thing missing is the smell of gingerbread men baking.'

Mary beamed. 'I can take care of that.'

'Not tonight you can't.' Pat and Ellen spoke together then laughed.

'Tonight you're doing nothing,' Ellen continued.

Pat nodded.

'We've brought everything. Even cornbread. You're going to sit, relax and enjoy all this.'

Mary obediently dropped into her large armchair and accepted the glass Pat handed her. 'Oh.' She lifted her glass high over the head of the little dog who followed her into the chair. 'You almost had this dumped on your head. You can sit here, but we're going to have to work on letting me get settled first.'

Dan and Karl walked into the room, both carrying beer cans. 'Outside lights are up and your lamp table, the lamp and all the other stuff you had on it is in the garage, covered with the old sheet like you wanted. You're now officially ready for Christmas. What's for breakfast Christmas morning?'

'I can taste it already.' Karl took a healthy swallow of his beer and went on. 'If we get a vote, I'll cast mine for that strata thing you make, the one with the chilies and the cheese. And those sticky buns. I do love Christmas.'

'You love the food.' Pat smiled and took a small sip.

'Speaking of which...' Dan looked at the women expectantly before he tilted his can and took a drink. 'All this Christmas stuff makes me hungry.'

'Everything's ready. We were waiting for you two to finish.' Pat nodded toward the table, set with Mary's outdoor tablecloth in deference to the casual menu. 'I thought we'd eat early since you each have another tree to put up tonight.'

Dan and Karl looked at each other and groaned.

'You want our trees up tonight?' Karl asked.

Dan sighed, tilted his can again and took another drink.

'I think we'd better,' Ellen said. 'You both get a lot of unexpected calls but so far tonight you're free. Pat and I thought we'd better get this done while you're available.'

'I thought you wanted to wait until Susannah was home.' Dan addressed this to Ellen's back as she disappeared into the kitchen.

'I thought you wanted Neil home too. That tree will keep another week if we put it in a pail of water.' Karl watched as Pat sat a large soup tureen on the table.

Ellen followed with a bowl of salad in one hand and a basket loaded down with cornbread squares in the other.

'I do, but that's not going to work. Neil has midterm exams and so does Susannah. We don't know when either of them will make it home. I'll keep a few ornaments back for Neil to put on.'

'I'll keep the ones Susannah used to do when she was little. The rest of them need to go on,' Ellen said. 'Let's eat, everyone.'

Mary thought Ellen sounded a little wistful. Families had their traditions and they were especially important this time of the year. However, this was Ellen and Dan's first Christmas as a family and they were sure to start some traditions of their own. Susannah would be a part of it, but only a part. It wouldn't be long before she would be setting up traditions of her own. The years went too fast. However, Mary would make sure Christmas morning followed tradition. She looked around once more and smiled. It would be a beautiful Christmas. A slight frown replaced the smile. At least, it would be if they could find out who had killed both Clint and Evan. With a small groan, she started to push herself up. Dan beat her to it.

'Give you a hand?' He smiled at her.

Mary smiled back and accepted Dan's offered hand to help her to her feet. Millie immediately looked up and jumped down from the chair before Mary could move, ready to follow her wherever she was going.

'You've already eaten,' Mary told her and headed for the table. She couldn't blame the dog for being hopeful, however. The spicy aroma of chili underlay the aroma of fresh baked cornbread and, suddenly, she was also famished.

Bowls were filled, salad passed and cornbread buttered before the conversation started again.

Something had been trying to get to the front of Mary's mind for a while and suddenly it was there. She put down her spoon and addressed Karl. 'Didn't you say Cliff knew where that little dog, Merlot, was?'

Karl nodded. 'He had the DNA sample. He had to have known.'

She turned to look at Ellen. 'Cliff's diary made it sound as if he planned to blackmail someone. Probably whoever has Merlot. Right?'

It was Ellen's turn to nod.

'So that would be the motive for murdering Cliff.' This time she addressed Dan, who nodded.

'It's a possibility.'

'OK. Let's say, for the sake of argument, it's more than that. Let's say someone stole Merlot and is breeding him. Cliff found out somehow and it meant so much to that person not to be exposed, they killed him.'

'It would mean more than being exposed. Whoever stole him could go to jail.'

There was a hard edge in Dan's voice Mary rarely heard. She hadn't thought of that, but, of course, Dan was right. Cliff's attempt at blackmail would destroy someone's life in more ways than one. So they destroyed his. But, for the hundredth time, why Evan? She went on more slowly, feeling her way.

'Let's say Evan also knew who had Merlot. Either Cliff told him or he found out accidently. I doubt Evan would try blackmail, but he'd tell someone, probably Dan, about his suspicions. Evan was an honest man. He wouldn't have tolerated either the stealing or breeding the dog.'

Pat leaned forward a little and pushed her plate to the side. 'He wouldn't have tolerated murder, either. How could Evan have found out? Cliff wouldn't have told him.'

Karl listened and finally jumped in. 'The toenails.'

'Exactly. The toenails.' Mary reached for her glass of wine and took a small sip. 'I'll bet you anything Sampson is from the litter Evan has for sale in his shop. He's about the right size. Maybe Cliff saw him, noticed his toenails were the wrong color and asked Evan about him. Then the puppy disappeared and Cliff died. Evan had to have been pretty upset. The person who owns the pups would have been also. He had to make sure Evan didn't talk to anyone, especially the police, so he killed Evan as well.' She leaned back and looked around the table to see how her theory was going over. The expression on each face was a little different, but everyone seemed to consider it.

'How do we know Sampson is from the same litter in Evan's store?' Ellen asked.

'We don't.' Dan looked over at Karl. 'Is there any way to find out?'

'Blood tests, DNA. That will tell us, but it takes time. We can go look at them. If any of the rest have clear nails on a black paw, that's almost a certainty they were all sired by the same dog.'

'Merlot?' Ellen asked.

'Merlot,' Karl replied, somewhat sadly.

'So, what do we do now?' Mary sat up straighter. Maybe, finally, they were getting someplace.

'I guess we could go look at the pups.' Pat seemed a little hesitant. 'We'd have to ask John and Glen, of course.'

Mary wasn't sure that was a good idea. 'Couldn't we just go to the store and look at them?' She studied Pat for a second. 'Is that where you buy your dog food?'

'Actually, no.' Pat seemed embarrassed. 'We carry a line of special food for dogs with specific problems, but for dogs and cats that board with us, we just feed a general good quality kibble.'

'I could do it.' Ellen was swirling the wine left in the bottom of her glass around and around, not looking at her husband. 'I buy Jake's food there, and we're getting sort of low. I could drop in tomorrow and just, you know, admire the puppies. I'll bet everyone who comes in the store stops to visit them.' She stole a glance sideways at Dan.

'Are you seriously thinking of skulking around that store looking at the puppies' toenails? Why? What do you think you're going to find out?'

'If one of the black ones has white toenails.'

'Then what are you going to do?'

'Come back and tell you, of course.'

'What am I supposed to do? Run out and arrest John and Glen? Last I heard it wasn't against the law for puppies to have different colored toenails.'

'That's not why you'd arrest them. It would be because...' Ellen stopped and shook her head.

Dan smiled. 'Exactly. Even if we think that litter might—and I repeat, might—have been sired by Merlot, that doesn't tell us much. It doesn't tell us who has the dog or who owns the puppies, and it sure doesn't tell us who killed either Cliff or Evan. Go, if you want. But don't expect much.'

Everyone went quiet. Ellen swirled her wine some more and Pat ran her fingers up and down the stem of hers. Karl stared at his beer. Dan took what seemed to be the last swallow of his.

Mary sat still and thought. 'Evan must have records.'

'What?' Dan put his can down and looked at her. 'What are you talking about?'

'Records. You know, who owned the pups, how much they wanted for them, what Evan's cut was, some kind of contract or bill of sale. I don't know. Something.'

Dan nodded slowly. 'You're right. He must have had something.'

'How do we go about finding out?' Ellen looked dubious. 'Ask John and Glen?'

Mary had a number of questions she'd like John and Glen to answer but didn't think she wanted to start with that one. She couldn't believe either of them was a murderer, but there were a few things that made her uneasy. However, she couldn't think of any other way to find out who owned the pups. 'Can you get a subpoena or something?'

Dan didn't say anything for a moment but the look he gave her was a little more than thoughtful. 'I've already requested a court order to go through Evan's effects, looking for clues to his murder. Why don't you want to ask John and Glen?'

She didn't want to tell Dan her suspicions. That's all they were, suspicions, but she couldn't come up with a way to avoid it.

Dan watched her, saying nothing, waiting.

She sighed. 'I just…there are some things… John was a surgical nurse. He'd know how to stab someone through the heart. At least, I suppose he'd know.'

'Go on.' Dan looked interested. 'There must be more than that.'

'Well, they inherited everything, including Millie.'

The dog pricked up her ears at the sound of her name.

Dan simply said, 'And?'

'I think they might be the owners of the puppies at Evan's shop. If they are, then they have Merlot.'

Dan looked startled. Apparently he hadn't been expecting that. Ellen sucked in her breath and Pat's mouth made a small 'o.' Karl looked as if he was going to say something but stopped when Dan held up his hand.

'That's a pretty serious accusation. What makes you think they might own them?'

'They were pretty free letting the children hold them. Evan didn't like it, but when John said it was all right, he backed off. I thought that was strange.'

'There's got to be more than that.' Dan's brow furrowed as he watched her.

'They have a couple of litters of cockapoos every year. Their dogs are cockers and they always breed to poodles. That's what got them in so much trouble with the purebred dog people. I think they didn't want anyone to know they bred another litter of cockapoos, especially since they bought two of Alma's cockers. No, bitches—that's right, isn't it? Girls are bitches?'

Pat started to laugh and Ellen joined her. The corners of Dan's mouth twitched.

'Not all of them,' Karl said. 'However, technically, you're right. Female dogs are bitches.'

Heat crawled up the sides of her face. 'Thank you.' She turned toward Dan. 'Glen evidently wears sandals with white socks on his days off from the bank. He's about the same size as Father D'Angelo. And, according to the very observant children, so does Luke.'

'Are you still trying to identify the footprints you found around the manger where Cliff died?' Karl asked.

Dan hesitated for a moment. 'Yes, but that's not what Mary is talking about.'

'Oh, oh. Something more has happened. What?' Pat's expression lost its amused look. Foreboding took its place.

'Someone was prowling around in the Mendosas' bushes the night before last. Whoever it was didn't try to get in the house but was under Ronaldo's bedroom window. We found a print.'

'Let me guess.' Karl looked a little pale and there was anger in his voice. 'A large sandal print.'

Dan nodded.

'What you and Mary are saying is that Glen and John, or one of them, could be implicated in all this, so you don't want them to know what we're thinking?' Pat looked as if she was having a hard time swallowing something.

'It's always a good idea not to let anyone know what you're thinking in a murder investigation.' Dan yawned.

'Then why are you telling us?' Ellen stood and started clearing the table.

'Because, for some reason, I always seem to. Need help?'

'No.' She smiled and picked up his beer can, shook it gently and put it on the pile of dishes she held. 'Why don't you and Karl run our Christmas tree over to our house, find the stand and get it up? Pat and I will clean up all this and we'll be right behind you. If we don't get it done soon you'll fall asleep and it'll be New Year's Eve before the trees are finished.'

'I have something other than decorating a Christmas tree planned for that evening.' The smile Dan gave her was amazingly tender for a man whose job did nothing to reward tenderness. New Year's Eve would be their one-year anniversary. Dan's plans didn't seem to include anyone else but the two of them. That was as it should be.

'You go along,' Mary told Pat and Ellen. 'I can manage all this just fine.' She pushed herself out of her chair but didn't move. Her leg was stiff and sore and her head ached. She reached for the empty cornbread basket, only to have it taken from her hands.

'You're supposed to rest. We're doing this.' Pat took the basket, stacked the rest of the bowls on top of it and followed Ellen into the kitchen.

Dan walked over beside her. 'Want an arm over to your chair?'

Mary shook her head. Big mistake. The room swam a little. Dan caught her under her elbow and walked her to the chair. 'Falling off boxes, slicing open your leg and getting bashed in the head would take its toll on someone far younger than you. Do us a favor. Rest a little.' He placed a small kiss on her cheek. Karl, who was right behind him, gave her arm a soft squeeze, and they both turned to go.

'Mary, forget murder, at least for tonight. OK? Your valiant police department is on the job. We'll find out who did this. I promise.' They headed for the kitchen.

Dan asked Ellen if she had her car keys. She murmured an answer, then the back door opened and shut.

Suddenly, Mary was very tired. Maybe she'd close her eyes for a minute. She let her hand rest on the dog, who had joined her. So soft. Why had she never had a dog before? She couldn't remember. Maybe because… she didn't remember anything else until a hand gently shook her and a quiet voice spoke into her ear.

'I'm sorry to wake you, but we're going and you really should go to bed. Do you want me to help you?'

Ellen leaned over her, amusement and concern equally mixed.

Irritation filled Mary, not for Ellen but for herself. Surely she hadn't dropped off to sleep? She never did that. But she had.

'The day I can't put myself to bed will be a sorry one, indeed.' Mary sat up straight, waking the dog, who seemed to feel no embarrassment about dropping off. 'You both run off and get your trees up. I'll be just fine. Go.'

Ellen hesitated for a minute.

Pat joined her. 'You're sure? Yes. I see you are. Promise you'll call if you feel… All right. All right. We're going. Do you want us to let Millie out one more time?'

'No. I'll do that before I go to bed.'

'Well, make it soon.' Ellen followed Pat toward the kitchen.

Mary listened for the sound of the old screen closing and looked around at her living room. It looked, and smelled, wonderful. She loved Christmas. Such a happy time of the year. Maybe she should take inventory of the presents she'd already bought. Or get the box of gift wrap out of the closet. She had some left, but how much? She wasn't ready for bed. That few minutes of sleep had left her wide awake, but not energetic. 'How do you feel about *Masterpiece Mystery*?'

Millie's snore was her only answer.

Mary took it as assent. 'I'll go get some Tylenol and a glass of water and we'll watch it before we go to bed. Who knows, maybe it will give me an idea as to who killed Evan.' She sighed, pushed the dog over and went in search of the remote.

THIRTY-FOUR

MARY'S EYES POPPED OPEN. She'd been dreaming, something…it had gone. It had something to do with murder. Something on *Masterpiece Mystery*? No. Something to do with Cliff and Evan. She'd been thinking about them, about what had happened, about the children… That was it. The children. She dreamed something had happened, only she couldn't remember what. What time was it, anyway? Three. Why was it always at three a.m. when she was worried? She sighed and pushed back the covers. There would be no more sleep for a while, so she might as well do something constructive.

Millie raised her head and looked at her questioningly.

'I'm going to use the bathroom. Do you want to go outside?'

Millie dropped her head back down on her bed and closed her eyes. Evidently she didn't suffer from bad dreams. Mary yawned. If she went back to bed, would she sleep? No. She'd only stare at the ceiling, letting a lot of questions roll around in her head. If that was going to happen, she might as well put them in some kind of logical order. She'd always found putting things on paper helped her to think. Maybe, since she had to get up anyway… She felt around for her slippers, made it to the bathroom then headed for the kitchen to find pen and paper and heat up any leftover coffee.

Mary stared at the paper, steam from her coffee mug rising silently toward the ceiling. In lots of the mystery novels she read people made a list and it helped them understand what happened and often made clear who the killer was. Only, she'd never done this before and wasn't sure how to go about organizing it. She had to start somewhere, so she divided the paper into three equal columns. At the top, she labeled one column 'suspects.' That seemed logical. The next column she labeled 'motive.' She sat back, took a sip, gasped and immediately set the mug down on the saucer. Even McDonald's didn't serve coffee that hot. She'd go back to her list while it cooled. She gave a small nod and stared at the third column. What should she put there? Connection to Merlot? There had to be one. Somehow, the disappearance and reappearance of that little dog figured strongly in all this. How did she go about finding out how?

She'd start with all the people who visited Evan's pet shop the evening of his death. Reluctantly, she wrote John and Glen's names as number one under suspects. They certainly had a motive. That is, they had if obtaining the pet shop was that important. Or was there something else? Were those puppies theirs? Had they stolen Merlot to breed to their cockers? The purebred people in town made their position clear on mixed breeds, but Mary doubted if either Glen or John cared much. They would, however, care a lot about going to jail and she was equally sure Dan was right: stealing a dog like Merlot would mean that's where they'd go. That changed things. Was that why they wanted to use Luke's dog? So any new puppies would carry the same genes? How did that work, anyway? John would know. Cliff had never liked them. If he found out they had Merlot, she didn't think he'd hesitate to threaten blackmail. But Evan. Would they... Evan wouldn't tolerate stealing a dog, and he certainly wouldn't ignore murder. Shutting him up would make them safe and also give them the pet shop. They'd been there, in the shop, right about the time Evan closed and they'd had more than enough time to murder Evan and get to San Luis Obispo to set up an alibi. As much as she couldn't bring herself to believe they were guilty, she had to leave them on her list.

Who else? Father D'Angelo. Should she even consider him? He had no connection to Merlot that she knew of, but he had one to Cliff. Had he ever forgiven Cliff for whatever he did to his cat? He must have. He was a priest. But Father D'Angelo had a temper. She'd worked with him on too many committees not to know he sometimes struggled not to lose it. She'd watched him turn beet red, seen his eyes flash and almost physically felt him swallow the words he so desperately wanted to say. But he'd never lost it, at least in public, and he would never hurt the children. Or did that keep him on the list? The murderer had brushed by the children, hiding his face with a hood. He'd made no attempt to hurt them. The sandal print under the children's window could have been his. So could, and probably was, the one in the crib scene. Did that prove anything? Probably not, but the children saw someone in a robe like the one he wore, and he was the victim of one of Cliff's mistakes. That alone had to keep him on the list. She finished filling in his name with sadness.

That brought up another thought. Had any of the other people she needed to put on this list worn a costume to the extravaganza? She didn't know and wasn't sure how to go about finding out. Bill Bliss, for instance. She couldn't picture him traipsing around in a medieval robe. However, he had been seen going into Evan's shop at about the right time on the day of Evan's murder. Why? He and Naomi didn't have any animals but he had a connection to Merlot. He once owned him. Insurance. Had he done something with the dog to collect the insurance? Had Cliff found out? Cliff found the dog. Was it Bill Bliss Cliff planned to blackmail? Mary didn't think she'd want to. There was something cold—almost, but not quite, menacing about the man. She'd be less surprised if he turned out to be the killer than any of the other people she'd been considering. But why Evan? The telltale toenails. That had to be it. Evan knew about dogs and evidently that recessive gene wasn't common. Had Evan guessed? If he had, he wouldn't have let it go. He'd have investigated and, if he thought something illegal was going on, he would have done something about it. Mary sighed. It was an idea, nothing more. She had lots of ideas, but nothing that came close to proof. She wrote down Bliss's name but left the other two columns blank. She needed to find out more. Lots more.

Who else was in the store that afternoon? Luke Bradshaw. No. Luke was the last person to have done something so brutal, surely. He was… Mary paused. What was he? Who was he? She barely knew him. A pleasant, helpful young man who seemed to like the children. A young man who had chosen to work in the library. Hardly a job for a vicious killer. A young man whose chosen career was sidetracked by Cliff. A young man who owned a son of Merlot. Was that a connection somehow? Cliff mentioned Luke in his diary that he wanted to make amends. He must have contacted Luke. Had he found out things he wasn't meant to know? What did this 'son of Merlot' look like? Did he resemble his father? If so, how much? Could this be a purloined letter affair? She threw down her pen. This was doing nothing but giving her a huge headache. There was someone else who was seen going in the shop that afternoon, but she couldn't remember who, and she wasn't going to try. She was going to take two Tylenol and go back to bed. First, she was going to give Millie one last chance to go outside.

The air was cold. The first frost of the season had been forecast, for once correctly. She shivered, pulled her bathrobe closer around her and hoped Millie would be quick. She was. Mary shut the door and hurried back to the bedroom without another look at the paper sitting on her kitchen table. It had done nothing but confuse her more. She was going to leave all this up to Dan. She had more than enough on her plate. Tomorrow she'd try to get into the beauty shop for a shampoo before she picked up the children. She had some shopping to do and had to see if dismantling the can tree was on schedule and the press would be there. She also needed to…she couldn't remember what else. There was something… It would come to her in the morning. Her eyes closed, but they jerked back open. There was something on her bed. What on earth…a wet nose nudged her arm and a small body curled up next to her. Millie. She'd jumped up on her bed. She'd have to get off. Mary didn't approve of dogs on beds. At least, she didn't think she did. But she was tired, tired and upset. The dog must be also. She seemed to take

comfort lying so close to Mary. Maybe she wouldn't
push her off. Having the dog nestled next to her this
way was warm and comforting somehow. Maybe she'd
let her stay, just this once. Tomorrow she'd be stricter.
Her eyes closed again and she drifted into a deep and
dream-free sleep.

THIRTY-FIVE

THE BEAUTY SHOP was packed. That meant, for this tiny
two-chair shop, there was one person in Gloria's chair
and one other waiting. Irene had been more than willing to squeeze Mary in, provided she could come right
away. Mary could and, at this hour, she wouldn't be in-
conveniencing anyone. Irene and Gloria were the only
stylists in the small shop. The two stylists and their two
early clients gathered around Mary.

'What happened to you?' Gloria Hugger, blunt and
to the point, stood in front of Mary, curling iron in
one hand.

'Were you really mugged?' There was horror and
Mary thought a little thrill in Alice Ives's voice.

'Is it true you found poor Evan?' This from Leigh.
She had on another workout pantsuit that had never visited a gym. Today she clutched something that looked
like an old burlap sack. Mary didn't have time to sat-
isfy her curiosity.

'Does Dan know who killed them?' Irene asked.

'If he does, he hasn't told me.'

'Are you all right?' This time Mary only nodded,
but Irene didn't look convinced. She took her by the
arm and guided Mary over to the empty chair in front
of the basin. She carefully draped the protective cape
around Mary's shoulders, gently wound a cloth around
her neck, tucked in the collar of her blouse, leaned her

back in the chair and gasped. So did the other women who gathered around the shampoo chair.

'What did he hit you with?' Irene gently touched the blood-soaked bandage that hung entangled in Mary's hair. 'I'm going to have to get this off. It's not doing you any good, anyway.'

'No one hit me with anything. I fell off a box.'

That stopped Irene in mid-yank. 'What were you doing on a box?' She finished the yank. The bandage that had been stuck on nothing but Mary's hair came away, but not without a sharp intake of breath from Mary.

'Looking for Evan. His car was parked out the back but the shop wasn't open. I was worried about him.'

'Turns out you had something to be worried about.' Irene ran her fingers gently through the hair around the stitches, pulling it this way and that, separating the blood-soaked strands. At least, Mary thought they were blood-soaked. She couldn't see them. They might be stained with butadiene. They used that with a more-than-liberal hand.

'Do I have any hair left there?'

'Some. After they take the stitches out, I can sort of comb what's left over this spot until it grows back. You'll hardly notice it. Right now, I'm just going to rinse around it and get the worst of the sticky stuff out.'

Lovely warm water gently washed away dried blood and grime. It effectively shut out the questions from everyone else. Alice returned to her chair, where Gloria resumed twisting her wispy hair into little curlers before setting her under the dryer. Leigh picked up a magazine, featuring a beautiful woman with a hair-cut that was never meant to be worn by anyone who took care of children, cooked meals for a family or attempted sleep.

Mary's eyes closed; the soothing warm water and Irene's fingers gently running through her hair. The familiar voice barely penetrated but it made Mary open her eyes. It was the sight of Leigh, magazine abandoned, wrapped in what appeared to be a burlap sack that made her sit straight up. 'What on earth is that?'

'Mary, lean back. You're dripping water all over. It's just Leigh in her choir robe.'

'It's too long, isn't it?' Leigh turned around with a swish, but if she thought the robe would swish with her, she was mistaken. The brown material hung heavy and limp from her shoulders, held in place at the waist by a coarse rope. It looked much like the one Father D'Angelo wore, only he never wore high heels. Leigh pulled the hood of the robe up over her metallic gold curls and fluffed it out so it framed her face. She was right. The thing was too long and the hood was too big.

'That's a choir robe?' Water dripped down the back of her neck, but she ignored it. Leigh looked ridiculous. She must have agreed with Mary because she squirmed inside the enveloping robe.

'Yes. We had them made special for the Victorian extravaganza and the Christmas parade. We wore them for the first time when we followed the *posada* the other night. You must have seen us.'

If she had, she didn't remember. If they all looked like Leigh, she was sure she would have. The only thing, other than murder, that stood out in her mind about the *posada* procession was the cow.

Leigh went on: 'I had to wear high heels to keep this thing from dragging and almost killed myself. I can't do that again for the Christmas parade and I don't know what to do.'

'Shorten it.'

Irene giggled, or at least Mary thought she did.

'Oh, Mary. I couldn't do that. I can't sew a stitch.' Leigh sounded distraught but maybe just a little smug as well. Surely she wasn't proud of not being able to take up a hem? Well, maybe she was.

'Get Bonnie to do it.' Irene put her hand on Mary's breast bone and lowered her back into place over the shampoo bowl. 'She made it for you, didn't she?'

'She made half the robes in the choir and got rich doing it. Why, she charged fifty dollars a robe!' Leigh sounded incensed, but Mary thought she wouldn't have done it for that. Those hood things looked tricky.

Irene finished rinsing. She sat Mary up and wrapped her head in a towel. 'I'd hardly say she got rich, but I'm sure she was glad for the extra money. It costs a small fortune to feed all those dogs and run that kennel building, especially as Todd's business has fallen off.'

A start ran through Mary. She'd never thought about that but, of course, Irene was right. Keeping up kennels must be expensive. She'd heard Todd was having a hard time competing with the big box store that had recently moved into town. Several downtown merchants were. However, she hadn't thought about it in conjunction with Bonnie's kennels. So, Bonnie was drumming up business of a different kind. Good for her. 'I didn't know Bonnie could sew.' She knew very little about Bonnie.

'She made a bunch of the robes. We'd been talking about what we could do that would be different for the *posada* and the parade. She suggested we dress sort of medieval and brought in hers to show us. They looked about right and they weren't that expensive, so we voted to go with it, especially when Bonnie said she'd make one for anyone who wanted her to, but it'd be fifty dollars and we would buy the material. Cheap at the price, in my opinion. She did mine.' Irene threw a look at Leigh that said plainly she thought Bonnie had treated them fairly.

'Do you think she'll charge me to take up the hem?'

Leigh eyed Mary as if she might ask her to do it. A retired home economics teacher should have no trouble putting up a hem and certainly had a sewing machine. Mary silently vowed this was one time she wasn't volunteering. She didn't mind helping. She went out of her way to help organizations and people, but she didn't care one bit for being taken advantage of, and that's just what Leigh had in mind.

'Call Bonnie and ask her.' Irene looked at Leigh, then down at her shoes and sighed. 'You'd better do it soon. That parade is coming up and you'll kill yourself in those things.' She stood in front of Mary, blow dryer in her hand, studying Mary's hair. 'I won't be able to do a very good job with this. I'm afraid of hurting your stitches.'

'They're already hurt. Do what you can.'

'I think we need to put a bandage of some kind back on.' Irene walked closer and examined Mary's head again. 'I've got a first-aid kit in the back. I'll go see what I can find.'

She laid her dryer on the stand and left.

Leigh moved in closer. 'Do you think I should ask Bonnie to take up the hem?'

'She made it. I'm sure she'll take it up.'

'Yes, but will she charge me?'

'Leigh, I don't know.' She paused as she looked at her. 'It seems a little big everywhere.'

Leigh looked down at herself and ran her hands down the sides of the garment. 'My James has mentioned he might like to join. He's in the choir at school. I thought I'd get it a little big so he could wear it too. That way I wouldn't have to pay for two of them.' She pulled the material out around her hips. There was quite a lot of it. 'Maybe I shouldn't have had it made so…big.'

Mary stared at her. 'How are you going to work that if you're both still in the choir?'

'I hadn't thought of that.' Leigh looked a little taken aback.

'How long have you been a member?' Mary put her hand up to her head and gingerly touched the shaved spot. It felt bigger than she'd thought. Drat. How long would it take for her hair to grow back?

'Not too long. I joined about the time John Lavorino left. Too bad. Everyone said he was one of the best tenors they'd had in years. Dog people certainly do get upset.'

Mary abandoned the problem of her hair, or lack of it, to give Leigh her full attention. She'd forgotten John was in the choir. She listened to them on Sundays, sometimes with appreciation, sometimes with a cringe, but she'd paid little attention to who was involved. 'When did he quit? Before or after you all ordered your robes?'

Her tone must have sounded a bit sharp because Leigh took a step backward and opened her eyes wide. 'Why, let me see, it must have been after. I remember thinking there went one hundred perfectly good dollars down the drain. It's not like we can wear these things for anything other than choir, and not very often then.' She stopped and the expression on her face changed. 'Why?'

'Was Glen a member as well? I don't remember that.'

'Probably because they buried him in the back row. Glen can't carry a tune in a bucket.'

Ignoring the cliché, Mary tried to remember who else was in the choir. She saw them every Sunday. Why was nothing coming? Bonnie played the piano for them, and she remembered Naomi… Naomi. 'Is Bill Bliss…'

'Of course not. Can you imagine that stuck-up man wearing a robe like this? Parading through the streets, following some woman on a donkey, singing "We Three Kings"? Hummp. Mr Bliss thinks he's the king and we're the servants. He wouldn't stoop so low as to mingle among us.'

Mary briefly wondered what Bill had done to engender so much dislike from Leigh, but her mind was going in a different direction and she pushed Bill aside. A mental picture of the choir was starting to form. 'Luke. From the library Luke. He's in the choir, isn't he?'

'He is. Nice boy.' She gave a little laugh. 'Can't help thinking of him as a boy, but he's a man now.'

'And Todd? Todd Blankenship? Bonnie's husband? Is he in the choir?' This came out a little faint. Mary felt a little faint. It seemed there were medieval robes everywhere.

'Mary, why all this interest in the choir? If you want

a list of the members, ask Bonnie. Actually, ask Misha Turner. She's the adult choir director. Or, if you want to get the contract to make the next robes, well, I'm not sure Bonnie…'

Mary didn't let her finish. 'I have no interest in making anything. No. I only wondered…such an interesting idea…it seemed there are a lot of new people in the choir…'

Leigh still stared at her, almost willing her to say more.

Saved by Irene. 'Found this gauze and tape. Let me put this bandage on before I try to fix your hair.'

Mary watched Leigh out of the corner of her eye while Irene tried to make the bandage stick. She seemed undecided whether she should continue to question Mary or not. However, she wasn't going to get the chance. Irene was asking the questions: exactly how had Mary fallen, what made her think Evan might be in trouble and did she have any idea why Cliff was in the manger, let alone at St Theresa's. Mary had no answers. Leigh listened intently for a few minutes then gathered up her robe and, wobbling a little on her high heels, left. Was she going to call Bonnie? She thought about all the choir robes. Too many robes. Too many people connected to these terrible events seemed to have one. It must all mean something, but for the life of her she couldn't figure out what.

THIRTY-SIX

MARY SAT IN her car in the library parking lot. After turning the car off, she leaned forward on her steering wheel and thought about what she'd just learned. Had she, though, learned anything of significance? The choir had robes that looked a lot like the one Father D'Angelo wore. Enough so two small children, in the dark and already scared half to death, might mistake someone wearing one for him? Mary thought it possible.

Luanne said half the town was dressed up for the extravaganza, but they didn't all wear robes like a Franciscan friar. There were Dickens-era carolers, elves and reindeer, Maids a-Milking, who had ruffles everywhere except where they were needed most. None of them would be mistaken for a monk. The Morris dancers with their ballet slippers, white pants and full-sleeved blouses and the lady who read stories out of a very large story book were out. So were the people who gathered around the Charlie Brown Christmas tree portraying the Peanuts gang.

There weren't a lot of monk robes she could think of. That narrowed the field of possible suspects but didn't mean the murderer had to be a member of the choir. She had no idea how many of them had anything to do with dogs. Mary was certain dogs came into this. They had to. Cliff had found the Blisses' poodle, Merlot, who she was sure someone didn't want found. Why was easy: they faced jail. Who wasn't so clear. She sighed deeply and got out of the car. She didn't know if Luke would be at the library today, but she had to make sure the cans that hadn't been used to make the tree had been picked up and the volunteers who would dismantle the tree were on track. If Luke was there, perhaps he could answer a few questions. If, that was, she could think of a tactful way to ask them.

Luke was at the counter, smiling at a little girl who labored to sign her name on a library card application. Her mother stood beside her, beaming. 'Your first library card. I remember when I got mine. It was a special day.'

'Did you get ice cream?' The child looked up with a hopeful expression.

Her mother looked a little taken aback but recovered quickly. 'I believe I did. Would you like to celebrate with an ice-cream cone?'

The child nodded, a small smile starting to form.

'Finish your name then. Have you picked out your books?'

The child nodded and pushed two books that lay on the counter closer to Luke, who picked up the card and looked at the slightly smudged signature. 'Good job, Clarisse.' He handed her a new card with a bar code on it. 'Keep this somewhere safe and bring it every time you want a new book.' He swiped the books under the scanner then gave them back to the child, who solemnly picked them up and tucked them in her book bag.

'Ready?' her mother asked.

Clarisse smiled broadly, because of pride in her new

library card or the thought of ice cream, Mary wasn't sure, but she smiled as well as they walked out the door.

Luke leaned on the counter as he watched them, then straightened and nodded at Mary. 'It's that kind of thing that makes me stay at this job. Kids learning to love books, old people who come to get ones they can't afford to buy, young people who don't have a computer but come in here to do research papers...' He gave a rather rueful laugh. 'It sure as blazes isn't the money.'

'No,' Mary said a bit slowly. 'I don't imagine it is. There have been so many cutbacks and it always seems the library and anything connected with music or literature are the first to go.'

Luke laughed, but there was more than a trace of bitterness in it. 'When I decided not to try for vet school, I thought I was making such a sensible choice. A degree in English Lit and a Masters in Library Science. Sort of a nerdy field, but one I loved and I'd always be able to find a job. I wouldn't get rich, but I'd have stability.' He shook his head, his earring sparkling. 'Didn't quite work out that way.'

There had been a lot of talk about money the last few days. The shortage of it, or the possibility of a shortage. She wondered...she'd never find out if she didn't ask. After all, he didn't have to answer. 'Is that why you bred your little poodle to Millie? Did Evan pay you?'

Luke's head jerked up and he stared at Mary for a moment, expressions coming and going like a kaleidoscope across his face. 'How did you...?'

'I have Millie, at least for right now. John and Glen have inherited her along with everything else Evan had, and they might want her back. I guess her puppies were pretty cute. So, I wondered, if you made some money by…what do they call it? Standing your dog at stud? Why you turned down John and Glen. Don't you approve of breeding to anything other than another poodle?'

Luke's mouth was slightly open as he stared at her. It seemed he'd forgotten to breathe for a moment, then he let it all out with a whoosh and a small laugh. 'Who have you been talking to? Whoever it is, they have it wrong. I love poodles, but I also love dogs and was happy to work out something with Evan. I don't want it advertised, but that's because I really don't want to get back into the dog business. Fred's a pet. He's pedigreed, and he's a really good dog, but I don't plan on showing him or standing him.'

'Then why didn't you let John and Glen use him?'

'Mrs McGill, it's very simple. They don't want to pay me. At least, they didn't want to pay what I asked. Evan only paid me one hundred dollars, but he gave me a year's worth of dog food for free, much of which I will now not be able to collect. Evan sold those pups for between three and five hundred dollars each. There were five of them. A lot for a little cocker like Millie. But, think about it. He did just fine on that deal, but so did I. Dog food is expensive, at least the special kind I feed. When John and Glen approached me, I said I wanted pay equal to the sale of at least one pup. They didn't want to do that, so—we didn't. Simple as that. Now, are you all right?' He peered at her closely, especially her bandaged head. 'I heard you got mugged, and your head looks pretty sore. Should you be up and around?'

'I'm a little bruised but fine,' she answered through barely clenched teeth. 'And I wasn't mugged. I fell off a box trying to see through the back windows of the pet shop.'

'The back window of Evan's shop? Why?'

Mary didn't want to answer. She'd told this story one too many times, but Luke looked genuinely upset. Repressing a sigh, she told it again. Millie barking all night, discovering Evan wasn't home and the shop still locked long after opening time, even though Evan's car was parked out back… 'So I decided to look in the window. The crate I found wasn't very strong and it broke when I tried to get down.' She paused, remembering the panic she'd felt when she saw Evan's crumpled body. If she'd just been a little more careful…

Luke appeared beside her, placed his hand under her arm and lowered her into a chair beside a table opposite the checkout counter. He pulled another up beside her.

'You haven't had such a great week, have you? First Cliff, then Evan.' He sighed deeply. 'It hasn't been much of a week for any of us.'

'Luke, you knew Evan well, didn't you?'

He nodded. 'I guess you could say that. I've bought all my dog supplies from him since he opened.'

'Did you know he had cockapoo puppies for sale in his shop?'

'Yes, I've seen them. Why?'

'Do you know who owns them?'

Luke's eyes widened slightly, apparently in surprise. 'No. I never asked, although I was a little curious. Since Millie and Fred had theirs, I've been more interested… but, no, I don't know.' He paused and looked at Mary intently. 'Where are you going with this? You wouldn't be asking unless you had a reason. A good one.'

Mary leaned back a little in the hard chair, winced

and sat forward again, using the table to rest her arms on. She opened her fingers and let them spread out across the worn wood. 'I'll get to that in a minute. First, tell me a little more about dog breeding. You said you only got one hundred dollars to breed your little poodle... Fred...to Millie. Is there a standard fee? What would you expect to pay to get dogs like Bonnie's, for instance?'

'Oh, boy.' Luke slumped in his chair and ran his hand over his hair, pulling strands out of its ponytail. It gave him, Mary thought, a somewhat frazzled look.

'You just asked for the half-hour lecture, and if you really want to understand it, plan on an hour.'

'Don't you have a five-minute version?'

'I'll try. OK. There are several things that determine the amount a breeder can ask for a stud fee. First, bloodlines. Does the dog have a lot of champions in his background and did they, in turn, produce a lot of champions? Then, has he been shown and how did he do? Is he a finished champion and, most importantly, has he produced champions? If you have all of those things, the stud fee can be in the thousands.'

Mary's mouth dropped open, but she didn't care. Thousands? Surely she'd heard wrong. 'Did you say thousands? Why would anyone pay thousands?'

'Let's say you have a really good bitch and you want top-quality puppies. You'd expect to pay what Bonnie's asking for that new dog of hers—twenty-five hundred dollars. The pups that were just born were his.' The expression on Luke's face was unreadable. 'She says she has them all sold for between two and three thousand each. Do the math. Take off a couple thousand for vet bills, food and running her kennel, and she's still ahead.

Nicely ahead. But, of course, it's not that easy. You're not always going to have a whole litter that's show quality, no matter how illustrious the parents. There will be some litters where no pup is show quality. Then you're looking at maybe breaking even. Not all litters will have five puppies. There are lots of variables.'

'Has she had many people pay that?' Mary's voice was faint.

'I haven't heard of anyone, so far. But maybe in the spring… I hope so, for her sake. She paid a lot for that dog.'

'What's a lot?'

'I don't know the exact amount, but if what I've heard is true…it could be upward of twenty thousand.'

A cold chill ran through Mary. She felt like one of those people on the *Antiques Roadshow* who had just been told their Aunt Bessie's ugly parlor lamp was a rare Tiffany lamp worth more than their house. 'How much?'

'Again, I don't know the exact number, but a dog like that, with his bloodlines, his show wins, has to be worth a whole lot of money.'

Mary did a quick calculation. 'You'd have to breed about eight bitches a year to pay for him, and that doesn't take into account all the other variables and expenses. Could you do that?'

'There are some kennels that can, but I'm not sure Bonnie's is one of them. She has good dogs and is fairly well-known around the central coast, but I'm not sure she's going to get out-of-state dogs to breed. Of course, if she starts getting really good pups from her dogs she can make a lot of his purchase price back selling them, but it's not going to be easy.'

Mary barely heard it when Luke changed the subject. 'Come look at the can tree. Most of the overflow cans have been moved, but we've gotten more. Did you contact the press? What time will they be here?'

'What?'

'What time tomorrow will the press be here? The real estate guys want to start pulling this down right after lunch.'

'Oh. Yes.' She shook off thoughts of dogs and murder and tried to concentrate on soup cans and newspaper people. 'I haven't called them yet. I wanted to talk to you.' She turned toward the tree, thinking how many people would have full tummies on Christmas day because of the generosity of the town and had a rush of pride. It didn't last long. The leashes Evan had given hung from dog food cans somewhere in the middle of the tree; dog bowls and squeaky toys lay on the floor in front of it. She became a little sick looking at them. 'I'll see if I can get some of the school kids who made those decorations over here around noon. I'm pretty sure I can get Ben to send a reporter over then, and I'll see if the local TV people can come.'

Luke nodded. 'Let me know. And, Mrs McGill, I heard you were heading up the Friends of the Library fundraiser again. Is that true?'

Mary nodded.

Luke beamed. 'Then it will be a huge success. Oh, oh.' He turned to look through the glass doors into the library. A woman stood at the checkout counter, looking around, fingers drumming on the counter. 'I've got to go. Talk to you later today?'

Mary waved her hand at him as he went through the glass doors into the library. She pushed through the vestibule doors out onto the street. The pet shop was directly opposite. She stopped for a moment, staring at it. The drawn blinds over the plate glass windows gave it a mournful look. Admonishing herself not to be morbid, she started for the corner and the parking lot, but stopped. A notice with a wide black boarder was pinned prominently onto the front door. How Victorian. She crossed the street to read it.

Due to the sudden and tragic death of Evan Wilson, this shop will be closed until after the funeral and memorial service. The shop will re-open under new ownership in time for all your Christmas shopping needs and with the same policies and standards held by our beloved Evan.

John Lavorino and Glen Manning

Mary stared at the notice for what she felt was a long time. She wasn't sure what she thought. There was no practical reason why John and Glen should lose Evan's customers, nor should the customers be left in limbo, wondering if they should find another place to buy their Christmas supplies. But there was something about the promptness of all this, the quickness with which the funeral was planned, with which the turnover of the shop was being accomplished, that made her a little...nervous. That was it, nervous. She supposed it made sense. Christmas sales were important to any store. It certainly didn't mean John and Glen weren't grieving for their supposedly best friend, but still... It was good business. Wasn't that what Luke had talked about? Breeding dogs? Running pet shops? It was all about business. Wasn't it?

She turned and, more slowly, walked around the corner, got into her car and headed for home. A glance at

her watch told her she had a little over two hours before
she had to pick up the children. Plenty of time to call
the newspaper and the TV station to see if she could
arrange coverage for the grand dismantling of the can
tree. But her talk with Luke wouldn't leave her alone.
Dog breeding was big business, with at least relatively
big money involved. Was that what was behind Cliff's
and Evan's deaths? Money? If so, it let out Luke. Or, did
it? She wasn't sure. However, she was sure, it let in Bill
Bliss and John and Glen. Who else? She put her foot
down a little harder on the accelerator and almost skidded as she turned onto her cracked cement driveway.
She needed to take another good, long look at her list
of possible suspects and their motives. She had some
revisions to make, and she needed to make them now.

THIRTY-SEVEN

MARY LAID HER purse and keys down on the kitchen table and knelt to stroke the wiggling, whining black bundle of fur that wound in and out of her legs. 'My goodness, I was only gone a couple of hours. Are you always this glad to see someone when they come home?'

She glanced at the clock on the opposite wall. One thirty. She had time for a cup of tea and a quick sandwich before she picked up the children. She'd swallow a couple of Tylenol with the tea. She'd put up a brave front for Luke and the women at the beauty shop, but her leg was aching something fierce and the back of her head and neck was beginning to throb. She was definitely too old to be falling off boxes. She suspected she was getting too old for a lot of things.

She opened the back door for the dog, who shot out gleefully. Mary watched for a minute then crossed to put on the teakettle. One eye on the back door, she rummaged in the refrigerator for something to eat that she didn't have to cook. Leftover chicken and rice soup. It would go beautifully with tea and all she had to do was heat it.

She absently finished the last bite, swallowed another mouthful of tea and leaned back, getting a small protest from Millie, who lay under the table, her head on Mary's foot. Mary shifted it slightly, wiggled her

toes and once more picked up her list which she'd up-
dated, adding every possible name to it, while she ate
her soup. Even Alma had a column. Mary thought that
was a stretch but she didn't want to overlook even as
remote a possibility as Alma. She had been in the dog
breeding business and she'd hated Cliff. Mary entered
a 'w' against her name. She had placed one next to the
name of all those who were or had been in the breeding
business. The only one it left out was Father D'Angelo.
He was also the only one who didn't have a dog. He
had an old grudge against Cliff, though. The children
had seen a man, a tall man, dressed in a robe, wearing sandals. No. That wasn't right. They hadn't said a
word about footwear. Only that the man they saw wore
a robe of some sort and carried a stick. A long, pointed
stick? Mary shuddered. That left out Alma. She wasn't
a man, she wasn't tall and Mary didn't think she had
enough strength to push even the sharpest of sticks
through someone's front. She set her tea down and
pushed away the mug. This was getting her nowhere.
She shoved back her chair, picked up her dishes and
headed for the sink, the dog right behind her.

'You're going to get stepped on, or trip me and, if I
fall on you, you won't like it.'

The dog paid her no heed. She sat by Mary's ankle,
watching while she washed out her soup bowl and put
it in the dishwasher. Mary turned, dried her hands on
a dishtowel and stared down at the dog, who stared
right back.

'I have to leave here in fifteen minutes. What am I
going to do with you?'

The dog whined.

'I can't take you. I have to pick up the children and deliver them to the winery.'

The dog cocked her head on one side, pricked up her ears and let her tongue roll out the other side.

She looks as if she's smiling. Only, dogs can't smile. Can they?

'Well, I do have a leash and the children love you.' She drained the last of her tea and put the mug in the dishwasher as well. 'I guess it wouldn't hurt if you came. The winery has had dogs visit before, but you have to be good. You can't…drat.'

The red light on her answering machine was blinking. Why hadn't she noticed that before? She walked closer and pushed the button. Father D'Angelo.

'Mary, I just hung up with Sister Margaret Anne. She says you'll be here this afternoon, picking up the Mendosa children. I have something I want to ask you. Would it be possible for you to come a little early and stop by the rectory? If you're feeling all right, I mean. I heard about your…accident and don't want you… If you can. I'd appreciate it. Thank you.'

What was that all about? Mary had never heard him sound so hesitant, so, well, distraught.

She stood for a moment, undecided, wondering what she should do. It settled one thing.

Millie couldn't go. She didn't want to leave her in the car, alone, but she wouldn't be very long at the rectory. What could he possibly want? Was it about the children? He knew they'd seen Cliff in the manger. He'd been there. He'd taken them to St Mark's. They hadn't wanted to go with him. Could that be because… they'd said they thought it might be him they saw. Oh,

dear Lord. Was he trying to find out if they'd seen…
if they recognized…

Could that be why he seemed so nervous on the
phone? Only, how did the puppy fit in? It couldn't be
him, but still…just the idea he might be involved made
her a little queasy. She had no choice. She'd go. One
glance at the clock said she'd better get moving if she
was going to see the good Father and pick up the kids
on time.

Millie whined, ran to the back door and gave a sharp
bark, then ran back to Mary.

'Are you telling me you want to go for a ride or that
you have another need?'

The small stub of a tail wagged her whole rear end.

'OK, we'll do both.' Mary picked up her purse,
checked to make sure she had her keys then opened
the back door. 'Go on. I'll be right behind you. I think
your leash is on the washer.'

The dog bolted out the back door. Mary followed,
carrying her purse, the dog leash and a full load of anxiety. What if he was trying to find out if the children
recognized him in the manger? Could he have been the
person in the bushes under Ronaldo's window? Surely
he didn't think she'd tell him…

Should she call Dan? And tell him what? No, she'd
see what the Father wanted and go from there.

Hopefully, she'd get answers to a few questions of
her own. Maybe she'd even get a glimpse of the devil
cat.

Mary went down her back-door stairs a lot more
slowly than Millie had and she didn't get into her car
with anything like the enthusiasm the little dog ex-
pressed as she jumped into the backseat. She just might

be on the way to unravel one more strand in this very
tangled mess, and she wasn't one bit sure she wanted
to. She backed slowly out of the garage, hit the garage
door opener and, with very mixed emotions, turned
toward St Theresa's.

THIRTY-EIGHT

MARY FOUND A spot under an old elm that still had some
leaves. The afternoon wasn't hot, quite the opposite,
but she wanted to make sure Millie would be comfortable so she rolled each window down just enough so
she could get her nose through, but not her head. Hoping she wasn't the kind of dog who chewed on uphol-
stery when left alone, she walked to the rectory door
and rang the bell.

It was answered promptly, as if the woman who
stood there, examining Mary, had been waiting for
it to ring.

'Good afternoon, Mrs Farrell.' Mary smiled.

The woman didn't smile back.

Mary gave up. Getting a smile out of this woman
would take more work than she was prepared to give.
She knew Margaret Farrell only slightly and had never
seen her smile. She'd never seen any expression except the one she wore today. Neutral, with just a hint
of suspicion. She'd never seen her in any kind of dress
but the one she had on. A black dress of some kind of
shiny material, buttoned down the front, with a white
lace fissure around the neck, black stockings, black
sensible lace-up shoes and a cover-all apron. The pattern on the apron changed, but not the style. A high bib
with straps over the shoulders crossed in the back and
wrapped around the waist to tie in front. The skirt had

two large pockets in front, always bulging. Mary wondered what was in there but never found the right moment to ask. Today the apron was made of bright blue, pink and white dots on a field of pale yellow. It was an incongruous sight over the severe black of the dress.

'I got a phone call from Father, asking me to drop by.' Mary waited.

Margaret Farrell turned her head slowly to look back into the dim interior of the house. Two hairpins fell out, landed on her shoulder then slid to the floor. Iron-gray strands fell from the bun that hung loosely on the back of her head. Mary suspected the bun had been tight early this morning but had loosened as the day progressed. Would it completely escape its confinement by bedtime?

'He did, did he?' Suspicion deepened on Mrs Farrell's face.

Mary nodded.

'Hmmm. Well, I guess I could call him. Tell him you're here.' She made no move to do so. 'He's due in the confessional in…let's see…about thirty minutes.' She paused and looked at Mary as if she expected her to respond to that statement.

Mary wasn't sure what was expected, so she smiled instead.

'Hump.'

There was more disgust in that 'hump' than Mary thought possible, and Mrs Farrell still hadn't moved. Finally, she sighed loud enough for it to be heard in the church next door. 'I'll tell him. Come on in.' She held the door a little wider and let Mary pass by her. 'Go on in there.'

'There' was what the builder had long ago dubbed

the formal living room. It was small with one window exactly in the middle of the wall that looked out onto the street. Mary walked in and looked around.

'Take a seat, if you've a mind to.' Mrs Farrell followed Mary into the room and gestured vaguely at the celery green plush-covered sofa that screamed it belonged in the seventies. Mary hesitated but sat. Mrs Farrell nodded with the first thing that looked like approval and left the room, closing the door behind her.

Mary took a deep breath in and slowly let it out. Why that woman exasperated her so, she couldn't imagine. She hoped she didn't have that effect on Father D'Angelo. If so, he must lead a very uncomfortable life. She sat up straighter on the elderly but immaculate sofa and looked around. It wasn't a very hospitable room. Mary had been in several homes of this floor plan over the years and was familiar with the layout. This room was designed for guests, or adults only. Off the entryway was a hall that led to two bedrooms that also faced the front. The master bed and bath, the kitchen and large family room were at the back.

In most houses this small room didn't get used much, but she supposed it served the rectory well. It was furnished as a cross between an office and a reception room, both a bit shabby but hospital clean. Nothing matched. The two wing-backed chairs were covered in a red, white and blue print much too bold for that type of chair and the pseudo-early American end tables held wrought-iron lamps in a vaguely Spanish style. The coffee table was blond modern, or what had passed for modern in the sixties. A desk sat in a corner at an angle so as to face the rest of the room, but it held no computer or much of anything else. A maroon swivel chair sat behind it. The bookshelves were filled with religious books and the wall decorations were either depictions of Jesus on the cross or paintings of The Blessed Virgin holding the dead body of Christ. There was one rather large picture of a nun in a brown habit and black veil. St Theresa, she supposed. She stood up to take a closer look but a click brought her attention back to the door, which opened and a smiling Father D'Angelo appeared. He was followed closely by a huge black-and-white cat.

'Mrs McGill, so good of you to come.' He walked quickly across the room and reached out a hand. Mary offered hers, which he gave a single shake before dropping it. 'I hope you're getting along…ah…feeling better. I heard you had an accident but were doing all right.' He paused to stare at the white patch Mary was painfully aware showed on the side of her head. At least her pants covered the blue wrap stretched tightly around her calf.

'You are, aren't you? All right?'

'I'm fine, thank you. Just fine.' She paused, giving him a chance to say something, offer her a chair or tell her why he'd called, but he seemed not to know how to start. Maybe she could help him.

'That's a handsome cat. Is he…' The cat had to be a 'he.' No female would have those heavy jowls, that broad front, the muscled hindquarter, '…the one Cliff gave you?'

The priest looked at the cat, who sat at his ankle, staring at Mary. She had little experience with cats, only with Ellen and Dan's yellow Tom, Jake, but she knew instinctively this was no ordinary cat. At least, he didn't consider himself ordinary. The stare he aimed at her was unblinking and the low rumbling in his throat was no purr. He was letting her know something... what, she wasn't sure.

The priest seemed oblivious to the cat's threats. 'Yes. Isn't he magnificent?'

'Yes.' Mary didn't know what else to say. The cat was, indeed, magnificent. And threatening. 'I thought... I was told...everyone said he's a holy terror. I wondered why Cliff would give you a cat...' She wasn't sure how to go on, especially as the priest seemed to regard the cat with genuine fondness.

'We had a few problems getting started, but he's really come around.' He paused, looked at the cat and a slight blush stained his cheeks. 'I must admit, I wasn't too sure at first. I even named him Lucifer. I'd change it now, but he doesn't seem to mind and he comes when I call.' He paused and smiled at Mary. 'When the cat first arrived, I wasn't sure if Cliff thought bringing him was some kind of joke or what, but then, I realized he knew the cat needed me. It was really an act of kindness.'

Mary tore her eyes off the cat to examine Father D'Angelo's face. Was he kidding? Everyone, well, almost everyone said the cat was awful. 'How long have you...has the cat lived here?'

'About six months, I think. I took him over to Karl... for an operation. You know.' The red got brighter and crept higher on his face. The look he gave the cat was almost apologetic. 'It took him a few days, but he started to get better. He's quit biting me, doesn't hiss when I feed him or tries to sit on the sofa. He even sleeps on the end of my bed sometimes.'

Mary couldn't quite control the little gasp she gave nor the immediate need to sit down. She sank down on the sofa. As if he'd been waiting for her to sit first, Father D'Angelo folded himself into one of the wingbacks. The cat immediately jumped into his lap and began to purr, loudly. The priest smiled and started to stroke his ears.

'He bit you?' Mary was pretty sure he'd bite her if she offered a hand to stroke him. It wasn't something she'd try.

The priest's smile got broader. 'He was scared. I knew that and was determined to make friends. I've always had animals. It was the hardest thing for me to give up when I became a Franciscan. Parish work let me have one again, and I chose a cat because…lots of reasons. I was determined to win this one's confidence. We're making progress. He still wants to wander at night sometimes and then I have to go after him, but he lets me catch him now and doesn't hiss or claw me. He curls up next to me on the sofa and I think he actually enjoys sitting with me while we watch TV.' He paused and laughed a little self-consciously. 'We both like the PBS stations.'

Mary felt as if she'd just heard Father D'Angelo's confession, a very unreasonable feeling given the nature of his 'sin.' Keeping a cat, being nice to it, rescuing it from a life on the streets was hardly something to condemn yourself for. It wasn't weakness to be kind, but maybe that wasn't what he felt. She wasn't sure, but she'd been given a glimpse into his life that she didn't want. However, he'd just given her the perfect opening to ask for information she wanted. 'Is that why you were at Evan's shop the night he died? To get…' She looked into the cat's eyes, where he sat perched on Father D'Angelo's lap, almost level with her...'Lucifer's cat food?'

Father D'Angelo nodded. 'I was just in time. I'd been trying to get there all day but things kept coming up... I don't like changing his food. He gets...you know... the runs if things change.'

Mary didn't know and didn't want to imagine. 'That was about five?'

The priest nodded. 'I snuck in just as Evan was pulling down the window shades. John Lavorino and Glen Manning were going out the door. Do you know them?'

Mary nodded. 'Was anyone else there?'

'Luke, I can't remember his last name, but the young man who runs the library...' He paused, as if waiting for Mary to acknowledge she knew who Luke was. She nodded. '...rushed in as I was grabbing the cat food. Evan seemed irritated and said he was closed, but Luke laughed and said he wouldn't want his dog to starve now, would he, and he'd only eat Evan's brand.' Father D'Angelo took a deep breath and let his hand rest on top of the cat's head. The cat started to purr. 'Evan muttered a rather crude word, then said, "Oh, all right" and went in the back. That's when I left.' Father D'Angelo didn't say anything for a moment, just stroked the cat's ears and seemed to listen as the purring got louder.

Mary didn't say anything either. She wanted to hear whatever it was the priest was trying to decide if he should mention.

Evidently, he made up his mind because he raised his head and looked straight into Mary's eyes. 'Evan was a nervous wreck that afternoon.'

Whatever Mary had been expecting, it wasn't that. 'What?'

'Evan. He was…not himself. Evan was a nice man, never snapped at anyone, never neglected his animals, but that afternoon…it wasn't only Luke's head he almost snapped off. Bill Bliss…' he paused at Mary's look of surprise, '…you know, the man who owns Golden Hills Winery? He came in and Evan told him he couldn't talk right then, to go talk to the florist.'

'Yes, I know Bill. The florist? Why would he send him to the florist shop?'

'I have no idea, but Bill went.'

'He did?' The thought that Evan had the nerve to send Bill Bliss anywhere was surprising, but that Bill went wasn't processing.

Father D'Angelo looked as if he was as puzzled as Mary. 'He seemed unhappy when Todd Blankenship said he'd be back with his truck to load the dog food he ordered. Evan said "Tonight?" as if it was the last thing he wanted to do, but Todd only nodded and left. I took my purchase and left as well. Evan was drawing the blinds on the front windows as I walked away.'

There was something wrong here. Something didn't fit.

'I feel terrible about all that's happened, and maybe this isn't the time to ask, but we're right up against winter and I don't know who else to approach…'

What was the man talking about? Not Evan any longer. It took an effort for Mary to bring her attention back to the shift in the conversation. 'Ask me what?'

'How I go about setting up the church hall as a shelter this winter for some of the homeless people who live under the bridge.'

'What? You want to do what?' Now he had her attention. The homeless population was growing. They would be among the first to have access to the food from the Christmas Can Tree. Only, it had never occurred to her this was what Father D'Angelo wanted to talk about. Why, she didn't know. Catholic charities were famous for the good work they did. It wasn't always reflected in individual parishes, however. 'Are you sure?'

'Oh, quite sure. I just don't know how to—well, organize...' His eyes shifted away from her and onto the cat, who hadn't moved from his side. 'We have the women's guild, of course, but they help plan activities for the school, raise money for textbooks and make sure they have funds available for our needy families, but to put up a whole bunch of homeless, well, none of them seem to know any more about how to do that than I do. However, someone needs to do something and...' The look he gave her was clearly tentative hope. Why her? She had more causes than she could possibly handle now. 'Have you talked to Bob at the food bank?'

The priest shook his head. 'No. I thought I'd talk to you first. Everything you organize runs so smoothly. I thought if you couldn't help, you might be able to tell me who to contact and how to...' The worried, helpless look in his eyes intensified.

Mary sighed. No wonder his women's guild shied away from this. She knew most of them and, while they had good intentions, none of them had much experience organizing anything larger than an eighth-grade dance. 'What do you have in mind? Shelter when it rains? Every night? Just for families with children?

Are you going to serve food? Have you talked to the city about permits?'

The priest held up his hand and drew back into his seat, as if the onslaught of questions had pushed him into it. 'I have no idea. I don't think we could open it every night. There are a lot of church functions that go on there, so maybe just in emergencies. Like, when we have a storm. I hadn't thought about food, but I guess... do we need a permit?'

Mary sighed again. 'Call Bob. He has contact with the homeless all the time. Did you know St Mark's serves a hot meal to the homeless once a week in the evening? Maybe we could work out something with them. If you plan to put people up for the night, you'll need cots and blankets and we'll have to see if the bathrooms are compliant. Do you know what the occupancy rate is on the hall?'

Father D'Angelo shook his head. 'It's posted, but I can't remember what it is.'

'Hmmm. We'll have to find out.'

For the first time, Father D'Angelo smiled. A somewhat tentative smile, but a real one. 'Does that mean you'll help?'

Mumbling things to herself like, *You're an idiot, you don't have time to do all you've signed on for, Christmas is coming, you have a houseful of people arriving for Christmas breakfast and you haven't wrapped even one present... You'd never forgive yourself if you'd done nothing to help those people living under a bridge. And in the rain!* 'Yes, I'll try, but I'm not promising anything and I won't chair any committee. Call Bob, tell him what you're thinking and have him call me. We'll set up a meeting. We'd better get going if

you want to get anything done this winter.' She glanced
at the digital clock on the desk and started to her feet.
'I'd better move if I'm going to get those children on
time. School is about to let out, isn't it?'

Father D'Angelo nodded. 'The bell will go off any
minute now.'

Mary had heard that bell and had no doubt everyone
on this block knew when school was out.

'Call Bob as soon as you can. Let's try to get together next week. You have his number, don't you?'

Again Father D'Angelo nodded, but this time with
enthusiasm. 'I can't thank you enough for offering to
help. Every time I think of those children, the only roof
over their heads the underpass of a bridge, no heat, no
bathroom, no lights to read by or...'

Mary waved her hand, as if she could wave away
the image he had so inexpertly but vividly painted.
She hadn't offered. She'd been shanghaied. However,
first things first. It was time to pick up the Mendosa
children. Telling him once more to have Bob call her,
she headed out the door and over to the schoolyard, accompanied by the clanging of the school bell.

THIRTY-NINE

MARY MADE THE now-familiar turn off the highway onto the road that led to the winery and to Bonnie's house almost on auto-pilot. The children sat in the backseat, talking about their plans for Christmas break and what Santa might bring, but Mary barely heard them. Her mind was full of her discussions with Luke and Father D'Angelo. She slowed, however, as she passed Bonnie's street. The house had the blinds drawn, giving it a solitary, almost sullen look. The big gate was closed and, for the first time, she noticed there was no sign proclaiming it as a dog-breeding business. Why? Wouldn't Bonnie want the world to know where her beloved dogs lived and wouldn't she welcome visitors? Perhaps it was some sort of zoning thing. No. The house next to Bonnie's proudly displayed the picture of a paint horse, Warrior something, loudly advertising his services. If they could, so could Bonnie. She drove into the parking lot of the winery, lost in thought.

Naomi was in the parking lot watching a young man place a case of wine in the trunk of a silver Lexus. She was flanked by an older couple, both with clouds of expertly cut white hair, both expensively dressed, both beaming at Naomi as they climbed into their car. It wasn't until they disappeared down the long drive that Naomi turned toward Mary and the children.

'Kids. You can't go in to see your mother for a while. She and Mr Bliss are busy.'

'What are they doing?' Ronaldo stopped trying to untangle Millie from the leash she'd managed to get caught around her legs in her rush to get out of the car.

'Going over the books. Your mother will have to take some time off, and we need to make sure everything is in order.'

Dalia took the leash from Ronaldo and unwound the little dog, who immediately sat and stared at Naomi. 'Of course things are in order. Mom doesn't like it any other way.'

A flush spread across Naomi's cheeks. 'I'm sure they are. However, it's always a good thing to double-check.'

Mary nodded. She'd spent more than one day cleaning up a mess someone had assumed was fine instead of checking. 'How long do you think they'll be?'

'Oh, a half hour or so. I have some soft drinks. Would the children like one?'

The children looked at Mary with hopeful smiles that turned into bright beams as she nodded.

'What may I offer you, Mary? Glass of wine? Coffee?'

'Coffee sounds wonderful. Thank you.'

They followed Naomi into the tasting room and down the hall to her office. 'Sit down.' She motioned Mary to the chair beside her desk, and pointed the children to a small sofa on one side of the room. Millie she stared at for a moment. 'I think I have one of Merlot's dishes in this closet. I'll get her some water.'

It was no time at all before everyone had a drink of some sort in front of them and had settled down to wait.

Naomi handed the children a copy of a dog magazine and it took only a moment before they were engrossed in it, comparing Millie to other cockers and Sampson to other puppies. Naomi watched them for a few minutes, an expression on her face Mary found unreadable.

Finally, she pushed her coffee aside and leaned over the desk and stared at Mary, her voice low. 'Are you all right?'

Mary nodded. 'Still a little sore, but fine.' News certainly did fly fast in this town. She wasn't sure she liked it, but Naomi had given her an opening. She didn't get a chance to use it. Naomi was in a talkative mood. Or was it nerves?

'It's terrible, what happened to Evan. He was a good person. I can't believe someone would do something like that.' She paused. There was the tiniest hint of a smile in her voice as she asked her next question. 'Did you really fall off a box, looking for him?'

Try as hard as she might, Mary couldn't repress the snort of disgust that escaped. Was there no one in this town who didn't know about that dratted box? 'Yes. I got worried when I found he wasn't home or at his shop, but his car was in the parking lot behind it. I stood on the box to look in the window. I only had time to see him lying on the floor before it broke.'

Naomi's mouth formed a soft 'oh,' as her eyes drifted up to the bandage on Mary's head. 'I just can't believe it. Why would anyone want to... Cliff had enemies.' She paused. 'Maybe not exactly enemies, but he made a lot of people angry.' Deep furrows showed in her brow and around her mouth that Mary hadn't noticed before. The breath she took before she continued sounded a little ragged. 'Evan…they were opposites in every way. I can't see any connection.'

Mary thought she could. There were a couple of possibilities and one, the more she thought about it, seemed distressingly possible. Dogs could be big business, at least in some circles, and that business, or some kind of business, was at the heart of all of this. John and Glen wanted the pet shop. Bad enough to kill Evan? She couldn't make herself believe that, but someone had killed them both, and dogs and the business of dogs seemed to be at the heart of it. There was one question Naomi could answer that might help. Mary wasn't in the least bit sure she would, but at least Mary could try. She stole a quick look at the children, who seemed absorbed in the dog magazine, put down her coffee cup and leaned across the desk, keeping her voice low.

'I heard Bill was at the pet store right before it closed. Did he say anything to you?'

'About what?' The furrows across Naomi's brow seemed to deepen and her eyes narrowed.

'About Evan. I heard he seemed…nervous. Did Bill think he seemed all right?'

'He didn't say one way or the other. He wasn't in Evan's shop very long. We're trying to take over the lease the flower shop has and, since Evan owns the building, we had to make sure he'd let us.' She gave a soft laugh, probably at the look of surprise Mary was sure was on her face.

'What do you want with a flower shop?'

'Nothing.'

The laugh disappeared, replaced with a look of faint irritation. Why? Did Naomi dislike the idea that where Bill was and why he was there was a subject of discussion in town? If that was so, Mary could sympathize. However, it seemed a legitimate question.

'It's not the flower shop we want, it's their space. We want to open a tasting room in town but haven't openly talked about it because we're not sure we can get the shop. It's a great location. Right on the town square, facing the library. Everyone passes there. It should do very well. The flower shop, for whatever reason, isn't. Bill's been talking to Evan about taking over their lease. Evan wasn't too excited about it. I don't know why. He's had some trouble getting his rent paid and if we went in, he knows…knew…oh, dear. I don't know what's going to happen now.'

'Do you know that John Lavorino and Glen Manning are Evan's only heirs? They've got everything, including Evan's mother, so probably they're the ones you need to talk to. You might want to wait a little, though. They have a lot of things to sort through.'

Naomi's face said she hadn't known. Her eyes widened, her chin lifted and something that might have been a smile grew. 'John and Glen? From St Mark's choir?'

Mary nodded.

'Well.' There was a speculative look on Naomi's face, a smoothing of the worry wrinkles that had creased her brow. Worry, however, soon came back. 'Are you sure?'

'That's what they told me. I think they were at the shop this morning. Someone put a note on the door, one bordered in black, saying the shop would re-open after the service, in time for Christmas shopping. I rather think John did that.'

Naomi laughed. Really laughed.

Mary wasn't amused. 'Is that good for you? Having John and Glen to deal with, I mean.'

'Glen has always thought our opening a tasting room in town a good idea, and I don't think he'd put up with consistently late rent payments for a minute.' Her smile spread. 'Yes, I think we can work out something with Glen.' Again, her face changed, but this time the distress was different. 'It sounds so callous to talk about our concerns when poor Evan…'

Mary nodded. 'I know how you feel. It's been a horrible week. First Cliff, then Evan.'

Naomi gave Mary one of the saddest smiles she'd ever seen. 'But I'll grieve for Evan.'

That was probably true. Naomi and a lot of other people. Evan had been well liked and respected, whereas Cliff… 'Luke, from the library Luke…' she paused and Naomi nodded, '…said he had one of your little poodle's sons. Did you breed him, Merlot, a lot?'

'Not as much as Bill would have liked. He sired two litters and, yes, Luke has one of the pups. He's a good dog and looks a lot like his father.' Her left eye twitched and her mouth pursed. 'Luke calls him Fred.'

Mary wanted badly to laugh but thought she'd better not. Naomi might not appreciate that and she needed an answer to her next question. 'How did you pick the females to breed with?'

Naomi's eyes widened in surprise and the hint of a smile returned. 'I didn't. They picked us.'

'I don't understand.'

'Merlot was in a lot of local shows. He was a finished champion and had three Best in Show wins. His pedigree was impeccable. People with female poodles contacted us and inquired about breeding.' She looked around the room, seemingly lost until her eyes stopped on the picture of the little dog she'd taken from Cliff's apartment. 'Cliff had been badgering me to stand him, but this place takes all my time and energy. Standing a dog like Merlot takes a facility, a lot of time and a whole lot of paperwork. I didn't want to get into it.'

'Then, why did you?'

'Bill, of course.'

There was more than a trace of bitterness in Naomi's voice.

Sympathy and a deep sadness, but no surprise filled Mary at Naomi's statement. 'What did you do?'

'I didn't do anything. Bill and Cliff worked out a deal with Bonnie. Well, with Todd. Bonnie, of course, did all the work. It didn't last long.'

A start went through Mary. She hadn't expected that. 'What kind of a deal?'

'We rented her barn. You know, the old one at the back of her property. Cliff was supposed to take care of the bitches who came in for breeding and do all the paperwork. We paid for the improvements, such as they were, and we put in the gate between the vineyard and their yard. That was so one of us could get over there without having to go around, but I don't think it was ever used. We bred him with exactly two bitches and the whole thing came to an end.'

'Why?'

'For the reason I wanted nothing to do with it. I told Bill, but would he listen? Bonnie was busy with her dogs. She hadn't bought that new stud dog yet, but she was looking around. I think the only reason she agreed was because she got all those kennels and things for free. Cliff, of course, made a mess of everything he touched. He never helped clean or feed. He was only there when the female dogs were brought in, but so was I. The only reason I let Merlot stay while the females were there was because of Bonnie. I wouldn't have trusted him to Cliff's care for one minute. He didn't do one thing right. It didn't take long before Bonnie got fed up and put an end to it, much to my relief and Bill's fury. That happened shortly before Merlot was stolen. We didn't make a dime on that deal, but Cliff made a couple of months' rent. I didn't even get a puppy.' The bitterness in her voice intensified and a tear appeared in the corner of one eye. Naomi roughly rubbed it away.

'What do Bonnie and Todd use the barn for now?' Mary's mind whirled. Could it be…evidently not. Naomi's next statement knocked her burgeoning idea to pieces.

'I was told they dismantled all the kennels we built and use the barn for storage for the hardware store. When Bonnie bought that new dog, I thought she might use the barn for visiting females. Her kennel building isn't very big, but no. She always said it was too far from the house.' Naomi shrugged as if she didn't agree. Mary thought she didn't care, either. 'I guess it hasn't been a problem. I don't think she's had a booking so far. She wants a lot of money to stud that dog.'

Mary had a lot more questions formulating, twisting and turning around in her brain, but they weren't going to get asked right now.

Millie started to whine.

'I think she has to go outside.' Dalia picked up the little dog's leash and started to her feet. 'I'll take her.'

'I'll take her.' Ronaldo got up as well and reached toward his sister's hand.

'We'll all take her.' Mary pushed back her chair and stood for a moment, making sure her leg was securely under her. 'Give me her leash while you two pick up your cans and put that magazine back where it belongs.' Millie's whine got louder. She started to dance a little and looked at Mary as if to say, 'I need to go *now*.'

Naomi scooped up the empty cans and grabbed the magazine. 'Go ahead. Take her out the big French doors and turn to the right. Go down the hill a little way and you'll see a sign that says "Visiting dogs." She can go there.'

Mary nodded, tightened up on the dog's leash and told the children in her strictest middle-schoolteacher's voice, 'Don't leave my side,' and started down the hall toward the spot the dog needed fairly urgently.

'Thank you,' she threw over her shoulder toward Naomi, but she had already gone back into her office. Mary heard the click of the door as she followed the dog toward the grass and relief.

FORTY

MARY STOOD ON the top of the slight incline, watching Dalia follow Millie up and down the slope, sniffing, stopping, trying to find the perfect spot. Finally, she decided on one and squatted. Mary's attention moved to the flat board fence at the bottom of the hill. Rows of young grapevines were the only thing between where she stood and the dirt farm road that ran along the fence and continued in both directions. That fence had to be the back line of the Blankenship property. She'd never seen it from this angle before. She could make out the roofline of the old barn, the door leading into the hay loft and the rooster weathervane, but she couldn't see into the yard. She backed up the hill to get a better view.

The kennel building, or the roof of it, came into view. So did the roof of the house, but the kennel runs, the driveway and the large gate leading from the road into the back of Bonnie's property were hidden. She let her gaze drift back down to the fence. It looked just as high and impenetrable on this side as it had on the Blankenships'. Where was the gate Naomi talked about? Her eyes traveled the length of the fence and finally stopped. There it was. Close to where the old barn was located. It blended in beautifully and she would have missed it, but a little light showed through a gap...a gap? Was the gate open? Should it be? That didn't seem right. Naomi said no one ever used it, even when they had a need to. They didn't now. Merlot was gone. There was no reason for anyone from the winery to go onto the Blankenship property, and no reason Mary could think of for the Blankenships to come onto the vineyard. Had one of the workmen…

'Mrs McGill, Millie's finished. Can we go in now?'

Dalia stood beside Mary, looking at her, Millie sitting at her heels. Ronaldo was down the hill, staring at a grapevine.

Mary tore herself away from the mystery of the open gate but not from the mystery of the murders. She'd been thinking, had an idea she didn't like, but decided, before she went further, she had to eliminate other suspects. There was one question she didn't think anyone had thought to ask, and it seemed a good place to start.

'Ronaldo, can you come up here?'

The boy looked up then back at the grapevine. He started toward them, but slowly. When he got close enough not to shout, he gravely said, 'There are little dried-up grapes on those vines. They look like raisins. I thought about tasting one, but thought I'd better ask you first.'

'Very sensible of you, but that's what raisins are. Dried-up grapes. I think it would be all right to taste one, but first, I have a question for both of you.'

Neither of them looked happy. Dalia's shoulders tensed and the interested look in Ronaldo's eyes faded. A look of apprehension took its place.

'I don't want to upset you,' Mary said hurriedly, 'and if you don't want to answer, or don't remember, it's not something to worry about. I wondered…'

She'd better not drag this out. They seemed apprehensive enough, and Millie was on her feet, looking down the hill. They needed to get inside, but first... 'Remember the night you found the puppy and the man in the robe brushed past you?'

Both children nodded. The look on Dalia's face plainly said it wasn't something she'd forget anytime soon.

'Did either of you notice what kind of shoes the man wore?'

The expression on Ronaldo's face went blank and his mouth opened slightly as he stared at her. He didn't have to say a word. He clearly had no idea what she was talking about.

'Work boots.'

'What?' Mary wheeled around to look at Dalia. The little girl's face was expressionless, but there was plenty of expression in the word she'd uttered.

'Work boots. You know, the kind Tony wears when he goes into the vineyard. They lace up around your ankle. That kind.'

'Are you sure?' The moment the words came out, she knew they were unnecessary. The child was very sure.

Dalia nodded.

Mary felt a little sick. This was not the way she wanted this to end. Admittedly, she'd wondered.

Enough of the ends fit. In a bizarre way, it made sense. At least, she guessed it did, but it all seemed so sad. Now what did she do? Did she have enough evidence to call Dan? Of course she didn't. All she had were a few threads and a gut feeling she was right.

'Hey.' Alarm sounded in Ronaldo's voice. 'What's she doing?'

Millie stood straight and tense, staring down the hill at the high wooden fence. Mary could hear dogs barking, faintly but barking. Suddenly, Millie gave one sharp bark of her own and took off, tearing the leash out of Dalia's hand, flying down the hill through grapevine wires, her leash whipping behind her.

'She's going to get caught.' Distress rang out in every word Dalia shouted as she, too, headed down the hill, but not through the wires.

'I'll get her.' Ronaldo was right behind his sister, trying his best to outdistance her.

Dalia ran through the rows until she got to a farm road leading down the hill toward the fence and the slightly open gate.

Millie outran them both.

'Don't!' Mary screamed. 'Come back.'

No one listened. The race was on and there was no turning back. There was only one thing Mary could think to do. She started after them. Trying not to turn an ankle in the uneven soil between the vines, she hurried as fast as she could and still see where everyone was headed. The gate was Millie's goal and the children seemed determined to follow her. Mary stopped for a second when she reached the downward sloping road, as much to catch her breath as to see where everyone was. Ronaldo stood by the gate, trying to pull it open a little more; Dalia was halfway through it.

'Don't go in there!' Mary shouted as loud as she could, but she had little breath left. 'Wait for me.'

Either she wasn't loud enough or the thrill of the chase had left the children oblivious to anything else.

'She went in there,' Ronaldo shouted. 'Don't worry.

We'll get her.' He disappeared through the gate right behind his sister, who was already out of sight.

'Oh, Lord.' Mary headed for the gate as fast as the steep terrain and her elderly legs would allow her. 'Let's hope I'm not too late.'

FORTY-ONE

THE YARD WAS QUIET. No dogs barked. No children spoke. No one in sight. What should she do next? She was on the road that wound around the Blankenship property, the one that ran past the front of the old barn. The doors were tall and looked new. So did the metal rails they rolled on. One of the doors was rolled back slightly, but no light came through and no sound. She looked toward the kennel building and the house. There was no car in the carport and no activity in the kennels. The front door was closed and no sign of dogs in the runs. Where had Millie gone? Where had the children gone? There was only one answer. Mary walked over to the barn, pushed the door back all the way and stepped in. She was greeted by an explosion of noise.

'Oh, Aunt Mary, look what we found.' That, of course, was Dalia, squatting beside an open kennel door, a puppy in her lap. A black-and-white cocker, obviously the mother, sat beside her, nuzzling the puppy then worriedly looking back through the open gate at the remaining puppies, who hadn't yet realized the gate was open. They would soon.

Mary looked at Dalia only long enough to be sure she was in no danger from the mother. Her eyes were drawn like a magnet to metal around the rest of the barn. It had originally been a horse barn, divided off into four large box stalls, the rest of the area probably given over to feed storage, tack and other supplies. The board fronts of the stalls had been removed and replaced with heavy duty chain-link fencing, a gate at one side of each stall. Three of them each contained a cocker bitch, the two whose gates were still shut barked in sharp warning at the interlopers, especially the one who had a pup by her side. One curled her lips in warning before she let loose another explosion of barks. Mary watched her for a moment but was immediately distracted by the dog in the fourth pen. A dog who watched her every move but made no sound. A small black dog, overgrown with hair, his long, pointed nose and straight tail gave evidence he was no cocker. He was unmistakably, even to Mary's eyes, a male poodle, and she was certain she knew who he was and where he'd come from.

'Merlot?' she asked as she approached his stall.

The dog didn't move. The look he gave her wasn't filled with suspicion so much as apprehension, as if he waited for her to do something he might not like. Fear? She didn't think so. Watchful, guarded, he stood his ground as she moved closer. 'Merlot?'

'Is that his name?' Ronaldo suddenly appeared at her side, causing Mary to startle.

'Yes, I think so.'

'How do you know that?'

Mary wasn't sure how to answer him, but she'd found the missing poodle, just as Cliff probably had. Who owned the puppies in Evan's store, or why he had been killed as well, was no longer in doubt.

'Where's Millie?' she asked him.

'Over there. Making friends with that dog. Why are all these dogs here?'

Good question, but one she wasn't prepared to answer. Instead, she took Ronaldo by the hand and hurried over to where Dalia sat with the puppy on her lap. There was one more thing she needed to see before she and the children got out of here, and that had better be soon.

'Dalia, may I hold the puppy for a moment?' She bent down and held out her hand.

The child hesitated but handed over the puppy. The mother dog looked up in alarm and started to get to her feet. Another reason for Mary to hurry. She turned the puppy upside down and pushed the hair back on one front paw. An all-black paw and all black toenails. She checked all four black feet. All of them had black toenails. She handed the puppy back to Dalia and started to edge past the mother into the box stall where the remaining three puppies squirmed and whimpered, protesting the absence of their mother. One was all black, one had one white spot on its chin and the third was what Bonnie had called parti-colored. She started with that one, keeping a close eye on the mother, who started into the box with an unhappy curl to her lips.

'Dalia, bring that puppy in here, please. I think it's hungry.'

The child looked down at the puppy. 'Are you hungry, little thing? OK. Let's go find your mother.' She walked into the box and put the puppy down under its mother's nose, who immediately lay down and started licking it. The pup ignored its mother's ablutions and headed instead toward lunch. At least, for the moment, the mother seemed to have forgotten Mary, who held the parti-colored puppy up toward the light. All the toenails seemed to be the appropriate color for the hair on the foot. She put it down close to the mother, who immediately started to lick it as well.

'Why don't you go stand by Ronaldo?'

The mother dog was occupied for now, but she still had her eye on Mary and the other pups on the far side of the box stall. If she got nervous, it would only take one lunge for her to get between them and whoever she thought threatened them. If anyone got bit, Mary didn't want it to be Dalia. She started edging around the side of the stall toward the last two pups, making shooing gestures toward the child while she moved.

At first, Mary didn't think Dalia was going to leave the box. It was obvious she didn't want to. Finally, slowly, she backed out to stand beside her brother. Neither child took their eyes off Mary.

'What are you looking for?' Ronaldo's voice registered confusion but not concern.

Thank goodness. They'd been scared enough. She wanted to get this done and get them out of there before they found out that, right about now, they should be petrified.

'Why are you looking at the puppies' feet?' Dalia seemed less confused, but more concerned. Not good.

'I'm looking at their toenails. As soon as I'm finished, we're leaving. Get Millie away from that other dog and make sure her leash is secure. I'll just be a minute.'

Millie protested as Dalia dragged her away but the girl took no notice. 'I don't like it here. Can we go now?'

'Yes.' Mary put the last puppy back down beside the mother dog and stood. She'd started to think she'd been wrong, that the poodle wasn't Merlot, but he had to be. It was the only thing that made sense. Then the fourth puppy had clear nails on a very black paw. Time to get the children, Millie and herself out of there. 'Let me go first. I'll just make sure the coast is clear. Stay right behind me.'

The children did as instructed, but it didn't matter. The coast was anything but clear. Horror closed down Mary's throat. The back door of the house opened and Todd appeared. He stood, staring right at the open barn door.

FORTY-TWO

'GET BACK,' MARY hissed at the children, who had appeared, one on each side of her. Millie squeezed in between her legs. 'He'll see you.'

'Who will?' Ronaldo pushed forward a little, trying to peer around Mary.

'The man from the hardware store, that's who.' Dalia's voice quivered and her hand went up to clutch Mary's. 'I didn't know he lived here.'

'The hardware-store man? Isn't he the one you thought...' Fear began to creep into Ronaldo's voice as well.

'Yes,' Dalia whispered. 'I wasn't sure, but his boots looked the same.'

The child didn't say the same as what, but she didn't have to. What did they do now? If Todd saw the children here, he'd be sure they'd recognized him. There was nothing she could say or do to convince him otherwise. She had to think of something, and quick. Her cell phone. Of course. She'd call Dan, or at least Hazel. He'd come...her cell was in her purse, which sat beside a chair in Naomi's office. She looked over the hillside behind the fence, up toward the winery. Maybe someone was in the vineyard and she could scream... No one was in sight.

Grabbing each child by the arm while trying not to

get caught up in Millie's leash, she backed away from the door. 'You have to hide.'

'Where?' Dalia didn't ask why. She seemed more than willing to hide and started looking around. 'In there?' She pointed to a door that led into what might once have been a tack room.

'No. That's the first place he'd look.' Mary's eyes scoured the room, looking for some corner, some safe place, something. They stopped at a set of stairs that led to the hayloft. It would have to do.

'Go up there. Now. Hurry. And, kids, don't make a sound. No matter what happens, no matter what he says or I do, keep quiet. Do you hear me?'

'What are you going to do?' Ronaldo's eyes were wide with worry and Mary thought she detected a tear.

'Fool him.'

'Shall we take Millie?' Dalia bent down and tried to pick up the little dog. 'Oh, she's heavy.'

'Leave her. She can help me fool Todd. Now, get up that ladder.'

'It's a stairway.'

Mary glowered at Ronaldo. 'I don't care what it is, get up it.'

They did and quickly disappeared over the edge. Mary took a second to let out her breath. 'What's up there?'

'Just a bunch of old junk.' Dalia's face appeared in the square opening above the staircase.

'Go hide behind it and don't make a sound.'

Dalia's face was gone just in time. Footsteps sounded on the road. She grabbed Millie's leash and pulled her over to stand beside her in front of the little poodle's pen. The gate on it worked with a latch. Hurriedly, she slid it loose and pushed the gate open just enough so it no longer locked. She had no idea if what she planned to do would work, but it was the only thing she could think of, and if the children stayed quiet no matter what happened to her, they, at least, should be safe. Todd couldn't know they were with her.

A shadow passed across the partly open barn door and Todd stepped through it. An immediate explosion of barking greeted him. Even Millie joined the chorus.

'Hush.' Todd shouted the word with impressive lung power. Silence fell instantly. He looked around at the dogs, staring at each one in turn. They stared back, but not one uttered a sound. Seemingly satisfied, he turned to Mary. 'Why, Mrs McGill. I didn't expect to see you here.'

His tone seemed pleasant enough and, at another time, in another place, Mary might not have noticed the hint of anger that underlay it. She did now, and the dogs seemed to have as well. What had he done to get them to quiet down so quickly? Right now, however, she had more important things to think about, like keeping the children safe and herself alive. She had no doubt Todd had killed both Cliff and Evan and had no reason to suspect he'd spare her. Unless, of course, she actually could fool him.

'Todd. Goodness. I didn't expect to be here, either. It was Millie. You remember Millie, don't you?' She had to stop babbling. There was no way he'd believe her if she seemed nervous.

Todd's eyes had fastened onto Mary when he walked in. He briefly dropped them to take in Millie before returning to Mary. 'Millie. Evan's Millie? How did you end up with her?'

The slightly disparaging tone he used made Mary stiffen. She almost said something but didn't have to. A low growl from Millie said more than Mary could have. Todd ignored it. The narrowing of his eyes, the faint menace in his voice told Mary he wouldn't be denied an answer. 'What are you and that dog doing in my barn?'

Crossing her fingers, Mary replied in what she hoped was her most convincing voice. 'I was visiting the winery, buying some wine for Christmas, you know...'

His weight shifted from one booted foot to the other. Lace-up work boots. The same ones he had on that day in the hardware store. It seemed a lifetime ago. Oh, Lord.

'Millie needed to go out...' at least that much was true, '...so I took her to that spot up on the hill. She kept looking down this way and suddenly she just ran. I followed her through that gate over there...' The look on Todd's face stopped her.

'The gate was open?'

Mary nodded.

'Who opened it?'

'I have no idea. I didn't even know there was a gate until Millie ran through it. Can you imagine my surprise when I found her in here?'

Mary uncrossed her fingers. She decided that was close enough to the truth to pass.

Unfortunately, Todd didn't seem convinced. 'You're saying your dog ran through the gate and into my barn? Why?'

'I don't know that either, but she seems to like this little black dog. He is pretty cute. He's not a cocker, though, is he?' Mary thought she could easily play the ingénue in the next production of the Little Playhouse if her performance today was one to judge by. Just to make sure Todd knew how innocent she was, she smiled.

Todd's expression changed from angry to confused to cunning. He glanced over at the dog then back at Mary and smiled. 'Ah, no. He's, ah, boarding here for a while.'

'Oh. Well, he's pretty cute. Millie thought so too.' She chuckled. She couldn't believe it. She hadn't known she could pull it off. Should she try it again? No. What she needed to try was getting out of there. Fervently hoping the children would stay quiet until she could get help, she raised her voice so it could be heard in the back row of a theater. Or the top of a hayloft. 'Well, I guess we'd better be going. Millie is a naughty dog to go running off like that, but no harm. I'll go back to the winery through the gate, if you don't mind. Do you want me to close it?'

Todd didn't answer. Instead, he seemed to be listening. A car engine turned off and a car door slammed. Who…not help. Of that Mary was sure. If she could just ease out of there before… Footsteps crunched on the driveway then hurried footsteps drew closer. She gathered up Millie's leash, ready to make a dash for the barn door when another shadow passed over it. Bonnie.

A chorus of barking broke out as the dogs caught sight of her. Only this time it sounded different. Joyous barking, welcome home barking. Dogs ran around in their pens and jumped up on the wire gates, begging to be recognized.

'Quiet!' The noise immediately stopped as Todd's voice overrode theirs.

Bonnie ignored the dogs, but she glanced over at Todd and looked hard at Millie and Mary, who still stood in front of the pen that contained the little dog Mary was certain was Merlot.

A look of sadness seemed to pass over Bonnie's face, but it was quickly erased. She sucked in her breath and let it out with a sigh. 'Hello, Mary. Just dropped in to say hello?'

'Actually, as much as I'd like to stop and visit, it was my dog I came to collect. I was telling Todd I was up at the winery and I took her outside to…you know… only she took off down here…'

'Really? How did she get over the fence?' There was no longer any trace of sadness in Bonnie's voice. Only sarcasm and the beginnings of anger.

'The gate was open.'

Bonnie wheeled around to stare at Todd. 'How did the gate happen to be open?'

He shrugged.

'I thought you were going to padlock it.'

'Yeah, well, I didn't. Must have been one of those tourists who keep wandering through the vineyard. I'll get to it this afternoon.'

'It's a little late, don't you think?' Bonnie's voice dripped with sarcasm. 'She's here and she knows. She's many things, but none of them stupid.' Bonnie looked around the barn, at the cockers in their pens, at Merlot then at Mary, anger building. 'One of the things you are is a pain in the rear. Why did you have to come snooping?'

'I didn't. The dog really did run down here. I just

followed.' She paused slightly, wondering if she should go on, but it no longer mattered. 'I did wonder, though. You said you hadn't bred Alma's dogs, but you have them and they aren't in your kennels. Plus the toenails. Merlot has that recessive gene for clear toenails. One of the puppies for sale at Evan's shop did also. The one Cliff brought to the manger before he was killed. There were other things. You didn't want anyone to think you ever bred any other dogs than cockers but cockapoos bring in good money, and you needed money. I started putting things together and wondered.'

'Then you followed that miserable little dog and no longer wondered.'

Mary decided that was more of a statement than a question and didn't require an answer. Besides, she didn't trust her voice to come out without a squeak.

Bonnie looked around the barn, as if seeing it for the first time, and shook her head. 'I knew we should have done all this someplace else.'

'Where?' Todd's voice held a weariness that suggested it wasn't the first time the subject had been discussed.

'I don't know. If I did, we wouldn't be here.' Bonnie paused and looked back at Mary. 'You know, Mary, I've always admired you. So efficient, so willing to help, and so smart. This town will miss you.' She turned toward Todd, who looked a little pale but seemed attentive to whatever Bonnie was about to say.

So was Mary.

'I don't know how you want to do this, but you can't leave her alive, and you can't leave her body here. You'll have to dump her somewhere, and try to think of how to blame this on someone else. How about

John and Glen? They had the most to gain from Evan's death.'

Mary had the most to lose by what Bonnie was obviously expecting Todd to do, but she wasn't going down without a fight. She reached behind and felt the gate. It swung backward under the pressure of her hand. She glanced back. The little dog was on his feet, watching it. Millie watched the poodle. Mary reached her hand down to touch her on the head.

'What are you doing?' Bonnie's voice was sharp and filled with alarm.

'She's getting nervous. I'm just reassuring her.' Mary's hand came off Millie's head and landed on the gate. With one hard push, it flew open. She twisted to grab Millie and the poodle took a tentative step forward.

'Run, it's your only chance. She'll kill you too. Run, Merlot.'

The dog paused to look at Mary as if in wonder, but he saw the wide open gate and headed for it. Bonnie saw it as well and threw herself forward in an effort to pull it shut. Too late. The dog dashed right between her legs, detoured around Todd, whose dive for him was interrupted as Bonnie staggered into him. The dog dashed out the door, silently intent on escape. Millie twisted out of Mary's grasp and followed, barking hard enough to wake the entire town, her leash flying behind her. Mary had time for one quick prayer they'd head for the winery before she was faced with a furious Bonnie.

'Why did you do that?'

'Do what?'

'Don't be cute, Mary. Letting that dog go wasn't a

bright move. Now we've really got to do something about you.'

'What?' Todd's voice was scathing. 'You jumped all over me for getting rid of Cliff and Evan, even though you knew I didn't have any choice. Now you want me to get rid of the old lady?'

Bonnie's eyes shifted toward him. The look she gave him was filled with contempt. 'Cliff was my friend. You didn't have to kill him. He wouldn't have given me—us—up, as much as he hated the idea of producing all these half-breed puppies.'

'Is that why he demanded money? He was so worried about your precious reputation in the cocker spaniel world he wanted us to pay him not to wreck it? Is that why he took the puppy from Evan's shop? Is that why he said he could prove it was sired by that blasted poodle and if we didn't pay him, he'd have me arrested for stealing it? He may have hated the puppies, but he sure didn't mind the money he wanted from breeding them. Some friend he was.'

She'd been right. It had all been about dogs and Cliff had been trying to blackmail someone. However, being right wasn't going to save her from ending up in a grave next door to him. Unless, of course, she could think of something...

'We can't let her go. She'd be yelling "you murdered both of them" before she got to the gate...the gate. Oh, Lord. The gate is open. Those dogs will have everyone out looking for her any minute. You'd better go close it and, this time, lock it.' Bonnie stopped. She seemed to assess Mary, looking for what, Mary wasn't sure.

'Never mind. I'll lock the gate. You get on with it.

And don't mess this up. She could send us both to jail for life.'

Without a backward glance, Bonnie hurried out of the barn. Todd turned toward Mary, and his body seemed to go very still. There was nothing in the studied look he gave her that spoke of hesitation, only deliberation. What was he planning? Before she could move, he grabbed her by the arm and was dragging her...where? Toward a familiar pile of dog food sacks.

He threw her at them and bent over, seemingly searching for something stashed in between the piles. He straightened, smiling, the missing barbeque skewer in his hand. 'Bonnie wanted me to get rid of this, but I knew I might need it again. Don't shake so. It'll hurt a whole lot less if you stand still.'

He had her by the arm, twisting it behind her, forcing it up between her shoulder blades. Did he really think she would just stand there and let him stab her? Besides, it hurt. Mary ducked, trying to twist around to free her arm, kicking out with her good leg.

'Quit it! Stop kicking. God damn it, stop...' Todd's hand went slack, the eyes that had bored with fury into hers went blank and he slumped to the ground, blood pouring from the side of his head. The loud thump she'd barely heard must have come from the ancient metal pail that now lay on the pile of dog food, blood staining the jagged rip on one side.

Surprise and shock kept Mary from moving as she stared at the unconscious Todd. At first, even the small voice coming from above didn't penetrate. When it did, she looked up to see two small faces peering down through the hole at the top of the stairs.

'Did we kill him?' There was a distinct quiver in Dalia's voice.

'No.' A twitch seemed to run through Todd and his eyelids fluttered. He wasn't dead, and he would soon be very much awake. They had to get out of there. 'Come down and hurry.'

'Are you mad at us?' Ronaldo seemed more worried about her reaction to their disobedience than how much damage they'd inflicted on Todd.

'For saving my life? I don't think so. But now I need to save yours, so hurry.'

The children exchanged glances and scurried down the ladder. 'What are we going to do?'

'Leave.' Mary took each one by the arm and started for the barn door. The dogs started to bark again, which was sure to bring Bonnie running back. She had to get them out of the barn, but she also had to know if Bonnie had padlocked the gate. If so, that avenue of escape was gone. How she'd get by her and out onto the road leading onto the winery property, she didn't know. She did know they wouldn't be safe until they got somewhere more populated. She was no match for Bonnie in any kind of fight. She couldn't outrun her, either. Bonnie was going to be a problem.

She was right. Bonnie walked through the barn door, stopped and blinked as she spotted the children. 'Where did they come from?'

'Up there.' Ronaldo pointed up the stairs toward the hayloft.

'Hush.' Bonnie's voice didn't have the force Todd's had, but it served to silence the dogs. 'You were hiding up there, were you?' She turned to look at Mary. 'Very clever, but you're not going anywhere and neither are they. Too bad you had to turn up when you did, but sometimes…well, sometimes things don't turn out the way you want them to.'

Mary thought Bonnie looked very unhappy, like she didn't really want to kill Mary and the children. Maybe not, but Mary didn't think it would deter Bonnie. As long as Mary and the children were alive, neither Bonnie nor Todd was safe.

Dalia's face flushed with fear and she trembled under Mary's hand. Or was that her trembling? Not only did Bonnie block the door, but she'd pulled it almost all the way closed. Mary'd better think of something, and fast.

Todd groaned.

'What's that?' Bonnie looked around the barn and took another couple of quick steps toward them. 'Where's Todd?'

As if in answer, he gave another groan and started to stir. Bonnie was close enough now to see him, or at least one leg. She pushed past Mary to stare at him. 'He's bleeding. What happened in here?' She wheeled around toward Mary and the children, who started backing up, demanding an answer, but she didn't wait for it. She dropped to one knee beside Todd and started to touch him all over as if to make sure nothing was broken or missing, crooning to him, tears threatening to cascading down her face. 'Are you all right? You've got to be all right. Oh, your poor head. Todd, say something. I didn't mean to yell. Todd…'

Todd only groaned but his eyelids fluttered again. This was their chance, their only chance, as far as Mary could see. She mouthed at Dalia, *Pail.*

Dalia grabbed it off the top of the pile of dog food sacks as they quietly backed up more.

'Get the door,' she whispered to Ronaldo, who immediately turned toward it. One quick pull had it open wide enough for the children to slip through. It needed one more for Mary to get through too and that was enough to jerk Bonnie's attention away from Todd and back to them.

'Close the door,' Mary called to Ronaldo. He was way ahead of her. He stood ready to roll it shut just as Mary slid through.

'Does it lock?'

Ronaldo shook his head.

Mary grabbed the pail from Dalia. 'Run,' she told the children.

'Where to?' Dalia looked around. 'The gate's closed.'

'Is it locked?'

'Can't tell.'

'That way.' She pointed toward the kennel building. 'There's a gate just past that building. Run for it and head for the winery. Get help. Don't wait for me.'

They ran.

Mary knew she couldn't keep up with them. She could only hope they got the gate open and headed up the main road to the winery. With a little luck, they could raise the alarm before she had to fend off Bonnie. *What did Bonnie have in mind?* Mary hadn't seen any sign of a weapon, but she was absolutely sure Bonnie didn't plan on letting her leave this property alive. Should she try and hide or head for the gate and hope she made it out before Bonnie quit moaning over Todd and realized they were no longer in the barn? The gate into the vineyard. It was worth taking the chance, and she didn't want to get trapped anywhere inside this fence. She started toward it, clutching the old pail, surprised by how heavy it was, and turned to check the barn door. It was open and someone stood in it, shielding his eyes from the rapidly setting sun. Todd. Blood still dripped along one side of his face and down his shirt collar, and he held onto the barn door for support, but the fury evident in the scowl on his face and the tight way he held the barbeque skewer at the side of his leg lent him strength. He seemed to spot Mary at about the same time she saw him and a small, mean smile replaced the scowl. Slowly, he started toward her.

Clutching the pail, Mary backed up, turned and ran, faster than she would have believed possible, away from the vineyard. She'd never make it past Todd. She wouldn't make the gate by the road, either. There was only one choice. The kennel building. If there was a lock on the door, maybe she could keep him at bay until help arrived. If it did.

She slid inside the door and slammed it shut. Was there a lock? There was, but it was only a thumb latch. That wouldn't keep Todd out very long, but long enough? How long was that? A tremor ran through her so strong she had to hold onto the door handle to keep upright. The dogs had started barking as soon as she slammed the door, and she almost missed the voice, high pitched and very distressed.

'Let me in. Hurry. He's coming.'

Dalia? Mary had the door open almost before the child finished speaking. She grabbed her by the arm, pulled her through the door then slammed it shut again, engaging the lock before she turned to face the little girl.

'What are you doing here? I told you to run for the... where's Ronaldo?'

Dalia seemed out of breath but, after she bent over, hands on her knees, and had taken a couple of deep breaths, she put her head up, looked at Mary and smiled. 'He's out by the gate, waiting for the police.'

Mary could barely hear Dalia over the frantic yelps of the dogs. 'Quiet!' she yelled at the top of her voice. She had no idea if this would work, but it wouldn't hurt to try. Silence descended, immediately broken by the high-pitched wail of police sirens getting louder and more persistent by the second.

'The police?' The dogs started again, this time seemingly protesting the screaming sirens.

'Here?' She had to mouth this last. Dalia couldn't possibly hear her, but she seemed to understand because she nodded her head and smiled—a smile that disappeared rapidly.

The door to the kennels shook on its hinges as someone tried to get in. Mary had no doubt as to who that someone was. She grabbed Dalia again by the arm and this time headed for the room where Bonnie kept the feed. Please, God, let it have a lock. She hoped Dalia was right and the sirens were, in fact, police cars coming to the rescue, but they'd have to be fast. The front door had just given way with an ear-splitting crash.

The feed room door had a lock, another thumb latch, but a lock. It wouldn't stop Todd, but it might slow him down. If Dalia was right, it would give Dan, or whoever was in those police cars, time to get in here.

'Help me drag this sack over there.'

Dalia grabbed one end of a dog food sack and looked around. 'Where?'

'In front of the door. We'll stack a bunch there.'

'Why?'

'Just do it.'

The sacks were heavy and unwieldy, but between the two of them, they managed to stack three before the door started to shake.

'You've trapped yourself nicely, Mary, and those kids as well. See you in a few minutes.' Todd's voice sounded faintly amused, but Mary knew it was because he thought he'd won, that there was no escape. Hadn't he heard the sirens?

Where was Ronaldo? Where were the police? The sirens had stopped. Did that mean they'd turned them off or that they weren't coming here? Police cars and ambulances weren't uncommon on Hwy 46. 'Keep stacking.' It was all she could think to do. That and pray like crazy. Todd was still holding the barbeque skewer last time she saw him and she had every reason to believe he still held it. The thought of it sticking into her, or worse, Dalia, made her break out in a cold sweat. Another crash on a door that didn't look as if it would hold much longer didn't help.

'Another one,' she told a panting Dalia. 'Heave.'

'How many more?' The child looked as if she was ready to give out, but keeping the door from caving in was their only chance.

'At least two.'

Mary had just grabbed the end of another sack when a commotion broke out in the hallway. Scuffles, yells, protests, Todd's voice above the others, shouting in rage, and another, familiar voice saying, 'Watch out for that skewer.' Someone else shouted something about handcuffs. The dogs were barking so loudly she wasn't sure about anything except the incessant attacks on the door had stopped. She and Dalia looked at each other.

'Is that the police?'

Mary let a smile spread, sank down on what was left of the pile of sacks and nodded. 'I think it is.'

Dalia took a deep breath and sat down beside Mary. She let it out then smiled at her. 'Good thing I finally remembered I had my cell phone in my pocket, huh.'

So that's what happened. Mary could do nothing more than nod, but that she did with gratitude.

'Dalia, Mary, are you in there? Are you all right?'

Mary found enough strength to answer. 'We're here and we're fine.'

Dalia found her voice as well. 'Where's Ronaldo?'

'I'm here. I opened the gate for them to get in.'

Pride was ripe in the boy's voice and Mary couldn't think of anyone who deserved to feel pride more. Unless it was Dalia, for staying cool and thinking enough to use her cell phone. Actually, for remembering to bring it. Looked like she had a lot of cookies to make for those two, but first...

'We can't get the door open.' Dan's voice. 'We want to get you out, but we'll need you to move whatever you barricaded it with.'

'We used dog food sacks. They're heavy. You'll have to wait a minute.' She pushed herself to her feet and stared at the pile, ten sacks high, each weighing fifty pounds. That last one felt more like a ton. How had they managed to pile so many? Adrenaline, which seemed to have deserted her. She looked back at Dalia, who hadn't moved from the sacks.

Her eyes were fastened on the door, still filled with fear. 'Is he gone?' she whispered.

'Yes. They have him. He can't hurt you, or anyone else, anymore.' Mary sat beside her and reached out, but the child wrapped her arms around herself and seemed to shrink into them, as if burying herself in a cocoon. 'I know.' The words came out softly and she shook her head a little. She seemed to shake all over. 'I know they won't let him hurt me, or Ronaldo, it's just that I...' She couldn't seem to go on.

'It's that you don't want to see him?' Fear mixed with adrenaline had carried the child just so far, but now it was almost over, there was nothing left of the adrenaline, but the fear remained.

Dalia looked at Mary, her eyes clouded with tears, and nodded. 'He's a bad man. He hurt people something terrible and he tried to hurt you and Ronaldo. And me. I don't ever want to see him again.'

'We won't open the door until I'm sure he's gone. I promise. You stay right where you are and I'll go ask Dan where he is.'

Mary walked close to the door and called. 'Dan? Where's Todd?'

'Standing beside the car in handcuffs, alternating between using some of the most inventive cursing I've heard in a while and proclaiming his innocence. Why? Is there a problem?'

'Dalia doesn't want to come out until he's gone. She doesn't want to see him.'

There was a pause and she thought she heard Dan

leave but soon he was back. 'He's in the back of a patrol car headed out the gate.'

'And Bonnie?'

'In another car, on her way to the station.'

'Did you hear? They're both gone.' Mary turned toward the little girl, who had already started to unwind herself. She wasn't smiling, but the tears were gone and resolve seemed to have taken their place as she joined Mary at the blocked door.

'Let's get out of here.' Dalia grabbed the end of the top bag and pulled.

FORTY-THREE

MARY SAT IN her rocking chair, an almost-empty mug of tea held tight against her, listening to the quiet in her living room. It had been a tumultuous afternoon and evening, starting with an unwanted and unnecessary trip to the hospital where she and the children were thoroughly checked and pronounced fine. Mary could have told them that. None of them had been hurt, just seriously terrified. It was going to take some time for the children to get over that, but they would. Their mother and Tony had already started the process. After the hospital and Dan were done with them and they were ready to start for home, they told the children Sampson would be coming for Christmas and he'd stay. Their excitement almost overrode the terror of this terrible day. Almost.

It had been after eight when Dan and Ellen brought her home. They had picked up In-N-Out Burgers on the way, a treat Mary rarely allowed herself, and Dan had pressed her with questions in between bites. Why had they gone through the gate? When did she realize Bonnie and Todd were responsible for all that had gone on? Why hadn't she left sooner? Why hadn't she called him as soon as she went into the barn? Those last questions came with an undertone of both relief and irritation—relief they were all alive and irritation she and the children had ever been in danger.

She swallowed the last onion ring and held up her hand. 'If you'll hush, I'll tell you everything.'

Dan looked a bit taken back; Ellen laughed. 'All right. Tell.'

Dan fidgeted while she took a sip of her coffee. She wasn't sure where to begin; her suspicions, then her certainty, had grown gradually. She'd start with the dogs.

'From almost the beginning, it seemed to me this had to be about dogs, not as pets, but as a business. It was the only connection I could see between Cliff and Evan.'

Dan said, 'What connection was that? Cliff took care of them, at least while he was still practicing. Evan sold them.'

Mary nodded. 'Evan did, but Cliff also worked with the people who bred them and showed them and made money doing it. Cliff's passion wasn't dogs for pets, but purebred dogs. He hated cross-breeding. He berated Glen and John for breeding their cockers with a poodle and he tried to bad-mouth Luke for breeding his little dog with Millie.'

The dog looked at Mary from where she had squeezed in beside her then let her head drop back into Mary's lap. Mary stroked her ears.

'Luke didn't care. Neither did John or Glen, which made them unlikely candidates for blackmail. Then Karl said the DNA test Cliff wanted proved Merlot was alive and close by, and so was whoever took him. Todd said he'd seen the dog go off in a car, but I started to wonder. They bred cockers and Bonnie was a fanatic about her purebred dogs and the reputation of her kennels, but she needed money to keep it going. Todd's hardware store wasn't helping. She bought Alma's dogs, even though they, like Millie, aren't show quality. I didn't realize that until Pat said Millie wouldn't fit in a top-notch cocker breeding program. Neither would Alma's dogs. She only had one that good, and Cliff ruined her. So what did Bonnie want them for? She didn't have them in her kennel building. It was when I learned how much cockapoos sell for that I started to wonder. She might be willing to breed Alma's dogs to a poodle, but that would mean finding one, arranging the breeding, all things that might get out and ruin her reputation as a cocker spaniel breeder and judge. I think that was more important to her than not paying a stud fee. But stealing a dog like Merlot could mean jail time. I didn't think she'd risk either so started to look elsewhere. Then Evan was killed. That started me thinking about John and Glen, but they had no reason to kill Cliff. Father D'Angelo did, and there were all those footprints, but he had no reason to kill Evan that I could see. By the way, I think he was the one in the Mendosas' bushes. He told me his new cat, who he named Lucifer, likes to get out at night and he goes looking for him.'

Dan gave a soft laugh. Ellen grinned at Mary, who smiled.

'The only thing that made sense, the only reason for Cliff to have the puppy with him, was blackmail. He wanted to prove to someone he knew about Merlot. Sampson has the telltale toenail. So do the puppies in the barn. At least one of them does. I didn't know that then, but things kept coming back to Bonnie. She made those dreadful robes for the choir. Todd could easily have gotten one. He knew the route the *posada* would take and that the lean-to would be unlit until they got there. He had plenty of time to arrange to meet Cliff and kill him. Bad luck for him, he lost the puppy, but even worse luck, the children found the rest of the barbeque skewer set and insisted on buying it. No one else would have connected it with a murder. I didn't—not at first, anyway. Then Evan was evasive about who owned the puppies he had for sale. Why? Because the breeder was someone who didn't want it known they bred cockapoos. Someone Evan trusted, at least where the health of the dogs was concerned. He trusted John and Glen, but they'd already produced cockapoos and openly planned to have more. Who else had been in that shop Friday afternoon? Todd. According to Luke, Todd said he'd be back to pick up dog food. Only, I remembered seeing a large stack of dog food sacks when I picked up the donations for the can tree. Why would Todd need food so urgently? Then Naomi told me Bill and Todd had worked out a deal to stand Merlot. It'd failed but Bonnie and Todd got all the improvements the Blisses had made to the barn. I wondered if that's where Alma's dogs were. When Dalia stated the man she saw wore work boots, the kind Tony wears in the vineyard, the kind Todd wears, I was certain, but before I could act, Millie ran off, the kids followed and you know the rest.'

Dan looked stricken. 'Work boots, not sandals. We asked those kids everything about that man but what he had on his feet. I can't believe it.'

That was when the doorbell rang. A subdued Glen and John walked in.

'We're only going to stay a moment.' John dropped a kiss on Mary's check and scratched behind Millie's ear.

She looked up and wagged her behind but made no move away from Mary. John sighed and glanced at Glen.

'What a terrible day.' Glen addressed them all with a wave of his hand. 'We just can't believe it.'

'Yes, we can.' John's hand rested on Mary's shoulder and he gave her a small pat. 'Bonnie was a fanatic about her dogs. She got all that from listening to Cliff all those years, I'll bet. As for Todd, he'd do anything Bonnie said. I think he adored her as much as she adored her dogs.' He shook his head. 'What a waste.'

'So tragic.' Glen waved away the offer of coffee Ellen started to make. 'We're not staying but wanted you all to know we're going to take their dogs, at least for now. The owners of the black dog are coming to get him, but we'll take care of the girls. So, Mary, we thought you'd like to know, since you seem to want to keep Millie, and she seems to like it here, we're going to give you an early Christmas present.'

He dropped an envelope in her lap. Mary opened it. 'What's this?' She pulled out what looked like a certificate of some kind.

'Millie's papers. We've signed them over to you.' They grinned at each other. 'You'd better take good care of her now. We'll be watching.' John laughed.

Glen joined in but immediately turned serious. 'This is probably the only good thing that's come out of today. When I think what could have happened to you, or to those delightful children...'

Mary wasn't sure what to say. She hadn't expected this, nor the feeling of relief and happiness she felt. 'Oh,' was about all she could manage. 'Oh, thank you.'

PUREBRED DEAD

'You're most welcome.' John followed Glen toward the door. 'See you next time you need dog food.'

Dan and Ellen left soon after, Dan assuring her he'd have more questions in the days to come.

That was fine, but right now…

'Are you sure you'll be all right here, all alone?' Ellen asked.

This time Mary didn't bristle. She let her hand drop once more onto the little dog's head. 'I won't be alone.'

'I guess you won't be at that.' And they left.

She and Millie sat there, warm and comfortable, enjoying the lights on the Christmas tree and the silence in the house. The mess Bonnie and Todd had made of their lives and the damage they had done to others weighed heavily on Mary, but there were a few bright spots. The children were safe, largely because of their own bravery. Furry Friends would continue to sell the supplies the local pet owners needed and she was sure John and Glen would follow Evan's high standard of pet care. Father D'Angelo had befriended a cat who appeared to be incorrigible and was on his way, with her help, to provide shelter for a lot of people who desperately needed it. Luke, from the library, would continue to take pleasure in his dog, his job and his help in making sure, through the can tree, no one in this town would go hungry, at least for a little while. Her job of protector had ended, mercifully, happily, and the Mendosa family would soon have two new members. Tomorrow she'd start organizing the reception to be held after Evan's graveside service and make sure they had room to put the first donations to St Mark's annual rummage sale in the church store room. She needed to make sure the children's ornaments with their Christmas wishes on them were all being taken from the Secret Santa tree in the church lobby and she'd better get busy on her package wrapping. After the New Year she had the library event, then the dedication of the new playground her parks and recreation committee had been planning and...

She sighed and Millie looked at her. 'It's not been the best day we've ever spent, has it, but it's over. All of it, and we have new things that need doing tomorrow. Are you ready?' Mary pushed herself to her feet. Millie jumped down and waited while Mary turned off the tree lights, then trotted beside her as they headed for bed.

* * * * *

Get 2 Free Books,

HARLEQUIN®
Paranormal Romance

Plus 2 Free Gifts—
just for trying the
Reader Service!